LAND OF OPPORTUNITY

Karl tried to count the stars on a fluttering flag with red stripes and white, atop the old round building. Then the words came to him, "Six hours leave, to go ashore."

He went to his cabin and counted out his money. "Four dollars in American money, that should be enough to show me the whole city of New York."

With four dollars in his handmade leather purse stuffed clumsily into the pocket of his uniform coat, Karl stood hesitant at the end of the gangplank.

Here, now, was that land toward which his great desires, his hopes had led him; and here he stood, half afraid to enter. Anxious, silent, in awe, he put his foot forward and stepped into America.

LAND OF STRANGERS, Lillian Budd's poignant portrayal of two Swedish immigrants in America, is the second volume in the Kristiansson saga, which began with APRIL SNOW and concludes with APRIL HARVEST, soon to be published by Avon.

LILLIAN BUDD
LAND OF STRANGERS

AVON
PUBLISHERS OF BARD, CAMELOT AND DISCUS BOOKS

The quotations from *Beowulf* are from the translation by James
M. Garnett, published by Ginn and Company

AVON BOOKS
A division of
The Hearst Corporation
959 Eighth Avenue
New York, New York 10019

Copyright © 1953 by Lillian Budd
Published by arrangement with the author.
Library of Congress Catalog Card Number: 53-8923
ISBN: 0-380-48314-9

First Avon Printing, January, 1980

Printed in the U.S.A.

To
Starr Lawrence Cornelius
Editor and Friend,
who spurred me on

"Vad som gömmes i snö
Kommer upp i tö."

"What is hidden in snow
Comes up in thaw."

SWEDISH PROVERB

ONE

"BIRTH IS THE BEGINNING for us all," Georg reflected. "Then, as the sun comes to follow the first light streaks of dawn, comes baptism, a beginning too."

In the little church on the mainland in Bohuslän, Sweden, he turned with the congregation toward the baptismal font. His eyes followed his good friend, Sigrid, as she carried an eight days' old infant to meet the Pastor.

Sigrid, his friend through all the years, his benefactress in times of illness or distress, she who had been born Sigrid Eliasdotter, beloved granddaughter to his old ship captain, Karl Ivarsson; she who had lived as Fru Peter Kristiansson, wife of the silent man from Smaland, those many years until Death came to claim him, sitting as he was in his chair with his pipe in his mouth and his Bible on his lap. Ah, well did Georg remember that St. Martin's Day when Peter died. Peter's favorite meal was spread, goose for St. Martin's Day. The children had come home from school, and Tuppie was there, little lame son of the new captain, Lennart Lindström, who had risen to take the stand of Captain Ivarsson and place his hands upon the helm. It was as clear before the eyes of Georg as if it had been yesterday: the *svart soppa*, the roast goose, red cabbage, apples, and prunes, and browned potatoes—aye, no better table spread in all the farmland of Sweden than at Norden, family home of Sigrid—the fruit soup they had forgotten to eat, because Peter was dead.

The sadness of it, that a man should die and leave no sorrow for what his life had been. Rather, Georg knew, had Sigrid felt bereavement for what her husband might have been, yet was not.

How had Peter read his Bible, to live as he had lived,

1

returning taunts and biting words and cruelty to the one he had taken to love and cherish, and to those he had given his seed?

The sexton alone, of all who knew her, was blind to lay the blame on Sigrid for her husband's laziness. "No chance did she give him to work as master of Norden!" he had said, and, "She, by her industry, removed his will to bend to the plough or spread the nets." Alas, how little such a one knew.

But Georg knew. He had watched, in those early months of marriage, to see how the woman in Sigrid had yearned to fill her days with woman's work, at the hearth preparing to feed the man who newly was her husband, with spinning and weaving and knitting and sewing for the infant to come within the first year, urging by praising Peter, proffering the help of her knowledge, gained by living on the place, in the barn or field until Peter should know the needs at Norden and take over on his own, or leaving to him the labor of the fields and barn as his right and duty as a man come to be master of a farmstead.

But what woman worthy of the name would sit while harvest rotted in the field, would sit cold for want of an armful of fuel, would let cattle sicken for want of feeding at their mealtimes, let milk curdle in the udders when milk and cheese and butter were the mainstays of the family's living? Not Sigrid. What woman would, as years went by, see her children hunger while her man sat nursing a spirit in which a cancer grew, reading the Bible on his lap, enjoying to the full the leisure clothed in his outward piety? Or had he been pious, in his own way, but hard for others to understand? Georg's brow wrinkled. Then a joyless faith, was Peter's, bringing no happiness to him nor to his family. Could a man be judged by his friends? Then could he, Georg decided, judge Peter, for Peter had not one. None had come forth to see his body carried to the grave, and mourn.

But Sigrid, as it had been with her grandfather, Morfar, her friends were legion.

Into that doorway, yonder from the font, had walked the Widow Sigrid, and out again, following the dust of the man she had served. Served, yes, for more of servant than aught else, had she been to Peter; and to those who knew, 'twas Peter's choice had made it so. The sexton was blind, so blind that he could say, as though it were right that Karl should do so, "Even the boy, Karl, blamed his mother," and not understand the blight the father had laid on the boy.

Sigrid had been doubly bereaved, for even before her widowhood, Karl, her eldest son, had gone from home.

Thanks be to God that the rush of daily tasks had filled her life, after Karl's going, like water rushing in to fill a hollow after the breaking of a dam.

Half without thinking, here in the church, Georg had counted Sigrid's footsteps. Eleven steps, one for each of her children that she had carried to that font; Elisabet—"Lissie"—first, then Karl—pride of the secret heart of Sigrid, breaking the long line of female succession to the home and lands of Norden—then Maria, little Johann, Herman Nikodemus, Marta, Oskar Rudolf, Agda, Sven, Hjalmar, and Patrick.

Sigrid. The mother. To him also she had been like a mother, although they were near to an age. Georg's eyes grew tender and his lips trembled; he could feel pity for those who never had known Sigrid. How, then, could they know the full meaning of the word "mother"?

Sigrid reached the baptismal font. All of the joy of the reaper of God-sent good welled in the eyes of the mother who carried a twelfth child to be entered into His church. All of the ecstasy of well-earned happiness shone in the aura surrounding Sigrid, the grandmother, as she stood at the font with Elisabet's child.

Lennart, the father, bent over her and raised the infant from her arms and passed it to the Pastor.

Aye, reaping the harvest of a life of love, Sigrid stood, and Georg watched her as he heard the Pastor give the name to Lissie's and Lennart's son: Karl-Johann. Karl for their old sea captain, even as Sigrid's own son had been named; Johann for Georg's bosom friend and shipmate, godfather to little Johann, the lad doomed to spend his life in a wheelchair but thinking it not doom, sitting twirling a crochet hook to make fine lace, the fame of which now had traveled through the land.

"Karl-Johann," spoke the Pastor, "in the name of the Father, and of the Son—"

Karl-Johann, together one name, to mark the difference between Lennart's child by Elisabet, and Karl—the son by Lennart's first wife who had died—called Tuppie now by all.

Sigrid, the grandmother. Georg smiled to see her radiant face beneath the black bonnet covering only the crown of her head, framing the braids over her brow. Small, tightly curled ostrich feathers peeped from behind and curled over the bonnet's edge.

No longer did a peasant's shawl adorn her head for the church-going.

Symbol of all the changes that had come in Sigrid's life was that bit of frame and feathers, brought by Johann, his friend, and now beloved husband to Sigrid. For into that wide church doorway one day, had walked the Widow Sigrid, and left behind the title as she recrossed the threshold, out into the sunshine, as Fru Johann Sandell.

Georg wended his way to the door and passed the basin of blessed water. Eleven christenings of Sigrid's children, here in the church; and she had borne thirteen. No less sacred, the washing away of the *arv synd* from the souls of her posthumous twins; not less blessed the water, to cleanse away inherited sin, for having been used by the midwife instead of the priest, and used none too soon to save the souls of the unborn.

Georg knew the pain Sigrid had suffered at laying away the three little ones, Oskar and Sven and Hjalmar, succumbed to the dreaded throat-sickness. No less, the pain, at parting with her eldest son. Ah, how often she must ask it to herself, "Does he still live?"

How could they know? The days had stretched themselves to years, now, since he had torn himself from home, and Sigrid's eyes still searched the sea; unspoken yearning written in those eyes. . . .

Georg answered Sigrid's smile as she returned to her place and joined her husband, and saw Johann's hand and hers knit in a close and tender clasp.

Yes. Sigrid smiled. As she surveyed the congregation and saw her friends and family there, she breathed, "Thank you, dear Heavenly Father, for all you have given to me." Her daughter Maria and David, her husband, had come for the christening, faring well, receiving recognition for their work. She could well smile when they told her that she was the model for the statue on which they worked, a statue so fine that a sculptor, come all the way from Stockholm, had praised it high. She, only a farm woman, model for a statue!

Truly, it was a pity that David should choose to mold her hand as it had been before: she looked down at her hands, lying on her lap, the angry-looking wen on the back of the right one was gone. It had grown bigger and bigger, until one day Johann hit it a smack with the Bible, and then it disappeared. The hand would be handsomer on the statue as it was now; but still not handsome, she chuckled to herself.

There, in his wheelchair, was little Johann, for whom the poet Heine might have written

> *Creating, I got better,*
> *Creating, I got well.*

There was Marta, whose violin spoke to the hearts of all who heard; all of her children well and here in the church, except Lissie, and it would leastwise be Sigrid to find fault with the new way of keeping a woman to the childbed for ten full days! Loving, tender Lennart knew that was the way it should be. Lennart must be right. Times changed. And who could deny that change was for the good—at times. Lissie would be stronger for the rest, and able to put her utmost into the service of the Churching of Women, when at the appointed day, a month after her delivery, she would come and give thanks and praises unto God for safe deliverance.

At this moment, the chances were, the faithful old midwife Erika Alvardsson was serving coffee and cookies to her two charges, Elisabet and the aged Widow Kvalvog. Who but Lissie would have been so able to couch a loving invitation to the old school teacher, that she would have accepted a home with one of those to whom her own home had opened in the past?

Except Lissie, all of her living children were here—and except Karl. Her thoughts returned to her own Thanksgiving after his birth, and she stopped where she stood and gazed upward at the stained-glass window, placed by Morfar in loving memory of her grandmother, and in whispers repeated the prayer so earnestly spoken in unison with her Pastor on that day: "Grant, we beseech thee, O Heavenly Father, that the child of this thy servant may daily increase in wisdom and stature, and grow in thy love and service, until he come to thy eternal joy; through Jesus Christ our Lord. Amen."

"Amen," said Big Johann quietly, and pressed her hand.

"Let him, O God, think kindly on his mother—let him—O, let him—come home." Silently she prayed as a heavy sob tightened her bosom. "Forgive me, Lord," and she stood erect. She had so much to be thankful for—that Elisabet's child should be born without a mark—so much—so much.

But oh, how she wished for a letter from her boy, to tell her how he had fared since leaving the homestead; how she longed that he might choose to return to Norden to be its rightful master. But if he felt he could not write as yet, she understood. A man had pride.

Still, she would never leave off praying that one day a letter might come from Karl.

Her arm returned the fond pressure of Johann's as he led her to the boat landing. They looked into each other's eyes and laughed, as in the same instant, like true parents both, they turned to assure themselves of the welfare of the infant in its father's arms, and of her children, tall and short, and of his namesake using wheels in place of legs.

As Sigrid's words had often been, "Yes, God is good," so were Big Johann's. She was his wife. Say it over as many times as he would, yet how could he comprehend that such wealth had come to him? How should a man believe the coming of full realization of a dream? As he felt, so might his soul feel at realization of its hopes for eternity, awakening on one bright day to find that Heaven is real.

"I think of naught I do not now possess, with her as wife. Thanks be to Thee, O God, for eyes to see her beautiful soul. And let me be worthy, oh, let me be worthy of her love!"

The sea had filled his life these many years, but now he was glad to leave the sailing to the younger men and satisfy his sight of it by standing on the shore, with Sigrid. Those younger men, deeming their young shoulders the only ones fit to wear the mantle of love! Youth, who sipped of the frothy bubbles of the fast-tumbling mountain spring of life, thinking they tasted full of life and love! They could not know the deep contentment, found in the bottom of the cup, when savored by taste grown keener through the years. They could not know, but he knew: autumn is no less beautiful than spring. More precious, autumn, for all the while we bask in its golden light we know it soon will go—leaving but one season more—

Reminiscent of by-gone days was this christening day at Norden, with heavy-laden board and fun and frolic for all.

At the end of the day Sigrid and Johann and Georg sat alone in the old house, while the family visited at the sister house of Elisabet and Lennart. The out-of-doors was heavy with dusk and storm clouds were hanging low. The three sat in the gloaming, silent. Dusk erased the shapes of their figures and of familiar objects in the big room. Parting was ever like this, too hard a pull on heartstrings, no words expressive enough to tell the feelings.

Georg Ahlgren, the old family friend, "Little Georg," as they had always called him, was going to America.

Johann could not trust himself to speak. He had so much; life was so wondrous good for him, and Georg was alone. Did they all three think of the Selma who had forsaken Georg? And now Johann's marriage to Sigrid had left Georg all the more alone.

Johann stared toward the window. His memory told him a little aspen tree stood there, whistling her plaintive tune, but the evening was black; all was in storm-shadow.

Suddenly a slender shaft of low setting sunlight came from an opening in the clouds and shone through one little aspen leaf— setting it apart—lighting it against the background of all the leaves darkened together in one mass—making it golden.

Thus was his Sigrid.

Would that Georg could know such gladness as he knew. Perhaps America would be more kind to the heart of Georg. A friend could hope.

From the light of the lamp flame inside the sparkling glass chimney the room now took on its old familiar look.

"We shall miss you, Georg," Sigrid spoke softly, and turned up the flame.

"And I, you."

"It is a long time you think on staying," Johann said, "too long a time."

"Oh, I can always come back any day—"

"Come back here," Sigrid interrupted, for this was the only home he knew.

"But," Georg's face brightened, "I do want to be in Chicago and see the great World's Columbian Exposition before I come back."

"America is large," Sigrid said, almost in a whisper, "aye, America is large—"

She walked as in a dream toward the chest room, but soon returned and in her hands she held her son's blue shawl, the shawl she had knitted for him those many years before, of fine blue wool, like a spider's web, begun at the time he was born; years in the making, knit in the patterns sent to her by the winter on the windowpanes and in the flakes of snow, in the color of the sea when it is peaceful, and the blue of his own dear eyes, and the blue of truth and honor.

"Karl must be in America." Her pleading eyes tore at the hearts of the two men. "Here—give him his shawl. Please, Georg, I know America is large, but take it, please. Your way may cross Karl's path."

She wiped a tear from her cheek and smiled, "The world is small. We never know—

"And if you meet him, tell him of his papa's going, and that Norden now is his. Give him his shawl, Georg, and tell him that its every stitch speaks of his mother's love."

TWO

KARL LEANED FORWARD and whispered into the ear of the horse, Elsass, and they shot forward like a breeze, leaving his riding companion behind.

He was at home on the back of a horse, part of a oneness that is rider and mount. Childhood scenes, all of his childhood dreams, rushed in upon him as he sped: he was with Hjärta, the coal-black stallion, with a white star on its forehead, that had been as much a part of his boyhood as his mother or the roof over his head or the summers' sun and winters' snow, or the sky.

Beyond the length of his memory it had been part of his life, for his mother had dedicated the little shining black colt to him before ever he was born. Hjärta—Heart—she had named it, because her own heart had gone out to it at once.

They had grown up together, the horse and he. One of the earliest of his recollections was of sticking the toes of one foot into the crevices between the stones of the rugged barnyard fence, clinging with the other foot to a higher stone, reaching for the mane, grabbing it and holding it tight to pull himself to Hjärta's back.

"Too young," he remembered his father saying, "to be allowed full freedom of the farmlands." But his mother had trusted him and over the fields he had ridden, beyond the pasture into the sheep lot, beyond the firs, through the birch swamps, to the peat bog, on the back of his beloved horse.

His mother had given him Hjärta, the most precious horse in all the world. Growing with the horse, it had shaped the plans for his future. He would be no ordinary farmer, guiding the wooden plow over the field, turning his ankles in the little trenches it made, dragging the old wooden-toothed harrow over the newly turned earth to pulverize and smooth it, striding along with a basket hanging on his front, dipping into flaxseed and casting it from him—far and wide.

Ah, no, his boy-dreams saw Norden's ground as carpet for the finest horses in the land. He would combine his two ambitions, his three. A writer he must be, for it was born in him to write. The trolls in the forest heaped stories on him as he rode, and the stories wanted only the putting on paper. And he would raise horses. Starting with Hjärta and the little farm mare, he would learn; then their colts would sell and the money buy him a pair of thoroughbreds—Arabian, Belgian, Flemish—or maybe he might do well to start with Suffolk Punch, accustomed as they would be to breathing the North Sea's dampness. The searching far and wide for the best sire of a strain would satisfy that third ambition, burning always inside of him, the Viking thirst for travel. And with travel, came adventure!

Soon he would own a chain of stables, branching out to the continent, supplying the mounts for a lady's riding or a gentleman's; from his stables would come horses for racing, for the cavalry, for mounted constables, for the King! For each use, its breed; and each breed the best.

The boy grew. His stallion grew. His secret ambition grew, and his knowledge. Choosing the finest specimens, he would wipe out any undesirable features of the breed, and improve the best ones.

So dreamed the boy he had been. All would come to him through Hjärta. His horse would start the chain, for anything was possible, everything was possible through his pet.

Horses. Nearest to the intelligence of man; and with his help the animals he raised would more nearly meet that intelligence, for he would control their breeding. It was not to be like Norden's family life, with his father and mother producing offspring almost each and every year without a thought of—

His father—

A low wail broke from him; his head drooped and his mount slowed. He was no longer that boy he had been. He had no horse of his own.

Reaching toward manhood, there he had lain, on that day, nursing himself with the mumps he should have had in childhood, while Hjärta was taken away and lost to him forever.

Lost, too, were his dreams. Because of what his father had done, all were for naught. His own father, whom he had been taught to respect and honor, who said the family prayers so eloquently that chills crawled up the boy's spine as he listened, who sat with his Bible on his lap; that same father had taken his horse to the mainland and sold it for money. Not because of hunger, nor necessity, had his father done so. No! But to pleasure himself.

Karl's heavy breast still felt the hurt. Something within him had died in that moment of shock when he heard his father say, "I only sold a horse."

Only a horse! God! He had sold a young man's future, taken away the symbol of everything that life could mean: the pride that comes with ownership, love, hope for successful enterprise, *everything!*

"Men do not cry." Karl blinked the tears from his lashes and tossed his head. "Dreams are a fragile stuff." He leaned forward, addressing the rented horse, and his voice trembled, "But what is a man without dreams?"

How could he have stayed on in the home, hating his father so, and with Hjärta gone? No. He had had to run away. Only one course left open for a boy betrayed, to search for opportunity elsewhere.

And how could he believe in God, after this thing that his God-loving father had done to him?

"Ho! Karl! You left me like a streak of greased lightning." His companion caught up with him.

"Aye, Rikard, Elsass is a good horse."

With feet toughened by weeks of marching at Kronobergshed, in training for the infantry, Karl and Rikard Eklund had not minded the mile from the military training heath to Jakob's *gästgifvargård*, there to obtain mounts for the trip to the Eklund homestead, where Karl was to find work.

"No ordinary rent horses," Rikard smiled and patted his animal's neck, "come from Jakob's innyard. I swear he has the finest of any innkeeper in Sweden."

Karl winced at remembering: "Come," Jakob had said, "if rent horses are all you have wish for, and you will not sup or stay the night, come," and he led the way to the barns. "Rikard Eklund will want the pert ones, yes, as he is accustomed to having?"

"Aye, *tack*," Rikard answered.

"There is not choice, much, for Karl Petersson," and he had

turned to Karl, "the black stallion is aught there is left in the barn. Elsass—come!"

Black stallion! The heart of Karl Mattias Petersson, eldest son of Sigrid and Peter Kristiansson of Norden, had it stopped beating? Or did it skip a beat only, or two, or three beats? Hjärta was a black stallion! Certainly not improbable that a good horse, sold once on the mainland in Bohuslän might be sold and sold again, finding its way at last to an inn in Småland! Karl's eyes looked heavenward.

No. No use to pray. But if there really were a God, now—*NOW* would be the time that He could prove Himself, and make this horse be Hjärta!

The innkeeper then backed his rent horse from the stall. Big eager eyes had turned full upon Karl, and he could not help but return the look of affection Elsass gave him. Animals knew, somehow, when men loved them. Coal-black was Elsass—no white star on his forehead—but a fine horse, for all he was not Hjärta.

No; Karl knew he had not really expected to find his own horse. But still, why not? *Why not?*

They loped along, and Rikard wondered at Karl's heavy mood. Was he not happy at the outlook of going toward the Eklund farmstead? Perhaps he was saddened at the thought of one going to his own home whilst he, Karl, headed toward another's? Rikard would not, then, force conversation on his friend. He leaned forward and spoke love words into Fanny's ear, and patted her neck crooning, *"Min lilla Franciska."*

Karl's look was dark. Why did his friend torture him thus? Could not Rikard treat the horse like a vehicle of convenience for a traveler, and not talk to the little mare as he would to a human—as he himself, he sighed deep, would have talked to Hjärta?

Why had he come with Rikard, after all? Because he had nowhere else to go, so he had told himself. Yet, if he gave his heart rein now, would this horse turn and speed its hooves toward Norden?

So deep the wish to know: how could a son who had torn himself in rage from his home, how could he turn his face again toward the homestead? How could he brave himself to meet scorn, if such should be there waiting? Or how could he beg forgiveness if arms were open? How?

The horse jogged under him. Why had he come with Rikard? His tent-mate at the training heath had written an elder brother, Sven, asking that a place be made for Karl, so he might have employment. The answer had come then from Sven Eklund. Would Karl Petersson come, with Sven's brother Rikard, to the home farm?

No. NO! His wish was to make more of himself than a tiller of the soil; and it was to America he wished to turn, to find the opportunity.

But, yes; what could he do but say yes. He had to have a place to sleep, enough to eat. The thought was unbearable of returning to the Granlund farm where he had worked the past year, where loneliness had built a solid wall about him, the only unmarried hired hand, eating alone in the corner of the kitchen, sleeping alone in the hayloft; through the whole year brushing against none near to his own age. Where else should he go from the heath and take with him his only possessions, the underclothes that stunk from his sweat in the linen bag?

Home? After the way he had gone from home? He could not. "For a while, yes, Rikard, I shall be glad to come."

There, at the Eklund homestead, his friend outlined, Karl would find a good home, farmwork to be sure; but also, had not Karl expressed the desire many times, during the weeks they had been together in training, to put his hand to sail again? Eagerly, with a *syskon's* pardonable pride, Rikard told of the older brother. No apter sailboat master in the whole of Sweden, than Sven, who planned to cut the waters this coming month of July, up the western frayed and fringed edge of Sweden, to Norway's coast. For Sven had known the dream to sail those waters every summer of his life, but had not gone in four years now for yielding to a newer, deeper love, that of his wife and child.

"Made to order with your knowledge, not only of the farm, but of the water," Rikard had urged.

Yes, he would be glad to come. Without spirit Karl had answered yes; but he took care not to bind himself by saying how long a time he would stay. Long enough, only, to add some to his purse for the going to America.

He took in the landscape about him. Beech trees, that furnished *bok* wood for the winter, now furnished shade. Now they showed that rare green color—as the sky can be a heavenly blue, this was a heavenly green.

"But," his head steeled himself against his heart, "at best, summer is short." And stones; all about him, stones. Småland was no richer than his own home place on the rugged stony island of Bohuslän's skerries! It was two years since he had left his home, thinking himself almost on America's shores because he had cut his home ties. Two years, and what had he, more than that he had not starved? Only a few *kronor* toward his passage to America. Money was hard to get, here in Sweden. Disgruntled, he looked about: a worn-out land, this, as compared to the new, in America.

Nay, Småland gave not of riches. Only a fool would have decided to remain here to find a bed and board, however temporary. Heavy with folly was he who, forelearned, should have been forewarned; every man knew the legend, repeated oft in Bohuslän as well as elsewhere all over the peninsula. Aeons ago Saint Peter petitioned to God, who had forgotten it in the making of the world, to let him make that part of the country which is Småland. And God denied him not the permission. Saint Peter, lacking the Craftsman's skill, without a lavish hand endowed the land, but skimped and skimped; and when he had done, the Master, viewing the poverty of the soil, thereupon was compelled to create the Smålanning. Hardy, and necessarily thrifty, infinitely persevering, thus was Småland's stock which, according to the story, could eke a living from a barren stone in the middle of the salt sea, if need be.

And with such he had chosen to cast his lot!

Uncountable, the many times he had smirked at the traits of those people of the sister province whose land lay east of Bohuslän, beyond Västergötland, fronting the Baltic. Disgruntled as he was, looking about him, as he rode, Karl knew it was no mere legendary illusion that it would take more than a plot of Småland's farmland to make a man rich.

Yet Rikard felt himself rich; and rich enough he was to provide employment for a friend.

Neck and neck, Fanny and Elsass carried the two young men, until, "There!" joyfully announced Rikard. "There, ahead, stands Lugnbo, the homestead of my fathers!"

Karl nodded. There stood a house, not so different from the home he—so long ago—had left behind, of Falu-red timbers with white trim outlining the windows. Some little difference, perhaps, as they drew nearer. This roof was not of thatch, but of thin strips of wood, like beechwood, lying flat. The corners of the house showed white, for there, defining the corners, were wide smooth boards painted to match the windows' trim. The house was taller than the home at Norden; instead of merely a loft room above the main floor, it must have rooms of the height of those below, for casements told of such. A one-story ell reached out to bind the tall house to the ground, and where there was no ell, high, thick and bushy foliage drew the outline—like foothills leading the eye to the peak of a mountain of only inconsiderable height—to the roof peak.

Peaceful and still the farm lay, with its stone fences, as at home. Carried away by the sight, nearing the yard fence, Karl gave the sign to his horse, and "Over, Hjärta," he whispered into the animal's ear.

But quickly he returned to the present, to Småland. He bade farewell to Ryssel, the boy who would lead the rented animals back to the innyard; but he turned fiercely from the horses.

He shook hands with Sven Eklund, his new master. Sture Sven, they called him, since Lilla Sven had come. He bowed before Eleonora, the wife, as she sat with her child on her lap.

They live well, these Eklunds, he admitted to himself as he looked about the room. The furnishings were plain, but rich. Fine tapestries hung on the walls. The candlesticks and wall sconces were not of brass, but of finely wrought silver, and there was a golden clock sitting on the shelf of the *kakelugn*. It must have cost a fancy *öre*, this stove of saucer tile, rich in white and purple-blue with gold trimming here and there, tall—almost to the ceiling of this tall room—with fancy designs around the iron door in the lower part of it, and framing the clean clear mirror of the upper half. Like little iris flowers, those blue blossoms scattered in regular pattern over the shining white of the tile. Had ever, he wondered, any such fine kakelugn graced a home in Bohuslän?

He found his new bed, soft with feathers and clean with white linen; but as a dreamer he walked and saw and spoke. His real self saw only the coal-black stallion which, if there really *were* a God, would have had a white star on its forehead—saw all of the promise that Hjärta had stood for—gone.

He put his brawn to the plow.

A hired farmhand, in two years, so far had he come. He had come no way at all.

Then Elin came to Lugnbo. She walked into the big room. A stranger? Nay, some likeness here, come to bedevil him. Karl stared. Then, in the dropping of his eyelids, the room became the big room at Norden; the kakelugn faded somehow into a corner fireplace, plain, with an overhanging flue of plastered brick following the lines of the raised hearthstone and supported at the corner by a frail-looking, turned spindle of oak.

Carefully, Elin placed her bundle on the hearth. So would his sister Marta have set down her violin. Or was it his sister Maria that Elin favored? She walked across the room to greet him. Her walk—a quick and rhythmic movement— Who, in his past, had seemed to float across a room in just this way?

Ah, yes, of course, his mother.

THREE

As Sven was twenty years older than his brother Rikard, so Eleonora was twenty years further in age than her sister Elin. "The granddaughter of a Riksdagsman," Rikard had said when he told of Elin's forthcoming visit.

Was it the tone of Rikard's telling, or was the inflection of certain of his words meant to bring home to Karl a warning that he was not to show interest in this fair child? He, son of a poor peasant farmer, was that what meaning Rikard had intended to convey? That was the way it was, here in Sweden: a better class, a lower class. No such distinction in America to wreck the amity of men, at least according to Axel Lindqvist who had read letters from the United States, to all who would listen, back on the military training heath.

Not one good word for Sweden, had Axel had. A man might almost come to the conclusion that he could be one of those rumored to be in the pay of certain steamship companies to stir up unrest and dissatisfaction so they could sell more tickets for passage!

Love of homeland had not lighted the features of this crooked-mouthed man when they stood singing the national anthem,

"Du gamla, du fria—"

only a hard glint shone from his eyes as he whispered coarsely, or shouted, depending upon the proximity of officers, "Compulsory military training in a time of peace? *Not in America!*"

Still, Karl ruminated, had Axel something there, after all? As he had listened to Axel, he was not sure in his own mind but that the hurt of compulsory service went deeper than the tender foot

17

skin where blisters came and were worn and torn away by marching. Was his individuality being jeopardized? Karl knew his pride was hurt; in that one word, "compulsory," was the shame of it. Yet, Rikard did not mind the name of "conscript." And he was one to claim that money, or the lack of it, would build classes in America as widely separated as any built by birth or blood.

But Rikard had refused to listen to the contents of the letters Axel had, and therefore did not understand that every man in America was rich!

Aye, that was it, only that Rikard Eklund did not understand; Karl's friends, the Eklunds, could not feel toward him as if he were inferior, they would not have invited him to come here if they did. No doubt but that Rikard's tone implied only that he held Elin as his own, looking forward toward the day when their two families might have a second bond.

"No need to fear, friend Rikard," Karl assured himself, "for I am a man, and she is but a child. Her bosoms do not yet swell out her bodice. And if they did, I care not for a woman. My life is charted on one course alone now, and that leads to America."

He swung his scythe. The sun was good; it made the sweat come; and the breeze was good, it blew on the sweat, cooling his skin. The world, in this moment, was good; he paused to rest, gratefully, as he saw Elin come across the field. She brought a pail of coffee, hot from the stove-top, and freshly baked "cock's combs." They sat together in the tree shade and had mid-afternoon *kaffe kalas*. She had baked the dainties, with her own hands, and described to him how she folded the rich pastry over almond paste filling and then with a knife gashed them along one side five or six times, before baking, to give them their shape. Some she had turned onto pearl sugar so the tops were sweet, and some she had dressed with sesame seeds. They sat together and ate and drank and talked and laughed. Never so good had fresh-baked pastry tasted to Karl. She did not seem to mind that he was of a lower class, this granddaughter of Halland's deputy to the National Assembly.

"So there you are," interrupted Rikard. "I thought I smelled coffee. *'Kaffetåren den bästa är, Av alla jordiska drycker!* Coffee is the best of all earthly drinks!' say I. Is there some left for me?"

Karl rose and returned to his work. He felt his guilt at having been caught with a resting scythe. Striking the blade viciously against the yielding stems, he moved away, maddened to frenzied endeavor, going to all lengths to leave the sound of laughter from Elin's lips as she and Rikard finished the kalas.

He scowled. Rikard could have left him alone with Elin for those few moments. He would have more than made up for the idle time!

She was good company, was Elin. When she was near, and Rikard far, it seemed good to be working on Sven Eklund's farm. To be sure he worked long hours, but he was never one to flinch at hard work.

Too bad, though, to have to share with Rikard the picture of yellow-haired Elin, standing against the dark red of the homestead, half in sunlight and half in the shade of old gnarled oak trees. Too bad he could not have to himself the sight of the gold of her hair shining against the clear blue water of the lake as they rowed, or against the green of tall pines on the shore beyond. But, inevitably, Rikard was sharing the rowboat.

Almost it seemed a pain that it should be so short a time to be near Elin, less than two weeks until Sven and he would leave for the seacoast to fit their boat and unfurl the sails for Sven's water holiday. Not many women like Eleonora, he would wager, to encourage a husband to sail for weeks on a holiday without her. "Such is what I love about you, my husband," he heard her say as they sat in the big room on a rainy evening. "You know how to play as well as to work. Go, rest your business head, and when you return fresh from the rest, you will be keener, and the other men will be no match for you."

What did she mean? It took no greater keenness than another man's to wring their daily living from this farm; that entailed no great competition with other men. And then he heard Sven speak of pine and cutting, and the price of logs delivered to the mill, of perfect timbers of such and such dimensions, of pulp; and he remembered the pine forests beyond the lake. As he had seen his mother bargain at the fish market, so Sven must have to bargain to hold his own, to turn the green pines into gold.

The color of precious metal, gold; the color of his mother's hair—the color of Elin's hair.

He closed his eyes, and in the closing, again he stood beside his mother at the fish wharf after the catch. "Fru Kristiansson shall be our spokesman," the men voted. "She can out-trade any man amongst us. Is it not so?" It had been so. There had been cheers for Sigrid Kristiansson, his mother. He had been proud of her. That was before he had noticed how she was different from his teacher at the school, how her body always showed the rounding with another and yet another child.

He bit his lip. He had been proud of her! But then, after the merciless treatment of his father, he had hurt her, and run away.

He had to run farther—farther—to America, so he could make it up to her and come back, not empty-handed, begging forgiveness, as now he would have to come, but laden with gifts. A silk dress, a hat—his mother always had wanted a hat.

Thinking on his mother, stories came to his mind, of the sea, of mothers, of sons who were strangers to their fathers. His mother had thought he had talent; he sat putting words together in his mind, the first step before putting them on paper, but soon his thoughts strayed, for there on the floor was Elin, amusing Lilla Sven. They darted, on knees and hands, first to one side of the room and then to the other to play "peek" with a little black and white kitten.

Karl's were not the only eyes watching Elin's dainty hands smooth out the long carpet runner, then hunch it up in the center to make a little tunnel. Rikard followed each move and his mouth curved into an indulgent smile when Elin started the kitten head first into the dark of the passageway under the carpet. He laughed outright when Elin squealed, and Lilla Sven squealed, as the kitten emerged from the other side of the carpet, only to see the playmates he had left at the other end of the tunnel. Rikard laughed again when, after another trip through the darkness, the Kisse-Katt sniffed around, looking for Elin and the baby; but they had hidden back of chairs, suppressing their laughter behind their hands. When Karl laughed, Rikard's face straightened from the smile. What was this look he sent? Karl puzzled over it. Since Elin had come, it was not the same between Rikard and him.

If Rikard were master, instead of the older brother, Sven, perhaps he, Karl, would no longer share the big room but would sit alone in the kitchen, as was expected of servants, removed from the Riksdagsman's kin? Was Rikard jealous, even of the little pleasure he derived from watching children play?

But in Karl's eyes, Elin seemed to grow fast into a woman, as she held Lilla Sven on her lap and rocked him until he fell asleep.

And the woman-thoughts she churned within her mind, how they would have surprised the young hired man from Bohuslän! How had it come about that a young man should offer to help her clean up the dishes after the evening meal? How had it happened that he should be trained in such a household chore, him, a boy, trained in woman's work? If no servants there, in Bohuslän, had he not had sisters in the home? Men did not bend themselves to hold the linen drying towel in a home kitchen in Småland, or in Halland.

But question she would not only revel in the kindness of his offer and his help. So fine a mother Karl must have had, she mused, to have impressed her training with such thoroughness upon him that in drying the forks—although, carelessly, he first had drawn the linen over the whole of them and flung them into the table drawer—as if his early training spoke, he had retrieved them all and run the towel between each tine, polishing as he went....

Elin seemed grown to Karl as she stooped to neaten the floor and spread the carpet runner smooth. Such a carpet; he wished his mother could see it, for the like of it was new to him. He stooped to examine it and he could see that, though the warp was of linen thread such as he oft had set up on his mother's loom, the woof was of thin strips of hide and hair from a long-haired rabbit. It made a thick and soft, fluffy carpet, and with Elin sitting there with its fluffiness around her, matching in color the little kitten in her arms, it was a picture to wipe out thoughts of disillusionment, and blighted hope, and the magnetic pull of a far-away country.

The unrest he knew when he was alone, what became of that when Elin neared? It was dispelled when she came running toward him and they walked together through the fields or alongside the lakes, until Rikard joined them.

Karl was from Bohuslän? Then he must tell her of the rune stones. Had he seen any of them, truly, with his own eyes? So he told her of the stories portrayed on the Bronze Age stones, of engravings of adventure and the enterprise of seafaring ships, of homely themes of everyday life, of themes of war. He drew pictures with a stick, in the bare ground to the north of the stone fence, to show her how the horsemen mounted on their steeds would appear if she were looking down upon a rune stone. The horse's body, the rider's body, and the spear, all were of the same width. Crude drawings in the soil, but he spoke seriously as he assured her that they were no more crude than the runic originals.

"Oh, they could draw better than that!" She laughed.

"But this is the way they look."

She did not believe him, but it was fun to watch him draw and listen to him tell of his home province. So, he was from Bohuslän; the world was small, her grandfather's farm in Halland lay neighboring the farm of one who had taken himself a wife from Bohuslän! Often Elin had spent her summers on her grandfather's farm, every summer of her life, in fact, before her sister Eleonora had married Sven Eklund and come to live in Småland. Now she divided her summers between her sister's farm and her grandfather's. Wistfully she told of the gentle little mother who, this year, was too frail to come. This was the second separation from her *mor* in all her life. For mor had gone to Bohuslän for a wedding that September the year before last, and Elin *almost* had gone; the fact was that only the measles had kept her in Halland while the others went.

"But, Maria, the bride from Bohuslän, oh, what a wife to David Henning! What fun she is!"

Karl started.

"You know the name?" Elin asked, surprised.

Quickly he turned their conversation, "And where do you call home in the winter months?"

She told him of Falkenberg, of the shops lining the cobblestoned Storgaten, the main street, of frame buildings and brick, shop signs sticking out from the faces of buildings, a large clock hanging at the roofline of one, tiled roofs, dormer windows, a green tree near the bend of the street, white awnings and an occasional striped one fluttering gently, flag poles pointing upward toward the sky, white stone steps inviting folk to enter deep-set doors, and of a sign over one of the doors, *"Privat Hotellet."*

Karl only half heard. So, his sister Maria was married to David Henning! Soon after his leaving home she had married, and they all had been happy and gay, and he had not been there to share in it! He had missed the dancing and singing and being merry, at Maria's wedding. There wasn't anyone's wedding festivities he rather would have shared, than Maria's! Tears flooded his eyes.

A golden band now circled one finger of those long, expressive hands that could mold soap or suet, as well as clay, into likenesses so real—so "breathing" real. Maria was married to David, and he was glad for her. But he should have been there! Red-headed, red-lipped, red-cheeked, blue-eyed David would take good care of his sister and make her happy: if only Elisabet could know such happiness. It was to poor Elisabet that he must bring the greater share of gifts after he got rich in America, for with the hairy birthmark on her face, what man would take her as his wife?

Absent-mindedly he strained to hear a distant bird song. Like the sounds from his sister Marta's violin. She would have been the one to play at Maria's wedding—

Elin looked at him. She bit her lip, tears came, and she stamped her foot and tossed her head. Rikard never looked beyond her so, scarcely noticing her presence! She would go and find Rikard!

Karl reached for her hand, "Listen, Elin," he whispered, "music."

The bird sang. Elin stayed.

"In my writing," he confided, "I could make stories for the mind, but music gives stories to the soul—"

Elin stared at Karl. "Stories, Karl, you mean you—?"

"Yes. If only I could capture some of the music of words, some of their rhythm."

"Of what would you write, Karl?" she asked, incredulously, the accent on the pronoun.

The accent went unnoticed, and he told her, "Of the sea."

They sat on a log. "The love of the sea," of that he would write, "a love, matched in all human hearts."

"Nay, Karl," she said, decidedly, "then you would not write truth."

"What do you say, Elin?"

"There are those of us who hate the ocean."

"Hate?" He looked hard at her. Let him think; yes, he could understand a dread of the water in one so small as Elin, a fear of the mighty clashing waves by one who had not grown, perhaps, to know the sea intimately from infancy; but could he ever fathom a hatred for the grand, albeit boiling churning heaving howling waters?

"Anybody can write little stories," she said scornfully, "about things they love, or believe. Even I. It would take a real writer to tell a story that made real something he did not, himself, feel— or know."

Here was a challenge, coming from Elin, questioning his ability to write a story of a hate he did not feel. Even as the trolls in the woodlands at Norden, in his childhood, had given him words to put on paper, so now this nearness of Elin, and her challenge, guided his lead pencil over both sides of the flattened-out envelope which had encased his *Flyttningsbevis*, to spill over and fill the margins beyond the printed matter on his church removal paper.

Beatta, he named his heroine:

> Beatta stood at the window, gazing from a height upon the sea. Standing in her fathers' home, that clung to the rock ledge, she watched the water breaking against the rocks in fury.

> Beatta's stomach churned. She sat herself on the sill. Her fingers trembled; a sheet of notepaper fell with her hand to her lap, and her hand crushed it. Her head drooped forward, the chin rested on her breast and her breast heaved with inward sobbing. Tears fell on her hands, on her full rounded body.

> She spread the piece of paper flat, and re-read its message. The sea had won again. Oh, how she hated it, the robber of her home! First it had taken her grandfather, then her father, and, she smoothed the rumpled paper over her knee, now the father of her unborn child.

> Her grandfather—her Morfar—but the sea had sent him home, from his ship's wreckage, without a mind— sitting, as a little child, blubbering—

> Her father—his body washed ashore—

> And now her husband. Lost in the sinking of his ship.

> Beatta screamed. Her son should never go to sea. Never!

At once she would leave the home where her forefathers had learned to love the sea because it fed them. She would go down and fill a bottle with water from the ocean, and when she found a place so far inland that none could tell her what liquid filled the bottle, there she would stay and give birth to her son. Her will would conquer the unconquerable sea!

She climbed down the rocky ledge. Heavy, the wind blew her clothing against her. Cutting, the sleet pained her cheeks and her eyes. But the sting of storm-weather was as nothing against the burn of her heartbreak, against her determination to cheat the sea of her son. He should never know the salt water—her son—and if he learned by chance of it, she would thwart both God and Fate by—

"Oh—h—" her cry was higher than the loudest wave-wail. Like a loosened stone she crashed down the ledge to the shoreline...

Again Beatta stood at the window of the small red house of her forebears. She looked down on the sea. The water was calm and rolling. A small fishing smack rode and dipped. It could be the selfsame one whose crew had picked her up and carried her back up the ledge on that day she fell, the day her son was born.

She had set out to win against the sea, and she had won. Her son would never serve as able-bodied sailor aboard a ship.

And yet the sea, unmindful, had lost nothing; still it lashed as before against the shore. Still its color was blue, changing to green, breaking into white foam.

She had won. But in the winning, "How much I have lost!" she cried, and covered her face with her hands. Still she could see the empty crib, the little new earth bed, the small gray headstone.

Finished, Karl read it to Elin. Tears streamed down her face. "Oh, Karl," she said; she could not tell him how she felt, that she had had no idea—that she must not waste his time when he should be spending it in such creative fashion. Instead, she ran from him.

He stood, forlorn, his arms hanging loosely at his sides. If only she had stayed. He felt lonely, sad. Thinking of the sea made him think of home, and he suffered.

The next day Elin did not come near him; in the evening she played checkers with Rikard, and he walked the winding road to the hilltop by himself. He missed the little game she played with him, plucking a buttercup blossom and holding it under his chin "to see if he liked butter." A childish thing to do and have done to a man. But he missed it.

Morning came, and it was Sunday. Would Elin show some interest in whether or not he was joining them in their trek to the little church? Would he go if she invited him to accompany her and the others? No. He might wish that she would ask him; oh, how he wished she would care enough to ask him, but not even for Elin would he break his promise to himself to ban worship in the church forever from his life. Only by keeping that promise would he show his disdain for the God his hated father worshipped.

But he waited for Elin to come from the little church surrounded by fir trees. Beyond lay the churchyard with old sunken stones. There, strewn with wilted flowers, was a new grave. "Small windows, a heavy door to shut men in, a cross— symbol of suffering and pain—and graves, speaking of death. No, the church is not for me," he said vehemently, "I want life— and living—and opportunity—and freedom!"

He waited for Elin in the lane.

She came walking sedately with the others, sedately, yet with that flowing grace. Annoying that her walk should be so vivid a reminder of his mother, the mother he had to forget. Must forget.

Elin's yellow hair fell around her shoulders; she had removed her bonnet and he saw that the silken hair was drawn tight back from her forehead and held with a little whalebone clasp at the top of her head. Her tiny ears showed fully, rosy-pink suffused her cheeks, her chin was firm.

But how tiny she was!

She saw him in his everyday clothes and her heart cried out in sympathy. Poor Karl, she thought, he would not come with us to church because he had no change of clothing. This one time she could forget her grown-up decision of yesterday, not to put herself in his way to interfere with his story writing; she lingered behind the others and he caught up with her.

"*God dag, Jungfru* Elin." He towered above her and as he looked at her it seemed his eyelids almost closed, he must look down so far, "Yesterday—"

"Oh, yes," she saw that Rikard was within hearing and she chose to omit mention of their experience, but perched herself upon the stone fence and spread her church dress carefully around her. "So, I was telling you of my home in Falkenberg. It is not like in the country. Almost all of the streets are laid of cobblestones, not mud roads like this one here; and in the mornings when the housewives come out and get down on their knees and hands to scrub the streets in front of their houses, oh, it is fun to stand and listen to them call to their neighbors while they wring their cloths out into the buckets. And the women laugh and some of them sing." She had forgotten he was a seasoned traveler, and when she saw him smile, she added, "Is it so in the cities where you have been?"

He boasted then, and told her more of cities than his eyes had seen. He told her, too, of Malmö and watched her as, fascinated, she listened to him describe Lund and the Cathedral there.

Had Rikard lingered all of this time at their side? Rikard snorted now, as if to discredit the knowledge of the traveled one, and walked away. Karl was glad. He raised one long leg and reached it over the fence, then sat astride the stones and leaned forward to tell Elin more. He told her of the little iron fence, in front of the fourteenth-century clock, whose openwork only partly reached to shadow the signs of the Zodiac; and there, between those Twins and the Ram and the Bull and the Balance and the rest—and the clock face above—was the miniature stage which held the gaze of all who waited for the large hand to show the hour of twelve noon. Not one, and this he'd vow, but came away in awe at the sight of the little figurines moving across the miniature stage with swords waving, their horses galloping to the tinkling staccato of the organ, sounding at the stroke of noon. Four little doorways, he had seen, and out from one—across the stage—and into another, came and went the little statuettes.

"That, one day you must see, Elin, that clock, set there in its arch."

Dreamily, Elin added, "Arches. Yes, we have arches, too, in Falkenberg. There is the Gamla Bron, all made of big stones, but arched so," and her arms moved gracefully to show the arches of the Old Bridge. As if she saw it there before her, she finished, "To let the river run through underneath." In the manner of extending an invitation, she went on, "And there is a place to walk, on top, over the arches. And the harbor, Karl, you must put in to Falkenberg, you and Sture Sven."

She loved her home; he could see how much she loved it.

"And my papa is not so rich as grandfather. Our home is not so grand as his, but our home looks like a fairy tale house. It sits on a corner, where two streets cross each other, and though the basement on the low side of the hill shows to be of stone, and the steps in the front are of stone, who can say of what the house is built?" She spread her hands out, palms upward, and Karl smiled.

"For there it stands," she went on, as if she now were writing a story, "with white-framed casements opening here and there on the two floor levels, and in the gable a pretty fan, but they peek out of green leaves and the shape of the house is solid with green leaves. My father tells that those vines have lived on the walls of our home for over a hundred years."

"I would like to see that house, Elin."

"Oh," impulsively, "you must come! You would be welcome, Karl."

"Yes, I would like to see it, but do not look for me to come, Elin. For I shall not stay in Sweden for too many moons."

"Where are you going?" Was there disappointment in the child's voice? Did it really matter to her whether he stayed or went?

"How old are you, Elin?"

"I am practically grown, for on the twenty-ninth day of July I shall be fourteen years old!"

"Because you are practically grown, I will tell you. I am on my way to America."

"America," her eyes grew moist. "So, too, am I—on my way to America."

Karl laughed. She was fast to catch on to an idea!

"Laugh, laugh, go on and laugh. But tell not of this to Eleonora or Sven—or to Rikard. But, midwife I *will not be*." She drew her dress skirt closer around her, and looked about to make sure no one neared, "Come, I will tell you."

He reached his feet to the ground and shifted his body weight so that he sat nearer to Elin. He sat and listened to her tell: her sister Eleonora had been trained to be a schoolteacher; her brother was to be a diplomat, but Algot had rebelled, and now they did not mention his name in the home because he had run away. Elin's voice was low, and Karl leaned forward better to hear. Algot had gone to America.

Each one of the children of the Nilsson family must be trained to earn his or her living in an honorable way, and as a trade for little *skälmaktiga* Elin, the mischievous one, they had chosen midwifery. She slid from her place on the stone fence and stamped her little foot, "I will not be a midwife."

Karl stood beside her, chiding her. Was this actually he, encouraging her to bend to her parents' wishes—he who had—

"I'll run away before I will go to midwife's school. They think because I am a girl I will not go, as Algot did. But Algot will send me a ticket, and I *will* run away and go to America, too!" She had given much thought to America since Algot went, and she surprised Karl with her knowledge of the new land. She, like Axel Lindqvist on the military training heath, was so fortunate as to have a letter from America.

Elin could see that Karl understood. There was this secret bond, now, between them. It brought Karl a comfortable feeling of being close to her, for he shared with Elin something that Rikard did not know. He found himself half wishing that she was more than merely a child.

They walked into the woodland and the sun peered through the pine boughs and lighted their way. They talked of books, and writing, and learning, and of the new land. Yes, she was good company, and when she looked up into his eyes and told him how smart he was, "smarter even than my grandfather, and he is a Riksdagsman," he smiled indulgently.

She told of her little terrier puppy which had played "peek" with her between the rungs of a chair when she was a little girl, and of how the puppy playfully had reached to greet her with his open mouth, and when she had come too close to the sharp teeth they had snapped together, catching her nose between them. "They killed my little *Tös*; they said she frothed at the mouth, but she only played." Elin stopped and looked up at him sadly, "And I cannot forget her. Do you see, much, the marks she left?"

Faint little scars, no, he had not noticed them. But he took her hand in knowing sympathy, and they turned to go back. Both saw, then, the fairy ring; they stood in the center of a circle of mushrooms. Bent over on its curved and down-covered stem, one showed its broad and pallid gills; as Karl moved slowly he watched the shadow pass along them. Here a cap was depressed, and it was filled with dew. Its full length gills and shorter alternates rounded out the shape of a bowl for fairy punch.

Caught in the center of a fairy ring! Almost roughly Karl dropped Elin's hand, and led her back to the dwelling.

Time came for Sven and him to put to the water, and to bid farewell to Elin. She would be far from Småland on their return, gone to her father's home in Falkenberg. There was a brave "God bless you both," from Eleonora, Lilla Sven's baby hand throwing kisses, and "Bon Voyage" from Rikard. Did Rikard seem to hasten him on his way? Aye. What a curse was jealousy—straining the bond of friendship between his friend and him—for it was obvious now that Rikard begrudged him his companionship with Elin.

"Farewell, friend Karl," she said.

"Farewell, Elin." He shook her little hand.

Suddenly he was glad to go. This child Elin tugged at his heartstrings in some uncommon way. She would grow to be a woman, and he wanted no woman entanglements to complicate his life.

FOUR

MARSTRAND LAY in the cool water where the Skagerrak and Kattegat merged. The Skagerrak—whose impatient parent, the North Sea, pushed gently now with lenient but insistent motion, with little pushes beginning at the gateway between Norway and her Danish neighbor's land, sending the clear blue water undulating toward Bohuslän's skerries, ending with a lapping, lapping against Marstrand's shore—in her turn pushing the waters of the Kattegat. Marstrand held her head high out of the water; her crown sat straight upon her brow.

Karl lay in the glittering summer water which lapped against him and flowed over him as he floated relaxed and still. His eyes were closed, for the sun was blinding in its brightness. To swim and float was good in this clear calm, sure to be followed by days of rain and heavy gales, in this heat of mid-July.

Salt water ran down from his hair and dripped from the end of his nose as Karl lifted his head and opened his eyes.

He gazed into the eyes of Marstrand, the windows and openings of grim old Karlsten fortress—older than six centuries of time—forbidding, gray, drawing its medieval outline against the sky.

Well he had learned, in childhood, of the building of the tremendous fortress here on this island so strategically placed as to guard the mainland. Well he had learned of the patriotism that was mother to the plan to build the mighty fortress here. First, sitting on the knee of his mother's grandfather, and then from his schoolteachers, he had been taught of the moats, the outer and inner moats, which in protecting the fortress protected the mainland itself. Proud, he had been, to be a part of Sweden, to know of Marstrand and her heroic resistance against the enemy; proud, now, with his own eyes to see her strength.

31

"Marstrand *is* Sweden," an islander had spoken, he too with pride. Aye, Karl knew, and he himself was Sweden. From time immemorial the blood of his ancestors had pulsed in time, and in tune, with the life's blood of Sweden.

So long had the love of Sweden lived in the hearts of his forebears, how could he be the one to tear himself away?

Was it that the innate love of travel and adventure, lain dormant in his fathers' blood since the last Viking boat had steered into the harbor, now gathered all in him, threatening to split his reason if he did not yield? Or was it that a heart could bear no longer to share the land with his horse Hjärta and find him not?

He tossed his head and splattered drops into the restless water. It was a man's ambition drove him to the land of opportunity. After his pockets were filled, then he could return to Sweden: he could build a bigger home for his mother, he could buy her a stove of saucer tile, a golden clock, and sconces of silver.

Even if he went home, never could he gather the wherewithal; too many to feed from the small plot of ground at Norden, and Norden had never given its owners such. Oh, to be able to find some way, here in his homeland, to attract the wealth that beckoned to him from America!

What was it, fighting within him, a love of the old and a longing for the new? A blend from the far past with the new was his homeland. Every age had left its recognizable mark on the landscape, jagged *cromlech* of the Stone Age to crown a hill, rune stones to tell of Viking exploits, castles, fortresses to speak of glory and martial majesty. Every age had left its mark for him: ice, stone and bronze, giving the forests of birch, aspen and pine, oak, linden and maple, giving the farmlands—pointing a way of life—for him.

From his forefathers had come respect for the land, its rivers, its trees, and its soft-contoured mountains; no raping of the land in Sweden, for they were not the only ones, they soon were taught; the land must feed their children and their children's children after them.

The land, and the people living off of it, one must take care of the other. The land. His land. Norden.

Norden gleaming in winter moonlight, what would replace that sight in America? The beauty of the farms—the red-house, white-birch and blue-sky beauty of the farms—hoarding the old-country scenes, could he be satisfied with those in the new?

All in the new world would be new. Clinging to ancient values, could he embrace the new?

Could he ski there, in America? Would there be hills of virgin snow for his ski to draw the first line across? Would there be mountains dressed with pine, valleys, or little lakes giving back its own azure to a summer sky?

In America did folk fold blankets over their feet and hot bricks, and ride in open sleighs, singing to the jangle of sleighbells, carrying torches on their way to *Julotta* early on Christmas morning after an Eve of giving and eating and merry-making? Oh, his body could live, but how much longer could his heart live without the dragging of a yule log over the wide expanse of snow from the woodlot, without Easter, without *Midsommardagen?* Oh, to go home! To sit at the hearthside, singing, reading with *syskon!*

Go home empty-handed? After the way he had left? In America he would be alone. Yet he must go. He had to have something, be somebody, drive up to his home with his own horse. He had to *show his father!*

His jaw set. They were poor at Norden; had always been poor, but they were rich in other than material goods. He saw it now, how rich they were in the heritage of strength and health, and honesty. That was why his father, after he sold Hjärta, stuck out like a sore thumb in this picture of Sweden, because his father had lacked integrity.

Go home? And watch hate searing the fabric of home life, warping the frame on which the cloth of daily life was woven, as he had had to watch it after his father had sold the stallion? No, he could not go home; his own father had robbed him of his birthright.

Thinking on his father's treachery, the timeless majesty of the fortress before him paled. With unchanged expression it looked down upon him, but Karl had changed. With thoughts of his father came all the memories of what might have been. Hate forced his reason into semi-consciousness. The words of Axel Lindqvist came, the contents of the letters he had read; the words of the island guide came, telling of the chaining of soldiers to iron rings so they could not move from their stations back of Marstrand's eyes, but loath must stand ready to receive the enemy's fire while returning shot for shot until the grievous end.

He had been taught of patriotism, but had patriotism held those soldiers to their posts? Had patriotism led his way—or the way of any of the youths he had met there—to Kronobergshed for the military training? The shameful answer was in that one word, "compulsory."

The water around Karl spoke to him, tantalizing him. It chatted of freedom; it roared; it whispered in sibilants, whispered of freedom! He swam furiously, rebelliously, away from Marstrand. Let the islanders ignore this landmark, or let their laughter rise and fall and echo from the yawning abyss which was the center of the tower; let them prate, parrot-like, as to visitors they told and retold of iron rings and soldiers, one holding the other to his post of duty!

His father! Sweden! One reminding him of the other! He turned and treaded water as he sent his voice toward the island, "Has Sweden come so far in all these years?" he asked. "What say you, Karlsten Fortress, to a man who still is chained to iron rings as strong as those which bound men to your stones, to a duty which is against his choice?" He swept his right arm wide, and slapped the water hard, "Is it not man's duty to be *free?*" He swam slowly back to the island, toward the land where he was born, but toward the country where, to him in this agonized moment no man was free. "In America, a person can go from place to place as he pleases; no need to carry a registration certificate and report every time he goes as far as from Bohuslän to Skåne, or Skåne to Småland!"

He would not soon forget the humiliation he had suffered on going to his parish Pastor, to clear through the records, as everyone was compelled by law to do—receive a removal paper from the Pastor of the place in which one lived, to present to the Pastor of the place to which one was going. He had run away from home, yes. But others, beside him, had left their homes; others had learned from the multitude of letters come to this country from America, and had responded to the promise of equality and a fine life there, others had grown tired of a daily fare of *sill* and potatoes, others had felt the Viking blood stir in their veins, or had compared the tiny worn-out fields of their home places with visions of that broad land, America. Ah, there was a land where a man, not bound by the restrictions of a military chain, could go from state to state as he wished, nor carry any registration paper to show his transfer.

And the American homesteads! Where was there land to be had here, with ten or twelve or fifteen children to be fed from practically every meagre home place?

Would he be able to forget, ever, the manner and look of Pastor Oskarsström as the minister had looked up from the record and bade him keep his mother and his home in his knowledge always? No judge pronouncing sentence for a heinous crime ever could have spoken a more forceful incrimination than came from the Pastor's eyes. Did the Pastor know that he had torn himself from home while in a rage? And if the Pastor did, had he a right to judge?

He did not need the Pastor's judgment; more cruel than any other, the judge that haunted his days and nights, the conscience that plagued him with memory of the way he had denounced his mother. Nay, he could not write to her; no letter could bridge the chasm he had dug with his sharp tongue.

He reached the shallows near the shore and stepped onto a smooth large slab of stone. Like a giant's open palm, it lay, reaching from its arm of granite ready to claim the rushing water as its own and hold the water there in the hollow of its hand.

Perhaps it was that Pastor Oskarsström and all the other priests deemed it not good to see their men harboring desires to emigrate to another land. Perhaps the churchmen saw the taxes they could expect from these men, for the support of the State Church, slipping over and past their palms, even as the water had slipped over the palm of rock?

Karl stepped swiftly to the shelter of a cove and came to the crevice where he had hidden his clothes. He lay for a few minutes in the sun, on the warm rocks, to dry, and then he smiled as he drew on his leather shoes. A far cry from that time when he had patched the holes in the only shoes he had, with bark from the paper birch. How it had cut into his sore and bleeding feet! But no, he would not dwell on the past, the bitter days of looking for work; he would not dwell on the days of never fully satisfied hunger, the days when gladly he would have changed places with any one of many a family cat, dreaming of a warm place by the fireside and of warm gruel in a bowl, nor of the days when, finding no work, hanging around the general store at the docks, he swelled by one the number of unemployed who lived on what they could get for carrying gentlemen's luggage or on what they could borrow from anyone foolish enough to pay heed to them. They were always "going to be rich some day, *när sture arv comer in*." Then, when their large inheritance came in, of course they could pay back what they had borrowed.

He had wondered if theirs would prove to be any bigger or better than his. True, he was the eldest son, and to him would come the home farm. Big enough to provide for such a family as his mother's had been, for she was an only child. Too small, much, to provide for all of the sons and daughters at Norden now, in addition to what family he could expect, one day, to have in the natural order of things. Oh, yes, he had known of eldest sons, without moral compulsion, who grabbed their inheritances for their own and put the families out, with a small dowry for the girls and portions in money or goods for the boys, to shift for themselves—not caring.

They were not men. He might have faults, but greed was not one. The rest of the children were as much entitled to the land on which they were born, as the eldest.

Besides, his father was still in a young age as figured against the ninety or one hundred years his forebears clung to life. Not knowing that Death long since had taken Peter Kristiansson, often Karl had repeated to himself, "I could grow old carrying tapestry bags and metal trunks before my sture arv will come to balance my ledger." And the cheap hostels! *Isch!* He had been glad to find the job in the blacksmith's shop in Skåne.

Well-forgotten, the past. He picked up the square leather purse and flung its strap over his head so that the pouch hung safely close to his skin on the left side. His sister Elisabet had tooled it for him, to carry his money when he should go to America. His fingers moved slowly over the smooth oily surface, tracing a pattern on the flap, following the letters of his name; then he lifted the flap and looked inside. His heart grew warm. There was a yellow buttercup blossom, pressed and dry, given to him by Elin. He would keep it a while longer; gently he placed it in the little pocket stitched to the back of the purse with even hand-run stitches.

A silver ten öre piece, a five öre piece of nickel, and two copper ören; a five and a ten kronor in paper money; so much had he saved toward his passage to America. Far, yet to go, with this saving. And there was, too, the fifty kronor in money it had been said that he had to have in his pockets, over and above his steamship ticket, before he could enter the new country. He buttoned the front of his linen shirt, reached back between his legs to catch the long tail and drew it up against the front of him, folded it and drew on his trousers. For these good clothes, his good health and full stomach, he knew he could thank Rikard, and his brother Sven who waited for him now near the bandstand. Karl must admit, however grudgingly, that he had been favored when he had heard the lips of Rikard ask him to stay in Småland and work for his brother, Sven. How strange that it was because he had chosen to remain in Småland that now he found himself in Bohuslän, his home province!

He left the bare rocks behind, and long strides brought him to where the smooth water of the three-doored harbor framed Marstrand's promenade. Vacationers strolled hand-in-hand or arm-in-arm; an old sailor looked over his only love, the water, where folk of all ages swam or came wading to the shore.

So beautiful, the skerries of Bohuslän; and the skerries of Bohuslän had been his home. Perhaps one of those sailboats there, heading toward Göteborg, was from his parents' home place. Wait! That one has a look of Norden's boats! Wait!

Should he run to the water's edge and call and wave? So near he was to home—to Norden—

His arms stretched forward, his feet took running steps, but his voice died in his throat; the boat was not of Norden's.

He turned from the water and followed the rise of the rocky island to its crown. Six hundred years of mellowing in the warm Scandinavian sunshine, six centuries of rugged resistance to ice and snow, sat lightly on its gray dress as the fortress looked down over little red cottages set close together on their granite foundation, down over the promenade, into the eyes of a confused and restless youth. Karl closed his, then. So close, so close to Marstrand was his home—

But no, there was no returning. Bohuslän was beautiful; but he could see how his home, his father, Sweden—which even now hid Hjärta from him—God, each had betrayed him. He could remember the frugality of the soil, the frailty of his father; for he had nothing.

His throat tightened and he swallowed hard to clear the lump. He felt the eyes of Marstrand follow him as he left the protected side of the island, and walked again to the naked lonely rocks around the bend. Like the eyes of the government, always upon him. Bound to the Reserves for twelve years of his life! He shivered. He saw himself chained to material poverty: what else had Sweden to offer him?

The gray of the rocks grew darker as the watery hands of the Skagerrak and Kattegat together tossed spray close to where he stood; and he watched a lone gull leave the safety of the harbor and wing its way westward, toward that land of opportunity, where men were free.

FIVE

THE MORE KARL THOUGHT of freedom, the more of it he knew he had to have. He knew Sven Eklund waited for him, but he climbed the fortress stairs; he could not bring himself to bear close contact with another. He felt imprisoned, as much so as if the portcullis gates should fall, now, at signal from the guard.

He rested against the parapet on the old gray tower and looked down over the island, the measured it in his mind, "About a mile from water to water, each way," he guessed. Slowly his rebellious spirit calmed. Again, as he stood high on the tower watching the water rolling toward the shore, seeing the sister islands, breathing the invigorating air, he felt the poignant beauty of Sweden. He sensed that the torture, the suffering that this fortress represented, was incidental, that patriotism, love of country, and the need for protection as well as heroic resistance against an enemy were the dominant reasons for the standing of the fortress here. He knew, in this calm moment, he was a part of this fisherman's coast, these waterways of the Vikings....

"There! Look!" One next to him pointed excitedly. "There comes the King!"

Gliding through the summer water came the King's yacht, fresh and untired-looking as though she had not come so recently the distance from Stockholm, through the Baltic, paying her respect to Gotland and Öland, saluting Bornholm and Malmö, stopping at Vinga's lighthouse to get her pilot for company to Göteborg. Vinga, where even so fine a Captain as his mother's morfar, had stopped in his day for pilot to show the way into Göteborg's harbor. Terrible in storms, that course, but calm and peaceful now. So was Karl calm.

A scolding voice shrieked to a child to hold its jaw, "*Håll käften*, young one, or we shall go on alone, and leave you here— tied to one of those iron rings."

39

The spell was broken. He plunged down the steps taking two at a time, sometimes three, "As long as I am so soon to leave this country," he said to himself, "I may as well go down and have a look at Sweden's King."

He stood agape as he saw that no great commotion attended the arrival of the King. Couples strolled along the promenade, girls on the left arms of their young companions. Did they not notice the nearing of their King? They did not even seem to see the small boat carrying King Oskar from his yacht toward the shore!

King Oskar II, he who had chosen Marstrand for his summer residence, came from the pier and walked along as any other man. Karl stood embarrassed; what should a man do in the presence of his King? With reverence, in awe, Karl looked about to see what others did, so he might follow their example. With astonishment he saw no scraping, no bowing; the people did not gape nor turn to stare. Were they all plough-boys that they did not recognize their King?

This man, this tall and handsome elderly gentleman in nautical uniform, walked from the pier, up Marstrand's sloping ground, to the music pavilion. The band burst forth with "Du gamla, du fria," and Karl's eyes filled with tears. Oh, why, when he had made up his mind once and for all that Sweden held naught for him and that he must leave her, why, thus should he be torn? Was here the true Sweden, in this man with the visored cap set straight upon his head?

He was so near now that he could count the points on the gold star, pressing the cap cloth high to make his tall King taller still. He watched King Oskar walk as any other man toward the benches set for the public before the uniformed bandsmen, and with his three companions choose seats in the front row and sit down to listen.

No, none would stare openly at the King, but now Karl saw many a passing glance survey the lines of his royal frame. What was there about this man to bring to Karl's ears the sound of love and respect murmuring, in overtones with the music, for Oskar, monarch of the five million souls of Sweden and all of Norway besides? The music stopped, but respect and love continued to permeate the air about Karl. The knowledge stunned him. How could this be?

He looked here and yon for sight of Sven Eklund, and moved

to search for him. Best to lose no time now in finding his employer, for Karl well knew he was late. Would Sture Sven, for the first time in the weeks he had served the Smålänningen, see fit to reprimand him? He moved among the crowd. A youth came toward him, reminding him of the days when he had brushed elbows with the unemployed in Göteborg. Too much of the bottle had slipped down his throat, and he lurched toward Karl and croaked hoarsely, "The Queen, you note she comes not to Marstrand. Nay—fairer and younger women are there here for our King to—"

Karl's fist doubled and in frenzy he landed it squarely on the jaw of the leering sot, sending him sprawling. Karl stepped back as folk gathered around them.

Sven Eklund stepped forward, and removed their hands from his young workman. With firm voice, he said, "I heard. Not one of you would have done differently if he had heard such as he," pointing to the ground, "use our King's name as then he did." Authority rang in his voice and the crowd fell back. Sven turned to Karl, "And now, why did Karl Petersson keep Sven Eklund waiting long beyond the hour of meeting?" There was no anger in his tone, and Karl opened his lips to answer, but his employer gripped his shoulder and turned him slightly, till he saw the hand of Sweden's King outstretched to him.

"Tack," and his King clasped Karl's hand and pumped it, and Oskar II walked away.

Sweden's King, his King, had touched his hand! Karl held it out in front of him and looked at it as if he expected it, somehow, to look different. When night came and he held it before him in the dark, would it glow softly because a royal hand had clasped it tight? He stood, dumb, and looked at his hand. Oh, how could he endure the torment within him, the feeling—which from birth, from home, from mother, from Pastor, and from school cried out of his *belonging* to Sweden—fighting now to kill his certainty that he wished to leave Sweden behind him?

Was even the King slightly stooped as he walked away? How sad his eyes had seemed. Was even his head slightly bowed? Karl watched the blue-clad back as it walked toward the bath houses. There was so much unfairness in the world, not even the King was free; at least, not free from gossip. Karl's stomach heaved within him.

"It is time Sven Eklund and Karl Petersson saw to the sails.

Come." He followed at Sven's words, and they passed the baths and the open-air restaurants under the trees where happy people drank strawberry soda, or had coffee with their rye rusks, or ale with their potatoes and fish.

"Would Karl like to sup here, now?" No, Sven Eklund, Karl would not care to sup. He had no stomach for food. All he had was a thirst, a consuming thirst, for certainty in his dry and aching mind.

Out from the harbor, out into the open water, sailed two silent men. Twenty-five feet on the waterline, built of oak, with her tall mast and white sail, their boat nosed northward over the jagged and uneven sea-bed toward the Norwegian coast. Marstrand had kept for her own the clear calm of yesterday and now as they left her, the North Sea pushed against the Skagerrak so that the waters danced and broke. Heaving to windward, Karl stood in his oilskins and watched the man, Sven Eklund, as he waited to feel a mackerel pull at his hand-line. His medium height took on a strange shape for a man, for his head was small and the oiled cap he wore, though short-brimmed, widened at the sides and fell long over his shoulders and his back. Sven's oiled coat was short and his body filled it full below the arms, for here he was built broad and heavy. His head and body together looked like a triangle, there, set upon two spare legs, for his shoulders were narrow. Aye, mused Karl, Sven had worn the coat of compulsory military service too long, needing now the artificial structure of epaulettes to square his shoulders to look like a man. Yet, now Sven Eklund was years past the age of military claim.

And while he stood, Sven Eklund pondered over the young man whom his brother had brought with him from the training heath to the home in Småland. Karl came from a good home; this Sven and his wife had been able to tell from the first. For he was as one of the family in their home, clean and neat and well-spoken. Manners his mother had taught him well; his book knowledge exceeded by far the knowledge of the common youth. Why had he left his home? Why was he so anxious to quit his birthland, saving every öre which came his way? And if, as Karl had repeated time and again—as if, by repeating, he could make his own self believe—he had no love for Sweden, why then should he champion the fair name of Sweden's king? Oh, he loved the boy for that!

So difficult for Sven to understand the jumble of feelings that he could see the youth experienced. About the church, though, there seemed to be no doubt. How it had cut him to hear Karl say, "What if a man does not believe in God, why then should he stay in a land where he would be taxed for the upkeep of His church?" Too fine, this lad, to harbor such a concept.

His home, this much they knew, had been in Bohuslän. But where? Would he, by any word or sign, give inkling as to where in Bohuslän his mother most certainly awaited word from him, so Sven Eklund could be the one to fill her yearning heart with knowledge of her son? Sven thought of Eleonora and their little Sven. He pulled his hand-line in hard as he prayed that his son should never leave his mother so.

"Confusion may beat Karl's heart's blood through his body," thought the landowner, "but salt sea water flows through his veins," as Karl guided the little boat with wind blown sail over the deep waters—the littoral now near, now far removed—on into the northern shallows of the Skagerrak. "Rough as all Hell," so Karl described them, and he and his companion were glad to tie to the dock at Strömstad.

The weather was less angry as they started on their southward way, weaving between the islands or hugging the mainland. Past Koster, from whose twin islands had come those most marvelous sea-boats of all time, past Havstenssund and Fjällbacka, past Lysekil, stopping at Mollösund, hearing the voices of Vikings echoing in the songs of the waves, often the two men stood, side by side, under the spell of the far past, listening, and neither spoke. Again, as they

> *"Went then o'er the waves, by the wind hastened,*
> *The foamy-necked float to a fowl most like"*

as one man, they chanted from the saga of Beowulf,

> *"Gewat tha ofer waeg-holm, winde gefysed,*
> *Flota fami-heals fugla gelicost,"*

but so deep in reverie was Karl, he did not heed that Sven Eklund joined him.

Silently now, their little craft ghosted along in the thin air, and Karl looked hard beyond the water. His eyes were strained to see all upon an island to their weather side. Again he was a child; there he had learned to swim. His brothers and sisters had learned to swim, too, in the waters caressing that island. Elisabet, the eldest, had taught the littlest ones. Poor Elisabet, she should have the finest of all the silk dresses, when he got rich, and ribbons for her flaxen hair.

His eyes strained; his mother would be working in the fields, unless she was having another baby. He thought of his mother's hands, hardly beautiful, but ah, what beauty grew under those fingers! Closing his eyes he could see the big room at home, the tapestries of petit point, the little dancing figure on the sill, the fiddler; and he could see the thirty-two chessmen she had carved. What had become of them?

Did he remember rightly that the white king was King Oskar? Aye, and the likeness was real; he knew this now, for he had seen his King.

Night after night, in the poor light, she had sat and carved the men, sixteen out of light clear birchwood and sixteen of dark old rosewood bits.

Knights, bishops, and rooks, so true had she carved them that the family was able to name them, almost every one. The pawns—Swedes against Russians—

Oh, God, and he had not even thanked her for the doing!

She had made them to sell, so as to get money to help him go to America. And he, blinded by rage at that last indignity of his father's, tearing his books to bits before his eyes, had blamed her—and left.

Oh, that he could swallow his pride and run home and grasp his mother's hand!

He gritted his trembling jaw and roughly drew his sleeve across his eyes. Why, why did he always have to think of his mother? Did she take this way to revenge her mother-spirit? Because he had chosen, like a fledgling bird, to leave the nest was she to haunt him always? Even to stamping the likeness of her walk on the walk of little Elin? Would she never free him of thoughts of her, and memories?

He watched the changing colors of the water lapping at the island's shore. Yes, again he was a child, holding Morfar's hand, gazing over these waters with feelings of terror changing to ones of adventure, listening to the old man tell the saga of Beowulf. Time-honored, the custom that each generation of Norden's children early be taught of the monster Grendel and the brave Beowulf. Rightly, this was the first of the sagas to be handed down from fathers to sons, for had not Grendel's lair lain beneath the very water lapping the island on which the family homestead stood?

Karl recalled the sea monsters, and a smile flitted over his features as he remembered how hard it had been to say the name of the transparent limpid jellyfish, so he had left it to the grandfather to call them by their big name and to him and all the other children they had been the "lungs of the ocean."

"Not of the earth, not of the sky, not of the sea, but a blending of all three," Morfar had quoted from the Greek geographer.

There, as a child, he, Karl of Norden, had stood and heard his mother and her morfar tell of Viking fleets of a hundred sail or more, come to these shores to hold their auctions and plan yet another exciting voyage. His teeth gritted; love of adventure, romance, bravery, all to be lauded in the Vikings of old, but let not a youth display a taste for wandering lest a Pastor deem it unseemly in a son and name him a traitor to his home!

His eyes burned for looking. There was the house in which he first saw day, but the house in which sill and potatoes were the backbone of the spread board. There was the barn. In that red barn Hjärta had been born, and lived. But over these waters that horse had been brought to the mainland and sold! How could even the Pastor show surprise at his running away from home after that?

So hard he looked toward the island, that his eyelids did not blink to moisten his searching eyes.

Long ago, standing there, looking over these very waters, his elders had taught him the saga of Beowulf, told of the terrible mother of Grendel—the restless death-demon—the avenging mother of Grendel.

His eyes saw red. Red was the sun-dyed water lapping the gray rocks of the island. Fit home for the father who had not honor—the land atop the lair of Grendel's mother—

> "... They in a dark land,
> Abodes of wolves, dwell, windy nesses,
> Dangerous marshes, where mountain-stream
> Under clouds of the nesses flows down below,
> Lake under the earth. It is not far hence

In measure by miles that the mere stands,
Over which hang the rustling groves,
Wood firm in its roots; they cover the water.
There one every night a strange wonder may see,
Fire on the flood: so wise a one lives not
Of the children of men that knows its bottom:"

He had spoken aloud and Sture Sven, standing close beside him, joined to chant on,

"Those who with Hrothgar gazed on the sea,
That the waves-stirring all was commingled,
The surge stained with blood..."

Karl turned, "Sven Eklund knows then of Beowulf." He hesitated, then, "And knows that once this land was known, not as Sweden, but—"

The older man nodded, "Geatland."

"Aye, and Beowulf, Prince of the Geats, he with the strength of thirty men in his hands," Karl spoke absently, as if only his tongue repeated that which he had learned by rote, "after he had gone to the great hall of Hrothgar and torn out the arm of the man-devouring Grendel, here he came."

"Here?" asked Sven, watching the youth closely.

"Here. Deep in these rocky caverns dwelt he and his mor. At night the fire still glows on the water to mark this place."

This water! Its phosphorescent glow had marked a little ripple over him when as a child he had lain calmly floating. This water! Over this water his Hjärta had been taken to the mainland! Fiercely he turned to Sture Sven, "See, even now the waters look bloody, as they did when Beowulf stopped on his stony way, to mark the lair of Grendel's mother!"

Sture Sven understood. He had watched tenderness spread over the face of his companion, then had seen the tenderness swept aside, and rage take over. He looked where Karl was looking, at the island; already he knew well the look of intricate channels and granite caverns in the clear water where the Skagerrak and Kattegat joined hands. He knew the youth had rested their sun-tanned sail and recounted the saga of early days so that he might—almost against his will—have time for one more look upon his home. And Sture Sven's memory marked the spot.

He folded his hands, "Our Father," he began, and faced the horizon where lay the Pater Noster Skerries, where in the bright sunshine of day oft he had seen them lie like a string of holy beads, a jewel-set rosary, sparkling. "Our Father," he began, then changed to the Latin to fit his mood, "Pater Noster—"

"Pater Noster," Karl muttered. Yes, there on the horizon they lay, those skerries; and there, against those unholy beads, had countless numbers of sailors been dashed to their deaths. Had the Lord's Prayer helped them? Bitterness drew a pattern over the fine features of Karl Petersson and a grudge, real and momentous to the young man, turned the corners of his mouth downward, "The islands are well-named."

Sture Sven finished his prayer as his ears heard, "Pater— Pater Noster—treachery—" and his heart grieved sorely when he saw the square young jaw that seemed to say that Karl had had enough forever of his home, his father, and his Father.

In silence they sailed southward still, close, close to Marstrand. Japanese lanterns, their candles flickering, swung lightly over the dance-floor built up in the open, and the music ended with a flourish sending the girls in colorful dresses, and their escorts, from the floor. Close to the promenade the sailboat came in the twilight and Karl knew the light made shadows on the gray rocks of the seaward side; he knew the light gray changed to dark, and mauve gray changed to purple. He almost saw the little heather blossoms nestling tenderly in the crevices. Tight fingers closed around his heart. From the bandstand came more music from the uniformed players, soft on the summer air,

"Barndom's Hemmet—My Childhood Home—"

Sture Sven, the triangle of a man on short spare legs, stood, helpless, looking at a youth whose shoulders shook and whose face lay buried in his open palms.

SIX

"NO MAN IS EVER FREE," Sture Sven spoke softly, "not even in America, Karl. A man is always bound by something."

"But—"

The older man interrupted, "He may be bound by his own limitations or by the limitations of his job, or by his family obligations, or—take your America, for instance—you think you would have freedom there because you would not be bound to the military." He hesitated for an instant and then changed his approach. "You think it would spell freedom because you would not have to clear the official records before you leave one place and when you go to another. But you must know, Karl, that that whole thing is only a question of the area of your restriction. Here, yes, the area is small. But, have you thought of it, that once you are in America, your freedom to return here is gone, unless you get a paper from the State!"

Sture Sven spoke, but even as he pleaded he knew he could not hold Karl, no more than Sweden had been able to stem the swollen tide of emigration. He would miss this youth, as Sweden missed the many who had already gone. How could he expect Sweden to combat the wholesale emigration to America when he could not dissuade one man?

That was the hopelessness of it, though, that Karl had some small point there, in his argument about the compulsory service. Sven well knew that, for fifteen years now, bitter contention had tossed about the political proposal of scrapping the *indelnings-verket* and reorganizing the military. But, once again, he would try to appeal to Karl, "And the few days of training—"

"Sven Eklund talks of the few days of service in training for the infantry. You are not so uninformed that you do not know that the future speaks of a training period of months instead of weeks." He turned to go from Sven, but turned again, "And you know, too, which is of even more moment to me, that the length of time to be held in the Reserves also may be increased by many years."

"Aye, but can you gainsay that such a program is necessary to assure the safety of Sweden?"

"What is the threat?" Karl hurled his answer. "And where is the gain if Sweden is to lose her young manhood to America because of such a program?"

"You—"

"It is not only I, Sven Eklund. Who was it pointed out, a long time ago, that 'If we extend the time of military service, we shall indeed have our officers here at home but our soldiers will be in the United States'?"

Yes, oft had Sven Eklund heard that pointed speech. He hung his head. What could he say? Karl Petersson was wise for his years.

Karl spoke on, "What will the emigrating of the Fritz's and the Adolph's, who object to militarism as a way of life, do to Germany? Is it not possible that those who remain in Germany—or in Sweden, for that matter—will come to think and feel from the point of view of the military?" Excitedly he thrashed his arms, gesticulating, "Will not, then, their philosophy destroy the culture of the land? Can a culture survive if the youths who remain bow to the call of service, until a country is little better than a military garrison?"

"You exaggerate, my friend," Sven replied, "you see Sweden not as she really is." Yet as Karl spoke, sadly Sven Eklund wondered. He knew that with growing gloom Sweden had listened to her youth malign their homeland and had watched them clear through the church records, to America, or when she denied them the right to sail from a port in their own country, had seen them step aboard an ocean liner at Copenhagen or at some other foreign city and sail toward the New World. Sven could understand his mother country's gloom now that he had brushed first-hand against the problem.

This youth would go, and he would miss him.

Karl continued, "I want to know the feel of having men work for me, not always that I should be the one to bend the knee. What chance have I? Where can I go, Sven Eklund, and reap a fortune here in Sweden? I want more than mere subsistence.

"Why speak you not? Where? Where? I ask you." Karl let his arms fall to his sides. "You cannot answer me, Sven Eklund, for you know that here I am bound—not only to the military—but fenced in by Sweden's lack of opportunity for the common man, fenced in by her lack of land—enough land—just as here in this field I stand, fenced in by heaps of stone."

"Here I stand, also, Karl, surrounded by fence of stone. But do I feel bound? No. To me these piles of stones are merely boundaries to mark where the planting of oats begins, or rye or barley plantings end. And I stand here, arms upraised to the heavens, thanking God that I am free—free to breathe His good clean air—free to think the thoughts that come with enlightened manhood." He lowered his arms, "For I am free, Karl. Any man is free only as he knows freedom inside of himself."

But Karl had to go. If a man tell himself over and over enough times, he begins to believe what he has told himself.

What should he do, thought Sven; should he send Karl to Eleonora's kin, the Englishman who was a big officer with the steamship company? Nay, help Karl out of Sweden, he would not. Help him, rather, to find a job to keep him in the homeland, so it could prove to Karl it offered opportunity. Sweden could ill afford to lose the like of Karl Petersson, even though her streets were not "paved with gold," as in America.

While the farewell meal was being set, Sven wrote and handed Karl three letters, addressed to friends of the landowner, one in Stockholm, and Sven thought Stockholm best; there in the Capital City was opportunity for a smart young man, if he but present this letter to Jon Bergman. Or, Johann Dalin, in Göteborg, he also would find a place for Karl; Sven was certain of that. Or Simon Svenning in Falkenberg. Sven had not seen his friend, Simon, since the year before, at the celebration of the extension of the *Vestkustbanan*, the railroad, into Falkenberg. Either of the three would help Karl find work, and here were Sven's introductions.

The good meal was under Karl's belt. "Farewell," he said—not au revoir. Rikard was not a bad sort, Karl conjectured as they parted, for Rikard's wish for his friend's future, of a certainty, was sincere and his handclasp tight.

Sven drove Karl to the *gästgifvargård*, and as they rode Sven watched the muscles in the hind ends of the team quiver and stretch as they chafed under the confinement of the cruppers and hip straps; like Karl, resenting any restriction. But Karl had a brain with which to reason, and these two things in front of them never would be anything but what they were.

Sven shook Karl's hand and sent the best worker he had ever had from him.

With the paper kronor, pay for the skillful sailor and tireless worker on the farm, neatly folded and placed close to the others in his purse—beside the ören and a dried, pressed buttercup— jauntily Karl waved farewell. His other hand carried a little rawhide trunk, with bindings of sheet iron, not new but sturdy and filled with underwear and a linen shirt, and socks made by the hands of Eleonora and blessed by her mother heart.

These folk were kind and generous, but he was glad to leave them, circumscribed, thinking themselves rich! That bit of land they had in this barren province, poor land indeed compared with what he expected to find, and soon. Let *them* look for freedom inside of themselves! Karl laughed.

Which was the best road to America? He set his little trunk down and looked at the three envelopes addressed in Sven Eklund's hand. No, not Stockholm. Too far, the breadth of Sweden farther away from America. Not Göteborg; too close, too close to his childhood home. He would turn his face toward Halland; he would clear the records and name Falkenberg as the place where he would go. He folded the letter addressed to S. Svenning; that he would stuff far down into the foldings of his sock.

He found S. Svenning at the address of the railway station, given on the envelope, the *järnvägsstation*, "102 kilometer från Göteborg," and "136 kilometer från Helsingborg." He read the big clock: eleven in the morning. Just so would he be able to read a clock in America. It was good to think of that, for even though he had much yet to learn in order to use the new language in a new world, here was one step he need not master, for the same kind of face would greet him from the clocks across the water.

His eyes followed the height of the terminus, then down until they rested on the iron tracks in front. He stooped and touched the track with his fingers as a little child touches an object to make its acquaintance. Oh, how the world moved on! And over these tracks he would move, on, on, farther and farther until at last he found what place he sought.

Simon Svenning sat behind a large oak desk. His thin hair was parted low on the left side and brought over, long, to cover a balding head. His brows were full and bushy, and his well-humped nose gave support to glasses which pinched to the sides of its bridge. The lenses were rimmed in gold and a large golden loop drooped from the right glass, and from it extended a black silk ribbon, ending under a wide coat lapel. His stiff white collar was low and broad spreading, filled in in front by a dark red silken tie with paisley figures, hunched up into folds and caught with a sparkling stickpin. The pin was long and it wove itself in and out of the silky tie cloth, making six holes before it left its point exposed, sharp and fierce-looking, above the tightness of a dark wool vest. All this Karl saw before he noticed the full short-clipped mustache move and from under their bristles come, "The gentleman wishes to see Simon Svenning?"

The gentleman! Never before had Karl been addressed so. He liked this Simon Svenning, and soon found he was one who held Sven Eklund in high regard.

Yes, if Sture Sven recommended Karl he could and would find employment for Sven's friend. Had Karl had his midday meal? No? Then they must dine together; and hungry, Karl so far forgot his manners as to refuse only twice before he accepted, and then he marveled that the man of high estate should treat him as an equal, and that there was never an indication on the part of his host that it was not a privilege to pay for the meal for him, who was a stranger.

"Now," pushing back his plate, "what can Karl Petersson do?" Herr Svenning asked.

"I can do any kind of work; none is too hard," then, answering the friendliness of this man, Karl outlined his ambition to go to America, his wish to fill his pockets with money.

"Money," sadly Herr Svenning repeated. "Money. And what happiness think you that money can buy?"

To those at the homestead he could bring joy with it, to his mor, to his sisters, his little crippled brother; Karl opened the door of his soul and poured forth his ambition—to have money enough to buy a hat for his mother, crutches for little Johann, an operation for his sister Elisabet: "so beautiful she could be without the hairy birthmark on her face!" All this he could do, if he could but get to America.

Simon Svenning removed his eyeglasses and ran his fingers along the golden rims, he held them by the loop and pointed them toward Karl. There could be work for such as he, here, on the Vestkustbanan. Herr Svenning laid the eyeglasses down on the table top and pressed his hands against his eyes. But, if it was America Karl wished, he would not stand in the boy's way, but help him.

Sadness clouded the eyes of the railway gentleman. His own son, he said, had wanted America. Maybe—if he had let him go? Perhaps the brain fever might not have taken him in America? A letter could have bridged the distance from the United States, but no letter ever came from the grave. Yes, he would help the young man to go to America.

Karl appraised the man sitting opposite him: so different from his own father, progressive—in everything—even in the wearing of a tie which was not black, and him in mourning for his son.

"God bless you, my boy," the aging man shook his hand and Karl found himself, not standing on the gravel of the station yard, but floating on the clouds. Here in his hand was a little card, the like of which he had never seen, a little bit of parchment, and on the face of it was Simon Svenning's name in deep black, so that Karl's fingers could feel, as well as see, the name. And there on its back side was another name and address, written in Herr Svenning's hand, "The White Star Line, Liverpool," and a magic name, a different-sounding name than all the Perssons, Peterssons, Johanssons, and "bergs" and "holms" he had known, a British name no doubt, *"I—S—M—A—Y."* He spelled it out and repeated it over and again as he thought it should be spoken. "Iss' may."

This man, Mr. Ismay, a friend to Herr Svening, would have a job for him there, at that address, to help him find his way to America!

His feet flew toward the parsonage. No time to waste, getting to the Pastor for his Flyttningsbevis! He passed a house sitting at a corner where two streets crossed each other, a house all covered with green leaves except that white glass-paned casements peeped through spaces almost overgrown.

But he did not see it. Nor did he see a girl with yellow hair who ran from a window to the street and cried when she found that the tall young man had disappeared from her view.

* * *

"Aye," he had served in the *Beväring*.

"Aye, and aye." But this was a lifetime of torment for Karl to have to watch as the Halland Pastor's hand held the pen, hesitating, over the lines of his paper. He wet his lips. Then the pen came close, to let ink flow to form the most important words of a man's life!

Oh, it looked good to see it there, written on his paper, "America." At last he was free to go forth to the rich land of the United States, and realize his hopes. He would get to the top in America! He would sit at a polished desk, even like Simon Svenning; for there stood his name, "Karl Mattias Petersson, *från Sveriges Rike*," there it told that he had been born on February 9, 1868, baptized in Bohuslän, and confirmed, not entered into the state of matrimony, *och-så-vidare*. Beautiful paper!

Beside the other precious belongings in his leather purse it would travel with him into the future. He read, and read again, the vital statistics of his life, through the and-so-forths; and there on the line numbered "nineteen," sat those magic words, "*Afflyttar till Evangelisk Luthersk församling i America lan.* Removes to an Evangelical Lutheran Parish in America land." Beautiful words!

Karl read once more, "*från Sveriges Rike*, from the Kingdom of Sweden," he was going to America.

His heart sank. Not only would he be going *to;* he would be going *from*; from the land of his forebears—from the land of his birth—to a land of strangers.

Heartbreaking word, "afflyttar"; it meant more than being removed: it meant being *uprooted*.

Fast fading in the September mist, Göteborg's harbor lay behind him. As on an early winter morning just before dawn, the whole world was a misty gray. Gray sea gulls hovered overhead or, resting, rode the waves. Karl leaned over the ship's rail to watch the busy hands of the Skagerrak weaving white lace to edge the gray-blue of the waves below.

On the stroke of one o'clock after noon, he had looked his last look at the bustling seaport. Farewell to the city, and harbor, the old East India Company Building, the open markets where morning and evening all was commotion, in the mornings to set up the wares in the market-place, in the evenings to take in the wares and wash up everything, even the street—farewell to the room in which last night he had slept, where he could lie in a bed and look up, out of the window, at houses sitting on a mountain. Farewell to the wharves with their wooden piles, scarred and slivered; farewell to the mists, the penetrating melancholy mists of this land where once had been his home.

The North Sea must be furious to push the waters of the Skagerrak so roughly against their bow. Karl could sense that this trip would be a rough one; but rough seas or smooth, it mattered not. A change had come in his fortunes. Beginning when the hand of Fate had pointed to that one letter of Sven's three, addressed to Falkenberg, so it had led him to Göteborg, and at the instant when, bemoaning the thought of having to separate the cost of a sleeping-room from his savings, he had seen the notice being posted setting forth that a coal-heaver was needed on the ship about to set sail for Hull.

Of five men being tried out to see which could shovel the most coal, he had been chosen. His muscles still ached from the pressure of that trial, pushing himself to the point of exhaustion. He comprehended now the dual purpose of the test. True, they had learned which man might serve them to best advantage aboard ship, but also, taking advantage of the ignorant, had gotten coal into the hold without cost for labor. Be that as it may, here he was, employed to do a man's work aboard a ship.

As firm his tread upon this rolling deck as any person's would be upon the solid ground. As much at home on Skagerrak's boisterous billows as on the little lake in Bohuslän. Best, though, to go below and snatch a few hours of sleep before being summoned to work with the night crew. To shovel coal for twelve hours would scarce be restful; he would lie down and dream of the rosy future that now, for certain, was to be his.

The bench was hard but the engines' rhythmic throbbing and the ship's cradle-like rocking lulled him to sleep, a happy, calm, and peaceful sleep. He was on the first leg of his journey to America.

It was still Friday afternoon when Karl awoke with a start. At one o'clock he had been able to prophesy that this trip would not be smooth. And now, at five o'clock, the ship, wending its way from Göteborg to Hull, tossed on the water like a plaything and threw him from his bench. The engines throbbed with anxiety.

Karl drew himself to his feet and went up on deck. Was every passenger aboard clinging to the rail, to a deck chair, or lying sprawled on the deck lifeless-looking except when, retching, they squirmed and groaned?

"Oh, the devil, best I stay below," he muttered.

"Petersson," the deck officer hailed him.

"Aye, sir."

"Go to the galley, they will give you bread to pass."

It was suppertime and Karl carried the big woven wicker basket in front of him, a hand in each braided handle, with the basket swung low so he could rest it on his knee occasionally. Heavy—with dark-bread sandwiches filled with liver sausage or strong cheese—when he started on his rounds over the ship, it had not lightened after two hours of walking and calling, *"Supe, supe,"* he set it down again in the galley.

Karl ate the sandwiches. For him the living was good. Was it actually twelve hours of shoveling that brought the morning of Sunday? More like twelve minutes it seemed now that the ship drew near to Britain's shore.

The North Sea had not made a friend among the passengers, and Karl listened with interest to the comments. "What a hellion of a sea," the men agreed. "Thank God the North Sea lies behind us," sighed the women. If the small sea could pound with such relentless fury, they cried, what then might they expect of the broad Atlantic? If only they never had heard of America, they would be safe "back home" where what they ate remained within them!

Britain reached out to take them to her as past Spurn Head on the starboard, past Immingham to the port, they ploughed through the river's wide mouth to Hull.

"Aye," to the deck officer's request, Karl gladly would help with the baggage. Would Karl also be willing to assist in cleaning and washing down the ship? There was no train until Monday morning and if he would work he could spend the night aboard and save the price of a sleeping-room, and he would be furnished a train ticket to Liverpool. He was more than willing to help clean the ship, thereby earning his travel to Liverpool, all the while leaving his savings intact.

At nine o'clock on Monday morning the train steamed out of Hull, and on that train were heavy hearts and light, and one of the lightest of these was Karl's.

This was, indeed, seeing the world. Karl craned his neck to see what might be seen as they stopped at Leeds, and at Manchester, to take on passengers. He sat, terrified, at the blackness of the tunnel knowing that others sat near and breathed; without conscious thought of it, his hand pressed hard to feel the leather pouch under his clothing. After six hours of riding, he got off the train at Liverpool. He cleared his entrance and left the railway station.

He found himself walking the streets, trying to absorb the feel of a new country, shying from the ever-present beggars, and lingering near folk who spoke—so casually—in another tongue. Was this the English language that they spoke, delivered so much faster than anyone would speak in Swedish? Only a very occasional word sounded familiar, or even anything like the words he had learned from his mother's Swedish-English dictionary.

"That must take a smart one," he said to himself, as he watched men in baggy woolen pants balance themselves and ride along on two-wheeled bicycles. Some day he'd like to try that himself! But when any neared, he stepped aside and gave the wheel and rider all the room he deemed they needed. When one came, silently, from behind and in passing brushed against the little trunk he carried, he jumped and called upon the devil, "*Fan*, that such an infernal machine should run loose to endanger a man's being."

The front muscles of his neck stretched as he looked high, to the top of the double-decked horse cars; he trembled as one came near, and as it made a turn he closed his eyes and shivered. A man should not be surprised if it toppled over and crushed him beneath it! And the horses. Not like his Hjärta, smooth and fine-limbed with graceful walk, small, but with head held high. These animals were huge, with unkempt manes and drooping heads; and their hooves, overhanging with shagginess, reached over the crevices in the cobblestoned street.

For an hour or more he walked the streets of Liverpool, and then he turned again toward the wharves. There he would ask the way by which to reach the address shown on the parchment card.

What misery he saw! Oh, quickly to leave the Old World behind for if the waterfront gave proper introduction to this land, then Britain was more cruel than Sweden to the poor man.

Not scores, but many more poor old men milled about looking for work, and Karl could see the stamp of hunger upon them. If only he were rich, he would put bread and tea within their reach: even sill and potatoes would be a feast for such as these.

Karl set his trunk down; glad that he had, with foresight, changed some Swedish money into small English coins against his arrival in Britain, he opened his shirt and reached into the pouch. He went among the wrecks of men and handed each a coin as long as his change lasted, and a film covered his eyes at sight of the thankfulness he saw and the blessings he received.

"I can earn more, for I am young and strong, and I spend no more this way than I should have if I had paid my way over the railway." He talked to himself, and wondered at the warm good feeling inside of him. Not quite so alone now, he seemed, as before. And as a uniformed steward came toward him, he smiled, and proud of his English held out the card and asked, "Show the way?"

"Yes, come with me," and the remainder of what he said was lost to Karl, so fast the stranger spoke.

They entered a building. The man whose name Herr Svenning had written on the back of the parchment card, this Mr. Ismay of the magic name, no, he was "not in." The gentleman in the office was kind. "Would you wish conversation with another?"

Not sure of his English, Karl did not know what to answer, but he knew he wanted work; he knew the English word for work, and so he added, "on ship?"

Long John Wicksells, who sat on a tall stool and who wore a green shade on his forehead, spoke to Karl in Swedish. There was no work on a seagoing ship for him at present; the winter season was soon to be upon them, but if he wished to work on figures and learn the English language while he worked, then Long John would help him find a room. The steamship company would pay him no fancy wages, but enough to get along on; and in the spring, then perhaps he could sail, even on one of the luxury liners of the White Star!

Figures wrote a language Karl understood. And the wages! Not fancy, perhaps, to Long John—but to Karl—more in a month than he had earned in a year, from Herr Granlund of Småland!

"Figures," he remembered his mother saying, "are like

another language, understood by Swedes and Americans alike." Yes, he would be glad to accept the job at figures.

Much he learned while working on the books of the White Star Line, sitting on a tall stool at a slanted-top table, with an eyeshade on his forehead and, over his white shirt, a black coat that felt as if it had been made of horses' hair. And Long John helped him learn. At night, after the long hours of work over lined and ruled sheets, they pored over books of ships and of shipping on the Atlantic.

It was not long before he knew to recognize that passenger ships with names ending in "i-c" belonged to their White Star Line; and that any whose names ended in "i-a" were owned by their rival, the Cunard Line.

Did Karl know that the Inman Line used names of cities for their ships, such as the *City of Rome, City of Chicago*, and so on? No? He knew it now.

So he learned from Long John, and learned that the White Star Line's finest ships had been launched that year, the *Teutonic* in January and the *Majestic* in June. How could he be able to grasp the knowledge that the *Majestic* could push ahead against the waves of the Atlantic with the power of eighteen thousand horses? He thought of the time when he had learned of the horses carrying shipments from the boats above the series of falls of Trollhätte Canal to the boats at the foot of the last fall; nine hundred horses, he had been told. But this was the strength of twenty times that many! He envisioned this ship, as long as the distance from the barn to the sheep meadow at home.

"How would you like to serve aboard such as her?" Long John asked him.

The *Majestic*. He dreamed of her at night. Already he seemed to belong to her. She was his. He read, and reading, pretended he was aboard her. The while he sat entering figures in the books— so many first-class passages at twenty-two pounds each, so many second-class at twelve pounds each, so many many steerage at but four guineas—he saw himself standing on the bridge of the *Majestic*, cutting the water, braving the high seas, steering into New York harbor.

One day Long John made him a gift. John had no use for it, he said. Karl turned it over in his hand and stroked its cover. A book. As if his co-worker had given him a handful of gold, he looked at it as he read, "*Från Nya Verlden*—From the New

World, Sketches of a Visit to the United States, 1875, by Ernst Beckman."

"But you should keep it for yourself," Karl remonstrated.

"No. I am satisfied here."

Satisfied. How could so smart a man as Long John Wicksells be satisfied? Why, a man might as well be *dead* as satisfied!

Long John wrote on the fly-leaf, in English, "To remind Karl Petersson of the many hours we spent together, learning. In friendship, John W."

Karl treasured the book, and through the winter they read in it together. "When I am on the *Majestic* I shall think of you, my friend," he would say.

In April of the next spring, the captain of the *Majestic* asked for Karl to be a member of his crew, as assistant to the purser. A uniform, so grand, replaced the shiny black coat, and a visored cap the eyeshade.

"We of the office regret your leaving, Karl," and the great Mr. Thomas Ismay shook his hand.

That name, it sounded even more magical when the Britishers spoke it, almost as though the "s" were a "z." Not quite a "z" perhaps, but they did not pronounce it "Iss'may," as he said it still. He would practice now, more than before, to say it "Ismay."

Often Mr. Ismay had smiled, but Karl did not know that the great man knew him as a person; he had not dreamed Mr. Ismay knew his name. He could not know that the philanthropist had happened to see him passing coins to those helpless old beings, those paupers on the dock. He could not know that this job, which was the answer to his heart's yearning, was the shipowner's reward to a young man for his compassion toward those less fortunate than himself.

A castle on the water, that was what she was, his *Majestic!* Smooth promenade deck twice as long as the longest barn he could remember ever having seen. Powerful engines to send her forward over the waves, yet almost no vibration! Electric bells, handy everywhere, so that the passengers could summon service from below at any hour of the day or night. And the lights! How could it be that, at only a touch, the thin wire inside of a blown glass bulb could come aglow and throw this yellowish-white light into the room? Only a little wire leading out of a metal socket, looking as if it had been wound once around a finger, and then running back again into the socket. How could it be? Oh, to be able to show his father this.

How glad he was that he had learned the English words so perfectly to describe the *Majestic*. "Superb." "Magnificent." With its midship saloon, a smoking-room, even a library for the use of the passengers, the richness of mahogany woodwork, the leather couches, and he, Karl Petersson, could call this his home. Luxury, the like of which he had never dreamed, was his. A cabin, to share with another of the crew, was his. Must he pinch himself every hour out of the day to learn if this was real?

His cabinmate, Bert Williams, laughed at his enthusiasm. After a trip or two, he wagered, Karl would not gape with wonder at the so-called marvels he found here on the *Majestic*.

Member of the Royal Naval Reserve, the ruddy-cheeked, mouthy Bert Williams laid claim to many a worldly conquest, and looked down his long nose at the naïve young Swede who was his roommate. Wine: he had been drunk in every port of call. Women: he could get next to the best or the worst of them. Song: who would bother about song when women and wine were more than plentiful?

"But, is even the *Teutonic* so fine as this?" Karl asked.

"'Chew-tonic'!" Williams bellowed. "Oh, for Lord's sake, Swede, say it 'Too-tonic' not 'Chew-tonic.'" Extremely well satisfied with his sense of humor, he added, "You don't chew your tonic, you drink it!"

Many of the things Bert Williams said continued, through the days, to puzzle Karl. "So, this is your first trip to New York? Ah, you have a lot to learn, my shipmate. Now, the first bloody thing they will try to sell you is the Brooklyn Bridge."

"But what would I do with a bridge?"

"Ha! Ha! Serious-thinking suckers like you is what they are looking for. Yes, I will have to take you in hand and show you the town."

There would be plenty of time to think about that, after they docked. Meantime, he wished Williams would let him alone. There seemed to be a sinister something in the British sailor's solicitousness which he could not understand. But he felt it. He worked beyond hours on the purser's records so as to keep his distance from the cabin, and Bert Williams; there was plenty to do, with the many records of passengers and their fares, and their quarters, and of disbursements from the giant ice-house to the galleys; so many deck chairs and furnishings and bars of soap and towels and sheets and other linens to keep recorded. But beyond his outlined duties, he offered his time so as to keep from spending leisure in the company of Williams, who would not so much as let him read a book in peace.

The ship came westward. Gone like a wink, six days. Karl leaned over the *Majestic*'s rail and watched the foam streaking along her sides. Not many more hours and they would be in New York harbor. Almost involuntarily he looked up to the shoulders of her; did she have wings, to span the ocean in less than a week's time?

Past Sandy Hook, she nosed into The Narrows. Karl mourned that he could not catch a glimpse of "Liberty" now nearing completion on the island in the Upper Bay, but that he needs must be at his desk balancing ones and sixes and nines. Williams was a fool to think that "Liberty" brought good-luck only to those whose first sight of America was the giant woman; such superstitions were for fools; but oh, that he could have known the thrill of seeing the lovely bronze-copper goddess, standing there on her broken shackles—welcoming him—

"The big ugly dame, with her flat feet," Williams had described the Statue of Liberty. But how could he expect Williams, who showed no respect for anything else, to show respect for the symbol of liberty?

Karl returned, to their rightful owners, the valuables entrusted to the ship's safe for the duration of the journey; then proudly he came up on deck and helped to supervise the disembarking passengers. The mate supplied longed-for information: there was Manhattan Island, and here on its southmost tip, Battery Park; and here the old round building, Castle Garden. Three hundred first-class passengers left the ship; over a hundred of the second-class, and then Karl watched the *Majestic* dump almost a thousand immigrants into the waiting lap of Castle Garden.

To be one of those! To stay, here, in this land of promise, and not be signed for the return trip, even on the *Majestic!* Karl tried to count the stars on a fluttering flag with red stripes and white, atop the old round building. Then the words came to him, "Six hours' leave, to go ashore."

He went to his cabin and counted out his money, changed

now to English pounds and shillings. So much for so much in American money; the purser would make the change for him. The rest he would put in the purser's safe. "Four dollars in American money, that should be enough to show me the whole city of New York."

With four dollars in his handmade leather purse with its long neck strap wound around it, and stuffed clumsily into the pocket of his uniform coat, Karl stood hesitant at the end of the gangplank.

Here, now, was that land toward which his great desire, his hopes, had led him; and here he stood, half afraid to enter. Anxious, silent, in awe, he put his foot forward and stepped into America.

SEVEN

LIKE A HAMMER DRIVING a nail into soft wood, each step he took on the promontory that Americans called The Battery, drove Karl's decision deeper into his consciousness. He had reached his goal. This was America. Now that he was here, he should stay. He had to stay. He would go back aboard and get the remainder of his savings; no one would guess what was in his mind. If one spoke of his returning for more money, that was easy to explain; he could say he was going to buy a bridge. Folk in America do strange things, he smiled to himself.

Roaming through the large old round building, he came near a hawker's cart. An immigrant, shy, newly come from Sweden, was being urged by another man to buy a billfold for his money and throw away the pouch he had carried from his home.

"Nothing will make people laugh at you so much as an old country money pouch. Start being an American, right now," Karl heard the urging one say. The other bought a money-holder, and Karl saw him throw his old pouch into the corner after he transferred what had been entrusted to it, to the new purse.

Karl could be glad that he had heard this. He would start at once, being an American, and walked boldly to the cart and picked up the first billfold his eye lit upon. "I'll take this one," he said, and paid for it. A whole dollar, from his four, now was spent. But it was worth it. No one was going to call him an immigrant, and laugh. He walked away from the crowd, to be alone when he transferred the money. He laid the three one-dollar bills in his new billfold, but slipped his Flyttningsbevis into his inside coat pocket.

His thumb and forefinger reached inside the leather pouch; the buttercup petals fell apart at his touch. He turned the pouch upside down and shook it gently, and the powdery petals fluttered to the floor, all except one. The tiny petal clung to the corner; what use to try to remove it? But he could not bring himself to toss the pouch away where someone else might pick it up. Elisabet had made it for him. No worthless fellow, picking up trash from the floors, should have the use of it. He would throw it into the water. He slid the new leather fold into the back pocket of his pants. Already he began to feel like an American.

Because he wore a uniform, timid frightened men and women asked him the way to the labor exchange, or inquired where they could find a streetcar to take them to Brooklyn, or why had not Aunt Emma met them as she had promised in her letter? Germans, Englishmen, Italians, Swedes, Americans, all breathing the same air, all treading the same ground. What a country, America!

"Five cents! Get *The Story of Castle Garden!* Only five cents!" A long-nosed, dark-complexioned man with penetrating voice pushed himself along with one hand and held up a fan of booklets in the other. Karl watched him. He had no legs, and his body was mounted on a small square of wood with little wheels at each of the four corners. His trousers were caught up and held by suspenders slung over his shoulders, but the beltline was under his armpits. No need for the trouser legs; they lay in folds on the square platform. A rush of tenderness swept over Karl, pity for this poor unfortunate who must be jostled by the crowd while earning his living five cents at a time. To what better use could that twentieth part of a dollar be put, than to help and encourage such a one?

"I will take a copy," and he removed one of the dollars from his new billfold. No one could guess, now, that he was a Swede, smugly he assured himself, and slipped the new purse back into his pocket. He smiled as he snapped the bill between his hands so it sounded like a shoe-shiner's rag in action, then handed the money to the vendor, selected a booklet from the fan of them, and reached for his change.

The cripple dropped a fifty-cent piece, two dimes, and a nickel into his hand.

"Twenty cents more, if you please," Karl asked, and extended his palm.

"Yer crazy. I said twenny-five cents," and the cripple spat at Karl's feet.

"Five cents, you said. You owe me twenty cents." Did the man think for a minute that he did not know his figures?

The peddler laughed at him, "Ha! Tventy cents, eh? Why doncha sing it, Swede?"

Karl's blood boiled. The peddler had laughed at him! The cripple cringed as Karl moved forward and bent, to hit—but no—he could not strike this thing in front of him.

"Why doncha learn to talk English before ya start arguin' wid Americans?" The cripple spread his palm to push himself away, and his hand met a blob of spit. He looked at it, then wiped it against the folds of trouser leg; again his hand met the floor of Castle Garden and he pushed himself into the crowd.

Karl stood benumbed. Was this America?

No, it was not America that had made that thing the way he was; it was misfortune. Imagine one's own self with such a handicap! If the thing had not laughed at him, he could find it in his heart to forgive him; it must be pretty hard to get along without legs. And the twenty cents: well, he was a bookkeeper, he would know what to do about that, just charge it to Profit and Loss. But there was something else, and this was important; he had said the word "twenty" in such a way as to give the cripple cause to laugh. That must be overcome. He said the word over and over as he walked, "twenty, twenty; not tventy, but—" he tried so hard, but it came out "thwenty."

He opened the little booklet and riffled the pages, glancing through it as he walked toward an exit. Now was a good time to throw away the money pouch, the article that would give away the knowledge that he was not an American. Fondling it momentarily, he threw it then far out into the water, pitching it flat so it swirled, disc-like, in a semicircle from him; and turned his face away. He did not look to see it riding lightly on the water, coming closer, closer, at last tapping against the stones below. Instead, he read in the booklet, "The big round building on the Battery was built as a fort in 1807."

Karl stopped in his tracks. "A fort!" he exclaimed aloud, "This, a fort?" Without forbidding high stone walls and turrets? And Marstrand had been a fort. If such was the difference between America and Sweden, then he could be doubly glad he had turned his face westward.

"But it never fired a shot."

He had read enough. No cells, no iron rings: no doubt was in his mind. He would return to the ship and get his money from the safe. He could discard the uniform coat and cap and buy a plain coat and hat in New York; the pants would serve. How about the pay for the trip over? Best to let it go; it could be repayment to the Line for his passage to America. At that rate he would not be cheating them.

The purser was in his office and handed Karl his savings, changed to American money, ready for spending. "Now, with all that money on you, don't go buying the Brooklyn Bridge," he admonished his assistant, laughingly.

What was this Brooklyn Bridge with which they all made merry? Where Bert Williams had been sarcastic in his warning, the purser seemed to be indulging in buffoonery. That Brooklyn Bridge was something he must see! Quickly and with long strides he brushed his way between the bewildered children of many nations, through the round building, out of an exit, off of the mole on which Castle Garden sat, and then he turned to look.

Beyond lay the *Majestic* with her three masts and two funnels, symbol of a day now past for him. And there stood Castle Garden. Two flags waved proudly from tall quivering poles; only a glance for the flag of New York State, for there to the right of the arched door out of which he had come, held unfolded and uncreased by the wind, flew the Stars and Stripes of the United States of America! Gulls hovered over her, dipping to the red and white and blue. A many-windowed tower rose to crown the round building; and there were the shuttered windows of its second story. Eyes—yes—but not like those of Marstrand. These were the eyes of a tender guardian speaking of freedom; windows with inside-shutters half drawn, eyes with their lids half closed, not too clearly to see a man leaving his ship, for good, no longer an outsider standing on the bank, but wading now in the shallow waters of this deep river which was America.

Into deeper water he would venture, deeper, until at last he would be a part of this swift current.

Oh, he was proud that he could read what it said on the big sign over the arched and columned door:

"Immigrant Landing Depot of
CASTLE GARDEN"

He walked away from sight of the old round building, past

hobbling old men with crutches or canes, past children clinging to their mothers' skirts, past thin women dressed in plain black with deep black hoods like sunbonnets hiding pale faces, past teams drawing four-wheeled open carriages filled with baggage on which the owners sat, onto the gravel walks of Battery Park under the budding sycamore trees. A late sun, setting, reflected pure gold into the windows of buildings on the shoreline.

There was beauty, too, in America.

Birds twittered their evensong while the rays of the sun stretched a horizontal pattern over the promenade and pointed out a sailor and his love, holding hands. Karl watched them; they might have been in the full flush of a first love. But no. Her pleading eyes looked up to his, and as Karl looked, he saw the sailor turn from the tear-filled eyes and look toward the water. Fools—to find themselves in such a position—for Karl could see she bore a child without benefit of paper bearing signature and seal, for the third finger of her left hand was bare.

He turned and looked over the bay. The Statue of Liberty!

"So there you are. I've looked all over this confounded island for you," Bert Williams broke into his reverie. "Come on, the time is short and I promised to show you the town."

Karl's spirits fell. How was he to rid himself of Williams? How was he to lose himself from the *Majestic* if this cabinmate insisted upon attaching himself to him?

"Go on, Bertie, go where you will. I want to get the feel of the new land. Let me spend my time in my own way. If I do not 'get to see the town' on this trip, there will always be the next time."

"Well, I'll be damned!" Bert Williams stood back and put his hands on his hips, and spread his legs wide apart as if he needed to in order to remain upright. "What has got into you? I thought you wanted to know America. I thought you could hardly wait to see it. *This* is not America; you've got to see New York to see America! Come on." He wound his arm around Karl's arm and pulled him along.

Karl balked. Now was the time for him to put his foot down and say no. What was the matter with him, anyway, that he found it so much easier to follow than to up and say no, he did not want to go? If it were Rikard Eklund, here in his place, he would say no and have done with it—or Axel—

"The hours are short. You'll feel better after dinner. I know a swell place to get a couple of girls and then we'll eat and maybe come back here, if you like it so well, and have time for a stroll in the moonlight before leave is up."

Karl could imagine the beauty of this place in the moonlight, a white sail made whiter, eery light peering through sycamore branches. Oh, well, maybe he could slip away easier from Williams later. Yes, he would go.

Broadway, Whitehall Street, The Bowery; it was good he had come with Williams, for now he was knowing somewhat of the city of New York.

"Gert will be waiting for me," boasted Williams. "God, how that girl can sing about The Bowery!" Solicitously he leaned toward Karl, "You don't *have* to have a Swede girl, do you?"

"No. No." Karl scarcely heard him. He was thinking of Axel Lindqvist and the military training heath. If Axel only could see him now, walking down Broadway in the City of New York, in the United States of America! Had he beat Axel to this country? He wished he knew.

"That's good," answered Williams, "because I don't know of a Swede girl. But Gert works next to a Norwegian, and she is all right."

"A Norwegian. For what?"

"For what! He says for what! Oh, Lord! What a stupid!" Williams stopped and lifted his right knee and slapped it hard with his hand, "Don't be a silly ass, just do what Liv tells you to do and you'll live through it."

"Liv. That is a fair name. You say she is Norwegian?"

"Yes, and how she'll love the way you say her name, as if it was 'Leev,' just the way she says it herself."

They turned into Grand Street and walked into a retail store. Long underwear hung suspended from the ceiling, as did cloths of varied hue. A crowd of chattering women milled about, pushing and shoving each other to reach, first-hand, a long counter piled high with boxes and bolts of dry goods. There were four women behind the counter, lifting down heavy bolts of colored and printed cottons, measuring against brass-headed tacks set into the counter-top, biting the selvage, then tearing the cloth across its width.

By the gleam of recognition in her eyes, Karl knew which was Bertie Williams' Gert, a plump grimy-looking girl with reddish brown, stringy hair brought upward and placed in a knot on top of her head. Short ends had loosened, from the strain of stretching and bending, and they hung around the neck of her black dress.

The shoppers turned when Williams yelled his noisy greeting, "Hello, Gert! Hello there, Liv!"

A wan smile spread over the Norwegian girl's face. Karl appraised her; she was tall and thin, her skin was fair—with a smudge here and there—her hands were large, her light hair hung loosely down her back and covered the bow of the apron ties at her waistline. A few strands had fallen over her shoulder and hung over the black dress covering her bosom.

So this was Liv. How sad she looked. Karl knew that once there must have been rose-bloom in those wan white cheeks. Blue fought with smoke color in her eyes, but the blue was losing.

"How about it, Petersson? She looks as if she could use a hearty good dinner, don't you think?" Leaning close to Karl, "Is it a go with you?"

"Yes." Karl watched the arguing and quarrelsome customers file out of the store. So they were supposed to be ladies! Not in his wildest imagination could he picture his mother acting as they! He felt sorry for Liv; he would be glad to buy her a good dinner. With that large frame she needed a good dinner.

"Lord's sake, Bertie, these fire-sales almost *kill* me!" Gert screamed and fairly jumped into Williams' arms. Embarrassed, Karl turned away when she kissed his cabinmate full on the mouth.

"Gert!" Bert Williams held her away from him, and then they hugged and kissed again. Karl saw that when they separated from the tight hold, Bert scribed a circle over the point of her left breast with his index finger.

"Your name is Liv? I am Karl Petersson," he held out his hand and the tall Norwegian clasped it and pressed it hard.

"You are from the old country," she greeted him. It was not a question. Her eyes had lighted and the blue gained for an instant, but now they were gray again, set in deep blue-black circles.

"Well, I see you two are getting along fine, together," Williams said. "Come, let's hurry so we'll have time for something beside watching shop-girls close up for the night." He drew his girl out of the shop door and Liv and Karl followed.

They went to a German restaurant, on the first floor of the dingy building that housed the two hall bedrooms that the shopgirls called their homes. "Four dollars a week! A girl can't have a fancy home on them wages," Gert volunteered; and, "Poor Liv, old Simon has not yet raised her to three, even!" She looked for sympathy, to Karl.

"Four dollars a week for ten hours a day, not even counting the time it takes to eat a 'sandrich' in the middle of the day." Karl could not bear to look at her, but looked instead at Liv.

The red and white checkered tablecloth reflected a little of its color to her cheeks, and hot coffee, fried potatoes, a pig's knuckle, red cabbage cooked with vinegar, and pea soup livened Liv. By the time they had finished a large piece of soggy *apfelstrudel* she leaned toward him and eagerly outlined the places in New York that he must see.

"Here, Swede, pay up the check and I will settle with you later, aboard ship," Williams handed him the waiter's bill. Fifty cents apiece! They were being robbed! That would be two dollars!

And would he have to pay for all four dinners? Williams did not know that he was not going back to the ship. Could he afford to hesitate in the paying, lest Williams guess what he thought to do? Suspicion plagued his guilty mind. No, he had best not give his cabinmate any opportunity to guess his scheme of action; a plan to leave his ship was one to surround with the utmost secrecy and discretion, even at such a cost. His glowering eyes followed Williams as his cabinmate left, with Gert, through the side door.

Liv took his arm and they went together out of the doorway into the hall. At the top of the first flight of stairs, a door closed after Gert and Bertie Williams.

"Come," said Liv, and she guided him ahead of her up the stairs, green-carpeted except in the center of each tread, where holes showed the slivered wood of the staircase. Karl thought hard. Now was his chance to get shed of Williams. But it seemed so easy to be steered by Liv. They passed the closed door, and Liv pushed him toward the second flight. No, he would leave; he would run fast, down the stairs, back to Battery Park. He could sit on a bench until morning and then he could start his new life in America. He turned. Liv, the big Norwegian, threw her arms around him, vise-like, and pressed her half-opened lips against his mouth. She, who had been so wan, now with the strength of a tigress, was aflame and the heat of her lips against his melted the strength of his decision to flee. Gently she pushed him backward toward the little room at the head of the second flight of stairs.

He held her close. Ah, so this is what his father had meant when he had spoken of pleasure at the inn on the mainland. Now he could understand the little innuendoes his father had sent his way, no doubt to prepare him for life and living. He knew in this moment that somehow, somewhere, he would partake of this living—but not now! Now he must get away! He thought of the sailor loosening the handclasp of the young woman who was not his wife. What if he could not loosen the big, strong hand of Liv?

She ran her hands up his back, and down; and his breath came heavier—

So this was a part of living!

And then he dropped his arms. Silly, what thoughts could enter a man's mind. And at such a time! For he saw himself, as a youngster, drying a fork between the tines...

All of his sensibilities revolted at being here as he was. With ten times the strength of his passion he threw Liv from him and ran down the stairs, past the closed door on the second floor, out into the street.

"Oh—constable—*hvar* iss Battery-en?" The English words he needed did not come. *"Och tiden?"* he stammered.

"Sure, and where is your cap, Swede?" the policeman laughed as he told Karl, and told him the time by his watch.

Twenty-three minutes left of his shore leave. But, no matter about that, no matter about the cap, he was not returning to the *Majestic*. He could buy a hat, he had intended to anyway; he had money in his pocket, all of his money that he had saved for passage to America except the cost of a billfold and four dinners. Nothing mattered except that he had rid himself of Liv and Williams, and he was in America. Tomorrow morning he would lose himself in the stream of people leaving the Battery, and find himself a job.

He stood stock still. His hand—the one that had accustomed itself to feeling of his back pocket, to send a message of all being well up into his consciousness, stopped—moved slightly higher, and slapped against him; moved to one side, the other, and then pressed hard against his back pants pocket.

No! Oh, no—no—no—

His pocket was empty.

EIGHT

SIX DAYS, eight hours, and fifty-eight minutes. Such a short time for all the crew—but one—the best maiden voyage yet recorded for the North Atlantic; such a long time for one who, traveling eastward, had left his dream behind. America. Just when he had his chance to know her, the Britisher and the damned Norwegian had had to spoil it all.

What choice had he had, other than to return to the *Majestic?* Could he have stayed in New York without money, and thereby call attention to himself in the uniform of the White Star Line, with his ship out to sea? Impossible. No, he had done the only thing there was to do, return to the *Majestic.* And now again he was poor, owing money for his new cap from his first pay. Not even the reimbursement for two dinners could he inveigle from Bert Williams.

"You can't get blood out of a stone," Williams said. "Wait till I draw my pay. Then I'll think about it."

Karl was ashamed to let his cabinmate know of Liv's robbing him. But why had not Gert robbed Williams likewise? Williams had returned to the ship, hours late, and sneaked aboard and bragged about how a few pence would shut the eyes and mouth of any watch. So he must have had some money left.

Shame, remorse, regret, haunted Karl's waking hours. But then again, he asked himself, was he entirely to blame? He had stood the test of strength against passion, had he not? Was it not so, that his mother had taught, that nobility of manhood could be his? Why, then, was he thus punished? Even Sir Stig had lain in the arms of the princess, the while controlling the rising desire of his manhood, but *he had lain in her arms!*

The ballads of the Middle Ages might better never have been taught him if, in this day and age, their lessons were to be for

75

nothing! Had his own mother taught him wrong?

He repeated aloud,

> *"She kisses him on his mouth so red;*
> *There lay Sir Stig as he were dead.*
> *She took him in her arms at once;*
> *He lay so still, child for the nonce."*

He had done no more than Sir Stig; yet for the Danish nobleman of old, his strength of will had laid the foundation of happiness, while instead, he, Karl, had been robbed and the whole course of his life changed! The why or wherefore he could not determine.

But this he did decide upon: better to stay with the White Star Line for awhile, to build up another nest-egg against his settling in America.

Like the shuttle at his mother's loom in the old home, forth and back over the Atlantic, flying from side to side, stopping only long enough to touch the waiting harbors, the *Majestic* carried Karl. Afraid to go ashore with money in his pockets, reluctant to go ashore without, he stayed aboard or touched the holy soil of the United States of America through the floor of Castle Garden, and dared not venture off the mole for fear he might be tempted not to return to his floating home.

He was glad Bert Williams had been left behind in Liverpool after that first trip, so glad, it was worth losing the price of the two fifty-cent dinners that Williams had owed him.

The month of May came. No tall pole dressed with leafy garlands, as at home in the summer, but Karl could see that the leaves of the wide-spreading sycamore trees in the Park shaded the crescent Battery. He watched the water splash against the rough-hewn stones facing the harbor, and looked with longing at the paved walk beyond the stone posts connected with the neat open railing. He knew now that there was Long Island, there Staten Island, and there the Jersey Shore. The sun seemed so close, here in America, almost as if it reached down to touch the tops of buildings. At home it had lived so much higher in the sky. . . .

Once he was in America he would try again to write, seriously, as an avocation, of the sea—of work on the sea—of adventure.

The months of June, July, and August found him noting tragic accidents on the North Atlantic; the hardships on the ocean would serve as background for a story of the sea. He noted this year of restriction against cotton cargoes on the White Star passenger ships, so afraid of fire they were—the year that brought illness to his immediate superior and brought Karl higher wages, bringing extra savings to the money bag marked "Petersson"—the year that brought its September, and Elin.

Karl sat checking over the passenger list and the name stood out in letters that grew as he looked, and came toward him until they smote him, "Elin Benedikta Sibylla Nilsson, age at next birthday, fifteen years; Falkenberg, Halland, Sweden. Bound for New York, New York, United States of America. To: Sponsor, Algot Anders Adolf Nilsson, brother, of the City of Chicago, Illinois, employed, declared citizen of the United States."

"Oh, Elin, why did you do it, Elin?" he mumbled as he finished checking the N's, the O's, the P's, down through the alphabet.

Aft, to the steerage quarters of unmarried women, he hurried, and sought and queried the matron in charge.

"Yes, I know who you mean. She must be on deck."

Thanks to the matron: then he, who had long since rejected Him, did not realize he spoke of God, as to himself he said, "Thank God the *Majestic* has decent steerage quarters, high enough in the ceiling so a breath of air can get through the place where she must sleep. Thank God for the bathrooms with that luxury she has never known—hot and cold running water, for the toilets, planned so that this child of gentle nurture need not wait until dark to be alone, in private, when she has need to use them." He reached the upper deck reserved for passengers of her class, and he saw the little figure against the rail. Oh—Elin! So different from Liv. How glad he was that he had repulsed the big Norwegian!

He walked toward Elin but she did not heed his coming. There she stood, the child; against the black of her plain dress her hands were white as death. Yellow hair hung free below the point of a fringed black scarf, folded three-cornerwise and tied in a double knot under her chin. She had been seasick, that he could tell. Her hands, those tiny hands, clasped a little wilted bouquet of wildflowers; the faded buttercups, the berry leaves, hung lifeless over the pale blue-white hands. Oh, to take her in his arms and comfort her.

Fog had obliterated the British shoreline and she stood staring into the fog.

"Elin!"

She turned, and there was a brief light of hope to brighten her eyes. But she turned again toward the spot where the shore had been; she did not even register surprise that he was there, "It is too late. I left my home and now I cannot go back. It is too late." Her eyes, deep pools of sadness, met his.

Karl took her hand, and went to take the poor bouquet. Quickly she moved it from his reach, "My mother put these in my hand when she said adieu." She took her hand from his and moved her index finger up the stems, so that momentarily each stood erect, to fall as she touched another, "These I will keep forever. My mother put these in my hand—"

She would be true, he knew; and he—he was a traitor—he had thrown away the buttercup Elin had given him, after promising her to keep it always. Regret—how could six letters group themselves together so as to spell such ache for human hearts?

"Why did you come?" Pleadingly he asked it.

"I would not be a midwife." None of the conviction was in her voice that had been there when she had told him so in Småland. "And so I wrote to Algot, and Algot sent me a ticket. I boasted that I would go, *not* to school for midwifery, but to America."

She could not stop, now that she had started talking. "My father said, 'Then go.' Up to the last I was brave. Oh, yes," she nodded, as much talking to herself as to Karl, "I meant to go— one day—but not, perhaps, so soon. Or perhaps I hoped that my father would relent, and even give me in marriage to Rikard who wanted me, rather than to be a midwife, but no. So stern was my father, so terribly stern. If to midwife's school I would not go, then, 'Use the ticket, go to your brother Algot,' he stormed. It was the first time the home had heard my brother's name since he went away. And then my father said, 'You are making your own bed. No matter how hard it gets, remember you made it yourself, and you must lie on it.' I think, up to the last, his pride would not let him relent. I am his daughter, and so did I have pride. And so I went. My mother—she is frail, and she is little, like me—she put these flowers in my hand, and cried."

In some way, he must help her. For the next six days he must try to bring some cheer to this little one who had left the nest before her wings were grown. He visualized big Liv and her ten hours of work, six days in the week, and not receiving as much as three dollars for her labors. Thank God, Algot would meet his little sister at the pier so she would not have to fend for herself and fall into the path that the big Norwegian had followed.

"I have a free time now," he said to Elin after he had given the matron a can of anchovies so she would look the other way when he escorted Elin from the quarters aft. They went below and he showed her the long smooth promenade deck. "There, peek into the banquet hall," and she drew in her breath, panting, when she saw tritons and nymphs in ivory and gold gamboling on the walls under an arched ceiling, brilliant with lights.

She and Karl peeked together into the library; no one was there, so they went in and looked around as if they belonged, and tried the softness of luxurious couches and chose which books they would read "tomorrow evening," and laughed. She was a lady, so of course he would not take her there, but he told her of the smoking-room with its beamed ceiling, oil paintings, and its magnificence.

He was making it pleasant for her, Karl saw, and by the time they were the third day out, the color was creep back into her cheeks.

"Where do they keep the cows?" she asked, and it was incredible that cows need no longer be carried aboard ship to provide fresh milk for passengers. "The ice-house must be like a giant's one to store so much of victuals!" she said, in wonder.

Elin enjoyed inspecting the boat, and was especially thrilled at the sights gained surreptitiously, for then she felt the chosen one of all those in the steerage. Like a child at gift-giving time she turned the electric lights on and then off, and marveled at the wizardry of the American who had invented the uncanny light.

Had he written any more stories, she asked Karl. No, but he would, if she wanted him to, he would; and his chest swelled with pride in his knowledge as she listened, eyes wide with wonder, to him tell of twin-screws and water displacements, and entries in a ledger.

But she carried a heavy burden and the dread she knew, of entering the new land, kept a full smile from breaking over her features. "I wish you were going with me, friend Karl, into

America. When I am with you I am not quite so afraid."

They stood at the rail and read the writing of the thin crescent of a moon, a broken silvery line upon the gentle wavelets of American waters. This was their last evening together.

"No, Elin, I cannot. I am bound to make the return trip." He could not tell her that even if he had decided to make this his last trip, her coming would not have altered his plan. For the adventure into America he had to be free, especially in the matter of a woman.

He could speak English now! It must not be that folk could tell from any accent, but rather called him "Swede" because of his big frame and Viking countenance.

Poor little Elin, how her eyes had shone when she said she knew "one English word"—one word, "greenhorn," spoken proudly, knowing she was it.

Poor, poor little Elin. He was glad for all the little kindnesses he had bestowed upon her during these past six days. It had not been hard to do, either; he realized now how much he, himself, had enjoyed these days. But more than that? Oh, no. Not to a woman did he wish to bind himself; only to America.

Because of Elin he would not go ashore at all this trip, much less to stay; to slip unnoticed into the country became more difficult, anyway, with every passing day now that the American Government was taking over the inspection and supervision of immigrants. "You would not wish for a man to desert his ship, would you, Elin?"

"No, friend Karl, no." She took his hand in her tiny one and held it. He wanted to pick her up and hold her tight in his arms, close to him. He wanted to press his lips, hard, against her tiny mouth. He wanted her, oh, how he burned with wanting her.

He loosened her fingers from his hand. He could be glad that he could loosen them. "Good night, Elin," he said, and turned to go to the matron to add his thanks to the bag of oranges already come to her in return for these few moments with Elin.

No "Liberty" to beam a welcome to Elin, waiting in line to disembark. No friend Karl to fill the yearning, agonized gaze of fear-filled blue eyes. Yes, of course, she knew he was busy, he with the most important job of all on this huge floating city.

No welcoming arms of New York harbor to greet the girl-child fleeing from unwanted schooling; only fog. A whistling buoy sent its melancholy warning through the fog-drenched air. A light's horn blew a dirge, "From fog to fog," it seemed to sing, and Elin shivered. From Liverpool's fog to the fog of New York harbor.

Her dampened spirits rounded her shoulders and made heavier the little trunk and woven knapsack. Poverty-blunted immigrants, pressed close together, shawls covering the women's heads, many with fancy, brightly embroidered aprons, stood loaded down with bundles. Children clung tightly to their parents' hands and huddled with them over piles of bedding, guarding everything in the world they owned. Elin looked at the women, almost every one of them bore the unmistakable imprint of hard and long usage in the service of the soil. Hope did not light their features. Why, then, had they come?

Many were weeping, but enough were there, of men, who shouted and pushed and jostled with over-eagerness to enter the new land.

Elin's left hand carried her knapsack, woven of many-colored yarns in vertical stripes. Inside were cheese and dark bread, packed by her gentle, weeping mother before Elin had left her home. Inside, too, were the rolls allotted to her on that first day when her stomach, remembering the tossing on the North Sea, refused to welcome them. If Algot should be late in meeting her, the contents of the knapsack would keep her from hunger. She reached down and inched the trunk ahead, too heavy to hold as she did the woven bag, she scraped it along the deck; and when she stooped to take a hold on the little iron handle she was all but lost among people, a forest of close-pressed tall moving "trees," their elbows, like branches, extending outward from their trunks to keep themselves from being crowded to the crushing point.

A dirty, milling crowd, and she was a part of it. So many in this crowd less fastidious in their habits than any human should be! The smells—and the fog holding them close—oh, to be home again in the fresh pure sunlit day of Sweden!

Karl saw her as she stepped into America. A thin line broke from the impatient crowd, and he saw her walking, bent low on the side that lugged the small wooden trunk. And then he heard them laugh—the crowd.

Too long had the knapsack lain in dampness, or perhaps a

thread had pulled to ravel the bottom of the bag, for from the cloth of Roman stripe fell cheese and a large loaf of dark bread, and rolls and a small serviette folded over a jar of marmalade. There, to the floor of Castle Garden, fell Elin's store of food, to the floor where men had spit.

Karl heard them laugh. "Let them laugh! To Hell with these ignorant fools!" He rushed to help her, but stopped short. If he went to her now, would he be able to resist staying longer in her company? And if he did—what might that lead to?

As he hesitated, he saw her kneel and gather up the precious food, and saw her stuff it high up toward the handles at the top, then roll the rotted, raveled part up close to meet the cheese and bread. He took a short step forward.

He was too late. Too late he saw Elin tuck the rolled knapsack under her left arm, pick up the iron handle of the heavy little trunk, and with head held high and proud, walk forward into the new land and become lost in the crowd.

NINE

FIVE DAYS of waiting at the receiving station for immigrants, Elin knew now that Algot would not come. Resigned, she sat where the officer had told her she was to wait. No use to ask herself why she had come. No use to ask, "Where is Algot?" But it was unlike Algot to forget her.

"This is my punishment—for leaving a good home—"

"'Elin Benedikta Nilsson, in care of the White Star Liner *Majestic*,' I guess this is for you, all right." The immigration officer smiled as he read the script on the front of her trunk and handed her a letter postmarked Chicago.

Trembling, she opened the letter and read. Far away lay her brother Algot, with ice packed all around his body, in a hospital bed. Oh, he must be ill, almost unto death, to be in such a place! And she, without sufficient money, unable to go to him to administer to his needs. "Oh, dear God, care for him and make him well," she whispered, then shuddered at what his illness meant for her, and added, "Take care of me! I know, I know that this is punishment to me for breaking Your commandment to honor my father and my mother. Oh, dear God, now I know! Please do not punish me more, for now I know how wrong I was. Oh, please take care of me."

She read on; a Swedish nurse had written the letter at Algot's dictation. It was a Swedish hospital in which he lay. They would take good care of him and soon, they hoped, he would be well.

"Acute appendicitis," written in English; what was this sickness? She never had heard of such a sickness at home. It must be bad to keep Algot from meeting her as he had promised when he sent the ticket. The letter repeated many times the admonishment to let her brother know, at once, that she had used what money their father had doubtless supplied to her, for a return ticket to Falkenberg. He would dearly love to see her, his little sister, but the ticket had been sent in a time of weakness. Perhaps, even, he might have had a momentary return of the bitterness felt toward his father, and by taking Elin from him, had tasted the sweetness of revenge. But all of that, now, was gone for he had had a close call in this illness, and since he had been stricken had had time to think upon this thing he'd done. The way in America was not so easy, especially for a young girl. "So shall I rest easier if I but hear that you have gone back home."

"If he only knew." The tears fell and blurred the blue ink on the letter in her hand. And yet, he should have known their father well enough: money—what money?

"And when you write, Elin, on the outside of the letter, use my name as Andy Nelson. I am an American now, and when I get my final papers they will show my name thus, for it is more American." Why had he chosen Andy? Because Algot was so extremely old-countryish; but his second name, Anders, had lent itself splendidly to the American "Andy." He knew she would understand. If she were to stay here in this country, she too would wish to change her name to one which would sound American. Everyone did.

His new name, her name, or the spelling of them, what did they matter? Algot was ill and could not come. The tears could not help. She wiped her eyes and folded the letter carefully and tucked it far down into the bosom of her dress. The officer who had brought the letter stood waiting while she read; he had hoped the communication would be the means of dispatching one more immigrant from the Garden.

"Do you speak any English at all?" he asked in Elin's native tongue.

She nodded, and pointed to herself she said the one word she knew. And then she told him in Swedish that her brother could not come.

"Poor little thing. Poor, poor little thing." What should he do with her? Only one thing, find work for her.

"*Arbeta?*" Oh, yes, yes! She jumped up at the prospect of work, and followed the kind officer as he carried her little trunk toward the office for placement of immigrant labor. She turned at the call of "Five cents! Five cents!" to see a cripple, without legs, pushing himself toward an oncoming crowd. Men pushed against him, and one reached out his heavy shoe as if to kick at the crippled peddler, but caught the sole of it under the square raft set on four little wheels. The cripple would have toppled, but he let his booklets fly and grasped at the floor with his palms, to right himself. Anger sparked and streaked from her blue eyes as Elin rushed forward and with outstretched arms, shed the crowd from him and stopped to retrieve the pamphlets. She sat on her haunches, then, and was the height of the long-nosed man in front of her, as on her lap she sorted the booklets. Most were in English, and some were printed in German. "And Swedish!" she exclaimed delightedly, and smiled in returning the booklets to the cripple, all but one printed in Swedish.

Elin reached into her skirt pocket and held out her hand, on which were spread the American coins her friend Karl had said might come in handy, when he had made the exchange. The cripple grabbed for a half-dollar.

"Oh, no, you don't!" The immigration officer set Elin's trunk down with a bang, snatched the fifty cent piece, and restored it to Elin's palm; he picked up a nickel and tossed it to the peddler, and said to Elin, "Come."

She turned to look again at the crippled man. How could she have felt sorry for herself? She was strong and healthy. She had legs! She pressed the little printed brochure close to her; this was her first American belonging. It would remind her of the legless man, reminding her to carry thankfulness in her heart. Under her left arm she carried *The Story of Castle Garden* and followed the immigration officer.

"Sit here. They will take care of you soon. Good-bye and good luck," he said, and Elin thanked him for carrying her trunk and setting it beside her.

Dear little trunk, reminder of home. She need have no worry about the bottom giving on her trunk, and spilling the contents, for stout bands of sheet iron held the corners and ran up the center, over the rounded top, down the back and along the under side. Even the top was reinforced with sheet iron, and where the lid rounded, the metal had been snipped into points so it could follow the shape of the arch; and it made a pretty design, with each point held securely to the reddish-brown wood with a square-headed nail at its very tip. She felt of her bosom, nervously. Yes, the key was there, to the lock fastening the long iron hasp that passed over a staple in the front metal band.

She moved her lips in reading the delicate fancy script, painted in white across the front. Curls on the "s's" and swirls on the capitals, spelled out her name, the names of her home city, province, and country. A hand-forged handle hung at either side, and the handle in the center of the lid was lying flat against the wood.

"Tired, too," sighed Elin.

Men and women sat in chairs lining the walls of the room. So many more to work than were needed; so many sitting there, bigger and stronger than she, would anyone want her?

A fine lady came, dressed in stiff silk, holding a pair of spectacles at the end of a long stick, and peered at a husky young woman across the room. She was not of the better class, Elin knew, for as she sat her legs were crossed, one over the other. The fine lady's dress looked, at first, to be green but as she swished it changed to black. Flowers rose to an exaggerated height at the top of her large-brimmed hat.

"That is the way I shall dress, some one of these days," Elin dreamed.

The lady felt of the arms, the thighs of the waiting applicants; then, satisfied, swept her hand around her well-padded rear, caught up her skirts, and with the strongest looking of the applicants, left the room.

Men came, and women, and as they went the favored ones followed them. Elin despaired. No one wanted her.

But there would be tomorrow. She would try to forget her anxiety by reading the story of Castle Garden. Blessings on the cripple who had brightened this day of waiting by selling her this booklet, for here she learned of the building of this huge place. A fort it had been, a public hall, a place where minstrels and music had attracted countless throngs, where the opera from Italy had reigned, where some man by the name of Samuel Morse had demonstrated his telegraph instrument. Wouldn't her friend Karl love to read of that!

First and foremost, this was the place where Jenny Lind had sung. Under this very roof she had sung her first concert in America. Here she had enjoyed her triumph!

Ah! Song lingered still in this old round building, for here Jenny Lind had sung. This was a binding tie to Sweden, and no longer need Elin feel alone. There, on the printed page, were words of a song, carried through Jenny Lind to every nook and crevice of this American edifice; and she, Elin Nilsson, knew them word for word! She hummed the tune but stopped, embarrassed, when she realized that two men stood before her.

"A happy little thing, singing, but—no—she is too small," the voice of one said.

"Well, all of the others we had today are gone," the immigration officer answered. "If you have to have female help, this one is all there is."

"But the word at my—"

"Come back tomorrow, then. You never know what may come in. We always have plenty in the mornings."

"But—I just can't go home—again—without help," the voice was anguished, and Elin wished she knew what plagued the young man who stood there. If only she could understand what he was saying!

"It's up to you," the officer said, shrugging his shoulders.

"All right, let me talk to her, then."

"She can't speak a word of English," and to Elin, in Swedish, "He wants to know if you can speak English, so I told him, 'Not a word.'"

Elin uncurled the leg she had been sitting on, and jumped to her feet. By her attitude she proved the immigration man wrong. "*Ja—ja*—greenhorn!" and she pointed to herself, proud.

The young man smiled.

"Please, dear God," she pleaded silently, "make him want me. I will show him I can do any kind of work that he wants done."

They talked through the interpreter, the stranger and Elin. Would she want to come to work for him, knowing that the work was hard and there was plenty of it? His wife was a consumptive and could be of no help, rather did she demand care. He was a dentist, only just begun to practice, and his patients were few, few enough indeed, so that he took roomers into the large brownstone-fronted house left him by his parents. She should have food aplenty, and a small room for herself, and seven dollars a month in wages. He wished it could be more. "Three floors with rented rooms on each, and an English basement where we cook and eat," that was the house size. Could she cook? Would she give nursing, of a practical sort, to his wife with the consumption?

He looked so tired. Would she care to come and work for

him? "Oh, God in Heaven, only let him decide that I will do!" and Elin nodded yes, and hoped.

The two men talked. "I think you'd better wait for a two-hundred pounder, with all that work to do. This one is only a kid, and I'll bet she doesn't tip the scales at ninety pounds."

"Yes, I suppose you are right," the stranger took a step toward the door, "and yet, my wife is sensitive to disappointment. She expects that I will bring a hired girl with me when I return tonight. And she is ill. If the little one will come, I will take her—Elin—you said was her name?" He turned and smiled, "Come, Elin."

God had answered her prayer. Elin, too, smiled.

The dentist took her knapsack from her, and carried her little trunk; he opened the door and allowed her to precede him out onto the sidewalk. They climbed to the open top of a horse car, and he tried by gesticulating and by enunciating words more clearly and speaking more slowly than was his custom, to tell her of landmarks as they passed. She smiled and nodded, and he felt that she partly understood. Only around the corner, now, and they descended steps to the English basement level of a brownstone front, and he opened the door for Elin to enter.

"Oh, John dear, you've brought someone!"

Elin stepped forward, unafraid; whatever bashfulness she had experienced at thought of entering another's home, left her. She was needed. No wonder the dentist was tired, she thought, as she saw that the young wife's nightgown, which peeked above spotless blankets wrapped around her in the big chair, was fresh and white. But on the window sill, a rose stood in water that showed bubbles clinging to the glass vase; the windows themselves should shine! Yes, she was needed here, she knew as she looked about the room.

An oval dark wood table was drawn close to the sick woman's chair and on its marble top were a book, a stack of small white cloths—a worn sheet, perhaps, torn into little squares—a porcelain container with a close-fitting lid, and a glass of water.

Elin took the hand of her mistress. It was overwarm, and two bright crimson spots burned high on her cheekbones. Her eyes looked glassy—open too wide—moist, as if tears hovered, not only on the brims but over all the eyes.

"Oh, John!"

He knew she was glad. Perhaps this little one would be not only a hired girl, she could be a companion. It was a kind Providence which had led him to Elin, to bring such happy welcome to his wife's eyes. He would help the new girl with the heavy work as much as he could. As long as she was good to Sara, that was all that mattered. He took his wife's thin hand in his, "Sara," he nodded toward her, "Elin," and they were introduced.

"Sara." He said it differently, with a little harder "a," but it was a name Elin knew. Sara; she said it over and over, out loud and to herself, until it sounded as when Doctor John spoke it. She looked at the pale hands of this Sara, lying spent on the blanket over her lap, slender, "like the kind of thin china that shadows of your fingers show through, when you hold it up to the light," thought Elin, veined in a delicate blue that appeared again over the moons of the rounded, grooved fingernails.

They recalled, too, the story of that other who was Sara; even the chapter in Genesis, Elin could remember, "—and Sara was an hundred and seven and twenty years old; *these were* the years of the life of Sara." But this sweet-faced namesake would never live so long. "I need not be a woman grown to see how it is with Doctor John's Sara," Elin mused sadly.

Without understandable words, man and wife welcomed her, and the answering look in Elin's eyes proclaimed her loyalty, her thankfulness to know a home once more.

The new hired girl helped Sara to her bed, and they laughed at Elin's efforts to understand her mistress and master. But they had enjoyed her cooking! And the evening meal was good, the whipped potatoes and fried perch, and coffee. Coffee for an evening meal for Elin, who had been too young at home for that, but must drink milk! How satisfying to know that someone cared, that Doctor John should pick up a teacup and hold it in his hand and say, "Cup—cup—cup," and have her say it after him until she knew at once what to call it when he lifted it. Only a few hours in this home, and already she had added four new words to her vocabulary of one: cup, spoon, knife, and bed.

Dr. John Osgood showed her to her third-floor room. Ah, how good the clean white iron bed would feel this night.

God was good; she knelt to say her bedtime prayer, but found it hard to keep her eyes from the beautiful shiny brass knobs at the top of each of the bedstead's corner tubing of white. The room showed in these knobs as the world did in the gazing globe in Grandfather's garden in Stockholm. Dear Grandfather, what had he said when he learned of her leaving? What would he say if he could know that now his "little pet" was hired out as a common domestic servant? He, who was so proud of his position in the Riksdag, what would he say?

He should never know. Not until she had made good in this land would she write home. She had pride, too. No, never would she tell them at home that one of the Nilssons should so have reversed the tradition of the family as to be a household servant.

But no ordinary servant would she be. To the doctor and his invalid wife she would dedicate her days, and nights if need be, until Algot would send for her: every waking moment should be spent in loving ministry to these two who were so good to her. Tomorrow the doctor would help her address a letter to Belmont Avenue in the City of Chicago, Illinois, to Algot, her brother who was now an American and so was "Andy Nelson."

So tired she was—but perhaps she and Algot, together, could some day return to Sweden. Sweden and Jenny Lind. America and Jenny Lind. As Jenny Lind had found her way back to her homeland, so could Elin Benedikta Sibylla Nilsson—if she worked hard—find her way back to Sweden and a little house at a crossroads, a little house covered with vines, their leaves singing in the summer rain as gentle drops, like muted hammers, met the marimba of leaves.

Sleep came to little Elin, and in her sleep she smiled.

TEN

EVEN THE electric lights shone with a dimmer glow; this *Majestic*, she was not so majestic as she had been those weeks ago when Elin stood at her rail. Much as he wanted not to, Karl missed Elin. Much as he wanted not to think of how he had let her go, the thought returned to torment him. If only he could live over again that split second of time when he had lost her, when he had let her walk away—alone.

Life was hard and unrelenting. Somehow, since his father had thwarted his boyhood ambitions, nothing else worked out for him the way he planned, either. It was as though life were singling him out to be given the rotten end of things; even America, what had she given him other than a memory of littered streets and an empty back pants pocket? For five American cents, he would give up the whole idea of settling in the United States, and sail—oh, for India, perhaps. Tomorrow they would dock at Liverpool. He would seek a job on a steamer bound for India and go, not only there, he would go around the world! There was something to make a man forget his troubles, a trip around the world. Plenty of time, after such an adventure, to think of settling in America; best not to go yet anyway, what freedom was there with such as Liv lying in wait to grab hold of him with big strong hands—with Elin there—against his wishes, pulling at his heartstrings?

She had been so out of place there in Castle Garden. Why, oh why had she chosen to leave her home? She belonged to Sweden, in Sweden. He could have found happiness perchance, in Sweden, with Elin. He could have brought her to his home, to Norden: his mother would have loved her. What a mistress she would have made, for Norden! Fru Karl Petersson, she would have been then, the little Elin.

91

Music came from the banquet-hall. Played with the Swedish passengers in mind, this song, for the violin told of the days when the birches swish their mild summer song; and he could almost hear his mother singing,

> *"När björkarna sussa*
> *Sin mild sommar sang."*

Karl strained his ears; no, that could not be the spray of the ocean's water swishing as the *Majestic*'s prow cut sharply into the Atlantic; it was the sound of birches in the swamp at Norden. Elin ... her yellow hair would have matched their leaves as they turned golden ...

> *"The Bow'ry, the Bow'ry!*
> *They say such things*
> *And they do strange things*
> *On the Bow'ry, the Bow'ry!*
> *I'll never go there any more!"*

Karl winced. There must be good in the hearts of Americans, why did they think it smart and clever to request the playing of songs with such coarseness as this?

The Bowery. Liv. Oh, yes, how out of place Elin was there. And he had let her go!

Elin—the birches—mother—Sweden—Norden—home! A woman's voice rose from the banquet-hall. The popular song, written by one who had come from the South, only to die in the Bowery—and Bert Williams had pointed out the very house in which Stephen Foster had died—came like his own heart's plaintive pleading, "Oh, Tell Me of My Mother."

Karl stumbled into the hatchway to find his office desk, and sit with his head in his hands, lonely, bewildered, and forlorn.

"The Captain wishes to speak with you, sir," a cabin boy broke into his solitude.

"Thank you," he answered, and doused cold water on his red eyes, and smoothed the wrinkles in his sleeves and set his cap straight, to report to the senior officer.

"As you know, Petersson, we have on board the aged mother-in-law of one of the officials of the Line."

"Aye, sir."

"Mr. Barker was to meet her in Liverpool, but we have been notified that he cannot do so because of the critical illness of a relative."

"Aye, sir," and Karl wondered what this had to do with him.

"It is our duty, of course, and our pleasure to escort the lady to the place which he has designated."

Karl nodded.

"Now, Petersson, we have chosen you. It is not only because you know the country that we have done so, and that you know the language—"

What was the Captain leading up to?

"But because you have proved yourself trustworthy and so fit to accompany Mrs. Geddes to Sweden."

"Sweden!" Karl's heart leaped. Was it that he had longed, in the past hours, and days, to go? Was that the feeling which had surged inside of him, almost to tear his inner self apart?

"You are glad?" The Captain smiled.

"Aye, sir; oh, aye, sir!"

"Then we are glad that you are to go. There will be time enough for you to accompany Mrs. Geddes to where her son-in-law waits, and have a day or so to visit friends or home, and still rejoin us at Liverpool in time for our mid-month trip westward."

Happily, arrangements were agreed upon. The Captain shook Karl's hand.

He would go to Falkenberg; the elderly lady should be no care to him, so the Captain had said, for she traveled well. If only Elin were still in Falkenberg! Maybe there would be time to call on Simon Svenning.

Would there be time to go home? Was he ready, yet, to go home? He looked at himself in the mirror and set his cap first so—then so—

Not yet was he rich, but in all the finery of this uniform could he bring himself to go home?

The *Majestic* docked. Karl and his charge sped from Liverpool over the land and through the blackness of the tunnel, to Hull; they tossed, as a cork might, pushed by the North Sea's uncompromising hands into the Skagerrak; they docked at Göteborg. "So beautiful the fish nets drying in the sun!" he said impulsively, and heartily his companion agreed. They rode to Falkenberg.

"Strangely does the hand of Fate write our lives," he said to himself when the carriage stopped before a house, knowledge of which already was in his memory, a little fairy tale house whose bare vines now strummed a solemn tune. For no longer illness dwelt at his companion's destination; Death had moved in, and a wreath of wax flowers hung beside the door to tell of his entry.

In the house of Death Karl met the stern father to little Elin. There lay her mother in the casket, a broken heart of flowers standing at her head. So Elin's mother was the kin to the official of the Line! Remorse lined the stern face of Elin's father. So this was the father who had sent the little one out into a world that had laughed at her. Where was she now, lying on the bed that she had made?

Karl heard someone say, "Ja, soon they will arrive, Eleonora and Sven, but they leave Lilla Sven behind with the housegirl."

He must go. There would be no fun in telling Sven Eklund and his wife of what he had learned out in the wide world, not here in a house where both parents had died of broken hearts, the standing one no less than the one who lay in the casket.

"Death—the end—so hopelessly the end—" he repeated sadly as he walked away. He stopped at a public well to drink. Just such a pump had he fashioned while working in the blacksmith's shop near Malmö, so long ago, the little shop, built up of big pink and reddish stones, and some gray, and some brown—against a green-grown hill—with its low shingled roof of black, its wide open door, its anvil with sparks flying as he forged the pump handles—and here was such a one, a long graceful handle and a delicate outline of metal forming a hand-hold in the shape of a heart—aye, he remembered. A marvelous invention, the pump, the ironwork bolted to a heavy, standing board—almost as tall as he, and he was tall—the snout now giving water fresh and cool to slake his thirst, the brickwork built up to catch the waste water and keep it from splashing on a man's feet!

His fingers ran over the curved top and down the length of the slender handle, as smooth as silk satin; no, it would not be one that he had forged. Try as he would, he could never make his hands do his bidding to turn out work which might be termed superior. He stared at their palms, their backs, and marveled again at the capable hands that were his mother's.

Oh, well, let them who willed, work with their hands; he

glanced down at his good suit with shining brass buttons, he had done all right so far by using his head.

He walked on toward the railway station, trying to put it out of his mind, but the face in the casket haunted him. Should he have told the father of his meeting with the daughter? What could he have told—that he had let her go—as she had gone?

Falkenberg welcomed him; his papers were in good order, but he would not stay. The järnvägsstation beckoned to him, and his time was short. But the scene before him was so calm, inviting him to linger, cottages meeting the streets, so clean—as Elin had told him—the streets scrubbed each and every morning, as well as the white scrubbed floors seen through open doors.

In friendly fashion he nodded to a woman carrying a market basket on her arm, and smiled as two gulls came toward him, tame, enjoying their shore leave from the sea. This before him, could almost be a picture of home. The woman could be his mother; the gulls, also, a reminder of Norden, of the pet sea gull his little brother Johann had; and that old horse, over there, beside the railway station, that, in the picture, could be Hjärta.

Oh, if there were a Father in Heaven! The peace of this country was something to love—the woman, the gulls, the black horse standing yonder harnessed to its wagon—oh, if only he could find *his* horse!

Karl stood meditating; he could begin all over again the plan to build up his stables, would add a pair of those big husky ungainly horses, to serve the market for them in Liverpool. All of his boyhood dreams could come true, after all, if he could find his horse!

Now that he was a man, he would know how to handle his father; and his mother, oh yes, he decided in this happy moment of make-believe, he could find it in his heart to forgive his mother for everything—even for having borne so many, many children—for—

Strange, but there did not seem to be much to forgive her for. The home, not so poor after all; thinking on it now there must have been a great deal more on the table than sill and potatoes. It would be worth being bound to the military, to go home with Hjärta; as Rikard and Sven often had said, Sweden had so long enjoyed peace, now, the chances were that the Reserves would make no great demand upon him. He would be glad to see the old home; Elisabet would be there, and Maria, and Herman Nikodemus, and poor little Johann—oh, all of them would be there—except Maria, and she had married David Henning and lived in Halland. Not too far from Norden, Halland.

Across the station yard stood the black horse. Almost, it seemed a time when a man might feel an inward urge to pray—

Some other man, not him. Time and time and again had he not hoped that some proud black stallion would, upon his coming closer, prove to be Hjärta? That poor horse there, with the low hanging head: "Even if it could be Hjärta, let God—if such there be—notice how I walk by, with eyes cast stationward, expecting not an answer to my longing, giving no further occasion to be scorned."

Quickly, he turned. After all, it was a horse. He loved horses and they loved him. No harm to go and pat the nose of that poor beast, whinnying now—a sickly whinny.

But no, he would not go. It hurt too much to draw near to any horse, only to be reminded of his own and the rosy future it had stood for, only to be disappointed again. As quickly he turned about and entered the door of the railway station, "Who but a dumb, believing fool would keep on hoping?"

Simon Svenning was away, so Karl must tell the station master of his adventures; and he told, spinning greater stories, even, than his rich experiences in travel. And they must go to midday meal together, with Karl as host, to show how big he was, so the station master would have plenty to tell to Simon Svenning, the fine Herr Svenning who had gotten him his job.

"Karl Petersson shall come soon again, I hope?"

"Aye, when next I have business in these parts, for the White Star Line," Karl's chest puffed out, "so shall I stop for another visit. But, what is the running about?" He quickened his walk toward the railway station.

The horse. Men ran toward where it sprawled upon the ground. Karl ran, "Here, I will help get him to his feet," he called. "I know horses."

"The old nag's done for, I guess," a boy remarked.

Karl knelt to feel the horse's nose, but he drew back. His eyes widened; they might have looked at roaring fire coming too close for safety as he rose slowly, drawing away, pushing with out-turned hands against nothing, until he stood. And then the world about him reeled.

"Oh, no!"

A white star was on this horse's forehead.

He rubbed his eyes. It could not be! But yet it was.

"Oh, God! Not Hjärta—this—"

It could not be that this poor hide full of bones could be his Hjärta! And that sickly whinny he had heard. Did life have not only to stick a knife into a man's heart, but turn it and twist it and bore it deeper—deeper? His eyes closed and he swayed. His mind saw then the family friends, Johann and Georg, come to take him, a boy, with them to the ski meet. Yes, he had hesitated: could he leave his beloved horse for so long a time, five days, even for such pleasure as was assured him at the meet? Then his mother had spoken, "Hjärta will never forget you, Karl."

Good God! Had Hjärta scented him and tried to call to him? *And he had turned away!*

He fell to his knees and with his finger-tip outlined the familiar shape of the white mark, he stroked the white star on the forehead of the still black horse. "Open your eyes," he begged. "Open your eyes. I am here. I am Karl. At last I am here. Do you not know me?"

His searching eyes found all the marks, the little scar above the fetlock, the tiny patch of white deep in the groin. This, this was his horse. This was the proud and frisky stallion that had grown up with him at Norden. This was the glistening, glowing hide that had shone under his rubbing hand. Oblivious to the gathering crowd, his uniform whitening from the gravel, his cap fallen and picked up by an urchin, Karl wept and pleaded, "Oh, min Hjärta, come, get up." He picked up the poor head and crushed it against his bosom. "We shall go home!" He crawled on his knees, to fit his fingers into the depressions between the ribs of the skinny horse, and tried with his fingers to comb the burrs from out the matted tail.

As to a little child, he cooed, "See, I take my linen handkerchief from my pocket and wipe the matter away from these bad, deep sores where the breast collar has rubbed."

Hysterically, he screamed, "Oh, Hjärta, to think that you should have come to this!" Then softly, "But we shall go home, and min mor shall make you well."

He wept, and his tears fell to make the short hair glisten as he stroked it. Fearfully, he crawled to lay his ear flat against the horse's body. Could he not hear, for the pounding of his heart? Did the life drain from him, now, as he listened?

There was no sound.

He lay with his head on the quiet body, trying to grasp the meaning of what he knew was true. His forefinger twisted the long hairs of the fetlock in loving gesture.

"And I turned from him. I—his master—in his last moments—I—turned from him!" he wailed.

If he had come to him at once, when first the horse had whinnied, he might have saved him. But he had gone, instead, to dinner! To show off how big he was! Instead of coming to Hjärta, he had gone to gorge his stomach! The food bolted from him and he stood and kicked gravel over it so he could kneel again.

He could thank his father for this. Oh, how he hated his father! Rage rose to choke him, rage so red that it colored his face, his protruding eyeballs, his distended neck, and he struck his fists out wildly, and screamed, "Whose—"

"The horse was mine," a huckster said.

Karl picked the small man up, and set him down, "There!" battering with heavy blows, "one for the starving of him—another for the starving of him—and another—and another—

"There, one for the sores from the ill-fitting harness—

"There," he wilted, "because he has gone."

He threw the beaten man aside and knelt again to clasp the head of the dead horse to him, sobbing, "Hjärta, min Hjärta."

It was one thing, resigning one's self to loss, when always in the background hope could linger; for he knew now that never once had he truly given up his childhood dreams of finding his horse, dreams of a future with horses, through his own.

But this was another thing, seeing the end of everything, here before his eyes. Never would he sit astride his own dear animal; no chain of stables now; not even could he write stories now.

"There he is, the drunken fool," the huckster stammered.

"Stand up, you are under arrest." Karl heard the words as he tried to rise, but the fury of his rage, the depth of his grief, had sapped his strength, and he was spent. He tried again to rise and staggered, to fall against the constable.

"The drunken fool! Lock him up behind the bars! He struck

me down, the drunken fool," the huckster yelled, with fast moving hands urging the arrest.

"Nay, constable," Karl driveled, reeling, "I am as sober as an archbishop, sir. And this horse was mine! I can prove it, sir, the horse was mine!" He saw the constable's billet raised toward him and he lunged, maddened by the sight, and would have struck the officer, had he not dodged to one side, quickly, avoiding Karl's fist. Karl sprawled, but rose again, unsteadily, to feel a firm hand on his collar.

"See—he is drunk!" the crowd screamed.

He wrenched himself from the officer's grasp. The constable raised his iron-weighted stick and brought it down on Karl's head, and Karl fell heavily.

The uniformed man of the law took the uniformed man of the sea by the neck of his suit and dragged him along the cobblestoned street, to the jail. The constable closed the cell door; in company with another of his kind the sailor could sleep off his load.

Karl woke. A wail broke from him, "Hjärta!" Tears flowed between fingers pressed close to his face to hold his throbbing head from dropping between his knees as he sat doubled over on the hard cot.

"Here, quick! Have a little sip—quick—before they come," his cellmate whispered hoarsely. "A man can't sober up like that," he snapped his fingers. "No man but has to have a little drink to help him, especially the crying kind. Here."

Karl could only look at him. What was the matter with the man, could he not see that he was sober? Couldn't he smell that he had not been drunk? Karl turned, disgusted, from the proffered bottle.

His head ached! His eyes, his ears, even his gums throbbed. But in his heart, no throbbing there; only a dull ache, and an emptiness. Now, for certain, all of his dreams were done.

"Keeper, keeper," he bawled, tearing at the door and rattling the lock. At least he could bury his horse's body if he only could get out of here!

"Would you like another taste of this?" the jailer came and twirled a billet round and round in front of Karl, but made no move to free him.

Karl sat again upon the cot. Yes, he should have known better than to give as much as the meagerest thought to staying in this land. This was Sweden for you. How in God's name could he, even for one minute, have given thought to a desire to stay in Sweden, considered degrading himself so as to be willing to bow to the military? How he hated weakness in other men; and he had been as weak—or weaker—than any other. Just harvest, this, for giving bed to the seed of weakness.

His horse was dead, and still the world went round and round; didn't anyone understand what this meant to him? Hjärta had lain there, on the gravel, with sores on his body and a gray scab on his ankle; "And he whinnied—*and I did not go to him*—" a moan of anguish traveled through the corridors of the basement.

Then rage again took over. "So I am drunk! So I am a drunken fool, eh?" He lunged toward his cellmate. "Give me the bottle! They have given me the name! As well, then, that I have the game!"

He tore the bottle from the cringing drunkard's grasp and tipped it upward as his lips encircled the neck opening.

"Only a little drink, I said, only a little one," whined the trembling cellmate as he clawed at Karl's arm.

Karl stopped and swallowed hard. "What do I care? There is nothing left for me! Nothing—except," he held the bottle aloft, "Skål, skål, to America!"

"What will *I* do now?" the drunkard had started quivering at the chin; now his hands shook, and soon his whole body trembled with the strain as he watched Karl's Adam's apple move up and down with jerky motion, and then—after one strangulating gulp—stop still, for the bottle was emptied to the last drop.

ELEVEN

HERE WAS the exact spot on the sidewalk where his feet must turn to the right if they were to lead him to the entrance of the White Star Line office. That was the place he was headed for, to report for duty, and to explain his delay in reporting.

Aimlessly Karl walked. What should he say to them, there at the office? What could he say?

He had missed his ship. But it was not his fault. Oh, *it was not his fault!* Heavy sobs shook his big frame, and passers-by looked twice at him to try to fathom what ailed the seaman, but he did not notice them.

How could he speak like a man and tell them about finding Hjärta, and not break down and cry like a child?

It was no use. The words would not form themselves for rehearsal. He stood for awhile and watched the men from the telegraph company wind wire around a new-set pole, to keep horses from chewing on it while they would be hitched there. Horses—always horses—everywhere—to remind him of what he must forget.

For the third time his feet hesitated at the spot on the walk where they should turn right, and then carried him by.

"How can I make it sound real to them, this thing that has happened to me? How? *How?* How can I say it all, so it does not sound like a cheap tale to be taken with a grain of salt—a cheap excuse for having been arrested and held in jail? How can I face them?"

Undirected, his feet measured the alleys and streets. Over the smells of the alleys came one lately familiar, breathing of easy answer to vexing problems. He turned into the pub; not enough to sleepen the wits in a man's head, only enough to help him put together the letters of the alphabet into words, into sentences, to explain his missing of his ship.

Now he lacked not fortitude. Now he could walk straight into the White Star Line office and tell them all. His feet turned at the place in the sidewalk. His feet carried him out again, from the office. They had not believed him.

He knew he had not been drinking when he was arrested. They had been his friends; why did they not believe him? On to the question at hand, he had not argued with them, he had admitted he was late for his ship. Was that not absolution enough, when a man admitted his error? Why, then, had they laid him off from his job? That is what he could not understand. Why had they not let him talk with Mr. Ismay, who was his friend?

Well, anyway, the Line had been decent enough to give him his trunk and the bag marked "Petersson" when they took back his uniform. Nervously, he felt of his front pants pocket; good, the money was there. But who did Long John think he was, to turn a cold shoulder on Karl Petersson, his friend? Best to stop right here and now and throw away the book in which John had written of friendship. He set the little trunk that Sven Eklund had given him down on the street and opened the rawhide cover, and picked up the book which spoke "From the New World."

The new world. That was the place to go. He put the book back again.

A hanger-on at the dock reached for the handle of his trunk, "Are you sailing on the ship to America?"

"When does she sail?"

"Tomorrow. Passengers are going aboard her now."

"You are sure she sails tomorrow?"

"That I am. The passengers from Gothenburg have been waiting at the hotel for three days now, and a poor bunch of travelers they are; not one of them has extra baggage for a man to carry so he can earn an honest piece of change."

"Sailing? For what port?"

"New York, the United States."

"Not a White Star Liner, sailing tomorrow," Karl spoke with assurance.

"No, the Inman Line's *City of Chicago*."

"Inmanlinen!" A rival company to the White Star. It would serve them right if he should buy a ticket on a competitor's steamship line, them laying him off from his job! But, again, he would hate to cross the Atlantic on that old washtub, the *City of*

Chicago, after spanning the ocean on the fast *Majestic!* That would be a step downward, to be sure. But, would he wish to travel on the Line on which he had worked so proudly, debased by having to seek quarters in the steerage? The little over forty dollars in his money-bag would not allow better. Could he walk, out-at-the-elbows, with the common run of immigrants, on a ship of his "own" Line? Now that he could think once more without that awful throbbing in his head, perhaps it would be best to buy a ticket to New York and go aboard the ship at once, before someone had a chance to steal the money from his pants pocket.

Was there never another color to bid "bon voyage"? The October sky was gray—the water, gray—the clouds showed no spot of white—the pier, the people's faces, all were gray; and Karl, who had met with more than a fair share of kudos in the employ of the White Star Line, drank the bitter cup of humiliation to the dregs as he walked up the gangplank on to the S.S. *City of Chicago* with a steerage ticket in his hand.

Where was the thrill which had accompanied him on his first trip westward over the Atlantic? He watched the other immigrants as the ship pulled out of Liverpool, and there was a trace of a sneer on his face at their hopeful excitement.

An old man came, carrying a large copper kettle, dented and unshiny. *"Mat för barnen!"* he cried loudly. Food for the children, bread and milk, but what for him? Now came the realization that he had been hasty in boarding the vessel. He had forgotten to provide himself with cup and plate. Extremely prudent, he had thought himself, in anticipating all of his needs, buying the thin mattress, a quilt, and a pillow.

Passengers began to crowd around the bare wooden tables, and draw benches up close, with scraping sounds.

"Are you traveling alone?" a middle-aged man asked him.

From his speech this man could be from Värmland, Karl surmised, before he answered, "Yes."

"Come, sit with us. Soon the potatoes will be passed, and we have bread and cups and plates aplenty."

"Tack, I will." Karl joined the family already drawn up around a table. The mother had spread a red and white woven cloth upon it. The older boy, of about eleven or twelve years, stood slicing a huge round loaf of dark bread. The ship rolled, so he had his legs spread wide apart to give him balance. The loaf nestled close to his body, pillowed in the curve of his left arm and he cut toward him, with a long sharp knife, slices enough for all the family, and for the guest.

He served his mother first. With a look like that which lies in the eyes of a believer when he speaks of God, Karl noted, he waited on his mother.

Across from Karl was Fru Lind, and she held a little one on her lap. Beside that babe, there were seven children.

Boiled potatoes were passed by one of the ship's crew, and boiled beef with allspice berries clinging to the half-cold fat. After a long prayer said by Enoch Lind, the father, Karl skinned his potato. One by one the children slid from the benches, accustomed as they were to stand to their meals at home, ill at ease eating in the company of grown folk, having been brought up to wait until their elders had done at table.

"It must be urgent, your reason for such a long journey," Karl made conversation, and his eyes circled the large family.

"It is the call of God, I answer."

"Oh?" Karl smiled to himself. God had called the woman at a most inopportune time, he would say, as the child slipped from her lap and he saw that she carried another.

"I have the promise of a church," and Lind cast his eyes upward.

"You are ordained?" Karl inquired.

"I have been serving as lay preacher and colporteur—"

"The Mission Covenant Society," interrupted the wife, almost by way of defiance to her husband, almost by way of apology to their guest.

"Aye," answered Karl. Not of the State church, not even recognized by the State church! This man was another fanatic like his own father, doubtless, governed by too great a zeal for Bible-reading; but certainly lacking in the strength of Sir Stig!

"Fitting that I should have passage on the *City of Chicago*, for it is to the city of Chicago, in Illinois, that I go. There I may be so favored as to come in company with the great Moody!"

Moody. The name meant nothing to Karl; and he was not interested, nor in this man who reminded him of his father, nor in the woman. So like his father and mother, these two, parenting a child each and every year.

Twelve days to endure the life on board the *City of Chicago*, twice the time it took for the *Majestic!* How would he be able to stand the crowded quarters, Karl mourned, with four men in a little section, sleeping on a hard bunk with the inadequate mattress, standing in line to use the toilets or the face-washing bowls. In the cool weather at home he never would have thought much if a week went by without a bath in the big round tub in front of the fireplace. But now that, from his days on the *Majestic*, he had grown to enjoy an almost daily bath—as it had been at Norden in the summertime and they all bathed in the sea each day—he felt dirty at the mere thought of going twelve days without a bath. And to think they had charged him over thirty dollars for this!

He found he could buy a tin plate and cup, so he chose to eat apart from the family from Värmland. The mother never reappeared; seasick, without a doubt, Karl deduced, and her so soon to bring forth another child. He was glad not to have to look upon her, her full rounded body reminded him of the repulsion he had felt when he saw his mother so.

And now on the eleventh day at sea, Karl came above to see the hands stretching a hemp line to rope off a section of the deck. "Someone has died," he heard a woman say. Yes, there came the coffin covered with an American flag. Then came the lay preacher from Värmland and his eight children. He would have no more from Fru Lind, for the childbedwoman had taken the ninth one with her on her longer journey. Not only the husband had received a "call from God."

An American flag over the Swedish woman who had never seen America; why? And then Karl remembered reading somewhere that a large percentage of the stockholders of the Inman Line were Americans. No doubt but that would explain it. In all of his trips, this was his first sight of a burial at sea. This was the first time he had traveled with the dreaded typhus. He saw a section of the rail let down, and four deck hands holding the four corners of the striped and starred flag.

"Unto Almighty God we commend the soul of our sister departed, and we commit her body to the deep," the Captain finished his words and the coffin slid from under the red, white, and blue covering, over the side. A splash, and all was still, unearthly still. Even the lapping of the waves was hushed.

Carefully the hands folded the flag, not a thread must touch the deck. A thrill crept over Karl. This was his flag now, for he would be an American. As careful, he would be, as these who folded it, to keep his flag unsullied.

"There!" shrieked the lad who had sliced the huge dark loaf of bread, pointing to the horizon. "See!"

His fists beat hard upon the stunned Captain's back. "Curse on you for throwing our mother into the sea! Curse on you for not waiting—as we begged you to—so we could bury her in the soil and plant flowers on her grave!"

The father pinned the boy's arms behind him and pushed him toward the hatchway.

"Land!" The cry was heard and carried from mouth to mouth. All but the family from Värmland would have forgotten the mother had not the shrill wild shriek of her son pierced the air, "Curse on you! *Curse on this ship!*"

Karl's eyes were cleared of the red veins which had throbbed almost steadily since the day of Hjärta's death. He picked up his trunk—what an infernal hole, stinking of chloride of lime, this ship had been—and dressed in European clothes, like any immigrant seeing these shores for the first time, he stood in line waiting to clear into America.

Mealtime came, and dried prunes were passed to the waiting ones. Karl took a handful and bit into one, then looked at the rest of it. Moldy; he dropped it to the floor and leaned forward, glad to deposit the remainder of the handful into the asking palm of an old man. Poor soul, subsisting on what the transportation company considered "good and sufficient food in cooked state during the voyage from Europe to the final place of landing!"

"Papers—?"

"Here," offered Karl.

"Father's name: Peter Christianson."

"But it is spelled—"

Paying no attention, the officer of immigration wrote on, chanting as he wrote, "Mother's name: Sigrid Christianson."

"But—"

"Mattias—hey, you—Orville," calling to a co-worker, "isn't Mattias in Swede the same as Matthew over here?" Turning again to the papers, "Thought so." He turned the paper around and pointed, "All right, sign here—Carl Matthew Christianson—just as it is spelled here."

"But my name is Karl with a 'K'—"

"Oh, we don't use it 'K' over here, for Carl."

"And my name is Petersson!" His exasperation almost made Karl cry.

"You *said* your father's name was Christianson—"

Karl nodded. Yes, he had said his father's name was Peter Kristiansson; but did he have to explain that he was Peter's son, so his name, according to the custom at home, was Petersson?

"Then," the officer shouted, "your name is Christianson, see?"

All in a minute, everything had changed. No longer would he be known as Karl Mattias Petersson. The paper in his hand showed who he was, and it showed Carl Matthew Christianson. This was the final break from his home; his own mother would not recognize him from this name.

He was in the United States of America. Now he stood and watched the more prosperous-looking ones do as he had done, drop mattresses and bedding into the water. Others lugged theirs along, carrying them by knotted cords or twisted, rusting wire. Such flotsam as rode and bobbed upon the water! Copper kettles, soiled clothes, tin cups, and yonder a junk salvager netted in driftage, keeping what he deemed of value, casting it into a wagon; the horse stood still, head down, waiting for the wagon to be filled. Always a horse—Carl turned away and looked over the water....

Fascinated, he watched the tugs darting in and out between ocean liners, between the driftage, finding the shore. "Like insects skimming swiftly over the pond at home," and he listened to their humming tune.

So fine the leather boots on that young man, what need had he to buy shoes from off a pushcart, he with an extra pair of fine boots in his hand? Carl watched the young man set his bundles on the floor, remove the handmade leather boots he wore, slip on the cheap new shoes, and with a satisfied, happy smile wreathing his face, walk to the water's edge and as if he performed a sacred ritual, drop one boot after another of the four into the deep. Serene, he listened for the last splash and hurried toward a carriage marked "For Hire."

"He is an American now," Carl thought, wryly.

This was a sight to remember: poorer-looking travelers than he had ever seen pouring from the *Majestic*, losing their aura of hope and anticipation, wandering dumb-looking and forlorn, now that they had reached—what?

"Batavia, New York, or Batavia, Illinois, which is it you want?" he heard a railway clerk ask impatiently.

"Aye, Nee' York och Illinois, ja, ja!" The woman newly come from Sweden smiled.

Carl stopped to help her make her want understood. She took a letter from her blouse and he read in it. "She wants a ticket to Batavia, Illinois," he explained; and stayed to help the many others, whom he could understand, by interpreting their needs for transportation inland.

Where should he go? He wandered about, then lifted his hand and signaled to the driver of a team and wagon. The man who held the horse's bit stepped forward, "Hotel?" he asked, and at Carl's nod, slung the little trunk into the wagon and sat on it, while Carl shared the driver's seat. Out from the hurry and bustle of the landing depot, through the section of the city where tall buildings lined either side of the street, until the road was narrow and it looked to Carl like farm country. He shifted, looked around, and "Where is the hotel?" he began, then caught the look the man beside him gave his companion. Carl shuddered at the feel of the pressure of something hard against his back. The driver draped the reins about the whipstand and said, "All right, hand over your money."

"Like Hell, I will!" and with lightning movement he turned and sent a swift cut to the jaw of the surprised man behind him, and the gun fell over the side of the wagon. Carl turned again and pummeled the driver. In the scuffle the trunk slid along the iron strips on the floor of the wagon, and out of the rear end. Frightened, the horses bolted. Carl stood teetering on the wagon's sideboard, braced himself, and jumped.

The trunk was heavy, nor did it carry well for being warped from its fall off the wagon; his feet grew too large for his shoes; he was hungry. God, he was hungry! At long last, following the deep-rutted mud, Carl found himself back on the Bowery. Cheerless middle of the night, or was it the blackness that comes just before the streaks of dawn? But, beyond was a lighted store. It beckoned to him. Music called. That was a song he knew!

"Oh, Susanna!" a calliope whistled.

The doors of the store were forehead height and ended near the knees, a pair of shutters meeting at the center. Carl peeped beneath them. Some playing cards had been dropped near the doorway, and he could see the dirty imprint of a heel upon them. A small black and white terrier sniffed at his trouser legs, torn when he jumped from the wagon, then wagged its tail in welcome. Carl pushed one side of the twin door open a crack; on the counter was a large plate on which were stacked dark bread sandwiches. Delicious looking rosy-colored ham protruded from between the slices of bread, and on the meat's white fat a clove hung ready to fall. He walked into the saloon and the two-way hinges swung the narrow shuttered doors in and out behind him.

A weary bartender stood pouring a drink into a glass held by the lone man standing at the bar. Another customer sat with his arms hanging limp over the back of a chair, his head dropped forward, his body straight, not sitting on the chair but stiffly held up by it, his feet stretched forward resting on their heels. One chandelier was lighted, its crystal-strung garlands hanging heavy with dust, and its full shape reflected in the large gilt-framed mirror behind the bar. It must be the film over the mirror that made him look so disreputable, Carl decided, until the bartender addressed him, "Whaddeya want, bum?"

"A meat sandwich."

"Got the price of a drink? Free lunch goes with the drinks."

He did not want a drink. No. Thinking back, he could never afford to take one. "I'll buy a sandwich, if you please."

"This ain't no restaurant. Free lunch goes with the drinks, see? Got the price?"

That ham, pinky, rosy-colored ham with browned fat at the edges! Saliva filled Carl's mouth and he swallowed; involuntarily, his tongue slid along his lips. His middle gnawed.

"Yes," and he pulled a dollar from his billfold.

The sandwiches were good—and the drinks—

Sure, he had money enough for another, and another.

The bartender played over again the song of "Susanna."

"It is so much finer in Swedish!" Carl said. "And did you know, that song, 'Susanna,' has been translated into about every language there is!"

The film over the mirror was clearing. Those pretty bottles

lined up in front of it—how his mother would like to own them—one light blue, with white daisies painted on the bulbous part; thin necks reflected in the mirror; one with milky white bumps all over it, even around the neck, one purple, one green. "Kimmel" bottles, the bartender called them. He would remember that, and buy some for his mother. She would put flowers in them. Elin would, too, put flowers in them, if she had them. He would buy Elin some, too.

He felt fine now. "Ya, shure. I can sing it in Swedish," he grinned:

> *"Oh,* Susanna, *du ar min frid och lust,*
> *Finns ingen man så glad som jag—"*

"There is no man as glad as I," drowsily he assured the man in the mirror as the calliope started over again. "Oh, Susanna—"

TWELVE

"NEW YORK CITY is not America."

Here were no abounding golden fields of grain, rippling at beckon of a gentle wind, rippling as did the laughing waters of the little lake at home. Here were no acre upon acre of cotton or tobacco such as he had seen pictured before ever he came across the wide Atlantic. Here were no homestead acres awaiting only a fructifying hand.

As he walked to his room he looked around him. Where were they all? Not in New York City.

The ghetto, dirty place smelling of garlic; Chinatown, with its pigtailed chatterers sluffing along in loose light-colored cotton pants and grass slippers; The Bowery, with its noise and its Livs, of such was New York City.

Where was the promise of America? Not in the job—oh, yes, he had a job, and jobs were hard to get—but where was the promise in a job that used only his brawn for twelve or fourteen hours a day, or more if a ship was in a hurry to load or unload and clear the port? Where could a longshoreman find opportunity to use his head? Or when could a stevedore find time to read? That was the matter of importance—when?

There was no promise, even in America, if a man could find no time to read. And he wanted to learn, everything there was to learn about America. He was going to be a good citizen; but how could he be that if he did not know the history of the country, its geography, and the stories of the men who had made it great? He must read more of Abraham Lincoln and George Washington and Benjamin Franklin. In such a manner as he had been taught the history of Sweden, from its beginning, through its wars and its kings, so did he wish to learn the history of the United States of America.

Most of the history of his birthland he had learned in the old home, from Morfar and his mother, not beneath the ceiling of a schoolroom, for so busy had the public schools been, teaching *Kristendomskunskap* to spare much time for history. Now, in America, where not any time need be spent on the learning of the "Principles of Christianity," he could learn, also without the schoolroom, but he would have to find time for the reading of American history; so good was the taste of it, enjoyed in the library on the *Majestic*, like fancy hors d'oeuvres giving appetite for the main course of a meal. And feed himself he must, with reading.

This job, that he had, would get him nowhere. Nowhere except to and fro, in the mornings waking before dawn to the shrill ring of a cheap alarm clock, eating two greasy stiff-fried eggs, a couple of pieces of bread—white flour puffed up with air, but like rubber to chew—and a big cup of coffee. Poor coffee. Maybe if the coffee was good, he would not mind so much the breakfasts. What was it his boarding-house lady said when he had remarked, casually, about the quality of the coffee? "And, Mr. Astorbilt, did I count your board money correct, or was it four dollars and fifty cents you paid me for the week—including laundry?" And when she bumped against his arm, making him spill the most of it, "When did you say you was movin' back to Fifth Avenue, eh?" and mouthed that horrid shrill screech that passed for her laugh.

Then, after the breakfasts, the walk to the docks: hour upon hour of hauling, lifting, dragging, pushing. A man was glad to finish the walk back to his room, gulp down the spare ribs and sauerkraut on Tuesdays, the hash on Mondays, the codfish balls on Fridays, and stretch himself full length upon the narrow iron bed.

Where was the freedom of America? Ah, no, New York City was not America. Bertie Williams to the contrary, Carl knew this now. There must be more to this land than this city with its dirt, its noise, and its saloons.

On Saturday nights—pay days—a little taste of freedom then, when all the dock hands left the paymaster in high spirits and went as a body to the saloon, for none would dare to brave the ridicule of the others if he did not share the fun. Enough to pay board and room for the coming week stuffed into an inside pocket, but the remainder from the pay envelope, be it one dollar or two, or had it been five, was spent before heavy feet turned toward the rooming house that sheltered the bed on whose counterpane that night the shoes would leave a muddy smear.

This job, it was no job for him. A job without a future, and without a present, for all of that. To hoist boxes, or push them, and never know what was in them; to put cargo aboard a ship, glance at the destination, and never know if it ever reached that place! What way was that to take a part in a living world?

God, he'd go mad if he did not stop thinking like this. He would quit the damn job, today, Sunday morning. He would go to the boss and say—what would he say? He couldn't tell the boss how he felt about the job; the boss would laugh, and then he would likely hit the man and get into trouble. He would just let the job go—and go, himself, somewhere—somewhere—

And yet, in that Saturday pay envelope was security, from hunger and cold, security.

"But have I come so far that I must force down the head of my life to bow before the false god of security? Does the sea captain know security? Does even the deer in the forest? Do the lion or the eagle know the meaning of the word? Does the farmer—even the King? Why then should I lean heavy upon such a crutch? No. Not yet have I paid my next week's board and room: 'Sunday to Sunday, in advance,' the landlady said."

She had not yet changed the towel to the clean one for the coming week. He would not be beholden for more payment by using this one to freshen up after working all night; he washed and dried his face and neck and arms, then dipped his comb into the glass of water standing on the bureau, shook the drops off the short oily teeth and combed his hair down smooth, bringing the part low on the left side. A spotted frameless rectangle of mirror showed his right eye to be higher than his left, and there was a bare space where his neck should be reflected. Through the plain glass he saw a bedbug crawling up the wallpaper.

He picked up the mirror and pressed its chipped edge against the bug. And then he itched all over.

On the back of the reflecting glass, a boarder of another day had pasted a part of the page of a newspaper, "The Patrol."

"Geneva, Illinois," he read on, "January 4, 1889." Over two years old, this paper. "Fine embroidered lambrequins, tidies, table scarfs, children's hoods, new style muffs—" women's stuff.

"Anarchists and Indians!" Now here was news; but as he read on, it said, "have no use for E. B. Shurtleff's soaps. A trial will convince." His eyes followed the columns: "The Chicago and North Western Railway penetrates the centers of population in Illinois—"

Maybe he could get a job on the railway! Ah, but now he knew Fate was the one who had turned the mirror in his hand, so he could read, "Short Hand and Type Writing." Shorthand.

Slowly his hand lowered until the mirror rested on the bare top of the blotched and marked bureau. Carl's eyes looked straight ahead. The pink-flowered vines' color faded even more and changed to hay color before those eyes. In his own barn, at home, sweet-smelling, slick, and cool, the hay surrounded him. He lay on his stomach, elbows propping him up and sinking deep into the straws, a shorthand book before him as he wrote hieroglyphics on the page of a blank book. Absorbed, he had not heard his father's step; but oh, he had heard the words, "God tells us to read *HIS* Book on the Sabbath," and he saw again his father's hands tear page by page into tiny bits and drop them on the hay.

That had been the last straw, after the selling of his horse.

Shorthand. That was the one thing more his father had denied him. His breath came heavy at the memory—after— after— That was what he had turned to, after his father had sold his horse.

Shorthand.

He grabbed the mirror and did not feel the cut its edge made where his thumb joined his hand. Flushed, eager, he read, "Board, room rent, and tuition in the above-named branch, at Wheaton College, cost only fifty-one dollars for the Winter Term beginning December 4th. For particulars address C. A. Blanchard, President."

Should he write a letter? Indeed not. He would go to Geneva, where the paper was printed, and inquire about Wheaton College, for this was Fate working in his favor, telling him where he should go—to find the promise of America.

Security? The security that was in this job? Throw it to the winds. He was young; he could afford to take a chance.

Would the first two weeks' pay, that the boss had held out from his wages, cover the way to the West? It must, oh, it must! Quickly, nervously, his hands folded his few belongings and with the book of the *Nya Verlden* lying on top, they strapped the cover of the little rawhide trunk. Already he was late for the day's work, but that was of no moment now, for he was quitting.

How the new men always gabbled among themselves about the unfairness of the boss' holding out their first pay, but now Carl could see how right it was. It was a help to a man, only that. Did the boss, though, put up any kind of argument when a man asked for those first two weeks' pay?

"You have been a good hand, Christianson, I hate to see you go."

"Thank you, sir." Carl was pleased; but it seemed strange, still, to be called Christianson.

"If you ever need a job around these parts—you come on back—see?"

"Thank you, sir."

The boss shook hands with him. Carl kept his left hand on the pay envelope inside his front pants pocket. How much was in it? Enough? He did not dare to look, for fear there might not be enough.

Lost in the warmth of genuine good feeling on the part of the dock boss, deep under the spell of an inextinguishable desire for learning, hearing again his mother's words of encouragement, "Shorthand is like yet another language," his lips moved, "Dear God, let it be enough."

So rapt was he, he did not know he prayed.

In silence he stood to pay farewell to the water; now that the moment had come it was as if, in parting with the sea, he had to leave a part of him behind.

The cardboard ticket lay in his hand. There had been enough! Not only the nineteen dollars needed to reach Chicago, but enough for the dollar and seven cents to pay for the ticket to take him the thirty-five-odd miles to Geneva. Only a few cents left over, but he was not hungry; and as soon as he reached Geneva he would get himself a job. Had not it stood in the paper, "Men wanted: local and traveling. Positions permanent or part time. Salary from start. Experience unnecessary. Brown Bros." Then he would eat, to make up for this lack; then he would work "permanent" until he saved up fifty-one dollars.

Shorthand. There was magic in the very word! Perhaps he would work "part time" after he got studying, but again perhaps it might be best to spend all of his time learning, as long as the tuition covered board and room as well. First, he would be a court reporter, then he would study law!

On to the railroad, and a fine one, this New York Central. What a means of transportation! Now to board a car and find a seat that was not occupied amongst the passengers, like himself, who did not have the five dollars extra it would cost to ride in a Pullman berth. There was a seat; but it was wise to look around first to see if there might be one so placed that his face would not, on sidewise glance toward the out-of-doors, meet a standard of polished wood. No, the windowed seats were filled, but by turning backward and stretching his neck he could see out of the window to the rear of this seat. He slid the rawhide trunk under it, and tried to make himself comfortable in the double seat.

His legs were too long. Even by sitting sidewise into the seat, he found cramped quarters for his legs, and so he drew them up and rested the knees high, and hard, against the puffed and buttoned velvet of the back of the seat in front of him. A shudder of the mighty locomotive, a puff, a blow of steam, more puffs, and Carl craned his neck backward to watch the trainshed pass slowly into the past.

Why should he feel excited? He was no stranger to travel.

Trains. Railroads. Destined, to be sure, to have terrific impact on a country like the United States, especially out in the wide West where, to hear the New Yorkers tell, Indians still danced in the streets of the cities, still made their raids in Chicago streets to capture white women! To such, the railroads would be bound to bring enlightenment from the cultured East.

The landscape flew by now—houses were far ahead—they were abreast—they were gone—like a little watchman's hut, like a *vaktstuga* alongside the Vestkustbanan at home, each slid by and disappeared.

Carl listened to the entrancing music of the "click, click" over the rails, as it penetrated the car, to the whizz of the train cutting the air, and he peered out into the fleeting landscape, knowing a strange feeling of sharing in a deep impermanence, the leaving behind of the old and familiar and rushing forward toward the new.

The railroad could mean a change in a way of life, and a man had not necessarily to ride on one to be affected.

"It is progress," he said to himself, "even now I hasten

forward on the wheels of progress. The old must make way for the new. His thinking came better to him—more words to think with—if he thought in Swedish. "Forever, I put the old behind me," and with the Swedish words, the old frustration, the old loneliness, that merciless encroaching wall, changing places with the tufted velvet in front of him.

"The old; can I ever put the old entirely behind me—wipe out the pictures of home?"

"Chicago! All passengers out! Chicago!" the conductor called.

Carl picked up his trunk, set his hat straight, and walked from the railway station. Pigeons flew down from the ledges of buildings and, unafraid, walked close to his feet. A young woman, holding a child by each of her two hands, smiled as she passed him, a warm smile of welcome. He walked, unknowing, and then stopped to ask a police officer where the station was, at which he might catch the train to Geneva, Illinois. The policeman directed him, then stood and scratched his head, perplexed, to see Carl walk with deliberate step, eastward, in the exact opposite of the direction he had outlined.

Carl had noted well the officer's directions; but his eyes had caught sight of, and he had smelled the water of the deep blue inland sea, reminding him of the past, yes, but bidding him welcome.

"Stranger here?" an old man asked him.

"Yes, just came into the city."

"You will like it here," the friendly voice assured him, "and," as an afterthought, "if you can't make a living in Chicago, you can't make it any place," and as he turned to go, he smiled. "Welcome to Chicago."

The old man, the kind courtesy of the policeman, the breeze skimming this big body of endless water—all the while whispering of rain—all, in some indefinable way repeated the words, "Welcome to Chicago."

As by main force, he pulled his gaze from Lake Michigan and headed toward the station of the Chicago and North Western Railway.

THIRTEEN

THERE WAS MORE to New York City than its dirt, its noise, and its saloons. Only two blocks from where Carl had hung his hat was a brownstone front, a rooming house in which clean towels were hung on Wednesdays as well as Sundays.

"Isn't it too much for you, Elin," Dr. Osgood asked, "to change them twice a week? I'm sure it is not expected."

Elin laughed and looked toward Sara, "*Yust* like a man! He don't seem to *ree-lice* then they only get half as dirty!"

The doctor had seen her scrubbing over the washboard. She was what any man could call a "good sport," taking to hard work the way she had. He grinned now, "Just what did you say, Elin, about a man?"

"I said it was *yust* like a man," and then pink rose from her neck, over her chin, into her cheeks, up to her hairline. "I mean, just like a man."

"That's better, that's much better. Now we will have to get to work on realize."

The blush grew deeper, and Elin bit her lip.

"Why do you pick on her, John?" Sara asked, but she was smiling.

"I don't mean to—"

"Oh, he does not pick!" Elin spoke quickly, "I want to learn! I *want* to learn!"

"It is re-al-ize, not *ree-lice*, Elin," and he had her sit down, although there were the beds to change, until she got the hang of it.

"Re-al-ize, re-al-ize," she left the room repeating it over and again, and held the pillows with her chin in a grip against her chest, instead of between her teeth as she slipped the clean cases on, so she could keep on saying "re-al-ize."

Except that she got so terribly tired by the time night came, it was not bad at all being a hired girl. If only it could be different with Sara, Elin knew she would be content to stay here. Anyway, where else could she go? Algot had never replied to her letters. She went to her bureau drawer and looked at the stampings on the envelopes which had gone to Chicago and come all the way back. "Unclaimed," and "No Forwarding Address." Those were the words Uncle Sam used to tell a sister that her brother no longer lived on Belmont Avenue, and had left the Swedish Hospital. But thank God the little square on the stamp, beside the word "deceased," was not checked by a thick black pencil! Algot lived—as Andy—but he lived, for that little square was bare.

One day she would go to Chicago and find him. Her savings were growing. Some people might think that all a person had to do was to kneel and pray, but she knew that you have to set about to do something to help yourself to get what you wish for, and then in that way prayers are answered. Hers would be; one day she would find her brother; she never doubted.

"Re-al-ize," she had it now.

Flicking her fingers daintily over the ruffles of the pillow shams to make them stand out fresh and saucily, she pinned them to the cotton tape stretched taut across the headboard. It took practice to make up a bed just right, without a wrinkle or a depression where the full part of a body lay each night, but of practice there was plenty in a rooming house. Elin ran her opened hand over the spread, a loving and thankful gesture to the work that gave welcome peace of mind and a good home.

My, but the second floor front was a lovely room, the nicest in the house. She carried clean sheets and pillow cases in and laid them on the bureau. This was the room Sara should have. Dr. John agreed with her, too, but he was a man of his word and once had promised Herr Schmitt, the music teacher, that this room was to be his as long as he wanted it.

"Ach! *Goot morgun!*"

Elin, surprised, turned to leave, "I—I shall come back later."

Herr Schmitt sat in a big chair by the grate. "No. Come along, I do not mind, but best you lay the fire first before you make the bed, it is a little *shilly*."

With an old whiskbroom Elin swept the fireplace bricks and

laid crumpled newspapers and kindling with one log slantwise above it all.

"You know, *machen*, you are too pretty to work so hard—like dis—" she heard him say, and tossed her head. She knew what she looked like; there were plenty of looking-glasses in this house. She could not quite like this man.

There would be plenty of time to do his room later; she drew up from her knees, only to feel his strong fingers reach at her back and close around her waist as he drew her to him.

"*Isch!* Let me go!" she said between clenched teeth.

"One kiss—one little kiss—"

Elin wheeled about and with all the strength of a woman enraged, she slapped his face. The force of the slap relaxed his facial muscles and he looked to her like a silly frog-faced clown. She could not help but laugh. His spectacles lay, broken, on the floor; and where they had pinched to his nose, the places were a dark purplish red.

"I get you for dis!" he muttered as she fled.

Doctor John should know of it, but she couldn't tell him. She had been indiscreet, but the experience had served a useful purpose. Now she could "re-al-ize" that she was growing to be a woman. A woman would have had better sense than to enter the man's room while he was present. Let this be another lesson. . . .

Sara was failing.

"It is not because you do not take care of her well enough, Elin, that I have asked Faith to come. You understand that, don't you, Elin?" Doctor John explained when he asked Elin to prepare a room for Sara's sister.

Only too well, she understood.

They were alike, these sisters, except that Faith had all the bloom of health that Elin wished had been divided between the two.

"Now John can take Elin to church," Sara said happily. "Now that you, dear Faith, are here to keep me company."

"Oh, no, I shall stay and Doctor John can take your sister!"

"I'll stay with Sara; you go on and go." Faith smiled and put her arm around Sara.

"I know how you have wished to go," Sara said weakly, then brightened. "And wear my hat—the bright blue velvet."

Faith set it on Elin's head.

"You are beautiful, Elin," Sara's eyes filled. "Take her and show her off, John; introduce her to them all as my friend, Elin, my beautiful friend."

"I can wear my old hat—"

"Oh, wear it Elin, please. I won't be able to wear it this season anyway," Sara sat up straight, "and next season we can steam the velvet and put different trimming on."

The doctor stooped to kiss his wife, "Maybe by then I'll be able to afford that surrey and team, for you."

It was a game they played, planning for when Sara should be well. But they were not fooling any one, least of all, Sara.

The bright white dove perched on the top of blue velvet soared through the streets of New York City on the fair head of little Elin, walking primly by the side of Doctor John. It bent to pray as Elin bowed in the little church around the corner.

Yes, there was more to New York City than its dirt, its noise, and its saloons.

There in the little church organ music and singing brought a glow to the faces of the communicants; and to Elin it was like being at home. She shared the hymnal with her employer, and she did not feel like a hired girl alongside him here.

"I should like to present our friend, Elin Nilsson," Doctor John said to many, and then he introduced her to the preacher.

"Your sermon was beautiful," she said, in her very best English, "thank you for remembering to ask blessings on the seafaring men."

"You come from over the sea, then," he shook her hand warmly.

"Oh, yes—from Sweden—but, sir, may I ask please, have you ever noticed a tall young officer of the White Star Line, name of Karl Petersson, coming here for services?" Eagerly she described her homeland friend.

Dr. Osgood looked quickly from the preacher to Elin. She had never mentioned—

"No, my dear," indulgently the preacher smiled, "I have not noticed such a young man, but you may rest assured that I shall keep a sharp lookout for him, and let you know."

Karl would have no reason now, as he had at Sven Eklund's, to stay away from church, with the beautiful uniform clothing him; it would have been good if she could have met him here....

The white dove fairly flew toward the brownstone front. She

must hurry back and get to work; she was a hired girl after all, but "it matters not what work it is, so it is work"; while hands were idling, a mind could travel too fast—too far—as far away as Sweden! Remembering hurt too much for Elin.

But remembering made Sara happy, and she laughed when Faith recalled, "Remember how we used to call the man who lived next door the 'galloping ostrich'? It was you, Sara, named him that!"

Yes, but he *did* walk funnier than anybody."

Though it was Faith who cheered her sister with reminiscences of their girlhood, it was Elin who served her mistress and waited on her, who nursed in the bad days of her sickness and in the long dread nights.

"When I go, Elin," once she whispered, "take care of John for me? Please, Elin, take good care of John?"

"Oh yes, oh yes," Elin had answered, "of course I will," and when Sara, with a contented smile, fell back against the pillow and slept, Elin asked God to forgive her for holding a reservation against her promise—"until I go to find Algot."

Each day, when it came time to clean the second floor front, Elin knocked loudly first, then stuck her head in the open doorway and looked about, and so afraid was she of the strong hands of the piano teacher, that she stooped and peered under the bed to make absolutely certain that Herr Schmitt was absent.

This day, in front of his bureau, she found a small gold coin.

"I found it as I swept, standing up in the fur of the carpet," she explained, handing it to Dr. Osgood.

"Oh, he always does that, sooner or later."

"Does what?" Elin's curiosity opened her mouth wide.

"He should be more careful of his two and a half dollars. Yes, Elin, he plants a gold piece as if he had dropped it accidentally, to see if a hired girl is honest."

Incredulous, Elin spurted, "There are some mighty *konstig* people in this country, queer enough to think that anyone would want money belonging to somebody else! And the strangest one of all these people is Herr Schmitt!"

"It is not that he mistrusts you, personally."

"I hate him!" Elin flounced from the room, to the surprise of her employer.

There was not room for hate in Elin's heart, for long, and on

Sunday mornings love nearly burst her heart as, overflowing, it helped her sing with the congregation.

"It is remarkable," the preacher said, "the way you have learned the language."

"Thank you. I owe my learning to Dr. Osgood's good teaching."

"I noticed that today you followed me in the Lord's Prayer."

"Oh, but Pastor, what would you say if you knew I was saying it *Fader vår som är i Himmelen?*"

"I would say," he answered, smiling, "no less *helige* is His name."

As they walked toward home she questioned the doctor. "Am I really getting to be American?"

He shifted to the outside of the sidewalk as they turned at the corner and pressed her elbow, helping her down the curbstone, "Yes, Elin, you are an American."

Blushing, self-conscious, she broached the subject which had long been on her mind. "It is time, then, that I changed my name."

He turned, startled. Did this have some relationship to the young seaman after whom she had inquired? He felt a sense of loss, "Why, how—?"

"Elin Nilsson, it is old-countryish." It was better to explain it thus; Doctor John was not the kind to encourage a girl to make a change of name that would make it nearly impossible for a searching family to locate her. She liked to dream that they cared enough to search, especially Grandfather. But not while she was a servant should Grandfather be able to find her; she could not strike such a blow against his pride.

"What would you change it to?" the doctor leaned toward her, asking seriously.

"I thought—to—to Ellen Anderson."

He laughed; oh, how he laughed, "So you think that is less Swedish?"

It was not that she wanted it to be less Swedish. More, if anything; nothing could be too much Swedish—not for her— but she couldn't explain.

"All right, from now on you are Ellen Anderson. But I am glad you did not decide on Yolande or Wilhelmina or some such name. It won't make any noticeable difference, Elin to Ellen."

Ellen's days were filled with dusting, sweeping, cooking,

cleaning. Her nights were filled with anxious sitting, nursing, watching. Filled were the days with singing as, like a bird, she flitted from one chore to another.

Singing, she dipped into a bag of moistened sawdust and cast it sparsely over the wall-to-wall carpeting, and swept. Like a spring rain bringing fresh colors to the flowers in a garden, her broom brought freshness to the large roses on the carpet as it brushed the dust-covered sawdust before it. Now the third floor was finished.

"Om den strolande solen viste," her voice rang and quivered through the empty upstairs rooms as she put her power behind the broomstick. The second floor was finished!

Her eyes smiled, but furtively now she glanced around, as a spinster thoroughly familiar with the contents of a clothes cupboard, who had an instant before shut the closet door, reopens it to peer inside to make sure "no man is hiding there." So far, she had not been surprised at doing this thing she was about to do. What if Doctor John should catch her in the act some time?

But he was with Sara in the basement dining room. It was safe enough.

Surreptitiously, Ellen gathered up her broom, the dustpan, the not-nearly-so-full-as-it-had-been bag of sawdust, pushed the white hair-covering towel back from her forehead, gathered up her skirts and caught them under the arm laden with utensils, lifted her leg and swung it over the balustrade.

Whiz-z-z-z, down she slid!

Too late, she heard the front door shut. Her free hand grabbed the rail and burned as she tried to stop herself. At Herr Schmitt's excited yell, her hand let go.

"Mein Godt!"

She felt her bottom slow for a speck of time, over the newel, before she crashed backward into the paunchy front of the music teacher. She felt him squirm under her before her feet could locate the floor.

Dr. Osgood came up the stairs, and stared. "What in the name of Heaven?"

Ellen stood, wilted, penitent, amid the shambles. "I'm sorry, Doctor John; it was my fault. I—"

"Ach! So it vass!" The old man pointed his finger at her face and shook it. "Too old—you are—for such a monkey biss'ness!"

And to the dentist, "I demand she *leaf* at *vunce!* Dis roof—it iss not broad enough that it should cover her and me!"

"Watch out for your dyspepsia, Herr Schmitt. I do not know what has occurred, but I am sure Ellen meant no—"

"I tell you vat has oc-cured, the vild Indian!" Fiercely, he told of the whirlwind of broom, dustpan, and hoyden descending upon him. "She leafs or I!"

Ellen saw wrinkles come to the corners of Doctor John's mouth, as he took the portly roomer by the elbow and led him up the stairs. "I'll help you pack," he said gently. "I'll help you."

They moved Sara up into the sunny second-floor front room. There was no reprimand for Ellen's unwomanly conduct. It was not even mentioned.

A spelling book and an English grammar lay handy on the table beside Ellen's bed. Some day she would find more time to study from them. She was doing pretty well, though; not nearly so often lately did the laugh wrinkles come around Doctor John's mouth as she spoke.

Today she must remember the extremely important message left by one of his patients, for the dentist. Every few minutes saw her feel in her blouse to make sure the ten-dollar bill was safe. She was to give it to him *at once*, with the message that he had made a mistake in making change.

"Let me know if you see him coming?" she asked Sara, propping pillows so the sick woman could see in each of the mirrors of the "rubbernecker" outside the window. Faith had brought it all the way from Philadelphia, so her sister could see the front stoop, across the way, up the street and down.

Away up on the third floor, Ellen heard the front door close. It must be the doctor, now come from his office. *At once*, she was to give him the message. Down the banisters she slid; but he had gone out again. She threw open the front door and saw him hurrying down the street.

"Wait! Wait! Dr. Osgood! Here! It is important—a message!"

He turned. "Yes, Ellen?"

So did the pedestrians on the crowded street, turn, expectantly.

"Here! Mr. Cropsey said to give you this, *at once!*" She held the ten-dollar bill out toward him as she ran. Excited, she screamed, so all could hear and laugh, "He said you made a steak!"

FOURTEEN

"TO TOWN?" The man on the wagon seat leaned over and bent low atop the wheel which partly hid the crudely painted word, "Express."

"To town?" he called to Carl, and smiled and patted the seat next to him, as the North Western train puffed its way into a thin horizontal streak of sunset beyond the mist.

Carl's thoughts were miles behind, how many he could only guess, in that place where the conductor had called out the newly familiar word, "Wheaton!" That must be the spot where the college stood, the one that taught the shorthand he was going to learn. He should have left the train there instead of using the full amount of his ticket and riding still further westward, slowing to cross the bridge that spanned a lively flowing river with tree-lined banks, and dammed to the north beyond a wagon bridge.

"To Geneva?" The sing-song cadence, the engaging smile, arrested Carl. The "G" spoken as though it were a "Y," struck a note of kinship and Carl smiled in answer, "How much?"

Joseph Arneson knew travelers well enough; when they asked the price, not much change rattled in the pockets of newcomers. "Make it five cents?" Better a half-fare than none.

Five cents! Carl's stomach brought full to his attention now how empty it was. Five cents was what he had intended to spend in Chicago, on coffee, and another five cents on a bun or something to eat with it, and he had looked at the lake and forgotten!

"Nay, tack, I can walk." He pointed south, "This way to Geneva?"

"No, that way to Batavia; and say, if it is the lack of *pengar* holds you back, come on, jump in—" he slid far over on the spring seat as Carl reached his long legs and climbed in beside

127

him—"it don't cost no more to drive back with you on the seat here, than if we go back empty, does it, Steena?"

The horse whinnied and turned north into the road. "Steena gets just so much oats, one way or the other, if we get a passenger, or if we don't."

The mare plodded along, reins laid carelessly across Joseph's lap.

"She is a lucky little one—"

The expressman nodded. Sharply Carl turned, surprised that his lips had uttered the words his mental preoccupation had led him to believe were only thoughts. He wished for no talk of horses. Silently he noticed how neatly Steena's harness fit her. No rubbing of collar or band against her curried hide.

"So, I have told you my name is Joseph Arneson. But you are—?"

"Carl Christianson." It seemed a lie to use the name the Government had bestowed upon him. He felt like shouting, "Karl Mattias Petersson, that is my name!"

Calmly Joseph queried, "*Af*—?"

"Bohuslän."

"Ack! Min Martina, she will be glad to see us for supper," and at Carl's quick, audible drawing in of breath, and before he could speak, Joseph continued, "Martina, she is the boss in our house." He smiled smugly, "What Martina says *goes* in our house, ya' bet your boots, and she says when anybody from Sweden gets off of the North Western, they must come for supper and tell her about home."

Was she from Bohuslän, Carl tried to ask, but Joseph gave him no opportunity to speak.

"Oh, she is the boss, all right. Why, do you know, years ago, I had saved enough pengar so I could go back home and show how big I was, how I had made good here in America! Well, I takes my express wagon down to the station for the last time. Ya, ya, down to the station for my last load, I goes; then would I go home to Sverige." He chuckled, and his head nodded acquiescence to his memories, "Well, here I comes, to that very same station back there, and off from the train comes the most beautiful young *flicka* I have ever seen. Oh, ya, plenty of work for Swedish hired girls, all the rich people wanted them." He slapped his hand against his knee, "Oh, my! Oh my, oh my oh, but she was fancy!" And so he had decided right then and there, never again would he give thought to going home to Sweden!

He turned briskly to his passenger, "Hardly a single word did she say all the way to the Freedlunds'—that was her *farbror*, the mister was; uncle, we say it here—and his name was the same as hers, Johnson, when he landed from the old country, but when he came to get a yob at the gluk there were so many Johnsons already that Mr. Pope asked him to change his name to Freedlund. He is in Washington, the District of Columbia, now, Mister Freedlund, big job with the *Governamint*."

Ah, so it was in America! Carl settled himself in the wagon seat, satisfied. There was a man, not born to high station—not even born in the United States—and he had reached so high as to be with the seat of the United States Government! A station of honor, come to the kin of this ordinary expressman's wife. What a country! What a land of opportunity!

Joseph's finger tilted his woolen cap, to scratch his head. "Where was I, now? Oh, yes, hardly a word the flicka said, all the way from the train."

Carl grinned. Unless the expressman had changed, what chance had she had?

"Ya, ya, by the time we got there, to her uncle's house, it was decided that I would not go home to Sweden, after all. She would be Mrs. Joseph Arneson, and I would meet the trains every day for the rest of my natural life, I guess. Oh—" he laughed—"she is the boss all right, all right, all right. So you might just so well give in and come home for supper. Tomorrow morning I take you to the Immigrant House, if you want to, and then you can always get a job at the gluk."

The "gluk." What was this? Twice Joseph had mentioned it, but try as he would, Carl could not intrude his question into the full-running, enthusiastic welcome of the expressman. "Ya, ya, they will always find room for you at Castle Garden."

Was the man right in the head? Castle Garden? Now Carl tipped his woolen cap and scratched his head, perplexed.

Martina Arneson slid her finger through the little silver-colored ring, jerked gently downward, then rolled the green shade up to the top of the half-curtained kitchen window. With the cushion of her hand she cleared a circle of steam from the pane and peered out into the misting dusk. There came Joseph.

Only an instant to accustom her eyes to the outside, and yes, a passenger sat beside him.

Over the heads of the stark last-summer's weeds she watched to see if they might stop at the hotel. No, the flickering light of the lantern swung constantly from the left side of the tailboard.

Tonight would be no different from the many other nights: Martina reached under the red-fringed checkered cotton tablecloth and pulled forward the hinged swinging leg, and set another place.

Her husband, God bless him, as on other nights would stop in the little shed outside the kitchen door, kick off his overshoes, and make their clasps jingle as he righted them and stood them like sentries, to one side. Then he would call, "Oh, min Martina," as he had done through all these many years, "see, I have brought a countryman from Dalarna or Närke or Uppland," or wherever. Martina's lips curled into a smile. "I knew how glad you'd be, Martina, for company; we eat so oft alone." And turning to the guest, "You see, Martina, she is the boss of the house and oh! oh! what would happen to me if I did not bring the latest news from Sweden, by messenger, in person—" and then he would hug his head as if she had struck him a blow, and dodge an imaginary missile.

Dear Joseph, he was a trial sometimes; even sometimes giving up his bed—and hers—when he brought a family home, so children could start life in a new place with a good night's sleep. A wave of sadness passed over her face: it was the least she could do for him, she who had never given him a child.

The wagon neared, and her head perked up. Such a friendly squeak in the rear wheel. Was it a Swede he carried with him tonight? It would be comforting, as her husband said, to talk of home and the sunshine of Värmland or Småland tonight after the gray, rainy early evening. A little laugh broke from her at recollection of the time when Joseph had talked so big about her not letting him go unpunished if he did not bring every newcoming Swede home for supper, and the passenger—when at last he got a chance to open his mouth—turned out to be an Italian who understood not a word of her husband's blustering!

But Joseph, he always found a way to make everything right; the next morning he took the *Eye-talian* over to Lencionis' and they welcomed their countryman with open hearts and home.

They were new to each other then, she and Joseph. "You did

not mind he was a Catholic?" he had asked her, hesitating; and oh, his eyes when she had answered, "Does not the same God watch over us all?" and the memory of his lips as he whispered, "Min Martina—" like violin strings trembling to give the vibrant message full from the deep instrument, which was his heart. *"Catt-lick,"* he had spoken it that morning; but "t-h" sound or no, she had never heard him use the word again. Never again had he felt the need to question her full acceptance of any and all the lonely or hungry travelers he brought to their home.

Martina reached her hand into the wooden salt box, hung over a long spike driven slantwise into the wall. Worn leather hinges let the lid fall with a cheery clatter as she rolled her two fingers against her thumb, around and around over the open soup kettle, sprinkling salt evenly into the simmering brew.

"Better you take off your shoes," she heard his voice outside the door, "we can set them on a newspaper near the stove to dry out. What a kind of day! Nice and bright and sunshiny, and then—all of a sudden—drizzle, drizzle. Just like April."

The clamps rattled. "Oh, min Martina—" he called.

The introduction was over, word for word, as Martina knew it so well, and tonight Joseph was in fine fettle. Had the stranger no trunk, she asked, no knapsack?

"Better, I thought, to leave it outside in the shed. It was damp and we can leave it there till after. Then we shake the clothes good, so there are no bedbugs in—" He turned apologetically to Carl, "You see, Martina, she—"

"Joseph, how you talk," she nudged him goodnaturedly, but so that the soup spilled over the edge of the bowl she carried, onto the plate beneath it. "See what you make me do!"

That soup; a sight to fill Carl's heart with gratefulness. How it made his mouth water! How it heightened the gnawing in his middle!

"Come, sit!" Martina called.

"—and bless and keep the guest at our table, for Jesus' sake, Amen," spoke Joseph.

"Amen," Martina chorused. Carl raised his eyes from his unclasped hands and spread his napkin on his lap. It was mere chance that had brought him to this home, not God's guiding hand, as Joseph had just said. It had to be.

His spoon hesitated over the soup bowl. Clear soup, it was, with small diced potatoes losing their precise and clear-cut outlines in furnishing a starchy thickening to the broth, carrots sliced across so thin that the bottom of the bowl showed through the delicately orange circles, short lengths of celery no longer than a thumbnail. Little shavings of fresh green parsley swam on top, now touching, now darting from tiny orange-tinted rings of fat.

Carl watched as the wife spooned up second bowls, and Joseph licked his lips and said, "Ah, it is good to know hunger."

"But so much better to know the breaking of it," Carl answered, his eyes following the journey of his bowl.

When Joseph heard that his visitor had not eaten since he left New York, "Come, min Martina, bring on the meat, too."

Martina turned to the stove. The meat she had meant to save for hash for the morrow—all of the meat from the big ten-cent soup bone—she served on Carl's and Joseph's plates and watched as they relished every bite. There went the few cents she had planned on saving toward goods for a new dress, so she should look fit, come the sixth of June. It was to be for the benefit of the kindergarten—the lecture at Mrs. Harvey's, and the ladies had put her on the welcome committee—to go with Joseph to the train to meet Miss Jane Addams—and she would like to look a little bit up-to-date."

"Try catsup on—it's good—" Joseph mumbled with his mouth half full.

"Cat-soop, what is that *utländsk* food?"

"Outlandish food, he calls it! Try it. It is made from tomatoes."

Hastily, Carl set the bottle down. No, indeed, he knew enough not to eat anything made from the love apple. What was the matter with Joseph that he risked his life thus, sitting and with relish dipping his meat into the circle of catsup on his plate?

Martina lost sight of forks raising meat to eager mouths, the talk of catsup and of men out of work, but always a yob at the gluk, and tried to picture Miss Addams in her mind, this woman who with her friend Miss Ellen Starr had established what they called a Social Settlement on South Halsted Street in Chicago.

Half-closed, Martina's eyes rested on her husband. She must be just like Joseph, this Miss Jane Addams. No treasure of his would he hesitate to share, or give, to one whose need he knew.

The plates were clear of meat.

"And the admission is twenty-five cents," a little voice inside

Martina reminded her, but she went to the pantry and from a lower shelf drew forth a mason jar of peaches, and watched their raggedy edges swim like little tadpoles in the rich thick juice as she jerked the screw-top loose. Three halves rested in each dish she served the men.

"Ah, min Martina," Joseph crooned. "Ah—!"

She would bring Miss Addams a quart jar of peaches; no matter about the new dress.

Martina licked her lips after the first sip of coffee. Not bad, for having only the shell in it, but the morning coffee, that would never do without the whole egg in to clear it.

So Carl must tell of Sweden, and Joseph's ears perked up and his tongue was never still with questions.

Carl's look followed Martina as she moved her chair to sit under the light of a small lamp on an oval table with marble top and fancy feet. Fancy. Rich-looking. At home the tables had been so plain.

She selected one magazine of three that hung suspended in two narrow lengths of weaving, nailed to the wall, exactly as the almanac had hung in the big room at Norden. *Harper's*, the name was, of the one she took to read.

Joseph saw Carl follow his wife's movements, "Those are Martina's magazines; she has some time to read—not like our mothers, sitting weaving and spinning—for goods can be bought by the yard here for all our uses, and the women have time for other things. See?" he showed Carl the other two, *Scribner's* and *Demorest's Family Magazine*.

Carl saw books, too, yonder in the darkened parlor. Uncomfortably cool in there, Martina had apologized: perhaps they had let the fire in the parlor stove go out too early.

So different, these two, Carl mused, in their adjustment to the new country. Martina had followed Joseph to America by years, and yet her speech was not mixed with the homeland tongue; where the husband said, "Yust so vell," coming from the wife it sounded, "Just as well." His "vee" was her "we," his "vas" her "was," and his "vere" her "where." "De Noordvestern" to her was "The North Western." She was the more American. Listening to her speak, he would never guess she had not been born in this country.

"Take the word 'moder,'" Joseph was speaking.

Carl started from his musing, alarmed. Did Joseph read his

mind? For his host sat telling him how folk from *his* province in Sweden never could be taught to use the "t-h" sound. So, try as he would, he'd never be able to say "mother." There was just something about it; so it was with everyone who came from there, his home.

And so the men talked, but mostly it was Joseph, while Martina cleared up the dishes, while she went out into the evening and shook Carl's clothes and brought them in and folded them neatly, to replace them in the rawhide trunk when the heat of the stove should have dried it out.

"But I must go—" suddenly Carl realized.

Go where? This was as good as the hotel, Joseph assured him. The little bed by the stove in the kitchen, that Martina would set up, it would not be much—but—oh, he might "yust so vell" stay. Already the wife displayed her welcome as she brought from the pantry a low pallet and set it up beside the range.

"But—you don't know a thing about me—"

"We know you are from home," Joseph stopped Carl. Again Martina smiled. Home. A large place, home, in Joseph's heart. Here on this cot had slept, not only men from Sweden, but Finland and Italy, and every country that she had learned of in geography. Excepting Africa, perhaps, but that would not faze Joseph, either, she knew.

He wished to go to where the paper was printed, Carl said. "No, not *The Republican*, but *The Patrol*," and he lapsed into Swedish, better to tell of reading the paper on the back of a mirror in New York.

"Aye. *The Patrol*. Mr. Bailey, he is *The Patrol* man." Joseph snickered at his play on words. "Tomorrow I take you to Mr. Bailey. Tonight he is in the schoolhouse, I know; I just took him there before your train came in, with the ex-Governor. He comes to Geneva tonight, the old Governor, to make a speech in the schoolhouse." Joseph turned as if in invitation to Carl, "It costs ten cents to get in."

"Shall you go?"

"Who? Me? No. I must meet the trains, every one of them. Martina, she always goes, but tonight," he asked her, "you will stay home—with the heavy rain—and your throat kinda sore, and so much dipp-theria around?" She nodded, and Joseph turned to his guest, "And you better go to bed after all this traveling from New York."

He slapped his hand on his knee in that cheerful way he had,

"Listen to this one. Mr. Bailey, he says in his paper that everyone should go; and call it what you will, bargain, *köp,* or *handel,* Mr. Bailey says if you don't like the speech, come to his newspaper office tomorrow and he will give you your ten cents back!"

"What does he speak about, this man who was the Governor?"

"He is a prohibitionist," Martina said, with conviction.

"Oh?" Carl looked up, to question.

Spreading his palms out wide, Joseph interrupted, "When you meet Mr. Bailey, you will know that all of those big men believe we should have prohibition, and *votes for the ladies* — that women like min Martina should vote—"

"And why not?" Carl asked, quickly. He looked at the fine, generous woman beside the kitchen stove. That such as she should vote was not a new and strange idea to him. Had he not heard his mother's morfar tell ofttimes in the home at Norden of his hope and certainty that one day woman would come into her own and speak her voice in equality, as a human being? How right it seemed. "Why not?" he repeated.

Joseph stood from his chair and solemnly, with deep regard, he grasped Carl's hand. "There are men," he said, "who say that it will cheapen the ladies to go into the voting booth."

Even in Sweden Carl had heard such words. But, so long ago as when Morfar's thoughts came alive from his bearded lips Carl had heard quick rebuttal. It was as if Morfar now shaped his lips to speak, as in Swedish Carl answered Joseph, "Words, words only. Rather do those who would deny women the right to vote, feel it would imperil the dignity of the franchise to share it with their women!" And as he spoke, Carl knew his lips spoke truly for his mind, and heart. He was all for the new: now that he was here in the new land, and it was a part of the new that women should have a share in the making of the laws they had to serve— part of the new, like railways, and speed, and lights such as there had been on the *Majestic,* shining at the press of a button.

By the light of the kerosene lamp he saw Joseph's face draw up in resentment against those who would discriminate against his mate, as he spat furiously into the china cuspidor set on a neatly folded front page of *The Chicago Daily News* beside his chair. And then, in full control, he laughed. "Of course, with Martina the boss in our house, I *have* to believe in Votes for Women!"

And Martina smiled.

"Here Kitty, Kitty, Kitty," she called out the back door. A ring-tailed cat dashed swiftly to a box back of the stove. Carl had forgotten all about her, when she emerged holding a tiny kitten with her mouth; up to Joseph's lap, and when the round soft bit of fur lay cradled in her master's cupped hands, she brought another, then two for Martina. The mother cat jumped from Martina's lap, walked slowly across the floor to where Carl sat. She sniffed of his shoes, his trouser legs, and he watched her; she walked back to the stove and rubbed against its nickel leg, stepped from the dark gray "Wall of Troy" edging of the fancy tin stove mat, to the wide white-scrubbed pine floor boards.

"Here, kitty," Carl called.

Haughtily she walked toward him, sniffed again, and rubbed against his legs, in and out between them. He drew his legs together to make a lap, and hung his arm down to reach and scratch her neck, the back of her head, "Nice kitty—"

Can a cat smile? Åsa was smiling as she returned to the box and brought her fifth kitten to Carl's lap.

"See?" Joseph's eyes sent a message to his wife's. "See? I knew he was a good man."

Rain beat against the windowpanes. It was good to sit by the warm stove. "Ya, stay home tonight, Martina, and keep warm and dry," and she stayed; tenderly she added her charges to Joseph's, and Carl listened to her tell of Woman's Suffrage, and watched her change from the mild, meek housewife into an orator, with fire dashing from her dark blue eyes. She spoke it well, her little speech, and she had learned it well: "The foolish, flimsy, selfish, one-sided arguments against Woman's Suffrage are all invented by the men. A great big five-foot-eighteen-inch man in his stocking feet—a sort of John Sullivan affair—*rises to state that his wife has a representative at the polls*. Fie! A representative! He never consults her wish before casting his ballot. As soon as we can free ourselves from the fetters of barbarism, we will break away from the idea that one represents the other." She seemed to be looking at Joseph and Carl as if they were a vast audience, and not once did she glance at the printed clipping in her hand, "It is based on the dogma, 'I and my wife are one, and I am that one.' That is all there is to it.

"Taxation without representation is tyranny, and woman is the victim. There are men in this town who cannot get credit for a sack of flour, or a drink of whiskey, but who can vote taxes on the property of women in this city, and the women must pay those taxes or have their property sold."

Joseph clapped. "Votes for Women!" he yelled.

Sadly, Martina added, "All women are not alike, no more than all men. Some of the 'four-hundred' in Chicago have petitioned the legislature not to grant the municipal franchise to women. Maybe they were afraid of what it will do to gentle women to be thrown in contact with men at the polls."

"But, Miss Frances Willard," Joseph interrupted, "didn't she tell the ladies, here, in the Methodist Church? I," proudly slipping his thumbs under his suspenders, "drove her from the station!"

"Yes," answered Martina, "she told us that 'if we must lay down the dust brush and broom to read, if we let our manners rust while our minds brighten, if, in fine, we must cast off the crown of womanliness before we can wear the laurels of scholarship—then—for the sake of humanity, we must fling away the laurels and keep the crown. We must gain without losing, or all is lost.'" She drew herself up tall, "This is our motto, given us by Miss Frances Willard, 'Womanliness first; afterwards, what you will.'"

Joseph clapped again, and so did Carl.

"Thank God," she went on, "the time is gone when only laughter met the one who spoke of Woman's Suffrage to assemblies. It will take the voices of the wives and mothers of the land to speak against the liquor traffic, and woe be to it then! But Joseph, Carl must be tired; and you must go early in the morning to Long's and buy some of that McKinley sugar—twenty pounds for a dollar—"

"Only one more train to meet tonight," Joseph said as he turned Martina toward their bedroom. While Carl pumped water into a basin and set it in the tin-lined sink, he bade the visitor take his rest. Carl washed, and pulled the roller towel to a wrinkled spot and dried on it there. He had imposed sufficiently; no need to soil the clean, unused portion of the red-bordered towel.

In his unionsuit he curled himself up on the narrow pallet and pulled the covers over him; and Martina returned to the kitchen. Gone was the fire and vim of the petitioner for suffrage, the worker for prohibition. Her thin gray hair was combed back tight over her head, and hung in a skimpy braid down her back, over the heavy robe that had replaced the black and white calico print wrapper of the evening. From the pantry she brought an apple, blush red on one cheek and faded yellow on the other, and handed it to Joseph.

Martina's hand pumped at the sink, filling the tea kettle; she covered the kettle quietly and set it on the stove; drew a feed sack part way over the box housing the kitten family. While she filled the woodbox from the neat stack lining the wall of the shed and laid a handful of kindling on the top, Joseph drew a penknife from his pocket, opened a blade, and honed it twice against his open palm. With precision he pared the apple, digging the point of the blade into the stem end, paring in thin narrow even peeling round and round until he finished with a tiny circle like a doughnut with a hole in its center, at the bud. Carefully he laid the peeling in a geometric spiral on the stove lid; he cut the apple into thirds and handed one piece to Carl.

There was the story of these folk—in the piece of apple Joseph handed him—one third of all they had they would give to a stranger.

Carl saw the look that passed between their eyes as Martina took the proffered third from her husband. His own eyes grew heavy. Through half-closed lids he saw the big hand of Joseph reach to hold the work-worn hand of his wife.

Different they were, yes, like the two sides of the apple's skin, but the meat was identical—the core—the heart, the same. Two sides of an apple, but together making the perfect whole. Joseph and Martina—so different—yet, together, not a man and a woman, but the perfect whole of Charity.

The sweet scent of apple rose from the stove lid. Strange, how a smell could bring back places, and forms and faces, the feel of a page of a book, the sounds of words, his mother's words.

He did not hear Joseph go, nor hear him return from meeting the late train. He dreamed of pears drying, after the monthly baking of *knäckebröd*, drying in quarters, away back in the deep baking oven to one side of the hearth in the big room at Norden. He was the one to watch them so they would be dried to a turn, just so, as the heavy iron door stood open, while his mother and his sister Elisabet quartered more and cut away the brown spots. And all the while Marta and Maria and Herman Nikodemus climbed to the tops of the trees in the lean orchard to pick every last piece of the fruit.

His nostrils dilated as he slept, in all eagerness feeding the wanderer's dream of home.

As the sight of a buttercup or an arch—so long as life would last—would bring thoughts of Karl to little Elin, so did pansies and columbine, a colt and stone fences, the sea, a book, bring thoughts of Karl to his mother. But leastwise had she expected this.

"Blessings on you!" Sigrid called, and bade the waves carry the words along.

At Norden in Bohuslän, Sigrid the mother stood on her boat-landing and waved to a man of medium height. His shoulders were narrow, but below the arms he was built broad and heavy. The cap that had covered his bald head waved now, high in his hand, as his boat drew from the shore.

Sigrid waved.

There, on that deck, her son had stood. His hand had pulled the ropes to loose that canvas rigging, and to furl it. Her son: he was as she had hoped he would be, and Sven Eklund now had told her that he was, honest and true, and loyal to his King, a good worker, a good student.

She fell to her knees, "Thanks be to God—and to you, Sven Eklund, His messenger!"

The boat became a speck. Still Sigrid waved.

Sven Eklund of Småland had searched her out. He had told all, of Karl, and she, his mother, could be glad. Ah, this was the reward of faith! One word of him was all she had asked.

Not knowing that he told, Sven had told too of Karl's blasphemy.

Time and her prayers would help her son to overcome this want of wisdom. As she had prayed for word of Karl, so would she pray for this thing more.

FIFTEEN

"WHOA!" Carl grabbed the idle reins from Joseph's lap and drew the surprised Steena to a stop.

The boy, there, was he hurt? Carl swung himself into the road. The mud made sucking noises when each foot withdrew from deep watery ruts in the main street. Over the height of uneven-sized stones built up to support a wide board walk, Carl's long legs scaled, and his foot met the walk. Down he went, sprawling in front of a shoemaker's shop as the wide plank, like a see-saw, lowered at his touch and raised at the end near the doorway steps.

For an instant the boy's crying stopped; he jumped from the step and gave a helping hand to Carl, but then the piteous wailing began anew. "It was the same one, the same one I fell on—" only it proved to be the spike, rearing its big rusty head, that had caught into the loosened shoe sole of the boy and thrown him. And his penny had flown from his hand! Where— where had it flown?

It was the penny he had earned by carrying wood ashes from the pan under the big pot-bellied stove in the Swedish Methodist Church all the way to Mrs. White's, load upon load of them, for her to fill in the low spot in her yard where water sat, so she could grow some special kind of plant there. And now it was gone, the penny, into one of the cracks between the boards of the sidewalk! All of the time since Harry Swanson had no longer come for them for the fixing of his family's *lutfisk*, he had carried the wood ashes.

The heartbreak of a child; how well Carl knew that heartbreak. Bending over the boy, patting his shoulder, he dug his hand into his pocket. So spare was the change there, but, "Here is a penny, boy," he said.

141

Good that the depth of sorrow of a child is not matched by its length; this momentary deep and bottomless abyss fled at sight of the penny, tears gave way to smiles and the boy's black eyes shown as he thanked the stranger.

"What is you name, boy?" Carl asked.

"The boys call me Dago, but Mr. Bailey, he calls me Tony."

"Tony," Carl extended his hand, "my name is Carl Christianson."

He shook hands like a man, this child, and as if to prove he had arrived at man's estate he walked to the edge of the sidewalk and spat into the street. With a smile toward Carl, he plunged his hands deep into the pockets of his poor, threadbare pants. The sign of the shoemaker's trade, a big black boot, swung on its iron bracket over the doorway, squeaking in the west wind, keeping time with Tony's whistle as he walked past the new horse sheds being erected at the Congregational Church, toward home.

Joseph could wait a moment, Carl was sure, while he borrowed a hammer to fix the walk; he turned toward the doorway. A hand touched his shoulder, and he saw that Steena was fast to the hitching post. Joseph's eyes were moist as they followed the disappearing boy. "Just as min Martina would have done. Just exactly," and his grasp tightened on Carl's shoulder. "The poor boy. Do you know, he has *never seen* his father sober—never."

They walked together up the wooden steps into the doorway of John Peterson's shop. "That is one reason why Martina is so hot for prohibition, when she sees such a boy, like that—"

He changed the tone of his voice to *"Hälsning!"* and greeted the shoemaker and his helpers. Lasts sat in orderly fashion on the shelves lining the rear of the shop. An old man sat, head down, his beard touching his chest, his upper legs cramped together holding a half-sewn shoe tight between them, pulling his thread, inserting his needle, evenly, rhythmically, unconsciously playing a tune as the sleeve of his shirt brushed against his gaping leather apron. A younger man removed small nails from his mouth, and came forward to shake hands with Joseph, and with Carl.

Joseph and John Peterson found much to talk about, the epidemic, reduction in wages, small little lasts, the McKinley Bill and its effect on the common man, Russia tan, three thousand people out of employment, but Carl soon followed none of what they said. He picked up a woman's shoe, one of a pair lying on the low wooden counter. How much had the apprentice been paid for his work on such as this? The tune the old man made became the singing of canaries, cages full of them, dozens of them—mountain canaries, chirping, singing, rolling—enough to make a man stark raving mad! Again Carl was a youth, newly come from home, and he had found a job as shoemaker's apprentice before going on to Malmö. Glad for the offer to be bedded in the shop, that first night he had worked until midnight, and then had fallen tired upon the coverlets laid to soften the hard earth floor.

Two o'clock in the morning, and the mad singing had begun; the cobbler had laughed when he inquired how Carl liked the alarm clocks he had swung from the ceiling to awaken his help!

Six pairs of baby shoes a week, cut, sewed, and finished, had earned Carl his room and board. If he could make the seventh pair, he would get paid. Maybe fifty öre. Maybe more. Maybe less. Never was he to learn the pay; his hands but barely met the stint of the six pairs.

"Small, little lasts," he heard. To Hell with shoemaking! He walked with long strides from the rear of the shop, out of the door, and slammed it after him. An astounded Joseph watched him reach the wagon seat, there to wait.

Joseph joined Carl, apologetically; too bad they needed no help there in the cobbler's shop. John Peterson was a fine man, a fine man; too bad Carl should have overheard those disappointing words, "No more help needed."

Carl nodded silently. If that was what Joseph thought, let him think it. He could not trust himself to speak when, within, his very soul cried out hysterically, "Too bad? How blind can such a man as Joseph get, not to see that the sight and sound of such a shop is torture, bringing back thoughts of Sweden?" He gritted his teeth and clenched his fists. Again he would have to take stock of himself. This sort of thing would never get him any place, and he had to make good in this country where making good was easy. In his temper he had forgotten to ask for the hammer with which to fix the loose board. Should he ask Joseph to turn around? No, he would not care to face them there in the shop, after his display of bad manners, so he sat thinking over the morning.

The smell of coffee had awakened him, good coffee, and

when he heard Joseph and Martina talking he had listened closely to every word. "Times are hard. So many men out of work. When the World's Fair in Chicago would be ready, then there would be work for all, and times would be good for everybody. In the meantime, oh, always get him a yob at the gluk!"

He had not been able to wait longer; what was this "yob at the gluk" business? And so Martina had explained. There was a glucose factory on the west side of the river, and it employed many Swedes, so it was a common thing around town, to hear of a man's getting a "yob at the gluk" as Joseph said it. There came the farmers, bringing big loads of corn, and there the factory ground the corn and sold the glucose, in barrels, back to the farmers for their stock. Mr. Pope was a fine man, he and his four sons ran the factory. And smart! Mr. Pope was the first person in the world to discover that corn syrup could be made from the heart of the corn!

Now, on the wagon, Joseph's voice interrupted Carl's thinking, "John Peterson, he makes the shoes for the Marshall Fields and the Potter Palmers!" Joseph's tone implied that he should recognize those names, but they meant nothing to Carl. Everyone wore shoes.

"The home of the Geneva Fluting Iron, and all kinds of sad irons," Martina had said of Geneva, and oh, yes, Carl would never do better than to find his place here and grow with this growing city.

He had left the home of Martina and her husband, carrying his trunk with him, but he would remember long the warmth of her handclasp, her "If you need anything, ever, always come to Joseph, always."

Joseph and Steena had driven him to Mr. Bailey's newspaper office. They would return, for Mr. Bailey was deep in grief; within the hour had come to him the sad intelligence that the dread diphtheria had claimed another child.

"Dipp'theria," Joseph had repeated, sadly, as the horse walked eastward.

Now they sat as Steena jogged along toward the Immigrant House. "Castle Garden," they who had set it up had named it, and just about every Swede who ever came to Geneva had stayed there at some time or other, according to Joseph. A family would all pile into one room together, and sometimes there were four good-sized families staying there, all doing their cooking in the same kitchen. One of the women would board Carl, Joseph felt sure, but he was not to pay more than three-fifty for a week's board, including laundry. They charged in advance, always. *"Sharjed,"* was the way Joseph said it, as he dug into his pocket and counted out the sum, in dimes mostly, and nickels and some pennies. "Here, you can pay me after."

Of course, Joseph must realize his pockets were empty, but how could he accept?

Joseph looked straight ahead, ignoring him. "A loan then," Carl said. "Tack, tack."

They were on the bridge and the slow, even clip-clap of a horse's hooves came toward them, echoing over the river. A light in the small brass-circled eye of a carriage lantern flickered weakly in the morning sunshine, on the right-hand side of a doctor's buggy.

"Dr. Gully, this epidemic is hard on him," Joseph said, "and he is not so young any more, over seventy," and his voice was sad. As they drew near, Carl saw that the reins lay over the dashboard. Hunched in the corner of the seat, near the lantern, was a crumpled form in black broadcloth, his chin rested on his chest and his hat had slid down over one eye.

Who was it, Joseph wondered, had sent a panting messenger to fetch the doctor? God forbid it was another child stricken with the epidemic; let it be instead that Mrs. Mettig's child had come into the world! Joseph's fingers intertwined in his lap as his eyes sought the heavens.

Carl watched the buggy closely, and leaned from the wagon to see what it was lay in the path of the ray of sunshine streaking through the isinglass window in the backdrop curtain of Dr. Gully's curtain. The doctor's hand lay across his lap. Out from a stiff-starched white cuff below the black broadcloth coatsleeve came a hand.

All of the comfort of a world showed in that hand. If he believed in God, such would he know would be His hand.

The doctor's hand. That hand could whip a horse to furious haste, or stroke the brow of a dying child. Only a hand, but mercy and sympathy and benevolence were written by its high blue veins.

Carl closed his eyes.

Oh, God! It was his mother's hand he saw!

Quickly, he opened his eyes.

He would not be able to stay in Geneva. Somewhere else he would have to grow with a city. Too many reminders here—that hand—that horse, serving as eyes to the sleeping doctor, bringing him home—safe—as Hjärta would have done.

He had been too long idle; he knew this now, after shoveling starch until six o'clock, when the glucose factory's whistle blew. Things were not so bad after all; he could sleep in the attic of the Castle Garden, and a fair sleeping room it would be now that spring was well on its way. Not much chance of an April snow drifting down on him through the opening between the shingles.

Mrs. Lofgren would wash his clothes and he would eat with the family of Lofgrens and they would pack him a lunch to take with him to work, and for not a penny more than the three-fifty. So that had been settled and Joseph had brought him to the glucose factory and Mr. Pope had put him to work at once.

What a decision his had been to make! And still he was not sure he had decided wisely. A dollar a day for day work, from six in the morning until six at night, *but* a dollar-twenty a day for from six in the evening until six in the morning. The same number of hours either way, but such a difference in wages! However, if he worked on the night shift he could not attend the evening school so handy to Castle Garden—right next door— and have to pay only five cents an evening for one of the finest teachers to give lessons in English speaking and English grammar, and preparation for the examination for citizenship in the United States! Of course, Joseph had said, and it was true, he would want to be naturalized as soon as possible. And he would be a Republican, that would be natural. Why, there was only one Democrat in the whole town!

Yes, better that he work the day shift. It would take longer to save up the fifty-one dollars to go to shorthand school at Wheaton College, but he would be learning meanwhile to be an American.

He walked along the river. In winter it froze, the men at the factory had told him, so they could walk across it almost any place and save time if they lived on the east side, and many of them skated. But now it was a lively flowing river, burbling with a clear voice, rushing over the dam. Carl quickened his step in challenge as he seemed to hear it say, "Wait up, Mr. Carl! Wait up!" but when he stopped to look back at the factory with its lights and its tall black smokestacks, there was the voice, panting now, "Wait up, Mr. Carl," and Carl saw his friend of the morning.

"Hello, Tony."

"I thought you would *never* stop. I want to show you Geneva, and walk home with you," he reached for Carl's hand and stretched his short legs with every step, to keep up with his new-found friend, and benefactor.

He had just come from his job, too. Yes, he worked for Mr. Brown, in his law office, caring for the coal stove. Twenty-five cents a week he got for it, and did Carl realize how much spaghetti twenty-five cents would buy? He hoped to graduate to Gust Carlson's job one of these days, at Gillingham's Grocery Store on Bennett Street, because Gust said he was going to speak for Tony when he left. Tony could do it in summertime when school vacation was on; in that job he'd have to work from seven in the morning until nine at night, but the pay was eight dollars a month! His hand tightened over Carl's; just think, if he could bring eight dollars a month home to his mother!

They walked along and turned up the west side hill. "Run, quick;" the boy pulled Carl and they ran until they had passed a narrow stone residence building. "We always have to run past Mrs. Myers' house," he whispered, "lean down, lean down and I'll tell you why." He pulled Carl's head down, level with his own mouth, "Because—" he looked about, then whispered, "because *she smokes!*"

Carl stopped and looked back at the little house. What manner of woman was she who smoked? Was she one of those who made merchandise of her virtue, or was she merely over-modern, employing such means to announce her equality with men?

Past grocery stores and meat markets, past the livery stable whose painted side advertised that soap which was ninety-nine and forty-four hundredths percent pure, past the office of Dr. Gully they walked; Dr. Gully, whom Tony knew only as one who made his own pills and put them on the roof to dry—and it was to laugh to learn that the birds came and ate them all up so he had to make more—the doctor whose hand had bid that cruel relentless memory of his to rise and haunt the morning. Past the corner building across the street, with its corbiesteps finishing the gable, steps on which a giant might walk up into the sky; past the shoe store, and Carl felt that now he must pull at the hand of his young companion and say, "Run, quick," until they passed it. Again his mood was heavy, in keeping with Tony's next pronouncement that there was the town's undertaker.

"See the wire? See?" excitedly screeched Tony. "Stretched over to the hotel?" and hardly could he contain himself for the excitement which arose at the telling of the day when the circus tight rope walker came to town and walked that wire—high above the street—all the way from the elm tree in front of the dental office to the hotel, *WITHOUT FALLING!* He had seen it.

They were going to have the rope walker again this summer, because Tony had heard the men sitting around the stove in the grocery store tell of how good business had been when they had brought such an attraction to Geneva. Folk came from all over the county, to look, and then they stopped to buy.

Carl and Tony crossed the street and stood and looked at the rich red and green colors of the big hanging flasks in the drug store windows, each flask with its own light behind it from a kerosene lamp set in a swinging bracket extending from the wall. Carl's dark mood left him.

The lamplighter came in his buggy, for he was lame and could not walk the route, and Tony explained how he measured the kerosene with experienced eye and hand as he filled the lamps to burn until the dawn: a little less oil each night than the night before, for nights grew shorter now. With his long matchstick he lighted the wick; with the cheery light came his cheery call, "Hello!"

Carl hurried his step, and Tony matched him. He could scarcely wait to reach the top of the east side hill, to look again at the little one-story red brick building with its lean-to addition at the rear. In that building he would learn to be an American.

Tony promised to help him. Much would Tony try to teach him, for now the boy pulled him down to whisper, "Here is the saloon." Then tall and straight, he adjured Carl: "Come—as far to the outside of the sidewalk as you can get. Now, hold your nose—tight—with these two fingers—and *shut your mouth!*"

Trying to make himself understood through clenched teeth and half-closed lips, he muttered, "Now, when we get by—"

He pulled Carl over an imaginary line, and danced in momentary agonizing fear lest the crisis find his friend unknowing and let the saloon-taste get inside of him, and then he shrieked, "Spit—*quick*—before you swallow!"

SIXTEEN

RUBBING ELBOWS, learning from each other, moneyed folk and plain, many of each, gathered in the parlors of the Bailey residence. Always open to receive, these rooms, always with the same friendly welcome.

Plainest of the plain, Carl knew himself to be as he sat listening; but how he had grown in knowledge and thereby in appreciation of music in such a short time through these evenings, with Mrs. Bailey—her face like that of an angel—sitting at the piano, playing. Like the piano on the *Majestic*, this one was.

Her fingers came to a stop and there was the clapping of hands. "We have a surprise for you this evening," she said, bowing. "It is a privilege to have with us our neighbor, Thomas, whom many of you know."

Yes, Carl had heard of Thomas. "Odd," in the parlance of the young fellows at the factory; odd, because he played the piano. "Woman business!" they scoffed.

Thomas swirled the seat of the stool to lower it, raised his cuffs slightly on his wrists, and sat down to play. Carl smirked. He could do as well as this, all a sort of blur, and just as Thomas started on something that might be called a "tune" he smothered it by striking a lot of discordant notes. Wrong notes, to be sure; no human being could play with such speed and be hitting the right keys all of the time. He was not playing music, that was a cinch, he was practicing finger gymnastics!

He finished. For an instant there was a hush, and then clapping began. "Well done! Well done!" Mr. Bailey said, appreciatively. "One of my favorites, Liszt's arrangement of the Overture to the opera *Rigoletto!*"

Thomas glanced in his direction, and Carl felt ashamed at

his non-clapping hands. But Thomas returned his fingers to the keys. Ah, there was music. Carl listened intently. "Fine! Fine!" he said, and applauded loudly. "What is the name of that beautiful piece?"

"'Listen to the Mocking Bird, with Variations,'" Thomas answered him. "So that is what you like?"

This was on a Saturday, and on Monday Carl met Thomas in front of the County Courthouse.

"So you didn't like the piece I played the other night?"

Quick to answer, Carl assured him, "Oh, I did not say such a thing!"

"I could tell." Thomas appeared bewildered that it should be true, but brightening, said, "Let's go to Mr. Bailey's—right now—do you have time? I'd like to show you something."

They sat down together at the piano, and the musician played the simple motif around which the Overture to *Rigoletto* is built.

"Do you like that?"

"Yes, I like that," Carl replied.

Thomas played it again, embellishing it with part of the accompaniment.

"But now I lose track of the tune—"

Thomas played it again, pounding out the melody, louder. Over and over, he played it. Carl recognized the tune now so that the accompaniment did not interfere, and Thomas worked through the entire Overture in that way, pointing out how the melody shifted from one hand to the other.

"On Monday evenings I am free, Carl. If you want to come over to Mr. Bailey's every Monday night, we'll have a music appreciation class, you and I."

"How can I repay you?"

"I learn while I teach. It will be a pleasure for me, I assure you."

Through Thomas' patience, he was learning to be an appreciative listener to music.

Music. Not sufficient that it gave peace and contentment as he listened, it led to yet another broadening of his horizon. For as he listened words came to him telling of places and people he had never seen, and he left Thomas full of this heartfelt rush of words, and hurried to his room to put them on paper.

Onto lined foolscap went the story of the old man who carried a sawbuck over his shoulder and went from door to door asking for work. The old man never spoke—nobody ever heard him utter a single word—and never knocked, but announced himself by flicking the steel of the saw to make a humming sound. Could he not talk? The story need not tell; only would Carl tell of the fear and horror the old man knew at thought of dying in the poorhouse and being buried in the potter's field.

Carl wiped his brow and shuddered at the memory of reading that one person in every ten who died in New York in 1889 was buried in the potter's field!

The old man, never asking a fee, doing the work for whatever was handed him, eating a biscuit and a cup of coffee as it was passed out to him, his table the back stoop; and each night he carried home his pittance, and when his savings grew to the amount of a dollar, he would have it changed into a folding bill and lay it neatly with the rest under the loose board in his garret room.

Carl bit his lip, and tears flowed as he wrote of the torment, the agonizing pain the old man suffered when he came to find the savings of his adult life—three hundred dollars—chewed into little pieces by the squirrels. They had built themselves a nest of it—a good nest—a very good nest.

The old man became so real to Carl as he wrote, he pitied the poor soul. Overcome with emotion, he was hardly able to finish the writing, but it had a way of carrying him on without his own volition, almost as if his mother guided his pencil, with the help of the old man, to the tune of Thomas' music.

Carl showed the story to Mr. Bailey. Mr. Bailey did not laugh. Instead, he showed it to Mr. Forrest Crissey, the writer, and Mr. Crissey did not laugh either, but said, "It is a fine characterization."

"A great lesson there," Mr. Bailey said to him, "you've done a splendid job at showing how temporal is man's desire."

Mr. Crissey put a few marks on the papers, here and there, and handed them back to Carl, to write up smoothly. Perhaps it could be sold to a magazine, Mr. Bailey said.

Twelve dollars! One dollar saved out of each week's pay from the glucose factory. Not bad. Not bad at all, even though as Joseph teased he stood well in the way of becoming as stingy as the brothers Torkilsen who dipped their *overhawls* into the horse's drinking tank and slapped them against the windmill base to dry them, for fear their old aunt, Tante Hannah, would wear them out in the washings, saving as they were so they could go back and live in the old country on American dollars.

He must be pretty good at the job, too, since Mr. Pope had raised his pay to twelve and a half cents an hour. It hadn't taken Mrs. Lofgren long to hear of it, though, and raise his board and room to five dollars. That was one thing about this town, everybody knew everybody else's business.

No, it was not bad. Twelve dollars toward the fifty-one he needed. But, he must save more, for he must learn; if only the tuition money could be accumulated before the Fall Term began at Wheaton College!

Fine shoes, these, on his feet. The advertisements showed good shoes for as low as a dollar and a quarter, but when a man came to buy a pair, only the ones that cost three dollars came in his size! And he had bought overalls. Oh, he could have saved more; but—the look in Tony's eyes when he gave the lad the bright-colored woolen shirt! It had not cost much; fifty cents, marked down from seventy-nine. And the new shoes, so the boy's flapping sole would not catch on sidewalk nails—and the pants—

Carl's eyes saddened as he recalled Tony, clinging to his hand, with choked voice, begging, "Oh, Mr. Carl—all the other fellas have—" and bursting into tears, "Please, Mr. Carl, can I call you 'Pop'?"

Tony, always at the factory door to greet him at the end of the day, to walk home with him and coach him in the sounds of "w" and "v."

Tony, who left him hurriedly at the door of Castle Garden so he could rush home and take his mother for her daily walk, she who was to have another child. Oh, no, of course his mother had not *told* him, but the boy knew.

Carl had looked at Tony, speaking of his mother. So had the lad from Värmland looked, on the boat, serving his mother, and her big with child. His old nausea returned at the memory: that lad, aboard the ship, who did the boy judge he was, anyway, to think that he could plant a curse upon a ship?

But Tony; when he spoke of his mother that same tenderness had shown from his eyes, and he was no old-country peasant. Almost as much help in teaching the English language, he had been, as the teacher in the evening school.

But Tony had gone from Geneva. When everything was going along so nicely, because his mother was in that common condition, he, Carl had lost Tony. No more would the happy "Hello, Pop!" greet him at the close of the working day. The boy had clung to him and cried, in the leave-taking. Thus did the selfishness of such a woman rob another; it was best for the mother to go to the home of the grandmother in South Chicago, no gainsaying that, but in the going he had lost Tony and Tony had lost him.

"Would that they could have let the boy stay," Carl came to the certain place on the sidewalk, turned toward the outer edge and walked past the saloon, playing Tony's little game without realizing it.

"Ha! Done with military precision," a voice startled him. "My name is Willis—Mr. I. W. Willis—and yours is?"

"Carl Christianson."

"Just the man I was looking for. You know, I've heard all about you. Work down at the cheese factory, don't you?"

"No, at the glucose—"

"Ah, yes, of course, of course, my mistake. At the glucose, of course."

Carl saw fiery sparks come from a pin in the gentleman's broad tie, from a stone as big as a thumbnail, returning the light with heavy interest from the weak lamp in the window of the White Horse Inn.

The stranger pumped his hand up and down, talking all the while. Mr. Willis had a job for him; he'd pay him three times as much as he would ever get at the cheese factory—ah, the glucose—he would make Carl a foreman, over scores of workers.

"Think it over, my man. Don't mention it to your boss, or to anybody for that matter, or they will want to cheat you out of the job by applying for it for themselves."

He knew human nature, all right, Carl could see.

A foreman. He could be a foreman! How Mr. Willis had laughed when he learned what Carl's wages were at the glucose factory. Why, Mr. Willis would pay him twenty-five dollars a week!

All through the next day Carl dreamed of the new job. He wished he had had the presence of mind to have asked Mr. Willis where the job was, what sort of work his crew would do; he could, then, have visualized himself handling it. Think of it, in a month's time, a hundred dollars! Enough to pay the term's tuition at Wheaton, and plenty left over!

But what if the job should happen to be in Chicago, for instance. He would miss the good friends in Geneva, miss sitting in Joseph's kitchen with an inverted sadiron in his lap, the handle held tight between his knees, cracking nuts with a hammer as fast as he and Joseph and Martina could eat the meats, with Åsa purring beside him, with Martina reading to them from *Harper's* or the *Atlantic*, or even the *Ladies' Home Journal*, or quoting, as she had last night, from the good Senator who said, "Come the dawn of the twentieth century, the United States will be governed by the people that live in them. When that good time comes, women will vote and men will stop drinking."

The light in Mr. Willis' stickpin was a puny light compared with the fire that shot from Martina's eyes as she denounced such as Tony's father, and read, "We are told that public sentiment is not ready for Prohibition. I answer that if God had waited for public sentiment to get ready, we never should have had the Ten Commandments!"

Martina and Joseph must never know that on occasion he had drained the bottle.

Narrow-minded? Yes, but smart, Martina was. Smart as a whip, and she had taught him much in these several weeks. What could all of this learning lead to, that he was receiving in this little town? As much as the shorthand he would learn if he had the fifty-one dollars? Possibly so.

Through Mr. Bailey he was learning that a judicious use of money could minister to artistic tastes, not only to make life comfortable, but to make it interesting and exciting! For now Thomas had promised the "reading" of Beethoven's Sonatas to the group.

Could he leave all of this?

He was beginning to know the real meaning of the word "culture," more a state of mind than a display of things—such things as the diamond stickpin in the tie of Mr. Willis.

No, he could not leave Geneva.

The cordial hospitality, the ring of sincerity in the "Come again, and *soon*" that left with him at the door of Joseph's and

Martina's home, and at the door of the Bailey home, all of this would keep him here.

He could not leave the evening school, either. Session upon session, learning—learning—no, he could not leave the evening school before the term was ended.

And his attic room at Castle Garden, his home: a little row of books stood there now, *Nya Verlden,* a *History of the United States,* given to him by Mr. Bailey, *The Life of Lincoln,* and *English Rhetoric and Grammar,* and they were his own, to pore over far into the night. It wasn't too hot, even in the summer, for the west wind blew through and out the east window, while he read.

The end of the day came, and his mind was made up.

No Tony was there to meet him. As he walked alone toward the main street he practiced the word the boy had been helping to pronounce, "answer." Not "ans-were," but "ans-er." "Ans-er, anser," he repeated to himself, and reached the place of meeting decided by Mr. Willis.

'C-C-C-Carl C-C-Christianson?"

"Yes." This was not Mr. Willis, but an emissary sent to bring Carl to the gentleman, who remained at the hotel.

"You can tell Mr. Willis that I have decided no."

The man started nervously. Carl had better deliver that message himself! They walked together to the hotel.

"W-w-wait here, and I'll t-t-tell Mr. W-W-Willis you have c-c-come."

Carl sat in the lobby. Sadness hung over the waiting room. The epidemic. He heard a gentleman read, "The little lives went out through the direful disease diphtheria."

He picked up a last year's paper lying on the table shelf; it was opened and turned down to page two, and Carl read,

The following as a cure for diphtheria, is said to be recommended by Dr. Delthill, of Paris: "Pour equal parts of turpentine and liquid tar into a tin pan or cup and set fire to the mixture, taking care to have a large pan under it as a safeguard against fire. A dense resinous smoke arises, making the room dark. The patient," Dr. Delthill says, "immediately experiences relief; the choking and rattle stop, the patient falls into a slumber, and seems to inhale the smoke with pleasure. The fibrinous membrane soon becomes detached and the patient coughs up microdiades. These, when caught in a glass, may be seen to dissolve in the smoke. In a course of three days afterward, the patient recovers."

Choking. Rattling. Membrane. That was the dirty-white phlegm! Now he knew what this epidemic was! It was the throat-sickness such as they had known at home, come to the island from the mainland to claim the lives of the three little ones, Oskar, Sven, and the baby Hjalmar. And here, in his hand, was the cure that could have saved them! And he had not known! His mother had not known. He must ask for a copy of this, so he could send it home. Yes, yes, he would write a letter home and send the cure for the throat-sickness.

"C-c-c-come on up," a voice called.

Dazed, his mind centered far away—as far away as Bohuslän, in Sweden—Carl walked each step of the red-carpeted stairway, to the top.

"Carl Christianson! So glad to see you. Trust you had a fine day at the chee—at the glucose! Yes, yes, and now to get down to brass tacks! But first, let's have a drink."

Carl stared at a diamond stickpin, but his mind cried out for cessation to the pain of memory—of seeing those babies at home—choking to death—seeing his mother, putting her open mouth over the mouth of the gasping Oskar, trying to suck the deadly membrane from his throat!

But Oskar had died in her arms. And Hjalmar, even the opening she had cut into the throat of little Hjalmar—it had not helped—

Such were the burdens he should have stayed to ease; he was his mother's eldest son. How could he know but that *right now* she needed him? He pushed the empty glass toward Mr. Willis and the bottle. The glass was refilled, and emptied.

Now he was a bit relaxed and calm. Now he could look this job business square in the eye. There was something to what the Willis gentleman said: he had come here to get away from Sweden, hadn't he? What was this place if it wasn't just a piece of old Sweden, with its population two-thirds Scandinavian, with its Midsummer's Day Festival over in the grove by the river, with its *limpa* in the bakeries and its *lutfisk* in the butcher shops?

Was it an *American* that he wanted to be, asked Mr. Willis; then certainly he should be wise enough not to stay in this Swedish community. Clannishness—the bane of this country! It would take bright boys like Carl to break up such clinging to the ways of the old country.

The warm amber color of the liquid in the bottle lessened.

It took a fellow like Mr. Willis to make a man realize that he was filled to the point of surfeit with things Swedish.

"If you had wanted to stay in Sweden, you would have *stayed* in Sweden. Right?"

"Right," Carl answered, and they shook hands solemnly.

An American, that was what he was going to be. Not a Swedish-American, like—like Joseph—he bent his head over his arms on the little table, and cried. Joseph, the friendly warmth of Joseph; no, he could not leave Joseph—and Mr. Bailey—and—

Once again Mr. Willis saw to it that the liquid in the bottle lessened.

Joseph! Carl jerked his head up. What was his game, anyway, trying to talk him into buying one of those lots in the new subdivision just west of the North Western Station! He should pledge himself to pay a hundred and twenty-five dollars for a lot! Like fun.

A good investment? Yes, maybe, for Joseph! Most likely he stood to get a commission on every lot he talked some poor greenhorn into buying! And Martina—a fanatic—wouldn't she have a fit if she could see him here, drinking? Her, and her bottle of Lydia Pinkham's sitting on the sink. "A baby in every bottle!" Who did she think she was anyway, a Sara?

He was a free man, wasn't he? He had come to this country to obtain freedom. He did not have to ask Joseph or Martina or Mr. Bailey what he could do. He was free! He could go where he jolly well wanted to!

"Of course, you couldn't possibly get ready to leave tonight. No. No, of course not. That would be out of the question; wouldn't give you time enough," Mr. Willis urged.

"Who can't get ready?" Carl smote the table, "By God! I'll show you who can get ready! Get your rig and we'll go up to Castle Garden and get my things *right now!*"

SEVENTEEN

"BANG! . . . WHIZZ-Z-Z, SPUTT!"

The Fourth of July! Independence Day, in the town of Tom's Lake near the Wisconsin border. An auspicious day, for the first in a new place.

Such thirst as he had, though, after awakening from a night of oblivion, to have to revisit the spring, time and again, to drink deep from the rusty-seamed dipper. Symbolic of his future, no doubt, his arrival on Independence Day. Carl's aching head would let him think no further.

Sky rockets bursting in clear night air sent showers of red, white and blue stars—or a golden waterfall—Roman candles sizzed and shot their balls of fire; the thunder of cannon rolled "taps" to the Fourth of July.

The fifth of July. Why had he come? How had he come? The memory of it all was gone. He was here. No, Mr. Willis was not about, said Jim, the nervous one, but he had left word: the real job of foremanship would not begin until the first week in August. Did not Carl know?

"Know what?"

"That c-c-cucumbers are not ready for picking until then."

Cucumbers! Picking cucumbers! Was the man crazy? That was farm work. He grabbed Jim by the shoulders and shook him so that his head bobbed back and forth, "Don't fun with me! Foremen are in factories—like the glucose—I know that much!

159

Go ahead, tell me. What is this job all about?"

Assuredly, Jim stuttered, Carl would be foreman to the scores of Swedish immigrant youths who would gather cucumbers for the pickle factory. Where would the youths come from? Oh, from Wesson Street in Chicago, or Belmont Avenue; Lakeview was full of them wanting to come away from the city streets, those highways and byways that were nothing but mudholes gradually being lifted out by dumping stove ashes into them.

Oh, yes, a big foreman he would be, come August. Meantime, he was to go with Jim to the farms, and hitch up the horse, and draw the cultivator between the vines. And that meant between the corn rows too, for it was in the shade of the sweetcorn that the cucumbers grew.

The sixth of July, the seventh, the eighth, and the ninth and the tenth, the blistering hot July found Carl cultivating the corn and cucumbers, from sunup to sundown. Even so, he saw he could not uproot all of the weeds that grew among the crops. Jim soon called to his attention the pesky growth that nestled close to the crop stems, and introduced him to the American hoe. If these weeds were not subdued, they would get the upper hand; then there would be no big crops of cucumbers to pick, and then there would be no sense in getting the youths out from Chicago—if there was nothing to pick—and then Carl could not be a foreman and would not earn his twenty-five dollars a week. The more Carl saw of Jim the more he loathed the stuttering fool. But the thing that made him maddest was that he had allowed himself to be duped.

But, he wondered, was this the usual way of employers in America? Mr. Willis had not so much as mentioned farmwork to him. He might as well be doing farmwork back in Sweden, on land which one day would be his own, as sweating like a fool here. Yet—and it made him furious to think of it—he had brought this on his own damned self!

Only one bright spot in this whole picture, the horse.

But that Jim; always calling him "Green Swede," and smirking. For two copper cents he'd pack his belongings and turn his back on these rows full of useless weeds.

Yes, he would tell them all to go to blazes, and let Jim have it from his fist for all his sneering superiority, and go so far, as far as his legs would carry him, if it were not for the horse. Never had the animal been tended as he should have been, till now.

In the day they shared the fields, the lightly falling rain, the blistering sun; and at night they shared the barn. When the young fellows started drifting in from Chicago, Carl sent them to sleep up in the hay mow so he alone should share the stable with the horse. True, he was no child, but he could pretend, couldn't he, that the horse was black with a white star on its forehead?

"Fine work! Fine work!" Mr. Willis praised when, on the Saturday before the first of August, he came and "on account" handed Carl a dollar to go to town and "have himself a time," and "of course, take the boys with him."

A dollar. Was he a "Green Swede" indeed, to be satisfied with such an expression of payment? Here he had worked for almost a month with no return except his meals and a place to sleep.

"Might as well wait and settle up all together so you'll have a real bank roll," Mr. Willis said and slapped him on the back. That sounded fair enough, and Carl thought of the feel of the horse's damp nose nuzzling against his face. With the dollar stuffed into his pocket, he walked down the road with the boys from Chicago.

"No." They must not help themselves to the green apples on the neighbor's tree; but how should he discipline them, these boys who called their foreman "scared cat!" The neighbor, they said, never would miss a few apples with all the trees he had, full-bearing. This was not stealing. This was only *the American way!*

No, Carl did not care for any, thanks. The crunching of teeth into the fruit, the breaking away of the bites from firm apple meat, hungered him; but as clear as day he heard that voice from his childhood:

> *"Börja med en knappnal,*
> *Sluta med en silfver skal."*

Such a little thing, an apple, as was a pin; but "begin with a pin, and end with a silver bowl," were the words of his mother's teaching. And in the morning he knew how right she had been, when colic knotted up the boys who had followed their so-described "American way."

Now was the beginning of the foremanship. Naturally, Mr. Willis said, now Carl would want to work all the harder to set a good example for the boys. It was back-breaking work for one as tall as he to bend, day in and day out, over those straggling vines, hunting for cucumbers. When they were filled, the bushel baskets were too heavy for many of the boys to lift. Carl lifted them. Fifteen hours a day; could he have endured them, he wondered, without the uplift he got from the thought of building for the future with an education, paid for by these hours of work—without the rosy vision of that payday when frost should come, and the pickle factory be satisfied, the day that would be followed by the opening of the Fall Term at the shorthand school? No, he never would have stayed, despite having given his word to Mr. Willis, despite the closeness of the horse, were it not that the money from this work would pave his way into the future.

Now frost had come. The boys were on the train, riding fast toward Chicago, eager to arrive there so they could get their pay. "Not safe to give young boys money, so far away from home," explained the big boss, Mr. Willis. And now, for work well done, early in the morning he would take Carl in his rig to the bank in town and have a check drawn to pay him for his work.

A check!

Carl beamed. A man had to be *somebody* to see his name written on a check!

He slept, for the last night, next to the horse. Soundly, he slept. He did not hear the wheels of Mr. Willis' rig crush the gravel of the main road, and disappear into the night.

"He l-l-left this f-f-for you," Jim said, the next morning, and cried, "he l-l-left me with nothing—nothing! I was to g-g-get a sh-share, a quarter of the t-t-take, and he l-l-left me with nothing!"

Carl read the note. Mr. Willis was a little short, but would see that Carl got the balance of what he had earned very soon. Here was ten dollars on account.

Carl folded the bill and put it in his money holder, and looked at Jim. "Green Swede," he himself was, no doubt at all, but no greener than Jim, who was an American. They both had been rooked by Mr. I. W. Willis. He handed Jim the dollar, the one he had not spent, the first money Mr. Willis had paid him "on account." They would go together, he and Jim, and find work. That was the only thing they could do.

This could be a lesson to him. Let this be the lesson that would remove forever that name that he was being called, "Green Swede."

Miles beyond the cucumber farms they walked into a barnyard, and for the tenth time offered their services.

"I'll take the Swede," the farmer said, but at Carl's nod of acceptance, Jim screamed, "Y-y-you c-c-can't do that!"

"Why not?"

"People don't d-d-do that in America. They s-s-stick b-b-by! We c-c-come here t-t-together. You c-c-can't leave me alone—w-w-without a job "

"All right, get goin', both of you then," the farmer said.

It was hard, this learning to be an American. But the stigma of being a green Swede must be removed. He would do the American way.

That way proved also to be that they should not walk where there ran a railroad. Jim showed him how to jump a freight, and riding the rods they came to Blue Lake, where Jim's cousin lived. Sure, there was a place there for an extra hand, but only one. "I'll s-s-stay," said Jim.

"But you can't do that!" Carl remonstrated. "It is not the American way. You've got to stick by."

"That all d-d-depends on which f-f-foot the a a shoe is on," laughed Jim. "You c-c-can always g-g-get a job—they're all lookin' for g-g-green S-s-swedes."

Carl's fist met Jim's twitching, stuttering mouth before he turned and followed the road toward the city.

There was no one a man could trust.

"Experience keeps a dear school and only fools learn in it," Mr. Bailey had warned him.

Mr. Bailey was wrong. Carl knew better: "Experience is a good school, and it is only fools who don't learn in it."

Never would he trust anyone. Never.

EIGHTEEN

"EXTREE PAPER!"

"*City of Chicago* sinks!"

"Extree—extree—extree paper!"

Carl turned over in his bed. The ruses these newsboys used, to get rid of remainders of last night's papers, were absurd—selling them as "extras" and getting two cents for their left-over penny papers! Well, he was not as green as some might think. He had learned a lot in these past months. Imagine anyone believing that the city of Chicago could sink; that was as ridiculous as anyone trying to sell the Brooklyn Bridge.

"Wuxtree poiper!"

"Wuxtree—"

Carl rose from the bed. Maybe the people across the street would not notice him, in his underwear, if he stood to one side of the window and reached an arm over to shut it.

"Them darn newsboys—" he caught himself. "Those darn newsboys—"

What would the home folk at Norden think, he wondered as he reached for the sash, if they knew that people in America slept with their windows open all night, the year around!

"Read all about it!"

"Wuxtree—"

"Inman Line Loses *City of Chicago!*"

Inmanlinen! Good God, it was the ship *City of Chicago!* Forgetful of his state of undress, Carl moved full in front of the window.

Trembling, his hands picked up his trousers from where they hung over the back of a chair. Loose change spilled to the floor. He let the pants fall and picked up a coin, and threw open the window wide.

"Here, boy, throw one up—and keep the change—"

The nickel fell into the newsboy's waiting cap. He pitched a twisted paper toward the second-floor window and into Carl's hands.

"Wuxtree poiper! Read all about it!" the bearer of news turned the corner and was out of hearing.

Why in God's name did they have to twist a paper so? The sweat poured from Carl; he sat for an instant on the bed, then stood to read the headlines, "Inman Line Loses *City of Chicago!*"

The flap of his unionsuit slapped away from him and against him as he strode from wall to wall of his room, looking at the paper. "—a very useful, though not pretentious ship—" he read, "Coming up Channel in the summer fog she stranded, and just when prospects looked bright for her salvage she swung broadside on to the land and broke her back—"

He sat again upon the bed. Mental agony thrust his eyeballs forward in their sockets; his hair must stand on end, straight upward, and so his hand reached up to smooth it down.

The curse upon that ship, laid on it by the lad from Värmland, it had come true!

"Curse on this ship!" Carl's hands pressed over his ears, but still he heard the plaintive shriek of the boy.

No mere sinking of a ship was this. He picked the paper up, and cast it down, then picked it up and folded it and slapped it against his hand, his thigh, the bedpost. No mere sinking of a ship, *this was the ripping apart of a man's reason!* This was the swirling, as if it were torrents of water, of the ground under him, carrying him—where—?

His hand clutched one of the center iron rails of his bed, and it bent under his grasp. Unseeing eyes looked, and the hand moved to the outer rail, three times as big around. Carl stared at the wall, papered with ugly red-splotched stuff, but saw only a boy from Värmland, tenderly waiting on his mother—not ashamed of her full rounded belly.

He turned his head, trying to escape the picture, but there was the boy, proud. Proud of his mother, and she was with child!

Stupidly he handled his pants; where were the legs to put his own legs through?

"Curse on this ship!" The heartrending cry of the lad filled the room. Yet this was Chicago, Illinois! Carl sat again, now fully dressed, upon the bed.

So confident had he been in heaping ridicule upon the lad; but now that curse had spelled the doom of the *City of Chicago*. Could he, ever again, be sure of himself? Remembering, would doubt crawl in to beset his every thought or act? This was unthinkable, that he should stand in all humility, and yes, in fear, before the vision of an ignorant farm youth. Yet—if that lad could prophesy this thing, could he not be justified, too, in his respect for his mother?

Was the lad the one that was right and had he, all along, in everything, been wrong?

In his scorn for the family life at Norden, in his disgust for his mother when she bore her many children, in his leaving home— oh, God—had he been wrong?

He turned to the little table that he used as a writing desk. There lay the months of work, his writing. Yes, he had written; ever since he had left the stuttering Jim that day and come to this room on Clark Street, he had been writing. Every evening, except on paydays, when it was the thing to do to stay out late with the boys, he had filled the pale blue lines on this foolscap with his story—his plea for tolerance toward those newly come to America, a story telling of the heartache, the pain, the humility, the agony borne by those who also bore the stigma of "Green Swede." All of the heartbreak that a man could know, from ridicule, was there.

He had polished up the other story, too, the one he had done in Geneva. These were to serve as excuse for going back to Mr. Bailey, to ask for advice about the writing, but in reality to let him bask once again in the circle of friendliness and culture and encouragement.

But now, his self-confidence shattered, he ripped each sheet across, and tossed the pieces into the basket for waste papers.

He was afraid—of life—of everything—

Wretched, insecure, a part of him forever gone, Carl left his room, to go to the job where he was learning to be a helper to the carpenter's trade.

Carl learned. He learned, just as he had upon answering the want ad in the *Chicago Tribune* for a painter's helper, that such a job did not mean that one would assist a portrait or a landscape artist, but that in America painting simply meant a craft and not an art.

He learned that he could go to the Public Library and sit for hours, or days, and read: that Chicago offered any man a chance to learn, and as far as he could see, a chance to work if work he would. And more, it offered the opportunity to stand on the shores of its great inland sea and feel the power of it surge through his veins, watching the whitecaps roll toward shore.

Gray was the wonted color of the sky of Chicago, a lower sky than the heavens, painted and set by the pall of smoke that hovered over the city. Gray, then, was the color the lake reflected; but sometimes the gray dome parted and Carl stood to see the blue of the lake merge with the blue of the sky—so rare a blue.

He learned of the boldness of this city that encouraged voices to speak of a future that held an eight-hour working day, with Sunday free at the end of the week, voices that clamored loud for protection to the working man against accidents, a city sobbing at news of casualties.

He was pulling himself out of the slough of despond into which he had been thrown at news of the sinking of the Inman ship, for now he was a part of something big. Ah, it was good to bathe in the limelight of publicity that shone upon the home of the World's Fair. And he was a part of the Fair! For he was helping to build the World's Columbian Exposition!

His hands laid plank roads where the soil was sandy and shifting; his broad shoulders and strong back pushed lumber-loaded wagons out of holes as teams sweat and strained leg-deep in mud. His back—never too tired at day's end—lent itself again to push the horse car up the little grade beyond the river, north on Clark Street.

No less of music than that which had poured from under the fingers of the young man, Thomas, in Geneva, was the whir of the grip-wheels of the cable cars in downtown Chicago, the grinding to a stop, the ringing of the gongs, the clatter of horses' hooves, the scream of one too nearly hit by the crazy racing cable trains, and the scurry of feet on sidewalks. Music. The music of growth—and he, Carl, was a part of it all—growing—growing—

Learning.

Yes, he felt akin to Chicago; big, blundering greenhorn of a city that she might be. Perhaps that very thing was what made him feel akin to her.

Learning. How could a man keep from learning, with the daily newspapers giving, each one, an education in itself? Think of it, full story of the nomination of the Democrat, Grover Cleveland, for President of the United States, all for one cent! To read the daily newspapers was like reading history. But it was reading history as it was being made, sharing in the making. Within that leaky building there on the lake front, the history of the nomination had been made; and by means of the daily newspapers he, and all who would, could know all about it almost before the sound of the chairman's gavel had stilled.

By this means a man could keep up with things, to know that women's clothes were leaning from the frills and bustles to give more ease of action to the ladies; and never in any city were women so on an equal with their men, as in Chicago. Let Easterners sneer, Carl deemed it good. Here the ladies were now playing lawn tennis—with the men!

John L. Sullivan, his two hundred and twelve pounds of idolized flesh, beaten by the one hundred and eighty-nine pound Corbett! Yes, reading the newspapers, a man could not do otherwise than keep informed, and learn. With all of this, the shorthand faded in importance.

The "horseless carriage" came to Chicago streets. What his eyes would have given to see the contraption, with its long steering handle grasped by a man dressed in a tan duster; but a working man must put in his day, and it was good to be able to read about it in the newspapers.

Chicago "took the cake," all right. No doubt about that.

And as Chicago could turn the waters of her river backward, making it flow into the Drainage Canal, so could he learn to reverse his thinking; and somehow he felt taller than his height after stopping to hold open the door of Marshall Field's big dry-goods store for a woman pushing a go-cart, and her bearing another child.

But the door closed after her: Carl slumped and grew shorter as he stood, hat still over his heart, in the driving rain which had cut short his working day. Merely the sight of a woman in such a condition could bring before him the vision of the boy from Värmland, the headlines on an extra paper, bring back that overpowering rush of insecurity and doubt, a misery so deep his mind could do naught else than fail to form the words describing it—bring back the fight against remorse at thought of his mother—bring back the brooding, haunting memories of home, the way he had left his home.

"Only the heart describes the pain," thus had his mother spoken of grief, and it was grief he bore, put to the rack of loneliness, and fear. Such were the times he found it hard to pass the swinging doors of the saloons, his reason crying out to pass them by, his feet carrying him along, turning him into the entrance, the soles of his shoes bearing down and swiveling slightly to make a circular pattern in the sawdust.

Lights. Amicable chatter. Music. Forgetfulness. And again, oblivion.

And yet again, his feet did not find it difficult to walk past the shuttered doors and on to the lonely room with its welcome of darkness. Not lonely long, nor dark, for a match brought the cheerful gas flame, shedding its yellow light upon the pages of a book.

The shelf was almost filled now, with books, a shelf four feet long made from a plank the carpenter boss had given him, resting on its fancy cast-iron brackets screwed into the wall, planed smooth and rounded at the free corner. The angled end was tight to the corner of the room. With each new acquisition the bookstop moved closer to the end of the shelf. A good bookstop, the six-pound iron with "Geneva" molded into its handle, come with him from his attic room in the little Castle Garden, packed into his rawhide trunk with unremembering hands.

"Sure," he could learn from books, and as well as if he were one of those rich men's sons who now would study at the big new University of Chicago on the South Side.

Chicago—noisy, generous Chicago—what poor reward she reaped for all her giving, on that morning of the first day of May in 1893.

Rain.

This opening day of the World's Fair should have begun with a sun-splashed sky. As disconsolate as if it fell into an open grave, rain dripped mournfully upon the President of the United States, streamed from the backs of the high-stepping horses that drew his carriage, fell on the pitiless push of fainting women and crying children.

Carl uncovered his head as the President passed by, then

smoothed his damp hair back with a clean white handkerchief. It was clean, all right, but the corners did not meet squarely, but humped out at pressure from the point of the iron. His mother never would have turned out a job looking so *slarfvig*.

President Grover Cleveland reached a pudgy hand to push the electric key in its purple plush casket.

Where was the thrill at sight of the President? Carl shifted his position and drew his feet from under those of the ones who crowded him, and looked away ashamed. Here came no rush of blood through his veins, such as he had known upon looking at King Oskar, at sight of this man with a chest like a barrel! Here was no oratory to move hearts, but a "boom, boom" from the mouth of a man whose voluminous voice reached thousands who had not heard a word of the proceedings before he stood, but had to be satisfied to see the speakers wave their hands and arms.

The President touched the key, and at his touch the sounds of Heaven and Hell and earth, combined, broke loose: flags broke from their furlings, bands blared, circus lions roared, guns from the warships on the lake gave forth their deafening roar, frightened gulls rose screaming from their coverts, and the sun came out and shone brightly on the Liberty Statue as her veil fell.

"Ah—h—!"

"Ah—h—!" Carl echoed the crowd. From the carven, bloodless statue, from the Stars and Stripes fluttering up the mast in the middle of the Plaza, came the same excitement he had known when first he had beheld his King!

Inflamed with the thrill of being an American, Carl clutched the Columbian half-dollar deep in his pocket. This he would keep always, memento of his part in the World's Columbian Exposition. Gosh! Were all of the million and a half of Chicago's population here?

No dip should be able to reach into his pocket and remove his lucky-piece. A thousand memories would this half-dollar call to mind in years to come—moving sidewalks on the pier; the Yerkes telescope; the Transportation Building; handwork on canvas, like his mother used to make, sewn by Queen Victoria, and not a whit finer than his mother's work; rough diamonds brought from Africa; the Swedish Building, brought from Sweden, shipped in sections and rebuilt here at the Fair; the burlesque show, where he could see rows of lace on women's pants, and lace ruffles hanging from tight white pants' legs over sleek black stockings.

Hard times? The world was crazy. "The Democrats are in; now we will have hard times," Carl smiled to hear the word go around. Two hundred and sixty-four feet in the air, as his seat on the Ferris Wheel reached the high point, he looked at the throngs below: they had paid money to come from towns and villages all over the country, they paid their fifty cents admission, and some lost money to the "three-shell" man. No, there were no hard times in Chicago!

Looking at the Liberty Statue, how glad he could be that he had come to America! Let him never again spend time chewing on the cud of regret for having left the old country. How in Heaven's name could Sweden retain a man, with the military training extended as it was to ninety days, and the time to be kept in the Reserves lengthened to twelve years in the Beväring and eight in the *Landstormen!*

He had been wise, all right, to come to America when he did. Never again would he allow loneliness to rob him of his wits, never again stand as he had stood in the Swedish Building, suffering that pain of homesickness.

Chicago Day; and now he owned another tangible reminder of the Fair and liberty—an engraved souvenir ticket, about two inches by four, showing an eagle on its front, and on the back, a picture of Fort Dearborn, Chicago, 1833. This was the anniversary of the Great Fire of 1871.

Just think of it! All but wiped out, and look how Chicago had come back in a mere twenty-two years! Years less than his own lifetime, and look how far she had come. Yes, he was glad to grow with such a city as Chicago.

All things must end, and so the World's Fair ended; so came the end of the maintenance carpentry work for Carl, came the end of the life of Mayor Carter H. Harrison through the bullet of Prendergast, the murderer. Carl followed the many mourners past the Mayor's bier in the City Hall. Was it a law of life that sorrow must follow joy? Did a pendulum always swing thus, to bring tragedy to follow good fortune?

Not so much as a mourner for the man who had been Mayor, did Carl follow the line, but a mourner for the way life was.

Chicago learned that panic was to follow her carnival, and

with her Carl learned. He learned what it was like to pawn his overcoat and some of his precious books so he could pay his room rent of two dollars; he learned to look away when beggars pleaded for the price of a piece of bread. He learned how a man could feel when his savings account book was only another piece of cardboard. But he learned, also, of the generosity of a city; he saw the heartbeat of Chicago when in the cold of winter she opened up the corridors of her City Hall so men might have a place to sleep—not only Chicago's own—but men come from far and wide to the city, with forlorn hope of finding work. He saw the soup-kitchens open to feed, not only men, but women and children. He ate of the "free lunch" in "Hinky-Dink" Kenna's saloon, although his pockets did not give the price of a drink. He learned to share what he had with others, his bed, the shelter of his room.

His landlady was of the best, the very best; yes, if she wished it, he would be willing to double-up with the young man who had been occupying the hall bedroom on the third floor.

"He's really awfully nice," she said, "and maybe you can straighten him out. I wish you'd try."

"My name is Andy Nelson."

Carl reached his hand, "And mine is Carl Christianson." He liked the way the stranger shook his hand, "I ought to know you, living in the same house, but—you work nights? That is why I have never seen you."

"I *worked* nights."

Carl learned another truth, that no matter how anxious the saloonkeepers were to sell their wares to employees of their neighbors, the Saloonkeepers Protective Association had decided that they wanted none of a bartender who drank what he measured out to others. And so Andy had been fired.

Carl knew at once he could be a friend to Andy Nelson. Was it heart-weakness on his part to feel moved by pity toward one who was nothing in the world to him? Perhaps it was that this youth reminded him, in a way, of someone he had known; could it be Rikard Eklund?

Too young, this Andy, to have his fingers tremble so, to have that beaten look about his bloodshot eyes.

Where was he from? Sweden, of course, but where? From a good home, yes, for Carl could see refinement in his every word and manner, but so besmirched by drink he was! Carl could be glad he was one who could take a drink or leave it alone. The habit would never get a hold on him, as it had on poor Andy, who broke out now in a sweat, begging as a child would do, for the price of one drink, instead of the soup or meat he better could have used.

Yes, indeed, Carl was glad he was only what might be termed a "social drinker," taking one drink or so in the evenings after work, except of course on pay days. Poor Andy.

It was Andy who found the advertisement for carpenter's helper, that got Carl a job at two-fifty a day.

It was Andy who spoke to an erstwhile customer, an influential citizen, and had Carl released from jail.

The injustice of it! All he had done was to stand and listen to an orator speak for the eight-hour day, only one of the audience, but as he heard, "—fie to the industrial moguls—" spill from the corner of that mouth there atop the soap-box, he recognized Axel Lindqvist!

He had pushed his way forward, as any man would do, to speak to one he knew, "Axel—" he greeted, just as the policeman put his hand on Axel's shoulder.

"You damned anarchist, I thought we told you," the officer spoke, and his partner took Carl into custody. There at the jail they had branded him, too, what Joseph called an *arnachist*. He, who was as good an American as any who were born here!

But Andy had gotten him free.

He owed it to Andy to help him break from the drinking habit. And so he brought a bottle to his room and as Andy sat with him in the evenings, keeping away the lonliness and dread that at times, came to face him, he apportioned a bit at a time from the bottle to his friend, only enough to keep Andy from the saloon. Only enough for himself to keep Andy company.

By silent but mutual agreement they never spoke of home. Even the amber-colored liquid, time-proved discoverer of secrets, did not break down this wall of silence. Instead they talked of labor, and the free coinage of silver, woman's suffrage; and Andy was impressed at his host's knowledge.

"'Alas, that gold should be so dear and flesh and blood so cheap!'" Carl's memory was keen, to repeat Martina's quotations from Frances Willard's words, and he walked up and down the room, importantly, his left hand tucked into his coat front and his right gesticulating. He sat, and leaned over the table, confidentially sharing news with Andy, "'Light is thrown upon the temptation to crime in great cities by the fact that in Chicago we have women who make twelve shirts for seventy-five cents, and furnish their own thread, women who "finish off" a costly cloak for four cents; children who work twelve hours a day for a dollar a week.'"

They were in agreement on politics, on women, on Votes for Women. But on God, no. Andy did not argue. He was firm; superior, it might be called. Then Carl became quarrelsome, and for every once that he filled Andy's glass, he filled his own glass twice.

"You think so much of your own self, you cannot bear to think that a universe can run without you! Is that it? You think you are so necessary—you, a little insignificant speck in a whole order of things—that you can't even imagine a hereafter without you!"

"I only know what I believe."

"You think that it is impossible that your stinking body could be of no further value—after you're dead—so you have to—"

"Some day, Carl, you will know—as I know—"

So sure was Andy.

"Well, by Heaven, if that day ever comes, it will be the end of the world! You can put that in your pipe and smoke it!"

Summer followed spring. Early Queen Anne's lace stood proud in the bathroom's drinking glass on the center of Carl's little table, gathered by the trembling hands of Andy Nelson; all proud but one stem, bent weakly over the glass. Feathery pollen and delicate white flowerlets on the table top marked the size of its flat-topped umbel, hanging upside down.

Andy lay shivering on the bed. It had been so hot outdoors, so very hot, how could he possibly feel chilly now? But he did. He had to get warmed up. One small drink would warm him and stop his teeth from chattering so! He tried to stand; he couldn't stand, he shivered so. There, in the clothes closet, was a half-full bottle. He knew, he had seen Carl hide it behind his ulster, or maybe in the pocket. He crawled to the closet, reached, and crawled back to the bed. There wasn't enough. Oh, there wasn't enough to make him warm! Why did not Carl hurry and come home?

Andy groaned. If only he could get warm.

Carl opened the door; his room was dark. Where was Andy? Struck on the seat of Carl's trousers, a match showed Andy on the bed.

"So, come now, what is the trouble?"

"I feel sick, Carl, sick as a dog."

"I'll get the doctor," Carl turned quickly. Andy was sick, no two ways about that.

"No, please, only one drink—to make me warm—and then, I promise you, no more ever." The taste for it was gone, Andy was sure of that. This last one would suffice for all time.

Carl walked down Clark Street to the doctor's house. He was not in, but would come as soon as he returned from the baby case he was on. It might be late, the wife said, babies took their own good time, coming; but he would call.

It would do no harm to bring Andy what he craved, a little more could not hurt him, saturated as his blood was. Carl sorrowed that he had failed with Andy. Perhaps it might be better to take Andy to the Swedish Mission, they were doing a good work with just such as he. They should know better how to help him.

Andy got up and sat at the table.

"Skål." He lifted his glass.

"Skål," Carl answered, but the hand he raised was empty.

The evening wore on. "Ya, shure," Andy felt better now.

Carl shifted and glanced frequently at the alarm clock. Why didn't the doctor come?

"Skål," said Andy. He had the strength now to spread a little tidy under the glass of flowers, *"Så var det himma—"*

So had it been at home.

Carl saw tears in the eyes of his friend; but he could not afford to talk of home—not with that tempting bottle there.

"Himma. Yes. But leave us never talk of home between us, Andy."

"Right as rain, Carl—never talk of home."

"Never again."

"Never again."

"Skål!" Andy's hand fell heavy to the table, with emptied glass. The flowers shuddered.

"What shall we sing?" Andy asked.

"What do we know?" Carl answered nervously. Andy looked

so—so—the hands of the clock kept going around and still the doctor had not come.

Heavily, hoarsely, flatly, half through his nose, Andy began, "Du gamla, du friska."

"Nay, so goes it not," Carl reverted to the Swedish now, "Du gamla, du fria—"

Andy let his fist drop so the drooping flower sent a shower to the table top, "Nay, 'Du gamla, du friska,' I ought to know!"

"We are friends," offered Carl, and he talked as he would have talked to one of his littlest syskon, "good friends; let us not let a *fria* or a *friska* come between us."

"Ya, Carl."

They began again, each with his own words, and sang.

"Never—never—talk of home—again—" whispered Andy.

Their right hands met; Andy's head fell forward to the table, the bottle tipped, and whiskey ran over his benumbed fingers.

The fine thin face of Andy Nelson lay white against a cushion of black satin. He had carried a thousand dollars' insurance, so the undertaker had dressed him well for this last display.

Carl Christianson, his friend, stood looking down at him. With furtive glance Carl reassured himself that no one else was in the room, then touched his finger lightly to Andy's overlapped hands. The thin white fingers were hard and cold.

Carl's teeth chattered. He wanted to hurry out into the sunshine, but this was so cold a place for a friend to lie—in the parlor of a stranger, not as at home, as Morfar had lain, in the corner of honor in the big room—he would keep Andy company. He looked again at his friend. Fine black silky-looking broadcloth made the suit Andy wore. He had not realized Andy's legs were so long. Or was it the sharp crease down the trouser legs that made the legs look longer? The black patent-leather shoes were too pointed, they must crowd poor Andy's toes. The open front of the coat, above the four-holed buttons, displayed a crisp white pleated shirt front, brass studs, a stiff white collar, and white bow tie. Andy's dark brown hair was combed straight back from his forehead, as he was used to combing it. That deep resemblance, to someone Carl had known, was greater now. It must be to Rikard.

He reached again to touch the cold hand of his friend. Hard

to believe he would never clasp it again in friendly, warm, comradely gesture. Hard to believe this was the hand he had grasped only a night or two ago.

Trembling, he turned to leave.

The undertaker stopped him. "We have telegraphed to his nearest relative; we have found his sister, but until she gets here, we will take full charge. Burial will be on Sunday at two, in the afternoon. Rose Hill Cemetery."

Carl inched away.

"We will engage the minister, and we will see that the notice is placed in the *Tribune* and the *Daily News* and the *Inter-Ocean*."

These undertakers! At Norden they had had no need for such; why couldn't the man leave him alone, he did not care about the *Tribune* or the *Daily News*. His friend was dead.

"We think it would be well for you to meet the sister, if you will, at the train—as Andy's friend—and find a room for her." The man had a notepad in his hand, "Your address, please? And we will notify you at once of the time of her arrival, as soon as we hear, so you can meet her train."

Carl gave his address. Yes, he would meet the sister of his friend, Ellen Anderson of New York. It was good that Andy had named her on his insurance papers, for no one here at the boarding house had known he had a sister. Now she would know about Andy's sudden death. She must be Mrs., or else her name would be Nelson, like Andy's.

The carpenter boss was kind and understanding. Of course, he could take time off until next week, to see to the burial of his roommate.

He found a room for his friend's sister at Mrs. Binney's boarding house on Clark Street, near to his own, and paid a fifty-cent deposit to hold it until Sunday. Not a fine room, but passable, and as clean as any Irishwoman kept a room.

Andy was gone. Somehow, he was glad Andy had known "what he believed." There was peace on the face lying so white against the black of the coffin. Andy had not been afraid.

But he was afraid. He was afraid of Death.

What if it had been he, instead of his friend, about whom the doctor had written on the report, "—slipped from coma into death. Sunstroke, aggravated by acute alcoholism."

Let that last drink, that he had taken, be his last. He was afraid.

Sunday. Chugging and hissing, the train came to a stop. Carl walked along the side of it. Ellen Anderson would arrive; that was all he knew. How should he recognize her? "Look for a sad and tear-stained face," the undertaker had said. All right, he would stand here, and wait.

Tired-looking, the faces were, but none who looked bereaved, until he saw the little one.

"Elin!"

Her name had changed, but Elin had not changed. Thinner, and wan, but it was Elin.

"Karl!"

He took her hands; held her, sobbing, close to him and patted her soothingly. For a moment they stood thus. In front of Carl's eyes was the side of a railroad car, but he saw, instead, far away and long ago—and, he wondered, did Elin see as he saw—the two of them standing together in the center of a fairy ring.

Rain from a low gray sky fell into Andy's grave in Rose Hill Cemetery.

Carl glued his eyes on the minister. As long as the cleric was getting paid, he might not have seemed to be in such a hurry; he could have said a kind thing or two about Andy, even though he had not been a member of the church, Carl complained to himself. What would the sister think, at no eulogy coming from the lips of the minister, only the bare and necessary words of commitment?

He could have spared his concern. Ellen heard only that last farewell, said so long ago when hopes were high, the last words she had ever heard him speak, the last she would ever hear from her brother Algot.

Sad, sad it was that she should have lost all trace of him, till now. Doubtless he had thought she had returned to the home in Falkenberg. Only Dr. Osgood's keen searching eye had found the "Personal" in the New York paper, which told of the death of "Algot Nilsson, later known as Andy Nelson," and the request that the sought-for sister telegraph her address to the undertaker. Otherwise she might never have known.

Poor Algot. Dead from sunstroke. She owed it to her parents to write them now, of this. She could send them the clipping from the Death Notices; her father would not care to hear from her, stern, he would not have relented; but her mother would like to know that Algot lay in the shade of a lilac tree—that wild roses would rise to lay a pink-petaled coverlet over his grave— that robins would sing to him.

Yes, at last she would write home.

Hardly would she have known him, Algot's hair was so dark as he lay there. She should have been prepared, for he had written of losing his light hair after the typhus fever on the boat coming over, but she had forgotten it. She saw him in her mind, always, as he had been at home. Strange to see Algot with so white a face against the dark of his hair, he who had been so fair of hair and ruddy of cheek.

"O God," the minister finished, "whose mercies cannot be numbered, accept our prayers on behalf of the soul of the departed, and grant him an entrance into the land of light and joy, through Jesus Christ our Lord. Amen."

"Please, God, take care of Algot," Ellen prayed, and bent on her knees, and pulled away from Carl's touch, watching the spadefuls of earth fill in the yawning hole. "Weep, weep, skies— for Algot—who should not be here, so. Oh, Algot! Algot!"

She stood, but would not leave until the grave was filled. Over the top the gravesmen spread a blanket of red roses. Wide white airy ribbon shrunk in the rain, but golden letters gave their message, "Beloved Brother." Ellen plucked one rose. This she would press between the pages of her Bible.

A grave, one rose; all that was left of Algot Nilsson, except a memory. Ellen thought of the years she had worked, to save enough money to try to find him, gone. But she had found him; she knew now where he was. And she would send the clipping home.

Carl stood reproaching himself: why had he not thought to send a flower to Andy? Andy—who had loved even the flowers of the fields—he would have been happy to know that a little gentian had kept company with the roses there, even a dandelion with a ribbon on it, "Beloved Friend."

All he had done was to mourn his loss in losing again to Death. Why had he not thought to send a flower?

Carl was kind, to want her to stay; Ellen thanked him, but no later than Tuesday she must leave. She had her work, and it was all she had. The dentist would be missing her. She must return.

The dentist; what was this Dr. Osgood to Ellen that he claimed her loyalty? Jealousy ate at the heart of Carl.

Her eyes had softened at mention of him; it seems he had laughed when she had said it would be good luck in a new place to change her name and call herself Ellen Anderson. She had spoken the dentist's name so fondly when she said he laughed. She had gotten the idea for a surname Anderson from Algot's name, Anders; from it he had chosen the name of Andy.

Carl wanted her. He would not let her go to this Dr. Osgood. She must not go back.

"Stay—and marry me, Ellen—"

"I promised I would return within the week."

She had told him of the wife who died in the consumption. But he dared not ask her outright, what was the dentist to her?

"Ellen, do you not remember the fairy ring? You know the meaning, Ellen, caught in a fairy ring—our lives were bound together."

If only she could think; if only he had not let her go alone that day—from off the ship.

"It is three times now that Fate has brought us together. Three times, Ellen. Can you ask further proof that you belong to me? That, and the fairy ring?"

Yes, she had loved him, did love him; and it was four times, though he did not know of the time she had seen him back there in Falkenberg. Deep in her heart, since first he had come to the home of Eleonora, she had loved him. But she could not tell him so; her mother's last advice had been to warn her against such unwomanly display to any man. But did he love her? His lips had spoken, yes, but they had not said the words.

"Please, Ellen, marry me?"

"But you have not said—"

"What have I not said? Tell me."

"You have not said you love me, Carl. Speak the words, and I shall prepare my answer then."

Carl dropped his arms from her shoulders. He could not say that he loved her.

It was not the kind of thing a man could explain. She might laugh at him if he tried. Anything, anything in this world, than to have Ellen laugh at him!

If he should say that he loved her—he might lose her! He had loved Hjärta. He felt his chin quiver at thought of his loss. Everything he had ever loved, he had *lost!* The child, Tony; and in a friendly way, he had loved Andy.

He could not afford to love. He would have to take what

came to him, and never again let anything touch him as deeply as had his affection for Hjärta—then he could not have his heart torn right out of his chest and dangled before him while he bled.

He wanted to *have*, yes; but not to love. Then, if he lost what he had, he could keep on living.

How could he say this to Ellen? I can never *love* anything or anyone again—because once I loved a horse!

How could he say that? O, God—for the words to use!

"Is it not enough, Ellen, that I want to make you my wife?" He crushed her to him, "Ellen, I want you—"

He kissed her.

She had saved her lips for him. Now she was glad.

NINETEEN

LOVE LIGHTENED the load of sorrow carried in the heart of little Ellen.

Worker of wonders, love, that she could sit on a bench, so long that the minute hand would travel the entire circle on the face of the clock, looking at Grant's Monument in Lincoln Park and turn away unable to describe a feature or a single line of the statue, knowing only the feel of the pulsebeat in the big hand enclosing hers.

They stood together, she and Carl, on Lake Michigan's shore and watched ridge upon ridge of gray, or sometimes blue, edge toward them to break in foamy white ripples at their feet, coming forward, retreating, slipping back for one more lingering caress of the land, another and another, even as Carl caressed her and found it hard to let her go.

It was God's will that she should marry Carl: He had brought them together again. Bringing her into Carl's strong arms, He had brought a peace the like of which she had not known since leaving Sweden. She would belong to someone; she would have someone to care for her; it would be good, for she was tired.

And Carl was hard put to contain himself. Why should they wait? All of the pent-up yearnings and ambitions of his life would now be realized. He felt the urge to write again. Thoughts came in rich profusion. Words came like poetry into his mind.

"Let us get married tomorrow, Ellen?"

Not until her trunk came, would Ellen marry. "Dr. Osgood will send it right away. I know he will, he is always so dependable. It will be here soon; then Carl, I will marry you."

Women were hard for him to understand. It was silly to have to wait. What difference would it make if she should come to him now? She was going to be his anyway. A day, or a week,

what difference as long as she was going to be his wife? He was
full of the urge for creation: the sound of the streetcars, the rat-
tat-tat of his hammer on the job, everything was music, sending
the words to him with which to make stories. His fingers itched
to guide a pencil over the foolscap—to tell of the beauty of
lavender frost flowers, as Andy had seen their beauty—to draw a
line of scarlet across the white of winter snow, a streak that is, in
words, the cardinal bird—to draw, in a little circle that is the eye
of a child, the joy that comes when a mother reads to him—

Of progress, too, he must write; the sitting in a train car,
dashing forward into the future, like the scene from a moving
train window, only a passing blur before the eyes. But giving
such promise of what is to be found ahead!

After Ellen was his, his writings, mayhap, would give
pleasure and comfort and hope to those who would read them.
Books printed in this country sometimes were translated into the
Swedish: maybe even his mother would read them.

But first he must have Ellen.

He brushed his hair down smoothly after he parted and
combed it, and on the way out appraised his appearance in the
long mirror in the hall stand. If he did say it himself, he looked
swell. Ellen would never be able to resist him tonight; she would
be his—his—

Whistling "Daisy, Daisy," he fairly ran down Clark Street.

Why turn the knob of the doorbell only a fraction of the way
around? Might as well swirl it all the way—the full circle!

"Wal, ye don't have to wake the dead, ye know!" Mrs. Binney
opened the door for him. "Good evenin', Mr. Christianson, and
how're ye?"

"Fine as silk!"

"She said to tell ye she'd be down in a minute."

"Oh, I think I'll go right up." Hardly anybody called him
Swede any more; he spoke like an American, and the realization
brought a smile to his features.

Mrs. Binney stood her big frame to block the carpeted stairs,
and folded her arms across her chest so the elbows stuck out
toward him, "She *said* she'd be down in a minute!"

How he hated big women! He flushed and looked down at
the carpet, and scuffed the toe of his shoe at a worn place near
the door.

"All right, I'll wait here."

"By Gawd, and that ye will," she swung defiantly toward the kitchen.

He was glad Ellen was small. He could not have taken to her at all if she had been one of those big women. It would have been different at his place; his landlady knew he was all right, never checked up on him.

There was Ellen, starting down the stairs.

"Hello, Carl."

As soon as he saw her again, he knew again she would be his when she was rightly his. Her bearing, her damned delightful elusiveness, those dark and deep-set eyes reminded him without mistake that one move beyond the code of propriety would lose her to him.

The summer trolley stopped at the corner for them, and Ellen gathered her full skirt with a long sweep of her left hand, over the bustle and down, then drawing the skirt upward she placed her foot on the low step. Carl caught a glimpse of her ankle, and his pulse quickened. She wore low shoes. So up-to-date, so stylish, this girl who was to be his wife: so slim and dainty, no danger of her ankles growing thick and ugly from wearing oxford shoes!

He noted the stares of the occupants in the trolley, all of them men, one with a tall silk hat and a gold toothpick hanging from his watch chain. Carl threw out his chest; his girl was a stunner, all right, all right. And he was as big as the rest of them: he dropped the two nickels he had ready for the fare back into his pocket, and clung to the rail as the horses started, all the while maneuvering a five-dollar bill from his moneyfold. With a flourish he handed it to the conductor.

"Which one do you want?"

"Which one?" blankly, Carl asked.

"Yeah—which nag?" The conductor waved his hand toward the horses, and the passengers laughed. The driver turned and laughed and looked back into a small mirror that he had tacked to the ceiling of the car platform, and twirled his blond handlebar mustache. Red-faced, Carl pocketed his change and sat beside Ellen on the caned seat.

Now it was his turn to laugh. A gust of wind blew down the opened narrow ventilating window under the roof and lifted the straw hat neatly from the head of the man seated in front of them.

Ellen raised her hands to catch it, but Carl brushed them down.

"Good. It serves him right. I hope it rolls all the way to Van Buren Street."

"All aboard!" The fat conductor swung with one hand high in the air, and they all sat waiting while Mr. Jones or Mr. Houlihan ran the last half-block with cane upraised, or hat in hand, to catch the trolley. They were on their way to pass through the turnstile of the new Field Museum, and they were jolly.

But there were moments when faces clouded with trouble and over the racket of the trolley and the horses' hooves, Ellen heard mention of Eugene V. Debs, and strikes at the Pullman place, and martial law, and President Cleveland and Governor Altgeld, and "scabs." Then was when she reached for Carl's hand, and the warm pressure brought reassurance that all was well.

Beautiful, happy evening; and on the way home Ellen asked, "Are you happy, Carl?"

In the dark, halfway between the lights of street lamps, on Clark Street, he crushed her to him so that her breath was forced from her in a quick gasp. "I shall be happier when you are mine."

"Look, Carl, there is a hack in front of Mrs. Binney's."

"Some new boarder must have a half-dollar he doesn't know what to do with, too high-toned to ride the horse-cars."

He must be going to stay, because—see—the hackman is helping him carry in his baggage. He is not too high-*tuned* to help carry his trunk—"

A trunk!

Ellen ran from Carl's side and when she reached the housefront she called back, "It's mine!" and he quickened his pace to catch up with her. High-*tuned*. He smiled; he was going to have to help her with certain of her vowel pronunciations, in English the "o" did not take the sound of "oo" as it did in Swedish; but now she finished the steps, two at a time.

The front door stood open and a man shook hands with Mrs. Binney.

"Dr. Osgood! Oh, Doctor John—"

The newcomer took her hands, and Carl saw him place an arm around Ellen's shoulders. Didn't the man know she was *his!* His ready fist clenched. If the Irishwoman would only go into her kitchen he would go into that hall and demand an explanation! Instead he walked slowly up the last two steps and entered the hall door, in time to hear the stranger say, "I had to come, Ellen."

"Good evening," Carl interrupted.

"Oh, Carl, this is Dr. Osgood—and this is my Carl."

They shook hands. The gentleman continued to address Ellen, "I came, because I had to make sure you knew what you were doing."

"And what is it to you?" Carl asked glumly.

"Ellen's future means a great deal to me," Dr. Osgood began.

What was this man to Ellen? Jealousy planted a seed of doubt at this moment. He didn't like this Dr. Osgood. He felt the hot blood surge into his face, and mad thoughts raced in his mind. Dr. Osgood had been close to her, had set the bridge of seven upper teeth into her mouth after her own had decayed so soon after coming to America. Ellen had told him of that.

How could the dentist have come so close to that sweet young mouth and not have kissed it?

For years Ellen had lived in his home! And his wife had died, too, in that second year that Ellen had been with him; and now for two years she had lived in the same house with him!

"After only a few days in a strange place," Dr. Osgood was saying, "Ellen plans such a step as marriage." He turned to her, "You have been too near and dear to me, Ellen, for me not to—"

So he bragged about it! Carl could comprehend no more; but he looked at the Irish landlady and unclenched his fists. "It is late," he said, shortly.

"Forgive me," Dr. Osgood shook hands with Ellen and the landlady and heard Carl's curt "Good-night."

Carl watched the doctor's hired hack drive away until it faded into the summer dark, and he walked to his room. So Dr. Osgood was going to "stay to see Ellen married." Didn't the man trust him? And how fondly Ellen spoke his name!

Carl's hammer pounded with a force all out of reason, the next morning on the job. What was he doing here, anyway, leaving Ellen to the company of the doctor? What if the New Yorker beat his time, and he should lose her to him? By noon, Carl could stand it no longer. "I would like the rest of the day off," he addressed the carpenter boss. "And tomorrow, too— because I am going to get married." He felt himself blush, and could have kicked himself for blushing.

There were congratulations and hand-shaking. It was after

the hour of one before Carl reached Mrs. Binney's boarding house, and she said, "Ye'll have to wait here, sittin' in the hall. Ye can sit on the hat rack seat, there." The parlor had been rented, and two iron beds set up behind the sliding doors. "Git all the rents ye can, while the sun shines," was her motto, Mrs. Binney said, and Ellen was out, "eatin' luncheon at the swaggerest restaurant in Chicago with the gent from New York; at Kinsley's, no less!"

Carl fumed inside, and waited.

Color had risen in Ellen's cheeks. Gaily she waved good-bye to her escort and turned to find Carl waiting for her.

"He bought us a wedding present, at Marshall Field's!" She danced into his arms.

Carl would look at it later. Now they must plan their marriage.

"Tomorrow?" he pleaded.

"Any time now, Carl," she answered; and she was glad that her old friend and employer had come to see her side of what had nearly become an argument about her marriage. Or had he merely seemed glad for her when he saw that she was intent on going through with her plan to marry Carl? Why had he begged her so to wait until she knew her affianced husband better? She had known him since she was a child! How better could she know him?

"Wait. I shall show you why I wanted my belongings." She tripped up the stairs and when she came again to sit beside him on the hall rack seat, she held upon her outstretched palm a little crown of gold.

His eyes questioned her.

"I could not get married without it. It is the *brudkrona*—the bride's crown—the virgin's crown," her tongue tripped, she spoke with such excitement, "worn by every daughter of my family—through all the years."

Six-pointed, the crown, half as large across at the base as the palm of his hand, and no taller than his fingers were long. The points flared outward, and each tip ended with a little golden ball. Basing the points, a dainty filigreed scroll encircled the crown, with six oblong-cut aquamarine stones set evenly in the pattern. Over a slim arch between the flaring points rose a snub-ended five-pointed star, and a tiny golden heart hung suspended, dangling from a ring below each arch. The hearts quivered as he held the brudkrona in his trembling hand.

He was ashamed. The blue of the semi-precious stones—the blue of her honest eyes—her virgin's crown, he looked at them. And he had doubted her.

Well, not so much her, as that Dr. Osgood.

"So will the little hearts quiver, matching my heart, Carl, as I walk down the aisle."

The import of her words did not pierce his mind; in it there was not thought of church aisles.

"Eleonora," Ellen went on, "she was so beautiful. I can remember her, wearing this bridal crown."

"But in Bohuslän, in my home, they said the brudkrona had seven points?"

"No. Six-pointed, always," Ellen affirmed.

It was the coming of the dentist that had made him edgy; why else should he feel as now he did, inferior. True it was, he had never seen such a crown of gold. The peasants among whom he had been born and reared could not afford such luxury. Not even in the church on the mainland had there been one for use by any or all of the young women of the parish, much less a family rich enough to possess one of its own. But he had heard folk speak of the seven points of the bridal crown; was it not old Elsa Kvalvog who had spoken so?

Six points, or seven—what matter?

Damn it, it mattered much. It placed him in the class of an ignorant peasant, not knowing!

But it was a dear and costly object. How had she brought it into the country? Surely it had not been in the colored, striped knapsack, for he had seen its contents strewn along the street.

"Did not the customs officials find this in your trunk?" he asked, "How, then—"

"You were not there, Carl, you did not see. But when I left the ship at Castle Garden, the bottom of my knapsack burst open, and my bread and cheese and all my store of food fell to the ground. The people laughed. I saw even the United States Government's customs officials laugh!" She straightened her shoulders and held her head high, as he remembered she had done on that day.

"But they did not see, Carl, that I laughed too. For into the big loaf of dark bread, my mother had baked the bridal crown."

She held it close to her face. The mellow old look of the gold took on some of the color of Ellen's cheeks.

"For an instant I stood there, turning to stone. What if the loaf broke open, and the crown fell full into view? But God and my mother's blessings were with me. And now I shall wear my crown."

"Your mother—"

Now he told her of her mother's death. Too soon, this blow upon the other. She clung to him; he would have to be all in the world to her now. Not even the hope left, of some day seeing her gentle mother once again.

No doubt it was kindness that had kept Carl from telling her sooner; but, he had let her write home of Algot—not knowing—

"Oh, Carl, be good to me, be good to me."

"Tomorrow we will get the license and get married right away."

"Have you seen the minister?" sadly she asked him.

"Minister? No minister for me."

Ellen was stunned. Who else would marry them? A Lutheran minister, it had to be, of course.

"Ellen, let us never have our first quarrel—"

"But it is not marriage unless it is in the church! Marriage is a sacrament, Carl! There can be no blessing on a marriage unless it is performed in the church."

"I do not go to church, Ellen."

He saw tears fall from her brimming lids; she had had a lot to bear, and he felt sorry for her, but not church—he simply couldn't.

"The legality of marriage, that is the thing that counts; so a marriage is performed in accordance with the laws of the country."

She made him feel small, made him feel as if his words were silly, but he was right. He knew in his own mind that he was right!

"So it is legal, Ellen—"

Half-heartedly, she picked up her bridal crown, and with a sad "adieu" she mounted the stairs.

Carl walked along the street, and walked and walked. He had been so happy in the thought of marrying Ellen, but now he had caught some of her sadness. Should he have told her at this time of her mother's passing?

And yet, he knew it was not the contagiousness of her sorrow that ailed him. It was something else: it was inside of himself, this something that cast a shadow over his heart.

Instead of snatching at each little word and look to try to attach some base import to it, why had he not been glad for all that Dr. Osgood had done for Ellen? What if she had been picked up by whiteslavers, there in the labor office, and her not knowing a word of English? The corners of his mouth lifted, "— not knowing a word, *except one!*"

What if a shopkeeper had taken her and she had fallen into the ways of Gert and Liv?

The doctor had given Ellen a good home.

He walked into the jewelry store and bought a plain wide gold band the size of the piece of string he took from his vest pocket, and his blue eyes became a deeper blue when he said to the jeweler, "And please let me have that set of cuff links— there—those—yes, they will look fine on my best man."

The pink, printed paper was in his hand, and Carl and Ellen read it over together as they walked down the corridor toward the Judge's chambers. Dr. Osgood walked, discreetly, to one side. Out of the corner of her eye, Ellen saw him push up his coatsleeve to take another look at a handsome cuff button. Dear, dear Carl.

"'Marriage may be celebrated, in the County of Cook— between Mr. Carl M. Christianson and Miss Ellen Anderson—' signed by Henry Wulff, the County Clerk," Carl read aloud. "There is where it gets filled out by the marrying person," he explained, pointing to the lower half of the license.

"Marrying Parson, it should be," said Ellen to herself. It was almost too bad that Dr. Osgood was here, or she would have had conversation enough with Carl to persuade him it should be parson, and not person. She could have done it, if she'd had a little time. But she had pride; she would not let Doctor John see her disappointment in this. She pinched her cheeks to give them color and bit her lips to make them red.

Justice of the Peace John C. Murphy stood, and they stood before him, with Dr. Osgood as witness:

"I now pronounce you man and wife."

"Congratulations!" the best man shook Carl's hand and turned to Ellen, "Well, my dear, there was no 'obey' in that one! Lucky girl!"

The judge smiled, "Few women now, in this day and age, take that vow 'to obey' without mental reservation, so why include it?"

"How is that?" Carl asked.

"Several things have contributed to this, the constant progress of higher education, the enormous increase in the number of women who are able to earn their own incomes—"

He turned to Carl, "Do you read *Harper's?* I read not long ago where Colonel Higginson was saying that either of these experiences expands the wings of a feminine nature, and a return to the chrysalis is thenceforth impossible. A man who takes a woman to wife, today, must do so knowing that it is out of the question to keep her in that prostrate attitude she occupied in bygone days. And soon, you mark me, she will have the vote!"

He shook Carl's hand, "Good luck to you. And to you, Mrs. Christianson."

Mrs. Christianson! Ellen paled. She was no longer Elin Nilsson, nor Ellen Anderson, but Mrs. Carl Christianson. She looked hard at the wide flat plain gold band on her finger. Did her heart jump inches, inside of her? Up to this moment she had not realized the seriousness of this step she was taking, not truly. She would have to go home with Carl—to his room—or he would come to hers!

She knelt and placed her head on her folded hands against the judge's chair seat. Silently she pleaded, "Dear Heavenly Father, help me, help me! I am afraid."

Solemnly Judge Murphy handed her a scroll and as she read, she brightened. There were their names, Carl's and hers, "United in Holy Matrimony *According to the Ordinance of God* and the Laws of the State of Illinois, on the twenty-fifth day of July in the year of Our Lord—"

"*According to the Ordinance of God.* Thank you, Judge Murphy, thank you," she choked, as tears rolled down her cheeks.

It was His sacrament: she had been married in His sight; He would understand, as in the little room she would walk, trembling, toward her husband—wearing the crown—

Carl took her in his arms, "My wife," he whispered.

"Will you come with us?" Dr. Osgood urged the judge, "for dinner?"

"No, thank you. I shall have several more couples to marry before you have come to your dessert." He smiled.

At that rate, Carl decided, it was no wonder they had named him "The Marrying Judge."

The Boston Oyster House was where they should go for a proper wedding supper, and Dr. Osgood would be the host; but on the way, of course, they must stop at the tintype-galleries so they would have pictures to keep for always, of how happy they looked on their wedding day.

A proper wedding supper it was, and with much reminiscing. Did Ellen remember Mr. Cropsey and his ten dollars? They must tell Carl of it.

"So now I see why you pronounce mistake, *mis'*take!" he laughed.

Oh, they could laugh now at the many trials in the learning of a new language!

"Do you recall," asked the doctor, "how I stood, hesitating, fearing the work was too hard for you, and you so little?"

"You could not know how glad I was when you said I would do."

"The work was too hard," the doctor spoke seriously, "but oh, how happily it all worked out for me."

"And for me," Ellen added.

He thanked her with his smile, and continued, "You were never like the man from Paris, Ellen, who was learning English from a book."

"Tell Carl." She laughed, and speared a blue point from its half-shell.

"The Parisian said, 'In small time I can learn so many English as I think I will come at the America and to go on the scaffold to lecture.'"

Carl smiled at Dr. Osgood's tale. He was almost beginning to like the man.

"And do you remember the long red radishes?"

Ellen blushed. "Well, I had never seen carrots like those in Sweden; but this was a new country, and it was to be expected that carrots could be different."

"How many hours did you boil them?"

"Oh, three or four, anyway, and when they didn't get tender I asked Sara, and she told me—"

"Sara would have loved to be with you, Ellen, on your wedding day. And you know that Faith would, too." They sat in silence for a spell, then "I must go, Ellen." He clicked open the face of a large gold watch that hung at the end of a heavy gold chain looped from vest pocket to vest pocket through a buttonhole, "Just time to catch my train."

From the window of a New York Central train he waved to them, and was gone.

"I shall miss him," Ellen said, and Carl saw that her eyes were filled with tears. He could not trust himself to speak. She had said the man had been like a father to her, but he wasn't too much older than she was herself.

Silent, they rode the trolley. This was a great moment in their lives, in her life, and Ellen could not speak. She could understand Carl's silence; she was shy, and so must he be. After this first evening together they would understand each other better. She would understand him.

She sat with her hands folded in her lap. The light from the swinging kerosene oil lamp in the ceiling behind her made the shadow of the flowers on her hat dance on the dashboard in front of her. She watched, fascinated, at the nimbleness of the driver, and leaned far forward to see how he guided the horses so one of their hooves would hit an electric switch, to run the car up to a curb to pick up a passenger.

She and Carl; they were wife and husband.

Where would they go? To his room, or to hers? Hers, of course, because her nightclothes were there, and men always slept in their underwear anyway.

And Carl sat. The bulky hinds of the horses rose and fell in front of him. Like whirling snow, his mind saw the events of the last two days—Ellen's gaiety in the company of Dr. Osgood— and he felt again the hitting, stinging, biting sleet of jealousy.

Mrs. Binney was in the hall, "Before ye go up I'd like a view of the certificate."

Carl thrust it before her eyes. She read, and kissed Ellen, and cried, and wailed, "Gawd have mercy on yer soul, child!" and spreading her hands out wide, "I always do this at weddin's."

He left Ellen at the door of her room. "I'll walk around the block, while you—get—ready."

He could not go in with her while this damnable doubt crowded him; it wouldn't be fair to her. Oh, God, did other men ever suffer such torment, inside, as he experienced? As if another person than himself thought thoughts, and sometimes made him act upon them? If only he could throttle that other self, that voice which spoke to him! He began a second turn around the block.

Ellen's fingers grasped the front steels of her corset at their bottoms, and slid the eye-steel forward so it would slip off over the knobs of its steel mate.

Wasn't that just like Carl? Was there any other such considerate man, as her Carl? To think that he would leave her, on this first night, to herself while she undressed and donned her nightclothes and waited her turn for the one bathroom in the house. Dear, considerate Carl.

My, but it was warm in the room. Drawing on the batiste nightgown, she could be glad it was sheer. But she could be thankful it was made full; the fullness made it show less of her. Such a pretty nightgown, made with a wide ruffle of French embroidery over the shoulders and across both back and front, to form a square yoke and epaulette-like shoulders atop the long, tight-cuffed sleeves.

She brushed her hair and let it hang over her shoulders, and set the crown on top. But it was cooler with the long hair braided, cooler, too, with the white batiste sleeves pulled up as far as the cuffs would let them go, and the five pearly buttons in yoke and collar undone.

Carl's step came close. She set the little crown on top of her braided hair, and opened the door for her husband.

Eagerly his eyes met hers; then they traveled to the crown. The joy of anticipation wilted from him and he walked into the room. Why had she put that reminder there, belittling him— who was only from peasant stock—too poor, ever to have seen a bridal crown?

His fingers fumbled in trying to remove his new stiff collar, made of that same material of which piano keys were made, "finer than the finest celluloid, whiter, with a higher polish," so the clerk at Marshall Field's had described them, with a flourish, under the light of the Edison bulbs. He had paid twenty-five cents for that collar—and fifty cents for the matching cuffs—so he should be fine-dressed on his wedding day.

And now, despite his will to erase it, the question came again, obsessing him: what had the wifeless dentist been to Ellen? It was the devil himself stood there at his elbow, sticking a pitchfork into him, egging him on, but he had to know.

Great was his effort to be calm; but calmly, evenly, he asked, "Why did you not marry Dr. Osgood when his wife died, Ellen?"

"Why, he never would have thought of such a thing!"

"Not thought of marriage?"

"Of marriage, yes," she smiled, "but not with me. I was only a servant in his home."

"Not good enough to marry, was that it?" He had been right in his first judgment of the man. His Ellen—not good enough for that damned dandy!

"Dear Carl, you are tired, but you don't have to be nasty; surely I must have told you—yes, I remember that I told you— you could not have been listening; he married Sara's sister only two months after her funeral."

Carl slumped. Ashamed, he rose and looked at the flickering gas flame, then turned it out and raised the window shade. Now he despised himself.

"Sara would have been happy, if she could have known it, here."

"Here?" He felt like a fool, but he had to say something— something.

"We all know she knows, up there, where she is," said Ellen.

"Bah," shamefacedly he said it, and in all humility he turned toward his wife. Overcome by contrition, overwhelmed by shame, repentant, he reached to remove the little crown from atop Ellen's hair. Soft, mellowed, the gold shone in the weak light coming through the window from yonder street lamp.

He did not speak as he sat beside Ellen on the bed.

She could understand: he was distraught, he was bashful, he was embarrassed. She cradled his head on her breast.

A heavy sob broke from him. Why was it that he had to be a living example of what St. Paul said, "The good that I would I do not; but the evil which I would not, that I do." How could he have thought as he had allowed himself to think?

Overcome by remorse, he whispered, "Ellen, forgive me."

She stroked his hair, "There is nothing to forgive."

Their lips met. Carl drank deep, overwhelmed by the love which flowed from Ellen's lips, overcome by the joy of a consummate union.

TWENTY

"INCOME TAX!" Carl smirked and looked over the top of the morning paper, "See, I told you they could never put it through. Why, the common people would never stand for such a thing!"

"But I remember, the first year I came over, the People's Party demanded a tax on incomes so that the rich man would pay more than the poor man, and Dr. Osgood said that was fair enough."

Carl winced at Ellen's mention of the name, "But two percent tax on incomes over four thousand dollars a year. Ridiculous! The Supreme Court knew what they were doing—you can bet your life on that—ruling that a tax on a man's income is unconstitutional."

Ellen started to speak, but stopped short. She had read about how close the decision was; five to four, and only five to four the way it went because one justice had changed his mind at the last minute. But she would not argue with Carl; not in the morning. She had seen how hot-headed he could get in the morning.

Too bad they had had to move from Mrs. Binney's; she was so generous, giving Ellen the empty flour sacks for her future home. True, they needed bleaching, but they would make all sorts of lovely things for the little flat, within their means, that she was sure one day to find. She could even sew several of the sacks together with tiny seams and after bleaching they would make excellent bedsheets.

Yes, it was best not to cross Carl in the mornings. How afraid she had been, that Sunday, that he was going to hit Mrs. Binney; fighting over such a thing as the McKinley tariff!

It was to tremble still at the thought of it, when Mrs. Binney had walked up close to Carl, "So ye think we cannot git along without a Protective Tariff, eh? Sure and ye're like the big burly loafer who, when the night gits cold, pulls the bedclothes from his little wife to wrap them about his full-blooded form, and then the next day beats Hell out of her because she has caught cold."

And Carl had sworn at her. Sworn at a woman!

"Oh, well," Ellen answered him lightly now, "four thousand dollars a year—we have nothing to worry about, either way, with $2.50 a day—when there is work, or when it does not rain."

Carl laid his paper down. "I'll be making more than four thousand a year before you can say *sju tusen, sju hundra, sjuttio sju*," he reached for her hand and pulled her toward him, "then there will always be plenty, my Ellen." Then he would buy blue ribbons for her hair, a blue silk dress—silk-satin!

She sat on his lap, "And blue shoes, Carl? Blue silk-satin slippers?"

"And stockings to match!" He danced her around the room, singing, "—and you'll look sweet, upon one seat, of a bicycle built for two!"

He had an idea for an invention. A perpetual motion machine! Yes, they were going to be rich.

Ellen did not quite understand; but it would be good, for at the rate they had been going, she would be able to say "seven thousand, seven hundred, seventy-seven" many a thousand times before they would see so many as four thousand dollars in a year! Or one thousand.

The way money went! Two dollars a week for a room, and her meals, and the substantial ones that Carl must eat because he worked so hard, took almost all the money that he brought home; yet they were not really living—in a furnished room—

Still, she could feel that they lived like kings when she gave thought to the hundreds of thousands of people who were out of work in the country. While Coxey's Army marched to Washington—and, by the way, why did Carl say he was well-named "The Lunatic," that Coxey, to suppose that a Federal Government would lend itself to such a project as the building of roads to give men work; what was wrong with that?—but while Coxey's Army marched, hungry, she and Carl could afford to see the Chicago White Stockings play that exciting game, baseball. They could go to the theatre and laugh until they leaned against each other, to see performers double dance, and break, take three sidesteps, solemnly raise a hand toward the audience while clasping the region of the heart with the other, draw in a long deep mournful sigh, "Ah-h-h," and repeat hilariously,

> *"While strolling through the park one day,*
> *In the merry month of May—"*

They could sit and hear musical glasses give forth the tune of "Marriage Bells" and in the back row of the balcony where they sat, none could see her rest her cheek against Carl's.

So warm were her cheeks when nighttime came. So warm her love for her husband.

Only a man as smart as he would know all about the gold standard, would be able to "tell his boss" the pitfalls of Mr. Bryan's plan for the coinage of silver at the ratio of sixteen parts of silver to one of gold, would go to evening school to learn the "Bases of Americanism," and learn by heart certain parts of the Constitution and the Declaration of Independence.

Oh, he was happy while studying!

One day he would be a citizen. Then, too, would she be one, through him.

"Ta, ta," Carl waved, on his way to the job.

Only a man as smart as her husband could dream up an invention such as this perpetual motion machine. They might have to give up the going to the theatre, and the weekly bag of popcorn on Saturday nights in order to buy the machinery he would need: he simply would have to draw pictures for her, it was too difficult for a woman's mind to grasp how, or in what way, under-sized bowling balls traveling along circular grooves in a big black machine could provide answer to this question of the century.

There might be things they would have to do without. But it would be worth it. Afterward—think of all they could have—think of it!

This was God working in His wondrous way; for Carl would be working on his invention on Sunday mornings, almost the only free time he had, and in turn she could feel free to leave him while she attended church services. Happily occupied, he would not then say he went to the saloon for company because she left him alone. Seeing him spend the remainder of the Sabbath drowsy, or dozing, she knew the price of going to church had been too high.

By now Carl must know how much she loved him, yet he could hurt her in this one thing. She shook her head.

But, this new interest that had sent him smiling into the day, was the answer to her plea to God, for help. Now it was her job to encourage Carl as best she knew how.

Each evening, five of them, he drew plans on paper and his eyes glowed as he spoke of the income they were going to have. Together they made lists of the things they would buy, for themselves, for their home. Of course they would build a home. There were three things every man wanted out of life, he said, to build a home, to have a son, and to write a book.

Ellen sat close beside him. This invention he worked on would provide the leisure he needed, to write; one day in the future she would hold in her hands a printed book and it would have her husband's name on it—in gold—on the front, and on the spine; and between the covers of the book she would see the words that he had written. . . .

He deserved a home to work in, a better place than this dingy furnished room. Anyway, they had to find a home—

Carl interrupted her dreaming, "A measly four thousand a year. Not for Carl Christianson! No sir-ree!"

The next day, Ellen's search rewarded her. "To Let," she saw a dusty, dirty sign leaning upside down in the basement window of a two-flat brick.

This might be it!

Down the well steps, she tried to peer in, but the windows were too grimy with soot and dust. She brushed the iron rust from her fingers and followed the outside steps to the first-floor door and pulled the bell. If she lived here, she would scrape and paint that wrought-iron rail.

"How do you do?" an old man opened the door and greeted her with expressionless voice.

"The flat—how much is the rent?"

"I am deaf."

She pointed down and made her lips say, plainly, "How much?"

"Six dollars a month—" and as an afterthought, "as it is. There is nobody here to clean it, so take it or leave it, as it is, but bring the key back right away."

She tried to tell him, with her hands and eyes, that she would return later. He hung the key back on its nail inside the door, "As you will," he said in a monotone.

Six dollars! They could afford six dollars!

"Please, Carl, please, please, come and just look at it?" she begged when evening came.

Reluctantly he humored her, and drew himself from his invention.

They found one large musty-smelling basement room, with dirty—although plastered—walls; hinged inside shutters of oak clung crazily to the only two windows, there at the front. More screws were out, than in, the hinges. By the unsteady light of the candle the elderly gentleman carried, they saw that the floor was of large flat stones laid into mud. To the rear, under the upstairs kitchens, was a small room with a soapstone laundry tub and beside it, a laundry stove with a little snub-nosed iron sitting on its rusted top. From this room led a door, and beyond was a cement areaway. Off of this, was a water closet. For use of all the tenants, nevertheless it had no lock; privacy could be the users' by hooking the large bent iron wire into a knothole in the wood, which served as an eye.

"Quite modern," Ellen said, "with water closet," and glanced up at the sweating oak flush box, reached into the little square cubbyhole and gave a tug to pull the string to settle the ball and stop the waste of water.

"Nobody uses it much," said the old man in the flat tone of one to whom no sound has come in many a year, "only once a day, or so, to empty the slops in."

Carl locked the basement door after them, and deposited the key into the landlord's palm. With much mock ceremony he folded the wrinkled fingers over it and patted them down, saying in pantomime a final "no."

"But I could fix it up," Ellen wheedled, and linked her arm in her husband's, skipping to make up for her short steps against his stride.

"That is no fit place for you," he pacified her, or attempted to, "it's like a dungeon, and it's filthy!"

"It would do so long—"

They walked, and he pictured Ellen in his mind as mistress of Norden. True enough, the home was small, but the big room was big, and oh, so clean. There were the acres of land to furnish room and air to breathe; and he thought of that basement flat. Stuff his wife into such a dirty little hole? Not him.

"You, my Ellen, shall never need to call such a place home."

As soon as his machine was finished, then should she sweep

the porch on a fine white house, with curls and laces of wood hanging low from the porch eaves between each rounded post— a big front porch across the front of the whole house, and extending the length of one side—and at the corner it would round around a rounded window bay, and in the bay the plate glass windows would be curved!

"But, only six dollars—" she pouted, and she saw him deflate as though she had pricked him with a pin and he was a balloon. But, it was imperative that she finish, "We could afford that now, so long, until, and we could—"

"For God's sake, Ellen," his voice raised, "and then you wonder why a man takes a drink—nagging—nagging—all the time!"

She bit her lip. "I know that you will give me all of this you speak of, Carl—in time—but it is now that—"

Again his chest swelled, "Give me six months, Ellen; or at best, a year."

She clung to his coat-sleeve. "But Carl, we cannot wait so long. It is now that we have to find a place to live."

"Live! Live! What's the matter with the place where we are living?" he almost shouted at her.

"We have to move."

"Move? *Hva' say-er du?* I've paid my rent!"

He was angry. Too bad to have to tell him thus, but, "Mrs. Lonergin came to our room this morning, Carl—"

"Well, I'll talk to her." He hurried his step.

"No, Carl, wait." She tugged at his sleeve, "She asked me," oh, this was hard, and Ellen hung her head, "She asked me—she said—was I 'going to have a you-know.'"

"A you-know? What in Hell is that?"

"You would not expect her to say it right out, Carl. But she meant, was I going to have a baby." Ellen looked down, "Because I vomit in the mornings."

"Ellen. Ellen!" He grabbed her shoulders. "You're not, are you? On the square, now, Ellen?"

"Yes, Carl. And she said of course we could not stay there, with all of her men boarders, and me in that condition."

"Ellen—Ellen." Ellen would be in that condition. He kept on saying her name. The news had stunned him.

But the evening brought a certain peace to Ellen. The heavy dread she had known in carrying the burden of her knowledge alone, was gone now that her husband shared that knowledge with her. She slept in the crook of his arm.

He lay awake. He was going to be a father. What had these few words of Ellen's done to him? Since he had been old enough to think, he had known for truth that such words could mean only a trap for a man; look at his father, with a look on life so warped that he had fallen to be little better than a thief, for it was stealing—nothing less, nothing more—to sell that which belonged to another.

A life no better than his father's, that was what lay ahead of a man caught in the mesh of fatherhood: so had he been sure the truth was.

Now he was to be a father. And somehow it was different now. Somehow it made a man feel—like—like—a man!

But Ellen would be *in that condition*. He would have to look at her for days, for weeks, for months, being as his mother had been!

No, by God, it couldn't be true. But it was. Ellen had told him.

Not by sitting sewing on a little garment, as any other woman would have done, to tell her husband. She had to find a flat—belittling him because she was the one who had to find it, in that way showing he was not the provider he should be—oh, he saw it! Belittling him. She, whose grandfather was a Riksdagsman! Who can help what he is born? He could not help he came from peasant stock. It wasn't his fault that he had been cursed with a father who had made the ground crumble under the feet of his ambitions! Looking on Ellen as she would be, it would bring back to mind all the torment, the pain of loss, the insecurity come with the thoughts of a boy from Värmland. *He couldn't stand it*. Ellen being as his mother had been—her little body, big—

Big with child, because of him.

Because of him!

The grandeur of it smote him between the eyes: from him, and from Ellen, would come another life!

From him!

He had never believed in miracles. But here was a miracle. Ellen would bring forth a life, and it would be his—his own—something that even a father could not sell!

Carl put both arms around his wife and drew her near to him.

Ah, it was good, this sharing the bed with Ellen. Dear little soul. In the morning, he would let her sleep: she would need all the rest she could get.

He smiled. He, who had thought to mate with freedom, had taken a woman and now she was with child. His child.

Who wanted freedom, anyway? What was freedom but loneliness? He drew Ellen closer to him, and close, they slept.

It was a sin, but almost she could wish that Carl had stopped at Mister Hinky-Kink Kenna's saloon, or Shannon's, last night. Maybe then he wouldn't have been cross with her and said she nagged. Maybe then he would not have slid out of bed this morning, leaving her to sleep, not waiting to have her breakfast with him.

Ellen glanced at the clock. Carl's work day was long since over, and he had not come home.

Six o'clock was the time he quit. It had been only a few minutes past six when the storm broke; she shuddered at remembering the thunder crashes and lightning bolts come within instants of each other, hurting her eardrums, ripping the sky. It was natural enough that Carl should seek refuge from the storm; but now her sin of wishing could well torment her, for where should he find shelter except in the saloon?

She pressed her face close to the windowpane. Disconsolate, the rain flowed like a river on the pane. Filled, too, were Ellen's eyes, with water, and the double screen did not allow her sight of the street.

Night of nightmares; Ellen spent the night alone.

Now she looked out of the window. The storm was done. Mother Nature must have raised her hands from the washtub and flicked her fingers of the suds, for over all the blue sky were little wisps of sudsy clouds. But up the street and down, no sight of Carl.

She turned, to pace the floor. It was morning, and Carl's side of the bed had not been slept in.

Did all men act so, at their wives' pronouncements of approaching motherhood? Awkward, and gruff sometimes, as he was, he must love her. Would he have come home the other night carrying a bottle of Peruna for her if he did not love her?

"Take some of this for that cough of yours," he did not know the fancy way to present what he brought, but he brought it. That was proof.

He was proud of her, too, or he would not have taken her to the dancing party at the North Side Turner Hall; even if he had gotten angry after, and declared they should never go again! But it was not her fault that a gentleman had come up to her and with his clean white handkerchief over his finger, rubbed it on her cheek to see if she wore paint. A walking advertisement for *Gloria Water*, and he had said she was, with such a soft and clear "peaches and cream complexion."

But now Carl had not come home all night. He was angry with her because she was going to have a baby....

He would get over it, though, as soon as he got accustomed to the idea. It must be a pretty big responsibility on a man, to know he would have a growing family to support. But she would help him; she would rent the basement flat and tell him about it afterward. There were still a few dollars left of her savings, even a few from Algot's insurance. The flat was not so far from Rose Hill but that she could take good care of Algot's grave, and keep the weeds away.

She studied the tintypes taken on her wedding day. Carl was handsome all right, her husband, half-reclining, half-sitting on the heavy chair carved with a woman's face below the arm and long flowing hair forming the leg. Casually, the two lower buttons of his tight-fitting suit coat were out of their buttonholes, so his fancy vest would show. The trousers, so neat, as if the cloth of them was glued on to his skin; hardly a wrinkle, even as he sat. And the big black cigar held between the first two fingers of his right hand—yes— he was dressed fit to kill, with his derby hat, just the right size, so the small rolled sides no more than sat flush with his ears.

That little way he had of brushing around the crown with his coat-sleeve before he set the derby on his head, brushing off every speck of dust—one of the little ways he had, that she loved.

Where was he? Sadly she looked at his side of the bed, at the table where his drawings were, of his invention, at the little compass made from a narrow strip of cardboard with a pin holding it to the table, and the little holes darkened from the lead pencil after he had made circles of varying size.

No more tears came, the pillow had taken all there were during the night.

If she had it to do over again, she would have smiled on her tintype, standing there so serious, her black silk-gloved hand pushing open a rustic gate. But it was a fine dress she wore, that one of Sara's, the one that was her Sunday-go-to-church dress in New York City. And it had been her wedding dress. Soft green silk-satin with plain skirt falling to the floor from below the double-breasted bodice trimmed with bias folds of self-material, it was nicely made; a pretty touch, the bias piece turned and twisted so it looked like a necklace at the high collar, below the ruching.

There was her wedding bouquet, only a little bunch of milliners' flowers, tucked into the bodice where it crossed over, but sweet; and the hat, the lovely hat of black milan straw, up in front and back and drooping at the sides, with lilies-of-the-valley standing high.

How had the tintype artist managed to show that flush on her cheeks, pink, against the drab light and dark of the rest of the picture?

Soon the pretty green silk-satin bodice would be too tight.

Oh, the misery of having to lean over the chamber to rid her rebelling stomach of the greenish slime. Oh, the gnawing grief of having Carl go from her at such a time! Her chin raised. It just wasn't fair. Maybe Doctor John had been right; maybe she really didn't know her husband after all, if he would do a thing like this.

So soon after their marriage, he could stay away from her, and all night! "Oh," she flirted her head and looked proudly into the mirror. "Oh, no—not with a woman! I know, I *know!*" But that the saloon might come first—ahead of her—perhaps. Where else could he be?

And he blamed her for nagging! After this he should learn what it meant to be nagged at! She stamped her foot. She, Ellen Christianson, would teach him!

"Mrs. Christianson, they've brought your husband home," the landlady poked her nose into the doorway and looked around inquisitively, but spoke in a manner that said, "I told you so."

"I'll be right down," Ellen said shortly.

Twice she adjusted her wire bustle and fumbled the tie-strings, so that it fell to the floor. Her shaky fingers scarce could fit the hooks into the eyes, of her skirt, and two of the buttons on the back of her shirtwaist were undone still as she started down the stairs.

She stopped, clinging to the rail. There Carl sat, in the parlor, near the hall door, sat slumped in a chair. His clothes looked wet, his hair fell bedraggled over his forehead, and his head hung forward. There must be someone else in the room, for he looked up and smiled; then his lids and head dropped again.

So this was what manner of man she had for a husband. And she in the family way. While she sat home and waited and worried, while she bade good-morning to the sun by retching, he had sat in some saloon! Here she could sit—in a furnished room—alone—what did he care for her?

"He will be all right," she heard a man's voice say to the landlady.

"Oh, yes, he'll be all right," Ellen almost spoke aloud, "but what about me?"

With firm step, angrily, she descended to meet this man who had brought her husband home. Was he Carl's tempter?

"I am Einar Swanson, Carl's boss," the man came toward her with both arms outstretched. "We are all mighty proud of your husband."

"Proud of him?" Ellen said, and disgust was heavy in her voice, "Like this?" She swept her hand toward him, and saw his face turn gray.

"The fire—didn't you hear about the fire? By gollies, as soon as Carl comes back to work, I'm making him a straw-boss!"

They helped him up the stairs and put him on the bed. Once he smiled sleepily at Ellen and spoke incoherently. The only word she got was "baby."

Then Einar Swanson told: on the way home from work last night the lightning struck, just as they passed the milk-bottling plant, and they stopped to help fight the fire.

Carl had been the one to rush in and save the papers and the files; Carl had been the one to cast a rope over the chimney and climb it, hand over hand, to reach the screaming figure of a man standing on the roof at the edge of the cornice, and grab him and lower the two of them to safety; Carl it had been who forced the crowd back, to allow the firemen room to play their hoses on the burning building, he who kept order in the crowd.

All night, he worked.

He was near to exhaustion when they heard the cry, "Look! That piece of burning timber—look—it shot right up into the sky!"

On to the wooden roof of a little cottage the burning timber fell. How could a rain-soaked cottage take a flame? The crowd ran, and in its lead was Carl.

"'My baby! Upstairs—in the front—the attic bedroom—my baby!' a woman screamed; a husband held his wife and kept her from running into the burning building.

"'A baby.' Carl patted her arm as he brushed past, 'I'll save your baby.'

"The roof fell, but he brought out the child." It seemed to tire the boss to think of it; he ran his hand over his forehead, over his hair, "But that wasn't all. Before we knew what he was doing, he had dashed in again, and out, and in his arms he had this," Einar Swanson's voice quivered, "this cat."

But Ellen's voice was steady. "I will take care of Carl. Your straw-boss will be all right. Tack! Adieu."

It was no cat. It was a tiny kitten, a calico kitten colored orange, black, and white. Ellen nestled it in her shawl on the chair seat.

She laid her body alongside her sleeping husband on the bed; she pressed close to him. His clothing was wet, as was his leather belt so that it made a sushing sound as she pressed herself against him.

She would fix him nice and dry, and get the doctor, just to make sure.

Rising, she stepped toward the bureau and leaned far over across its top, standing on toe-tips, pressing her nose against the looking-glass. She placed her thoughts of now against those thoughts of doubt that she had had, and through clenched teeth she muttered, "Ellen Benedikta Sibylla Nilsson Anderson Christianson, *I hate you!*"

TWENTY ONE

TODAY CARL would be surprised, on the job, when Einar Swanson made him a straw-boss! Ellen opened her little trunk and from a box in the false bottom counted out six dollars, and walked from the furnished room.

Wouldn't Carl be surprised if he could see and hear her now?

"I should like to have a receipt." She smiled at the old man, as he took down the dirty "To Let" sign.

He watched her lips. "No, no rats; we have never had any rats," he answered in that colorless, flat tone, but there was a smile in his eyes.

She should be sharing this pleasure with her husband, the joy of buying and owning a tin pail for scrubbing, the fun of bargaining with the rags-and-old-iron man for bits of mirror.

Was this deceit she practiced, this keeping the knowledge of a little store of money from Carl? No. There would be a doctor's bill to pay. Not deceit. Necessity.

Was it deceit, this shying from the truth when he inquired why she should look tired when evening came? "What have you done today?" he would ask.

"*Arbeta i dag,*" she would smile, and bring her hand back to train the wilful scolding-locks upward from her neck.

Then he would chide her and forget to question further. They were in America now. To speak Swedish was not right at all; let her instead say, "I have worked today."

Laughing, she would not promise. Teasing, she would hurry him off to be on time to his night school class. Afterward she would sit and sew on her curtains, hemming the edges, sewing ivory rings to the tops, or when he was at home, take tiny precious stitches on the little wrapper, cut from her wool flannel underskirt.

209

"Your hands are rough," one night he said. "In this fall weather you need something to put on them." Would he have brought a bottle of glycerine and rose water for her hands if he did not love her? No. No, and when their little home was ready, he would be glad.

Sniffing of her hands after applying the lotion he had brought, she was sure Carl loved her. What else mattered? All men hurt their loved ones at times; if there was not love, there could not be the hurt, for no one was injured deeply by a stranger.

She would try no more to tell him of the little flat; he should never again say that she nagged him, and tear from the room at mention of the place.

Sorry after, he always made it up to her, and would fondle her and carry her, the whole ninety pounds of her, into their room; and when he held her close she knew that the rapture of those moments more than compensated for the lack of softness on this bed of life, that she had made.

Enfolding her husband, she knew contentment—brief, momentary, but real.

She could arise then, more loving, more forgiving, than before.

How could this be? It was.

She was a woman: she should be ashamed. But such was not the truth. Of his little faults, she would not complain, for his was the knowledge of the way to keep her satisfied, knowing so well how to bring fulfilment after desire.

She loved him.

Surely her love would find the way to bring contentment to her husband and bring him, happy, home to her—and bring him to the church. . . .

How much he had to miss by not partaking of the pleasure of painting the little flat, and running at the call of "Rags-o-li-on" to the alley, to paw through the day's accumulation on Mr. Ginsberg's wagon, to see if there was something she could use, with the growing calico colored kitten running at her heels. Like finding a diamond in a trash can, was the sight one day of ten old outside window shutters!

"Oh, Mr. Ginsberg, how much? How much for all of them?"

"Vat vould you vant vid all of them? How many vindows you got?"

"Only two windows, but—"

"Say—you—you vouldn't be buying my stuff for resale, yet?" He looked her up and down, "At higher prices?"

"No—no—Mr. Ginsberg."

The big question of how to separate the basement room into two, so she could have both parlor and bedroom, would be resolved, if she could buy these shutters!

Six and a half feet tall, at least—and—she measured them with her eyes, "and about fifteen inches wide. Painted a bright clear yellow, Mr. Ginsberg, they will be heavenly!"

"Cheap, then, I give them to you cheap."

Put together with double-swinging hinges, set like an art screen such as her grandfather had had—painted yellow—oh, what a lovely, lovely inspiration for this room.

"Thank you, Mr. Ginsberg. And if you find a lamp? I need a lamp."

"I vill find. For you. Yes, it is good to talk to you. I get— whsst—" he snapped his fingers, "cheerful for the whole day." He stepped close to her, and in confidential tone, said, "I see you, already, talking to Mrs. Shaughnessy."

"Mrs. Shaughnessy?"

"The vun they call Crazy Gertie."

"Oh, yes, and I like her," Ellen replied. The poor soul, living in the tarpaper shanty, a hermit woman, picking her living from the garbage can back of Hulseberg's grocery store, picking her warmth from the stray coals alongside the railroad tracks.

Ellen saw tears in Mr. Ginsberg's eyes, "I vas her only friend, until you came."

People did not mean to be cruel, he was sure, they just did not know. The day after her wedding night her husband had been run over by the train. They picked him up in forty-nine pieces and carried the pieces to her in a bushel basket. They said he was drunk.

"I saw her agony ven she said, 'Edward Shaughnessy, drunk on the day after his wedding! Never!' She has not been quite herself since; a little confused, she is." He shook his head, sadly, "But you should see the altar she has built there in her shed. I have seen her, in the early mornings: she thinks she is a priest, and vid an old lace curtain over her shoulders, says the Mass."

Ellen listened closely. It was like going to church to listen to him.

"She knows the litany," he continued. "I am a Jew, but I have knelt before that altar of love that she has built. Where there is not love, there is nothing. But where there is love, miracles happen, and she has found peace." He looked in the direction of the shed, "She has never crossed the railroad tracks since; I think she could not cross the tracks for fear in some strange way they vould draw her to them, and she vould lie powerless before the oncoming train. Then, who vould say the Mass for Edward?" His eyes looked deep for answer, but Ellen stood, only listening.

"Crazy?" he went on, "Sometimes she does not say so vell vat her poor mind figures, but she is no ignoramus. Have you noticed her fine speech? And you, Mrs. Christianson, you talk good. Say, how long you been here?"

"In Chicago? Only since July."

"In this country?"

"Five years, almost."

"Thirty years I'm here." He nodded. "I like it, to hear you talk. You know, some people they are here years and years, yet, and they still talk vid de eccent!"

Ellen could smile. Dear old Mr. Ginsberg. What would poor Mrs. Shaughnessy do without him? What would she, herself, do without him? When their little home was ready, she and Carl would invite him for dinner, so he could see what use she had made of the things she had bought from his wagon.

It should be her husband, and not the old man upstairs, who followed with amazement the restoration of the musty basement; but she was afraid to try again to tell Carl.

How would she get him to come with her, now that it was almost ready? It would spoil it all if he came under protest, or heavy with anger, or even if she had to lead him there genial, but half full.

Ellen sang as she worked,

> *"You'll be sorry when you see me*
> *Sliding down my cellar door—"*

The month was up. Another six dollars must come from the little box.

"Let me see your last month's receipt," the landlord, old Mr. Ferguson, said.

"Here—"

He changed the date to a month ahead. It was so little to do for Mrs. Christianson, who had changed the whole appearance of his old house.

"Mr. Ferguson! How can I thank you? You'll see—I will paint the iron railing, too—and keep the front sidewalk swept—" on, on she went; he hearing not, but smiling.

And so came one Sunday morning in October.

"I should learn never to worry," Ellen said to herself, "the things I fret most about never seem to happen. God goes all the way, to help."

The door of their room closed behind Mrs. Lonergin. Carl sat on the bed, his knees spread apart with his hands hanging limp between them, elbows resting on the knees. He stared at the floor.

"She certainly doesn't give much notice," he complained.

Ellen recalled her telling him, more than a month ago, of the landlady's first notice; but she said nothing.

"Maybe down on Roscoe Street we can find a rooming house." He stood. "We might as well go right now, and look."

"Two dollars a week for one, not for two people," one proprietor said.

"What do you expect? There's twice as much water used by two, as by one—and two towels," spoke another.

"No vacant rooms for couples, only for men."

Deftly Ellen guided Carl, and they came to the basement flat.

"Different-looking, isn't it?" She beamed with pride, and held the key out to him.

"Do you mean—? Ellen, you didn't—not after I—?" But his quick anger faded fast, and sheepishly he followed her. He opened the door and there he saw sunshine reflected from the zig-zag screen of yellow shutters. The stones in the floor were scrubbed to whiteness: little white curtains hung at the windows, a pair at each lower sash drawn together, a pair at each upper sash open, to let the sunshine in.

"Such were the curtains in the little café *på Storgatan i Falkenberg*," she said happily.

He saw the outline of the Bennett Milling Company's stamp, still visible on each of the curtains. The inside shutters no longer hung crazily, and they too were yellow.

How she must have worked!

The walls were painted white, and there was a border of

autumn leaves glued near the ceiling. He looked close—real oak leaves, still showing grayish-green and deep red, or dark deep red with yellow near the veins—real maple leaves in all the richness only the golden maple knows.

"They are leaves I pressed in my Bible."

God! How she must have worked.

He peered around the screen. An iron bedstead stood white, with its counterpane and pillow shams to match. The Milling Company was represented here, again. He walked into the kitchen, for the little basement room at the back was now a kitchen.

He could have sworn there was a window there, where none had been before, except that the four panes of glass gave again the sight of rooms he had just passed through, and sent their own sunshine back to the yellow shutters. The walls were yellow, here, and she had painted a border of blue around the squares of mirror, and between them, so it should look like a window sash.

"Blue and yellow—Swedish colors, Carl."

"But we are in America now, Ellen," he did not scold her, but picked up the hem of one of the kitchen curtains, "Lots of stitches; no wonder you were tired when night came, but why didn't you tell me?"

"You would not let me, Carl." She struck a match and lit the gas, and swung the bracketed fixture so the flame repeated itself in the window of mirrors, to give twice the light. Carl marveled to himself; no trace of the dungeon, as he remembered it, remained. It was so clean. The laundry tub was clean. The little stove no more showed red with rust; polish had made it black, like new. It stood proudly, its tall black legs pushing the plain tin mat to the floor of mud and stone. Part of the stovepipe, where it flattened and joined the stove, was shiny new; the rest was new with stovepipe paint.

A coal scuttle stood to one side, and hard coals shone in the gaslight. There was a poker, too, and the silvery-colored wound wire handle matched the one of the lid-lifter. The little snub-nosed iron sat ready to take its share of heat, and Carl bent close to see "Geneva" molded into its handle.

"My God, Ellen, how you must have worked."

He took her in his arms and she rested there, happy. No need to call attention to their wedding present George and Martha Washington standing in their china finery on the makeshift mantle, in the parlor, a board set on two iron brackets and draped with a piece of green silk-satin, well-spared from the old-fashioned wide sleeves of her wedding dress, and edged with a dainty ball fringe.

Carl was satisfied; that was all that mattered. He was satisfied, and he was willing now to come to the basement flat.

"Let us go and get our trunks, Carl, and bring them here—bring them to our home."

He took her hand and they walked in the near-stillness of autumn—only the last leaves falling—only the sparrows scolding.

The Queen Anne's lace stood tall and stiff in the vacant lots—their umbels drawn tight together into a top-knot, like Ellen's hair, with some small pedicels, too short to reach the top, frilling against the stems like Ellen's scolding locks hugging her neck—stood tall and straight to meet the winter, as Ellen now could stand. She had a home for her baby.

TWENTY TWO

JUNE. SUMMER.

Flies followed the fishman's wagon down the street, or hovered buzzing expectantly around the spring scale swinging from the tailboard. Carl brushed one explorer from his nosebridge, and it flew back to the wagon to be on hand at the next slitting of a fish.

"Hold up! Maw's gettin' her hat on!" a boy yelled out of a second-story window. The driver pulled the reins and the trolley stopped to wait.

A little dog lifted its leg against the striped barber pole. White clouds chased each other across the sky.

None of them could guess about the big thing that was going to happen to him! Carl walked past the barber shop; through the window he saw the row of razors hanging like inverted V's over their hooks. He rubbed his chin with thumb and forefinger, turned, and entered the shop.

He guessed he deserved this luxury, a shave by the best barber in Chicago; wasn't he going to be a father? The boys on the job had all shaken hands with him, had made him realize actually how important it made a man to be as he was now.

The doctor had come twice to Ellen, and had gone for Mrs. Drekman. No better practical nurse in the country than Mrs. Drekman, for the confinement case, according to Dr. Cuppwyn.

"Any time, now," he had said.

Any time! Carl felt a chill come over him. He had done pretty well by Ellen, though, during these past months; had put shelves into the big wooden dry-goods box so it made a passable bureau with flower-printed goods shirred around it like a skirt. He had set up that Franklin stove in the parlor; even played dinner host to the junk dealer and his wife. Strange that Mr. Ginsberg should have married a Swedish woman.

217

On the barber-shop wall the big-faced clock set in an oak octagon ticked away the minutes; not like the olden clocks at home in Sweden, with only one hand.

Carl half shut his eyes. Ah, it would be fine when he was rich and could buy Ellen a sealskin coat. He should have been in a position to do it long before now, but it was certainly funny how everybody and his brother had taken up the idea of working out a perpetual motion machine; no use spending any more time on that. No, sir, this new ventilator was going to be the thing!

Now that he had its construction worked out definitely in his mind and was ready to make a model so he could get a patent, he would stop on the way home and get an empty cigar box; no, he would ask for two. Then he could cut the hole in either end of one, and from the other saw out the sections for the interior, sections as wide as the box but shorter so that when attached alternately to the top and to the bottom, about a half an inch apart, they would compel the air which entered the hole in the end of the box, to go up and then down, then up, then down, and so on until it came out the other end. No drafts! Burglar-proof! Ideal for bank buildings. He had better buy some little fine nails, too, for the making of the model—and some glue—

"You're next!"

Carl seated himself on the green plush chair, rested his head on the small square pillow; with the exaggerated moves of a vaudeville actor he made use of the plush armrests, and lifted his feet as the porter slid an upholstered leg rest under his shoes. This was the sort of thing he could do every week, when he got rich.

"Fine day, Mr—?" the barber said, and shook the hair from a large white cover cloth.

"Christianson." Carl settled himself in the chair.

"Shave? Haircut? Face massage?" Carl felt himself being lowered to a horizontal position.

"Yes. You might as well give me the whole shootin' match. Today is a big day for me."

"So?"

"Before the day is over I expect to be a father."

"Congratulations!" The barber pushed back the white cover and shook his hand. Four others, barber and customers, shook his hand. This becoming a father did something for a man, all right!

Carl's chest swelled. "Shoe shine, too," he said.

"Boy—over here!" the barber called, and then to Carl, "You are holding up pretty well," he grinned, "and what are you going to name him?"

"Tony."

"Tony! And you said your name was Christianson?" the second barber laughed. "Why, Tony is a wop name!"

Carl stiffened. His barber rubbed lather on his upper lip with a delicate touch of the little finger, "He ought to know," he offered, "his own name is Tony."

"And what if Tony turns out to be a girl?" the second barber teased. "Will it be Antonia then?"

No. But it was no business of theirs.

"Come in again, Mr. Christianson."

Carl dug into his pocket. A quarter should be a proper tip; he would not want to look small, and after all, this was a high-class barber shop.

The barber smiled, and the porter swished a yard-long whiskbroom over his clothes, and held out a hand.

Might as well go all the way; Carl dropped a dime into that hand. It wasn't every day a man became a father.

It was payday. His envelope was still in his pocket, but he had better go straight home. Maybe they would know by now, was it Tony, or—

"My God! What if it should be both!" Ellen had been so big, almost too big for it to be only one child; and it was not because she had eaten so much, either. She had hardly been eating anything, except soup, as the doctor had said for her to do; "Eat plenty of soup, and when you get tired of soup, change from soup to soup."

Carl hurried. What if there should be two!

The smell of carbolic acid greeted him, and the words of the doctor, "It is taking longer than I anticipated. She is having a hard time—a hard time. She's such a little woman."

Carl sat in the tall-backed cherry rocker that Ellen had varnished so it looked like new and given him for his birthday—fidgety—trying not to hear the smothered groans, the painful breathing, the hacking cough from her catarrh.

"She is brave, but I don't know," Dr. Cuppwyn came and laid his hand on Carl's shoulder. "If she comes through this, though, you had better take her to a throat specialist and see about that cough."

If she comes through! What was he talking about, if she

comes through! She had to come through. His Ellen—

On second thought, he should not have spent all that money at the barber shop; she had so little to do with. Just the thirty-five cents he had tipped them there would have bought a pork roast for Sunday dinner, and there would have been some left over for his lunch sandwiches.

But, was it a fault to be generous? No; generosity he would never concede to be a fault in any man.

Still—last winter—God knew he always worked and worked hard whenever there was work to be had—but last winter when scarcely a single man in the building trades could find a job, Ellen had done housecleaning for the neighbors and worked all day for little more than thirty-five cents, so they should have food and not go into debt. That was the thing she feared most, going into debt; more than she feared life—or death—or hunger.

He was sorry now he had lied to her when she asked him, "You are not running up a bill at the saloon, Carl? Surely you would not do such a thing as that?"

She would not have understood, though. You couldn't expect it of a woman. Why, even the swells on the North Shore ran bills. It was much more businesslike than to pay cash for every purchase.

But, poor Ellen, when she came home exhausted, and after supper went so early to bed, and when she fell asleep, and a circle of sweat formed on the pillow around her head—he had moved away from her because the sheet too was damp from sweat.

"Poor little thing, poor little thing," he cradled his head in his hands.

"Go take a walk up and down in front," urged the doctor. "I'll call you if—"

Carl stumbled up the steps, to the sidewalk. "If? If what?" Did he mean, if she should die? She could not die!

Poor little Ellen. What could he buy her to cheer her up?

When he walked from the corner dry-goods store his heart was lightened, and his pockets. She would like the pretty parasol—red taffeta with shallow ruffles over the whole of it—with a long shapely handle, hooked big enough at the end to hang over her arm.

The hitching post in front of the two-flat brick was unemployed. The rig was gone, but the doctor would return, Mrs. Drekman said.

Carl walked behind the screen, "Ellen—"

The exultation of giving birth had left a spark in Ellen's eyes; the agony of it had drawn her thin face into a mask. Her lip was cut from biting hard against the pain. On her arm lay the baby.

Only one. He looked around. Only one. But such a one! Almost as big as Ellen, in the face. And fat!

"Thirteen pounds, Dr. Cuppwyn said," Ellen whispered.

"Good Lord!"

"He said he would have to put her in the baby show," she closed her eyes.

Carl lifted the infant and sat on the bed. He stroked the baby hand, clumsily. This was the miracle. This was his own flesh and blood. His. A child of his own being—to watch as it grew—as it learned—a child of his own to play with.

He spread one baby hand on his knee, then laid one of his big hands over it, stacked the other baby hand on that and laid his second one on top.

> *"Rock af palta,*
> *Två par vante."*

"Coat of rags, two pairs of mittens," he chanted, making a miserable attempt at picking his lower hand out and laying it on top, pulling a baby hand out and placing it on top.

"Fool!" snapped the nurse. "With a newborn baby!" She snatched the infant from him, "Do you want to drop her?"

Her. A girl baby. What was it he had thought to name a girl? It was not important what he had thought. There was only one name, only one suitable for his daughter, especially his first daughter.

Sigrid.

Let Ellen choose the second name, if there was to be a second. Sigrid, the child would be, named for his mother. This Sigrid lying here, she had no hair at all, or at best only a little white fuzz, but she might grow up to be like his mother; fair, with golden braids making a halo around her face, with love shining from her eyes, for him. Oh, could he ever forget the light in his mother's eyes when she read the little stories that he wrote? So, now, would he write, to make his mother proud of him; he, who had created a child, could create works to bring that old gladness back to his mother's eyes.

Could he forget the day when she had stood and heard the cheers of the fishermen as they threw their caps into the air, showing their confidence in her way of trading with the fish merchant?

Could he forget her eyes, so full of pain, the day he left?

His mother. A sob caught in his throat. Once had his mother known this same joy that he knew now, at looking upon *him!*

Dr. Cuppwyn came back, "Have you decided on a name for your daughter, young lady?" he asked Ellen, "Or shall I wait until tomorrow?"

"Sigrid, that is her name," spoke Carl as he looked to Ellen for affirmation, and shook the doctor's hand.

"Sigrid. Yes, I like that," Ellen said softly, "it is a fine Swedish name."

"For my mother!" Carl thrust his thumbs under his suspenders and threw out his chest, "A finer woman never lived."

Ellen choked as she coughed, and drew the baby close to her. Oh, what the coming of a child could do, that it could open the heart that had locked itself with cold and icy bars. That it could so change a man! He had not ever said his mother's name, in her hearing, till now.

"A second name?" the doctor asked.

"Elisabet," Carl answered, promptly.

"Sigrid Elisabet Cecilia, so let it be," Ellen finished wearily.

"Cecilia?"

"For my mother, yes." Ellen looked at her baby, and ran the tip of her finger lightly along the downy fuzz which served as hair. It was a girl, her child; one day she would wear the little golden brudkrona.

The doctor folded the certificate and put it in his inside pocket. Chicago was very particular about the recording of births, he said, and he was one to coöperate.

"Good-night, and come for me at the slightest change."

It was hope that surged so full in Ellen's breasts. The coming of her baby, their baby, already had worked this miracle on Carl. She reached for his hand, "Tell me of your mother?"

And yes, he told.

"Write to her, Carl." Ellen's heart grew light as she saw her words make imprint on his mind, "Tell her of baby Sigrid."

He drew the little rickety table over close to her bed, and set the student lamp on its corner. "Like a winding staircase leading upward," Ellen said to herself, and her eyes followed the brass tubing, wound around the long base for the chimney, leading upward toward the glowing yellow glass shade—the golden light of hope. Such a path would her Carl follow, now that he had found the first step, upward toward the Light!

Only the nubby, pearl-handled pen with solid gold point was fine enough to write this letter to his mother. Then why did he sit there, hesitating, keeping the point from the inkwell? Why, oh why, and Ellen mopped her brow; why did he have to stop to tell again the story of its purchase at the World's Fair? Why did he have to explain again about the Columbian half-dollar? She knew it all so well.

Carl looked hard at the pen. So long a time had gone by since he had left his homeland. Things could have changed in the old home. A shudder ran through him; could he be sure that his mother still lived? She must! But, would she care to have a letter from the son who had—

Oh, yes, yes—what would it matter what that little bit of flesh in the blanket, there, would do to him? If she were away a hundred years—no less welcome would a letter be, from her.

He dipped the gold point into the ink.

"Kära mor," he wrote; and he told of Ellen and their home and how they had fixed it up fine, and of his work, and his invention, and his writing. And he told of Sigrid, her granddaughter—Sigrid, the American—born in this land of the free, born with her citizenship already accomplished! And no greater wish could he know, he wrote, than that Sigrid Elisabet Cecilia should be like her, his mor. He signed it "Your ever-loving son, Karl."

It must be mailed at once, this letter. He must go out to the mailbox.

Ellen looked at the baby, the child she had brought forth from her own body, "Oh, God, I know how her mother heart will sing Your praises—if yet she lives."

How would it be, to have a child, and to have done to one as she and Carl had done?

She curled the infant's fingers around her own, "Forgive me! Dear God, forgive me! Dear mother mine, in Heaven, forgive—"

Ellen woke to find the room filled with the pungent smell of a strong cigar. Carl sat on the bed and displayed the first book of what would grow to be Sigrid's library, *Andersen's Fairy Tales*. Ellen saw the tall-legged stork, on the spine, holding by its bill an infant slung in a checkered cloth; and cutting the front of the red bound book into twos, rose a wicked-looking witch against a sky of blue. So familiar, the pictures, as Carl turned the pages, of Great Claus and Little Claus, of the Snow Queen, and of the husband and wife of the tale, "What the Old Man Does Is Always Right."

"Yes," she read, "always it pays, when the wife sees and always asserts that her husband knows best, and that whatever he does is right."

She saw the penciled price on the inside of the back cover. Forty-five cents. Who was Ellen Christianson to quarrel with the great Hans Christian Andersen? But—for Carl to pay forty-five cents for a book for a new-born infant, when the infant had no garments except what had been cut from its mother's underclothes; not flannel for its diapers, but flour sacks.

Then, there was the red umbrella. Ellen's eyes grew soft and smiling. Yes, Hans Christian Andersen had not achieved greatness for nothing; he knew whereof he wrote.

Carl sat beside her and talked of how they must send Sigrid to college, how nothing should stand in the way of her learning: after high school they would send her to the great university in Sweden, where the sons of his mother's family always had been entitled to tuition. There should his daughter go, in place of his going. She should be a lawyer, leading the way for women in a great and honored profession. They might even send her to Upsala for post-graduate work, if she showed a bent for further study.

Soon a letter would come from his mother. Ellen would love his mother. One day Ellen should meet her, and little Sigrid, too, should know her grandmother. A child who grew up without knowing a grandparent—ah—how much it missed! In his home, there had been Morfar. Teacher. Example. Playmate.

Morfar. Carl's eyes looked far away as he stroked the cover of Andersen's book. If only Morfar could have lived. Then boyhood dreams could have been realized, would have been—

Ellen broke in, "Ask not so much as Upsala, do I, Carl. Only do I ask—"

"Stop. Don't say it. Don't nag me, Ellen. I know—you want—that I should hop on the water wagon."

She touched his arm. It wasn't what she meant to say, only that high school was all she asked for her child, she tried to tell him.

"Don't say it, Ellen. Don't make me feel that I am failing you—please—please."

"No, Carl, not that. Never that. But, as you bring it up, it is only that we have so little money for necessities."

Of course, she was right. He patted her hand. A man was a fool to waste money on whiskey; and then, as Ellen had seen the *politicianer* orating an election promise on the street corner, he stood and swore, by this new estate of fatherhood, by the mighty gods of Old Sweden, "—as the child, there, is my witness, I have taken my last drink!"

Ellen flinched at sight of Mrs. Drekman's unbelieving face. But, how good it would be, if only the source of this promise could be deeper than his lips.

Days have a way of passing. Pass, they did, but brought no answer to Carl's letter.

Bitterness welled in his heart. Why had he named his child for his mother, anyway? She had not cared enough about him to answer. Let him never, never, in any circumstance, upbraid himself for being generous. He must fight the heritage of stinginess. For it was a stinginess of soul that could keep a mother from forgiving her son. And here he had blamed his father most. Could it be, after all, that his mother's miserliness had made his father what he was, and so had been the instrument which had driven him, Carl, from his home? His father had known and told him, on occasion, how she laid away the money from the catch—against necessities, or so she said—hoarding it rather than ever to be big enough to enjoy a moment of generosity; making Mammon the god to worship, so his father had told him.

Easy to believe of a mother who would not write a letter of forgiveness to her son.

Everything was wrong. Nothing he tried worked out, not even the perpetual motion machine, that could have made him rich so that Ellen could have real cream on her oatmeal instead of thickening milk with powdered sugar, to "play" they had cream.

In aborting his youthful ambitions his father had cast a blight over him; even his writings didn't sound like anything when he read them over.

"What's the use?" He found he could not pass by the swinging door: he had put by his pride and written home, but his mother had not answered his letter.

Ellen could regret that it was true, but true it was that Mrs. Drekman knew her drinking men: Carl tore into the parlor and pointed to the new lampshade—such pretty red roses on the china globe, come that day for only ten cents from Mr. Ginsberg's wagon—set in the front window with the kerosene flame turned bright to welcome him with its reddish glow.

Did she want people to think this was the red-light district? Without eating the kidney stew he liked so well, he bolted from the flat.

It was only in worry or trouble or stress that he drank, he always said; but could Ellen begin to believe that the appetite was ever there, seeking out crises to give him reason to seek consolation?

"Are you going to put up with this sort of thing?" the nurse asked.

"What can I do?"

"You can leave him."

Leave him! Ellen shook. He was her husband!

"I had such a husband, and I left him."

"But," Ellen looked at the baby on her arm, "*I* have a child."

"I had two children."

Ellen gasped, "What became of your husband?"

"I don't know, and I don't care. I only gave him 'tit for tat.' I told him to go jump in the lake." Times were harder for a woman those years ago, when she had begun raising her children by herself. But she had come through! Her girl was in Swedish Hospital learning to be a trained nurse, and her boy was studying to be a minister.

"Without a father—" Ellen repeated dumbly, "Without a father—"

"Yes, and no more without a father than if I had stayed with him. They are a darn-sight—" quickly she clapped her hand over her mouth. "They are much better off without the disgrace of having a father who was a drunkard. I don't have much, perhaps, but I have my self-respect, and I have my health."

Ellen shrank from her. She saw a different woman standing beside her bed, not the kind and sympathetic practical nurse who had been attending her. She would discharge Mrs. Drekman the minute she did not need those Hamamelis applications on her leg any longer.

Heartless, the woman had let her unbridled selfishness send her husband out "to jump in the lake." Maybe he had!

Oh, no! No! Carl was her husband. She could never do such as that to Carl!

Besides, she knew he suffered. Over-casually, over-often, he asked, "Postman stop by today?" and she had to answer, "Not here." She knew he had clung to the hope that he would hear from home. Watching, hoping, herself, she knew what pain he suffered, and she could pity him.

A letter. If a letter would come! Only a piece of paper, yet long enough to be a bridge from country to country, strong enough to be a tying cord between a man and his family; a mystic link, binding a mother to her son.

"Please, let a letter come," she prayed. "And please, dear God, let him grow more lenient so, even if he will not go to the church, that I may have Sigrid christened by the Pastor." Dared she to use deceit in conjunction with this most holy sacrament, to save the baby's soul by baptism? If she did, and he should somehow learn of it, would he ever trust her again, in anything?

Oh, to know the right! At any rate, she dared not again question his "no." Still she could pity him.

And how she loved him when he came wheeling the baby buggy in to the room: a place for Sigrid to sleep in at night, a bit of magic for during the day, with Mr. Ferguson pushing it along the sunny streets, finding fresh air for the baby, finding a new interest for himself. It was the buggy she had seen in the bookstore window. Had Carl caught sight of her, she wondered, standing there one day almost worshipping it? She had gone in to inquire about the tinseled wallpaper—excuse to ask, incidentally, the price of baby buggies.

It was seven cents a roll for the wallpaper, and *twelve dollars* for the buggy. Oh, well, she supposed they had to make a living somehow; no store could be expected to do so, selling only books.

Extravagance? Indeed not. "A baby has to have a buggy." So it was Carl spent his week's wages for the beautiful ivory-colored rattan buggy, set atop huge hoops of steel to make it springy, with the green parasol—"Best for babies' eyes"—that could be raised or lowered, ruffle and all, as the baby woke or slept, and be folded up small enough to fit into a bureau drawer for the winter.

And it was Carl who fell asleep on the trolley and let his *Tribune* fall to the floor, unread, on the next pay day. He did not read in the morning paper of the packet of letters that had come to Chicago, salvaged from the sunken Atlantic steamer *Elbe*.

It was Gust Forsberg, in his steamship ticket office on West Madison Street, who gave particular notice to the news item about the luckless letter bearing the name of Karl Mattias Petersson; who went to the Superintendent of Mails and asked permission to examine the letter, but who found no clue as to the sender or to the street address of Karl Petersson.

"The name is the same," he scratched his head and wondered how long more he would have to hold the knitted blue shawl left in his keeping by one Georg Ahlgren of Bohuslän before he went off on another voyage. "Every Swede in America, so I am told, comes to Gust Forsberg at one time or another, for help or advice—" his countryman had said. "Please keep it here for him, and give it to him, from his mother, when you can."

He would hold it a while longer before he'd sell it; but, it was too bad, now that he was close to learning of Karl Mattias Petersson, the owner of the shawl, that the letter from the foundered ship should have stayed so long in the water.

It was not Carl who read the joyful cry from a mother's heart; instead, it was a clerk in the Dead Letter Office trying to decipher the home and name of the sender, erased and blurred as they were by the waters of the North Sea.

TWENTY THREE

"DEMOCRATS BRING DEPRESSION," Carl echoed the feeling of a multitude. "Always have and always will. Why, any Republican, even if he was an old rag doll, could win the election after these hard times in Cleveland's administration."

Unreservedly for sound money, Mark Hanna's Republican, William McKinley, became Carl's choice and the President of the United States. A good thing, too, Carl knew, for the Republicans stood for a full dinner pail, and hadn't he found a slip in his pay envelope saying, "If Bryan is elected, do not come back to the job. There won't be a job."

The thrill of this living in a democracy was great! What would they say in the old country to the cartoons in the newspapers, as during the campaign Bryan was depicted as an insect descending on the poor farmer with his Free Silver, his Free Riots, and his Anarchy, or was drawn blowing his bellows for 16 to 1? What if he had been elected? Could he have commanded the respect of the country, after such display? Again, Uncle Sam sat disconsolate outside of the White House while portly Mr. Monopoly strode in, portraying the danger if McKinley should be elected. Some papers were so bold as to print "D——," leaving no doubt as to what word was meant! Oh, there was free speech, all right; what a country.

His mustache was grown full and long, and he could twirl the ends of it as neat as the rest of them. His daughter was growing too, and how she laughed when he tweaked one toe after another on her baby foot, repeating,

"This little pig went to market—"

But Ellen's face kept growing thinner; her eyes grew darker and more deep-set.

Then came the long anticipated day when Ellen watched him raise his right hand high. Soberly, he took the oath. "Be it Remembered," read the certificate; as if either of them ever could forget.

Carl was now a citizen.

An alien he had walked into the large room that was the Circuit Court; an alien who had lived within the limits and under the jurisdiction of the United States for and during the full term of five years last past; and one year, immediately preceding this day, in the State of Illinois; an alien who appeared to the satisfaction of the Court to be attached to the principles contained in the Constitution of the United States and well disposed to the good order, well-being, and happiness of the same; an alien who two years previously had filed the declaration of his intention to become a citizen of the United States, according to the laws.

Having this day here, in open Court, taken and subscribed the oath required by those laws to support the Constitution of the United States, and to renounce and abjure all allegiance and fidelity to every foreign prince, potentate, state or sovereignty whatever, and more particularly all allegiance which he had in anywise owed to the King of Sweden and Norway, of whom he had been heretofore a subject, Carl became a citizen.

Admitted to all and singular the rights, privileges, and immunities of a Naturalized Citizen of the United States—and she was admitted with him—through him.

With Sigrid on her arm, Ellen linked the other around Carl's arm. Citizens, all three, they walked from the courtroom. The beautiful Stars and Stripes was now their flag. As to the obligation of citizenship, they would do their best to shoulder it with honor. Ellen could just see Carl, always the first at the polls on election days—rain, shine, or cold.

Of the privilege of citizenship, she knew Carl was away ahead of her in her desire to be worthy. He would be an American, first, last, and always, his loyalty undivided. But, about his love, what? Could he truly wipe from his inner heart the memories of childhood? Could it be possible that one could cut himself from his roots, and live? Transplant them, yes, and continue to grow, some more, some less; but in transplanting, did not always some of the parent soil cling to the main root?

For the seeing of the Stars and Stripes, was she to be denied the knowledge of the Yellow and Blue? Gazing on the bouquet of red clover, Queen Anne's lace, and chicory blossoms in her little kitchen must she see, less, the blue and yellow of the walls?

Was it this rending of the heart that Carl experienced, yet all the while building a wall of grim defense around himself so none should know?

Which was the man? Sober or full? Two different men: vilifying his parents and his home, when he was sober; when he was full and spoke of home, was that his secret honest heart spilling its yearning?

"Even Nature calls to my attention that this is a day to be celebrated!" he said jovially now, pointing out the wild flowers with a wide sweep of his open hand, confident his was the discovery of their patriotic colors.

"Bye-bye," not waving from the wrist, Sigrid's fat fingers opened and closed.

"Bye-bye," he waved, and wafted a kiss.

"Papa goes bye-bye." She spoke well for a two year old; even tried to tell time by using the tip of her nose for the center of the clock and drawing the position of the hands across her face with her forefinger. But she was so heavy to carry. Ellen hoped the doctor was right, that it was only natural that such a fat child should not try to walk. She'd most likely be bowlegged if she did.

Twenty-six degrees below zero. Winter was early this year. Carl stood with his back to the little parlor stove, and passed his hand down and up over his lower back and legs, to bring the warmth of his woolen pants into close contact with his skin. It felt good. But, the basement flat was fairly comfortable, at that, even though the icy blasts drove from the lake; too cold, naturally, for Sigrid to play on the floor, but she was all right on the bed, and could draw herself to her feet now by holding on to the iron spokes of the bedstead.

He liked cold weather the best. Summer was a season to make mollycoddles out of people. He would take the winter any time, except that in his line a man did not have much work when the weather was bad.

How was his old friend, Joseph, he wondered, and Mr. Bailey; six years now since he had seen them. He had half a notion to take the North Western out to Geneva and blow a little about this big step he was going to take.

Pillars of the community, with deeds to their houses in their pockets, they thought they were living! Ye gods, didn't they know what they were missing, seeing only from day to day? There might be a shade of an excuse for Mr. Bailey, but had the Viking disposition entirely passed Joseph by? With his ancestry, how could he have no heart nor mind for adventure?

Carl stepped away from the stove. How should he break the news to Ellen, of this thing he was going to do? If not actually with opposition, he was bound to be met with that cold silence that spoke disfavor.

He admitted it, his ventilator idea had not worked out very well, but had it been meet for her to question his judgment when he paid the second ten dollars to the patent attorney? Making money was like going fishing; you had to put out some bait. It takes money to make money. But she had been too stubborn to try to understand. Then, when the patent attorney refused to give him back his model and papers without his paying another ten-spot, she called the man a shyster. The patent business had left a bad taste in her mouth for his ventures, it would seem. But, of course, this was different.

He scraped a good-sized circle clear, from the frostwork, and looked out of the window. Snow had piled up and drifted down into the stairwell, and it glistened in the fleeting sunshine. Beyond the parkway trees, little columns of smoke rose upward, regularly spaced against the sky. They would be coming from little cottages set on twenty-five-foot lots, smoke from the fires of other men as tied down as he had been.

Back of him, to the north, smoke would be rising from Crazy Gertie's shack, out of the piece of stovepipe that served as a chimney, stuck through the flat tarpaper top. And if the wind changed to the south, smoke from the city's buildings would join with this neighborhood soot to change that clean white snow into a dirty gray, then black.

Not so in the Klondike!

The search of his life had been for freedom. A poor man could never know freedom; he had come to know this much. What was the answer?

Gold. And learning; the love of his life was for learning. Too hard for the poor to obtain. For learning, also, he must have gold.

With learning came power. A poor man could never have

power, but did not the man who was poor deserve to show his worth as well as a rich one?

For himself, a man could discount it, but for his family, he must find security—and with what, if not gold?

The Klondike. The Yukon. The answer!

The gold rush. He had to join it. It would provide, not only the gold, but the most important chapter in his career, the most exciting. He would put it this way to Ellen, that he had found a job. True enough, too, for could not the Klondike be termed an employer? No use, when talking things over with a woman, always to describe a spade as a spade. It might be months before the building trades opened up, and by that time he would be rich.

His feet stomped even marks on to the snowy steps when he went out to buy a map of Alaska, and doubled them on his return.

"See, Ellen," he said, bending over the map spread out on the table, "there is the famous gold-bearing stream; there it empties into the Yukon!"

"You mean—you would leave us here—alone?" Rigid with fear, Ellen asked.

"Only for a little while." And he would send her a pouch of gold dust every Sunday; she could take it to the bank and have it exchanged for hard money. She would have enough to do all of the many things he knew she had wanted to do; she could go to Marshall Field's and sit on one of the revolving stools and play lady and buy linens—and gloves. She could buy that potted aspidistra that she liked, and the fern, and he would soon return.

"Six months, and I will be rich! The fellows at the corner told me all about one Norwegian—he married the boarding-house keeper in Alaska, and she needed a broom, and do you know what he had to pay for it? A common, ordinary broom—like this one—" he picked up the one that stood on its handle-tip near the door—"seventy-five dollars! So free is the money there."

He must be crazy. She was half afraid of him as, mad with happy anticipation, he twirled the broom around his head and narrowly missed hitting the gas jet.

If it was panic had touched him during the hard times they had known together, then this was panic in reverse that now sent his reason overboard. Ellen stared at her husband.

He slapped his chest. He was the type who could stand the extreme cold at the Klondike. Born to it—brought up for it—it was his destiny. He did not ask her advice. He simply told her he was going.

The Arctic called. Hysteria gripped the masses, and commanded men to pack their belongings and ride in passenger cars, or on the rods, toward the west. Men from all walks of life felt latent emotions rise and packed their clothes, willing to take a gambler's chance for gold.

His good woolen underwear, the sweater Ellen had knitted, all of his clothes, and tin cans of sardines and anchovies, went into Carl's pack; and he was ready to go to the corner and bid the lagging or henpecked adventurers good-bye.

Could the Klondike be colder, he wondered, than this night when he stepped from the saloon? The whiskey must be watered, for all it kept the chills from racking his frame. He walked along the railroad tracks where the snow was not so deep, and threw his arms out wide, and thrashed them around himself, slapping his body hard, to keep from freezing.

"Forty-one, forty-two, forty-three," he heard a voice, mumbling. Against the snow he saw a figure, stooped low over a bushel basket. The head dropped to the chest, and then no sound came. Quickly the head snapped upright, as if caught napping but denying it, and then counted, "forty-three, forty-four—"

As he had surmised, it was Crazy Gertie; and though it was too dark to see, he knew her tongue would be pushing like rushing waters at a stump, against and around the long lone eyetooth, as she said her numbers. But, for God's sake, she had no outer covering except the old and ragged man's suit coat that she wore in summer to keep out the heat and in winter to keep out the cold. But not such cold as this!

She was already on the way to freezing to death, if she sat here longer.

"Come, Mrs. Shaughnessy."

"No." She shrugged off his hand. "I have to pick up forty-nine pieces!" Her voice climbed to a wail, "Forty-nine pieces— forty-nine pieces—"

"Yes, yes, I know," Carl soothed.

"Forty-five, forty-six," her head drooped again.

He picked up clumps of snow and rolled them in his bare palms to make them hard, and laid them in front of her so that her hands would meet them. He heard the smile in her voice, "Forty-seven, forty-eight, forty-nine."

"Now, come." He lifted her by her underarms, and leaned her body against him while he removed his overcoat, and wrapped it around her. God, it was cold. He half dragged her to her shanty and sat her in the chair beside the stove, and jacked the fire up, and left the damper open, and left her, to find his way across the snow to Ellen.

He stumbled into their parlor and fell senseless on the floor. The icicles that swung from his long mustache scattered droplets as Ellen tugged him to the bed and shoved and lifted and lifted and shoved until she got him between the sheets. She had known him to drink before, but never like this; and now he had left his overcoat in the saloon or some place.

He shivered so the bed creaked, and she covered him with all the bedclothes that she had, adding the rag rug from the floor. The little iron, heated and wrapped in a towel, and placed at his feet would help his "circle-ation."

If only some of the heat from his forehead would travel to his feet and hands!

His face was puffed. He was sick. She looked down at him. Well, he had brought it on himself. She would take care of him, naturally, until he got well; but how much of this sort of thing could he expect her to stand for?

His eyes opened. "Ellen—"

"Where did you leave your overcoat, Carl?" she asked almost gruffly.

He smiled.

"Where? Carl!"

"She was cold," he answered, "almost frozen to death."

She! Merciful heavens! Had he come to the point where he would let some hussy talk him out of his overcoat? She shook his shoulder, "Carl! Listen to me—where—where is your ulster?"

"I put it around Crazy Gertie—she was cold—freezing—"

"Oh, Carl. *Min älskade, älskade* Carl." Of course she would nurse him. She kneeled by the bed and stroked his forehead. Big-hearted, generous Carl. He had given his overcoat to the poor, unfortunate woman.

"I am young," he spoke with difficulty, "I am strong. I can always work to earn another overcoat."

"I suppose I should hate you," she told the unhearing form upon the bed, "when I think of what this means to us, but I love you, Carl—this is the sort of thing about you that I love."

Ha! Had that woman, Mrs. Drekman, ever thought for a minute that her words would sink into the consciousness of a true wife, to point the way away from her husband? Little did she know. Most likely she was the kind of a woman who would *drive* a husband to drink.

Carl would be warm, she would see to that. She would make an inner coat of newspapers—many thicknesses—and she would quilt them together with closely run rows of stitches. Yes, he would keep warm with such as that under his suit coat.

He did not need the overcoat for his trip to the Klondike. He went in his unionsuit, sometimes strapped to the bed rails, sometimes throwing the covers from him. "The pack—it is too heavy—I'll throw this quilt away," he screamed.

Thirty-five miles over the Chilkoot Pass, he'd have to stop at the summit and catch his breath. It must be the mountain air that made his breath come so short . . . the yellow metal! . . . "It is mine! I saw it first! I was here first! It is mine!" . . . Fighting . . . Exhaustion . . . "Well, there is more. I can find other."

The cold: he shivered in the cold. And all the while the gold eluded him. He held out his hands, and begged, and cried. He wanted the gold, so he could do for his mother—for his sister Elisabet—for little Johann—for Ellen—poor Ellen who had only one nightgown—and it hadn't dried after the washing—and she'd had to sleep in an old shirtwaist and skirt—he had to have the gold!

He looked searchingly at his hands; his hands were empty.

Pneumonia alone would have been bad enough, but pneumonia and acute Bright's disease! Ellen worried; they meant that she must find a way to provide coal and food for a long time, and doctor and medicine, and care. She would have to do work that she could do in the home, for there was Sigrid too to care for.

Washing and ironing—what else was there? She could sew pretty well, but she had no sewing machine.

The greatest of all God's gifts was hers. Friends. Mr. Ginsberg brought a boiler with a copper bottom, as good as new, and although he could have gotten fifty cents for it any day, he did not charge her a cent. Mr. Ferguson brought down two irons, one seven and one eight pounds, so that a couple could be heating while she used one; and both of them had pointed tips to get close to a belt or cuff with, when doing up shirrings. And he found, in his attic, two iron-holders of calico quilted over batting and bound with bias tape. They never had been used. And Mr. Ginsberg brought, from Mrs. Shaughnessy he said, a cone of ironing wax with a little wooden handle.

Best of all, he found her a customer. Dear, dear Mr. Ginsberg.

Things always worked out right somehow, Ellen decided. She had stood and looked at the clothesbaskets, that long time ago when she was fitting up her little flat, trying to figure out whether she should buy the big one or the middle-sized one, and something had told her to take the big one; and now she would need it big.

Dear Mr. Ferguson, to sit with Carl and Sigrid while she carried the empty basket to Mrs. Gallagher's house.

Dear God, to have brought the snow so she could pull the basket along like a sled, because when it was filled it was too heavy to carry.

Dear Carl, because of whom the smoke still rose from Mrs. Shaughnessy's shanty. Dear Sigrid, who took her first steps alone, as if to be of help to Mama.

It stood to reason that her days would be long, being mother and nurse and dayworker. So with the creaking of the milk wagon's wheels on the snowy icy street, she began her day. Before the wagon had reached the corner, with its horse starting and stopping to keep even with the milkman as he ran to the steps with bottles, she had the water on to boil. Oh, these were mornings that the bottle cap could rise to a height of a good three inches if a hand did not reach out to take it in before a quarter after three.

As they had hung their clothes to dry in the winters at home, she draped the dresses and underwear of Mrs. Gallagher's seven daughters, on ceiling lines above the stove. Rather than to hurt, the dampness would be good for Carl's breathing, Dr. Cuppwyn said. Sheets took up so much room, but by hanging them over two parallel lines in one thickness they dried more quickly than if they were hung double. Oh, she could figure out ways to do, and Mrs. Gallagher's girls would be proud to go to school in the dresses that she had washed and ironed!

Too bad that this would be only a temporary customer— while the mother recuperated after the coming of the boy—but, perhaps Mrs. Gallagher might have some friends, and if she was satisfied she might recommend her laundress.

It took more water to rub only a few clothes at a time, then rinse and hang them, but in that way she could start to iron as some dried.

The next day, resting between the edge of the sink and the kitchen table, the ironing board received piece after piece of this first job.

Ellen lined the basket well with newspapers and tied a pullrope to the handle, and delivered the washing. A whole dollar, a silver dollar, rested in her mitten as she pulled the empty basket back home. And they had insisted on giving her ten cents extra, for carfare, even though she walked both ways!

There was a saying, Mr. Ferguson said, about building a better mousetrap and people would find their way to your door. Soon she could have taken on still more customers, if there had been more days in the week.

For four weeks Carl's illness, then his general weakness, kept him in bed. Practically all he had had to nourish him was milk, but now the doctor said to begin giving him beef, so his strength would return. The pay that Mrs. Ward would give her today should buy some beef, and she would scrape it and serve it to him, broiled. Her own mouth watered at the thought of it!

Mrs. Ward, her richest customer, took Ellen into her parlor, asking, "Do you suppose you could do up these curtains? I wouldn't want to trust them to just anybody; but you, you do such excellent work."

"Thank you." Ellen smiled, and without realizing what she was doing, she curtsied.

"You sweet, old-fashioned little thing, you!"

Mrs. Ward hugged her. Embarrassed, Ellen looked closely at the window curtains. They were of fine rose-point lace, hanging the length of the window, to the floor, and then lay over the carpet for a foot or more. Pieces of bric-a-brac sat on the curtains there, but none were finer than George and Martha Washington in her own little flat.

The carpet was Chinese, the chairs purple and red plush, tufted, and with fancy hand-crocheted antimacassars in the shapes of fans pinned to them. Wide gilt frames shone around oil paintings of Mr. Ward's people. Every article in the home showed they were well-to-do, yet Mr. Ward worked for Mr. Seastrom who was richer still—and he had come from the old country just as Carl had done.

All kinds of thoughts raced through her head, but she must figure; what should she charge? These were rare and fine curtains, she would have to be awfully careful in handling them.

"Yes," she answered Mrs. Ward, "but I would have to charge twenty-five cents the pair."

A look of surprise flitted over Mrs. Ward's face. Ellen wished the words back within her throat; she had been greedy, and maybe now she had spoiled it all and lost a good customer, even for the plain laundry.

And then the rich woman said, "Of course, at that price, I shall furnish the starch and bluing."

Carl would have to wait, for his beef, until Mrs. Bjorseth paid her tomorrow. Today's money would go to buy a pair of curtain stretchers.

It was fun, this pleasing people. She was practically a business woman, now that she could keep the bills paid and could slip a little change, once in a while, into the hollow George Washington. Lucky that when he had fallen from the shelf, Mr. Washington's head had broken off clean at the chestline; the piece of newspaper rolled up tight made a perfect new spinal column to hold him together and nobody could notice the crack, and no one would ever guess what his feet and legs encased. Wouldn't it be wonderful if, one day, she could fill him clean up to his neck!

If banks were a little safer she would deposit the ten dollars Dr. Osgood had sent to put toward Sigrid's education; but she guessed it was safe hidden in the china man. One thing she was sure of, that money never should be spent for any other purpose.

Now that Carl was better, Dr. Cuppwyn lectured him. He had what was termed a Large White Kidney. It could be a residuum of the acute Bright's, but there was a possibility that it was a result of what drinking he had done. He must leave liquor alone. With such a fine little family, the doctor thought he would want to leave it alone.

He would. Yes, of course, he would.

He had a will; no man with will-power should find it a problem to keep his hand from lifting a glass to his mouth. He would be a man; every time he felt the thirst, he would take a cup of coffee even if it had to be the weak stuff Ellen cooked after the fresh morning brew, on the *sump*—used grounds—time after time, to keep the grocery bill down.

Yet—yet—it was deeper than the thirst that constricted his

throat muscles. The doctor did not understand. It was the need to forget—forget the disappointments that had made him what he was, a failure. A failure, letting his wife bring home the wherewithal! Letting a little woman support a big man!

He had to get back to the job, and right away. He had to make up to Ellen for all this hard work she had been doing.

Little Ellen, sitting there sucking her coffee through a lump of sugar—*caffe på biten*—would she never become an American? She clung so to the Swedish ways; always on Thursdays, during the winter, pea soup boiled on a ham shank. And never serving veal meatballs without their accompanying white cabbage soup, just like at home. And now, before Christmas, she had scrubbed and cleaned everything in the whole flat, washing the windows with alcohol because it was too cold to use water. They were in America now—

"Look what I found in Mr. Ward's shirt pocket," Ellen tossed him a peach stone.

"They must certainly be rich, to have peaches at this time of the year," he turned the pit over in his hands and looked hard at it. With the point of a blade of his pocket knife, he started flicking tiny dried particles of fruit from its crevices.

Ellen bent over the washtub. This was the last washing before Christmas. The rubbing over the washboard was done, and she wrung out a heavy woolen blanket. As she turned and squeezed, the blanket crawled up her arm like a snake and she coiled it high to keep it from falling back into the water. Her hands were strong; only a drop or two tinkled into the tub as she finished wringing after the last rinse. She was to deliver it wet, because Mrs. Ward had a big warm basement with a hot air furnace in it, and the blanket could hang and dry there.

Tomorrow would be Christmas Eve.

"You are coming with Mama, and we will stop on the way home and buy our Christmas dinner." Ellen and Carl watched Sigrid put her hood on, backward so it slid down over her eyes, excited; the child almost seemed to know that it was Christmas.

"Bye-bye to Papa," the chubby fingers waved.

"Bye-bye," Carl waved his hand and knife together. He sat, then, hunched over his working hands, and soon drew closer to the light. Measuring with his eye, drawing imaginary lines on the peach pit, cutting—carefully cutting—removing the soft kernel—scraping the cut edges to make them smooth—with industry he worked to finish this thing he made before Ellen should return.

His pockets were empty. But pockets at home had always been empty; still there had always been a little present for every one of them at Christmas!

The little basket was finished. Where the kernel had been, there was the hollow of the basket—or where the lower half of it had been—and a dainty handle arched above. Held between his thumb and forefinger, it stood the test of his scrutiny, against the gas light. But it had to have a chain, so his daughter could hang it around her neck.

A chain. At home, they would have—

With the enthusiasm of a child he fairly ran to the tea canister in the kitchen where Ellen kept the ball of string that grew bigger with every bringing home of a wrapped purchase from the store. Three lengths, and he tied them together in a knot at one end, and caught the knot with a pin to his trouser-knee, and started braiding. He slipped the finished braid through the basket handle, tied the ends together and held it while the basket pendant dangled.

"Louis the Fourteenth's fine lady had nothing on my daughter; she, too, shall have a lavaliere!"

He closed his eyes. It had not seemed like Christmas, until now.

If only he had a present for Ellen. How long was it since he had worked and had a jingle in these pockets? The penknife returned to one, and he stuffed his handwork in another. His pencil sought a paper:

> Nu är det Jul igen, Elin,
> *Now it is Christmas again, Elin,*
> *My hand digs deep into my pocket,*
> *but it comes up empty.*
> *No gold to buy a gift for you.*
>
> *Here are no candles on a tree,*
> *lighted by me, for you.*
> *My hands have garlanded*
> *no sprigs of pine, nor fir,*
> *for you.*

No Yule log, cut by my hands,
and dragged across the snow,
burns on our hearth to keep you warm;
to burn out all the wrongs
of the past year—past years—

I have no gift for you.

But Elin, I wonder if you know
that deep in my breast is a glowing flame
sending a fragrance from myrrh and frankincense—
to you?
Does grateful caroling come to your ears
from deep within me, Elin?

Oh, it is Christmas.

Although I have no gift for you,
you who are generous beyond belief,
give me a gift?

Help me to put together the pieces
of my heart
so I may know again
the joy of loving—
Help me?

I have no gift for you.

But know you, now at Christmas, Elin,
that if I had a heart so I could love,
my gift to you would be
my love—

"It doesn't read right." Discouraged, Carl crushed the paper and tossed it toward the basket kept for scrap papers, a bushel basket painted white with blue and yellow flowers drawn along the cross strips. It fell beyond, into the corner, on the floor.

Ellen carried Sigrid, and the blanket wrapped in last

Saturday's *Daily News*, to the trolley. Off to the neighborhood of the well-to-do!

How she would love to bring home a Christmas tree. But the cheapest ones were fifty cents. It seemed like only yesterday that she and Algot had walked three miles from Grandfather's house, in Sweden, to the edge of the forest and there had bought a beautiful tree for only twelve *öre*, so big they hardly could carry it.

"There is Mr. Schulz's butcher shop," she pointed for Sigrid to see. Brown rabbits hung by their hind legs over the edge of an open barrel. The Germans would be making *hasenpfeffer*. Inside, they could see, were red and green crepe paper flutings dressing up the gas chandeliers and long meat hooks hanging from the ceiling, and flutings hung in garlands on counter fronts and meat blocks.

Wet snow began to fall, covering the thawed places, making the Christmas trees look like real growing ones, leaning against saw-bucks in front of the grocery stores.

She would be glad for the holiday. Until now she had not realized how tired she was. It seemed so far around to the back door of Mrs. Ward's house: she wanted desperately to short-cut to the front door, but she was a washwoman. She set Sigrid down, looked at her closely, took out her handkerchief, spit on a corner of it, and wiped a smudge from the fat little face. Now the child looked presentable, and so she knocked on the back door.

"Merry Christmas!"

"Merry Christmas to you!" echoed Mr. Ward, "And so this is your little girl!"

They must come in and sit in the parlor while he poured an eggnog for each one. Sigrid's eyes nearly popped from their sockets at sight of the Christmas tree. She grasped Mr. Ward's finger and toddled toward it, but stopped short not to come too near the firelight of the candles.

"She is just old enough to appreciate a tree," Mr. Ward beamed.

The eggnog made Ellen feel strong again. "It is so pleasant here, but we must go."

"Not with an empty basket, on Christmas," said Mrs. Ward as she tucked a dollar bill into Ellen's hand.

"Much too much," Ellen remonstrated, "for only a blanket."

"Not on Christmas." And it dawned on Ellen now that the blanket had not really needed washing at all.

Would she be offended? Offended if Mrs. Ward tucked these things into that beautiful basket, woven with a design on each side; how could she be?

"They are not new, but they will be parcels to open," Mrs. Ward said, smiling.

"Thank you. God bless you, kind people, and a Merry, Merry Christmas to you."

"And many of them," Mr. Ward said, "to you."

"Here, take this umbrella, the snow is awfully wet. Don't bother to return it, it's only an old one. Bye-bye, little Sigrid," Mrs. Ward waved.

"Merry Christmas! *God Jul!*" Ellen called back.

Besides the meat she could buy lingon berries, and they would make it seem like home. Oh, they would have a wonderful Christmas! They stopped at the horses' drinking fountain and she lifted Sigrid, to let her break off the icicle that hung from the faucet, so she could hold it in her mittened hand and lick it, and play it was a candy stick. As they stood, the wind blew the umbrella inside out. The black cloth tore from the center.

There was too much to carry, would Mrs. Ward mind much if she threw it away, she wondered. She turned from it to look at Sigrid, blinking her eyes to rid the lashes of big snowflakes. Ellen grabbed her, as inspiration came, and hugged her, and with the umbrella stuck into the handles of the basket, she fairly shrieked, "You are going to have a Christmas tree! My darling baby, you are going to have a Christmas tree!"

Deep into the night she worked. No, it was not work; it was play to rip the cloth from the umbrella frame, to nail the handle to a board, so the frame stood upright, and cover the board with a sheet, ruffled to look like snow as they had done at home. It was fun to snip yeast wrappers into fine shreds and stick them with flour and water paste to the ribs of the half-opened umbrella frame, standing there on the little table like a pine tree dripping silver icicles. And, for the topmost tip, a star cut from cardboard and covered with the tinfoil.

"The Star that led to Bethlehem—*En stjärna gick på himlen fram*," she sang, as she knelt before the star.

Now the presents spread underneath: a cigar for Carl, a

nickel dolly for Sigrid, a cotton handkerchief for Mr. Ferguson. She wished it could have been linen.

It was a wonderful Christmas Eve, with lutfisk first, and milk sauce over it—and a little sprig of dill—with chicken fricassee and mashed potatoes, and dumplings made rich with egg, and lingon berries, and *risgrynsgröt*, traditional Christmas porridge in Sweden. Always would it be *risgrynsgröt*, to Ellen, no matter how many Americans called it rice pudding. And there was the gift of a month's rent from Mr. Ferguson!

Offended at the contents of the basket from Mrs. Ward? Ah, no; for there was a dress, a little big but she could take it in at the seams, of lavender and black stripe and with a wide ruffle at the bottom deeper at the front than at the back and sides, with full elbow-length sleeves with lace hanging out at the cuffs, and a deep lace yoke in the waist, and a rolling collar, and a crushed belt narrow in the back, widening to a deep point over the stomach—

And the zither, with its tortoise-shell thumb pick, and the lovely sounds that came from the strings—

And the mechanical bank for Sigrid's pennies, a Salvation Army lassie and her shepherd dog—

And the box of Smith Brothers Cough Drops

The eve of the birthday of Jesus, such joy as it brought to the heart of Ellen, when her husband—her Carl—drew from his pocket the peach-stone-basket lavaliere, for Sigrid. Made with his own hands, a dearer gift than ever money could buy.

"I'm sorry, Ellen, I have no present for you. When a man's not working—"

"Oh, Carl," she hugged him right in front of Mr. Ferguson, "this is a glorious, glorious Christmas!"

Not knowing, on a rumpled sheet of paper, he had given her the gift her heart craved most—love words.

Sometimes the lack of money was a Godsend.

TWENTY FOUR

LIKE FAIRY ICING, so real one minute—gone the next—a feathery coating of hoarfrost covered each blade of grass, each dandelion leaf, within the outline of the shadow of the roof next door, until the shadow moved; only for an instant, then, did the fairy frostwork hold its outline against the rising sun as Ellen watched.

Such was the fragile quality of her husband's resolves. So many promises to be temperate, so many elaborate works planned, but most unstarted, all undone. Not because he could not do, that was the pity of it.

But, Ellen mused, it was hard to fit a person's self into a new way of life. Born to the land, perhaps Carl never should have left the land. And it was difficult to fit one's self into the life of a new country. Here, each one worked so much alone. It was hard for a woman, standing ironing hour after hour with no company except the tick of the clock and the crackle of wood in the stove; not like at home, gathering for the community mangling parties.

Hard for a woman, this new way of life, but harder for a man where on a job it was "every man for himself," caring not a whit how he stepped on another's toes while seeking favor with the boss in order to advance himself.

Perhaps it was the working together that Carl missed, the sharing that had been so much a part of the life at home. Birth, death, illness, work, all shared by all. Community spirit; the only place he would be able to find a semblance of it was in the church, and there he would not go.

She had watched, that time, how he blossomed under the drive of his quest for help to rebuild the cottage that had burned on the night of the fire at the milk-bottling plant. "A few hours a week? Any man can spare a coupla' hours a week!" They had, too, and Carl had lined up plumbers and carpenters and plasterers, until under the auspices of the Odd Fellows, the little cottage stood again.

He had been happy, doing in the way they would have done at home, helping each other.

Why were there so many more fires, Ellen wondered, here than she had ever known there to be in the old country? Hardly a day but a home burned somewhere.

How would it be, she wondered too, to be married to a man from whom a wife might always know what to expect, or even once in a while might know? Certainly there was no drabness in her life with Carl, standing here before her offering a bunch of violets, held close in his big fist, with a fringe of leaves around them.

"But where is your pay envelope, Carl?"

He shifted from one foot to the other, "The McGinnis', their oil stove exploded; they stood there in the ashes of their home, Ellen, everything wiped out!"

Ellen stopped dead in her tracks at putting the potatoes on. Another fire!

"I knew you wouldn't mind, Ellen. I gave it to them."

"But our own rent, Carl?"

"I couldn't bear to think of those children—six of them— without a roof over their heads. And the grandmother," he sat and she saw his chin quiver, "as old as my own mother." He strode about the room, nervous, as he always became at mention of his mother. "I couldn't bear to think of those children, homeless."

Strange that he should not think of how homeless his own child would be if they could not pay the rent. He was a human paradox, her Carl, but no more could she scold him than she could a little boy who held out half of his candy—or all of it— toward a playmate.

She sniffed the fragrance of the prairie flowers. Any man might bring home a loaf of bread. But violets!

She could almost believe that a mistake had been made in his birthdate, he was so much a Gemini, moody, either in the depths, standing morose and silent in the shadow of the closed door of the past, or on the heights. Meaning well, standing on the threshold of the future with one foot forward held in readiness to step into some new get-rich-quick scheme or some far job.

Yesterday, tomorrow, they claimed him so that he forgot to live today.

Though carpentry work was plentiful, what with almost every vacant lot humming with Southern Europeans digging basements for new houses, Ellen saw little from Carl's pay envelopes. There were the gold-mine stocks that every man, who was a man, should buy to provide financial security for his family's future.

"Why do you try to gobble the whole future in one mouthful?" she asked him. "Spending your whole pay on gold-mine stocks?"

"I don't want you to grow old, Ellen, and not have."

"But we could save a little at a time."

"I try to look ahead. I try so hard, Ellen, to do the right thing. God knows I try. But everything seems to get so complicated—"

"Looking ahead at life, Carl, reminds me of looking at a knitting pattern. See, on this one, if you try to read it all at once, it is like so much Chinese, too much by far to digest if taken all in one gulp—even for me—who can knit almost anything.

"I'd go crazy if I tried to read it all at once. But taken one step at a time it is easy, I put 129 stitches on the needle, knit fourteen rows, start the pattern, and so on, and before you know it, the whole thing is done! Why can't you try to take one step at a time, one day at a time, and live it—today?"

He looked at her, blankly.

"It is of your own foolish choice, Carl, that the day you live holds little for you, that you forget to see the sunshine of now for bemoaning those bleak days that are gone and anticipating what is to come, and seek forgetfulness of both."

"I know what you mean, Ellen," sadly he spoke, as a man who cannot throw aside a heritage.

But at once his mood changed, and he "choo-chooed" Sigrid around the room, she sitting on the Bissell carpet sweeper. She had to grab her ankles and cup her chin between her knees; her legs were getting too long. Carl was in the heights now, for they were going to Schenectady!

How would they like to go to Schenectady? Now was the time to make a change if ever they were going to make one, before Sigrid would be starting to school. He had answered an advertisement; the job of foreman in a big plant was as good as gotten, for he had answered the advertisement.

After supper they sat at the table and he drew a line on the map in his geography book to show how they would go around the south tip of Lake Michigan, through Indiana, through Ohio. Oh, How they could live on a salary of forty dollars a week! Sigrid should have roller skates, not wooden, but ball-bearing ones. The house would have a screened porch on it, for Ellen to sit on in the afternoons, and read the *Ladies' Home Journal* and eat chocolate candies from a box!

Ellen smiled. Not so much as that would she ever expect; but a screened porch on which to do the ironing! Oh my!

So sure was he that he would get the job, he gave the boss notice and left, so he could help Ellen pack.

It was a well-couched answer came; his qualifications did not fit him for the position. They desired a college man.

Disappointment, discouragement, defeat deflated his ego and drove him to seek consolation in the only way he knew. Bravado accented his announcement, to Ellen, of his rejection, "There are no flies on me!" was all he said. "I got myself another job on the way home." But it was shoveling coal at the gashouse, for a dollar seventy-five a day. A twelve-hour day. The building boom had miscarried, and the foundations sat holding water, stagnant, to encourage breeding of mosquitoes. He was not the only building-tradesman out of his line.

Ellen saw that he who had been so keen and eager to speak with no revealing accent, slid backward now. He gave up going to night school. He had to with such long working hours.

She had to help him. She had to find a way to help him. She could do no less for him, her husband, than he was always eager to do for some poor unfortunate. "Never kick a man when he's down" was Carl's philosophy, which brought him home leading the poor drunken Finn, or the Swedish schoolmaster who had run from the old country to the new and here tried to drown the memory of a mother who had served the largest portions at table to an older brother—not to him. She had turned in revulsion from the Finn, "Isch! It's his own fault!"

"But Ellen," Carl had pleaded, "you do not know what makes him so, or how he suffers from injustice done him as a child, that makes him seek forgetfulness."

Silly, to think that men could lay a grown man's weakness to some incident in childhood!

Folly to think that just because Sigrid did not get an all-day-sucker when the neighbor kid got one, that she might grow up characterless.

Maybe men were different from women. Ellen wondered. Carl had been hurt in his youth, deeply hurt. But then—who hadn't been? With his intelligence, how could he live more in what he had lost, than in all that he had? He had always been so much brighter than she, who had left school at too early an age. How she wished now that she had listened to her parents!

But she would see to it that Sigrid had schooling. The child was bright, and deep-thinking, so deep that sometimes a mother could almost be frightened by the young one's brightness.

Yes, she had to help her husband, and earning money by washing seemed to be the only way; but Sigrid should be skipping, now, at play in this beautiful early summer sunshine, instead of walking alongside carrying her handle of the washbasket. The sun slid like a goldpiece into a bank slot and left the edge of the prairie, as Ellen watched. She felt that Sigrid's side of the basket slumped, then rested on the ground, and so she turned from looking at the sunset.

Was she at home that this sight met her eyes? She brushed her hand across them; for Sigrid knelt at sight of an approaching wagon, loaded high with hay. In deep humility mother joined daughter and they knelt bareheaded before the first harvest as it passed them by.

"Thanks be to Thee, ever-living, ever-loving God, for sending us our food," Ellen breathed, and turned to look at Sigrid. Could it be atavistic memory had bade the child to kneel? No, instinct could never be so strong as this.

"How did you know, to kneel before the harvest?"

"I saw Pa do it," and Sigrid hastened to explain, "He didn't see me—"

"Pa?" The one who long ago had ridiculed her for such as this?

"Why did he do it?" the child asked. "To make him feel good?"

"He did it, as we did, to give thanks to God, for—"

"But Pa doesn't believe in God—" the space left vacant by her vanished baby teeth made Sigrid lisp the "s."

"There's no such thing as unbelief," answered Ellen, and her smile dispelled the look of trouble on her daughter's face. "In his heart, he does."

They swung the basket between them, and Ellen quoted, as they walked,

> *"There is no unbelief;*
> *Whoever plants a seed beneath the sod*
> *And waits to see it push away the clod,*
> *He trusts in God."*

"Teach it to me," Sigrid begged, as Ellen finished,

> *"Whoever says, 'To-morrow,' 'The unknown,'*
> *'The future,' trusts the Power alone*
> *He dares disown."*

"That Kolze boy just knocked the robin's nest down," Carl called back as he left the front door.

Sigrid ran to help her father pick up the nest.

"He is a bad boy," Carl said. "He should be punished."

"There is a God above who sees," Sigrid lisped one of Ellen's admonitions.

Carl glared at Ellen. "What nonsense do you teach the child? God above." Ellen saw that he was losing his temper, as he always did at mention of the Holy Mysteries.

"Above is the sky, the whirling of sun and moons in space, the interplanetary—" he seemed almost more angry at himself than at her or the child, yet he finished, "oh, of what use to talk to fools!"

"Stay out of his way," begged Ellen, shrinking from him, but reaching to draw Sigrid toward her.

But Sigrid turned on Carl, "You are bad! You said the Kolze boy was bad, but you are bad. You are bad—bad—bad! Go on away, I don't like you."

Carl's anger dispelled itself. A hurt look came into his eyes, and for an instant they pleaded with Ellen's to ease the hurt. She wanted to run after him, to cradle his head on her breast, as she would a child's. Sigrid should get a licking for talking in such wise to her father! Ellen turned to chastise her, but stopped to see tender loving fingers caress the dead young robin. "Poor birdie," Sigrid stroked it, and looked at Ellen with a far-away abstracted look.

"She isn't dead." Now Sigrid smiled, "See, here is her mouth. That is where she eats." She opened the bill with two small finger tips, "Now it is open—see?"

Her head moved back and forth, from left to right, "Only her eyes are shut, she is not dead."

Little hands cupping it, holding it in position, set the bird upon its feet, "See? She sits. She hope—hops—hops—she isn't dead."

Ellen watched. Sigrid, six years old, so calm in the face of death, did she not understand at all?

"I'll put her here in the tall grass so she won't be afraid," gently Sigrid set the fledgling robin in the grass while two redbreasts flew over, with their futile chattering.

"She isn't dead, Mama, *she's only changed.*"

Chills crept up her spine and tears clouded the eyes of Ellen, standing in solemn wonder to see her teaching embroidered by His hand into this full and awesome faith.

Carl's job at the gashouse did not last, nor did the job of hod carrier. You would have to give the devil his due, though, Ellen told herself, Carl always found another job and worked whenever there was work to be had; but the building trades were a flighty business.

No help wanted. No help wanted. Each such sign that he read wrote discouragement deeper into his features. Poor Carl, he yelled out in the night about the signs, "No help wanted."

It was a good thing she had kept up with her own little business. The income was steady and in the past little over three years she had eliminated, one by one, the heavy general washings; and now the neat printed sign in the front window read, "Hand laundering of fine lace curtains. Work warranted." She liked that word "warranted." Not that she needed the sign, with all the work she got to do, but she had taken such pains with the lettering, it would be a shame to waste it.

Doing up curtains was child's play compared with all-around laundry. It paid better, too, and was so much easier on the catarrh. A nice little business, and she need not neglect her home in the running of it, and was right there to greet Sigrid when she came from school.

Few of the chalkmarks of the hopscotch squares remained on the front sidewalk, for school had kept for two weeks now. Enrolled for only a fortnight, and last night had come the note from the teacher saying that on Monday, Sigrid was going to be promoted. "Far advanced," Mrs. Murphy said that she was, and laid it to her mother's teaching Sigrid the alphabet, and the sounds of the letters, and the numbers. It was not so much what she had taught her, Ellen knew, as it was that she was naturally bright from having a brainy father. It was because of that that she was able to read all through the Holton Primer, even some of the blackboard lessons, clear through "Chicken Little," and had memorized, or could read—Ellen was not sure which—the verse that stretched across the two pages inside of the back cover:

> *"And now good-by, O, girls and boys!*
> *Good-by, your playthings and your toys!*
> *Until we meet, by hook or crook,*
> *Within some other story book."*

Yes, it was a splendid thing that she took after Carl in braininess. Not only in book learning, either, was she smart, finding her way to school all alone, skipping home, blossoming from the shrinking timid child she had been at first, sitting in the front of the schoolroom on a little red chair while the rest of the children sang, "Good morning to you," as they did to each new first grader, in turn. Ellen sang it now and her thumb kept time as it slid a lace curtain's edge over evenly spaced pins on the stretcher.

"Extree—"

Ellen caught the far corner of the curtain on a top pin, to keep it hanging free from the floor, and ran to the street. "Here, boy!" This made twelve cents now that she had spent on Extra papers since the President had been shot a week ago yesterday in Buffalo. She unfolded the newspaper.

PRESIDENT McKINLEY DEAD!

The shot, fired from the handkerchief-covered revolver of the anarchist, had claimed his life. Only the big black headline and the first few paragraphs were new; the rest repeated what had been said so many times in previous issues.

William McKinley was dead. Teddy Roosevelt, the cowboy, the Rough Rider, the rich man's son, would be President. What would become of the country now? What would become of all of them?

The President of the United States was dead. Why? This was beyond Ellen's ability to comprehend, for he was a sober man, needed by the country. There were plenty of other men, no good to themselves or to anyone else, who lived on and on. There was Mr. Brattle down the street who lay drunk in the gutter night after night; why should such a one live, and the President have to die? There was—

Oh, no! God forbid that she should have thought of Carl in the same breath! Abruptly she returned to the stretcher. Reproving herself, she unpinned the curtain hanging there; for her careless idleness she would have to dip the whole thing again into the wet starch.

Dipping and pinning, the days were much the same for Ellen. But Monday saw an excited Sigrid leave her home, skipping toward the schoolhouse and the second grade room. Oh, such a day; she would remember it with joy for all of her life, for she was called upon to stand and read aloud before the class! Holding the *Lights to Literature*, by Grades, Book One, with only one hand—with her right arm pressed close against her side, she read, "with expression, with verve," the teacher said.

She loved Miss Holliday. Her feet ran a few steps toward home, so she could tell Ma and find out what that "verve" was that she read with; then she skipped. She had to step off of the cement sidewalk every few feet so as not to get near the lines. "Step on a crack, break your mother's back—"

"Hold up!" Someone behind her called.

She turned. It was Gracie Shannon. Gracie was the richest girl in the class.

"I'll walk with you," Gracie said, patting and stroking her full plaited skirt, "if you'll wait up."

Of course, Sigrid would wait. Going to school was such fun. And now Gracie was going to walk home with her! The other kids would be jealous.

"My father is the biggest saloonkeeper in Chicago," Gracie bragged.

So that was why she was so stuck-up, always swinging her tail! Sigrid bit her lip, "Let's count white horses, huh, Gracie?"

"Aw, gee, hardly any are white any more," Gracie's lower lip hung. "All of Marshall Field's delivery wagons have those old sort-of-gray spotted things, and—"

"There's one!" With solemn ceremony Sigrid spit on her index finger, patted it to her left palm, then clapped her doubled right fist on it. "One up!" she squealed. "I'm one up on you!" and waved thanks to the grocery boy for having a white horse hitched to his wagon.

They stood, open-mouthed, to watch an upright piano being hoisted up the side of a two-flat brick, into an upper window from which the sash had been removed. A big wheel at the roof's edge squeaked under the weight.

"Gee, what if the pulley-line should break?"

They ran from the nearness of the building.

"What does your father do?" Gracie prodded.

"He works," Sigrid replied, and trying hard to stick her nose as high in the air as her companion's, "Isn't school fun?"

"Huh?" Hadn't Sigrid noticed? Nothing was quite right in the old public school; the teachers weren't very good, and the chalk always split, and the drinking cups never looked clean. Suddenly Gracie wheeled around, "You are not going to be teacher's pet, are you, and be a tattle-tale and tell on me?"

Poor Gracie. School was wonderful. Sigrid knew that; and she knew that her mother would be watching and as soon as she turned the corner, Ma would drop her work and hurry to make ready slices of homemade bread with butter and sugar on. Gosh, but it was good. Ma had promised one day to make grape jelly as soon as the grapes got cheaper. Maybe today was the day!

> *"Hippity hop*
> *To the barber shop,*
> *To buy a stick of candy.*
>
> *One for you, and*
> *One for me,*
> *And—*

Gracie, do you want to come over to my house and play? We'll have some bread and butter and sugar on, and maybe milk."

"Gol-lee, yes," Gracie's face brightened. "Let's run! Where do you live?"

"Right here."

Gracie started up the front steps.

"This way, dummy." Sigrid laughed, turning down the well steps.

Gracie drew her skirts close to her, "Down in the basement?" she shrieked.

Sigrid stopped, her mouth open.

"What is that sign?" imperiously demanded the guest.

Sigrid's composure returned. She could read. She could even read in *The Wonderful Wizard of Oz*, about the beautiful City of "Emzeralds": Giving herself airs, she repeated the wording on the sign.

As an actress would do, registering exaggerated horror, Gracie slapped her hand against her cheek, "Oh, my goodness, you mean that your mother takes in *washing?*"

Weeping, Sigrid watched Gracie walking away, backwards, scraping one index finger along the other pointing finger, yelling, "Shame, shame, double shame—Sigrid's mother is a washerwoman!"

Half-blinded with tears, Sigrid opened the door to her home. Curtain stretchers were braced against each wall. The back yard would be full, too. They had always been a part of her home, something to be careful not to brush against, but now they were something of which to be ashamed.

Home. What was a home supposed to be like? This was the only one she knew, where her father came home after she had gone to bed, where her mother cried softly after she thought "the young one" was asleep.

Home. What was the one like, that her mother had known, that it made the word come from her mother's mouth sounding like a singing string of the zither? Or like the call of a bird before the dark? Why wasn't her home like that?

"Come, Sigrid, we'll have our little teaparty," Ellen bent over the kitchen table and spread their afternoon repast. She waited expectantly; sometimes Sigrid came and leaned over her and put sweaty hands over her eyes, and she must guess who it was.

Small fists beat against Ellen's back; furious lashings stung, but not so sharply as the words, "I hate you! I hate you!" Sigrid stamped her feet and screamed hysterically, "Take down that old sign! Take it down, do you hear me?"

Stunned, Ellen removed the sign from the window and stood tearing it into tiny bits. Her loving daughter, the placid Sigrid, what had come over her, now sobbing out her broken heart?

Sigrid calmed. Sniffling, she came and threw herself into Ellen's arms. "I'm sorry, Ma; I'm sorry, but she said Shame on me, Double shame on me, because my mother is a washerwoman."

"Who said?" Ellen asked, tenderly stroking the light hair back from Sigrid's flushed face.

"Gracie Shannon said—"

A firmness settled over Ellen's thin face. Maybe her daughter was too young to understand, but say it she must, "Don't you mind, *min lilla vän*, what Gracie Shannon says. It is her father, and his ilk, who steal the very bread from the mouths of other men's children. It is *because* of Gracie Shannon's father that I take in washing."

She sat with Sigrid on her lap, and as the child bit into homemade bread, Ellen chanted, "Shame, shame on Gracie's father, for he is a saloonkeeper."

TWENTY FIVE

"Two little girls in blue, lad,
Two little girls in blue."

ELLEN SANG as she cut two fronts and a back from blue plaid goods, only three cents a yard off Klebo's remnant table, and plenty in the piece for at least two schooldresses for Sigrid. Two sleeves; she pinned the newspaper pattern to doubled cloth and brought the pin's point through the top of a big "K" and out at the bottom of it, "K" for Keeley. She cut around the edge and brought the sleeves to the lamp, better to read about "The Keeley Gold Cure."

What a sad commentary on the will-power of men that such an advertisement should be necessary. Anyone, even she, knew that in the path of drinking walked intellectual decline. Carl had been so smart to correct her when she said "high-tuned" instead of "high-toned," and "Boo-peep"; and what had he done? Poor Sigrid, proud to go out and be the first to send the important news abroad among the children that the Pope in Rome had died. And how had Carl said it for his daughter to repeat—? "The Poop is dead."

To think that he, who was intelligent, should bring such aching sadness to the eyes of his own daughter; how sorry a thing that a little child should be too grief-smitten for tears. That had been over a month ago, and still she chose to stay in the small back yard, or in the house, so the children could not taunt her.

It was hard, no doubt, this being a child—in America. Though it was summer, Sigrid's face had a pinched and wintry look. If only she could have been brought up in Falkenberg!

A double collar now, two double cuffs; maybe the blue plaid dress would make her happy again. It was too bad, though, that

259

Sigrid was so sensitive. "Other children have fathers," she shook her head, "and fathers do not always do as children would like to have them do."

It was mightly generous of Mrs. Fitzgerald, a bran' new customer, to cut off her new Butterick pattern and give the newspaper duplicate to her, for Sigrid. Her child was only two weeks younger than Sigrid, so they both wore the eight-year size.

As if by intent, the pieces of the newspaper pattern delivered a three-part sermon. The lesson on the sleeves dwarfed those on the skirt, but Ellen read, "He who leaves a trail of nauseating smoke as he threads a crowd would commit no other parallel rudenesses; he who enters a car redolent of tobacco would not willingly enter it smelling of his stables; he who stands in the vestibule of a limited train and enriches the indraught with cigarette fumes would stand for hours to give an invalid his seat, but he never realizes that his smoke will cause a lasting headache. And so it goes, courtesy, high breeding and self-forgetful generosity in all the lighter and graver relations of life, smoking too often excepted."

A fly buzzed around her. Now where had that come from? Since she had replaced the flypaper with bunches of dried clover blossoms, not a fly had stayed in the house, till now. She folded a section of newspaper and got ready to swat. " 'I'm stuck on you,' said the fly to the flypaper," she sang, half under her breath as she played hide and go seek with it, then bang! With the squashed fly scraped onto the edge of the coal scuttle, Ellen returned to her cutting.

Oh, the newspapers told of women's smoking, but they were few and far between—fast women.

But, here was a worry for the mother of a girl! Ellen read the third lesson, "Can gum chewing be regarded as to any degree harmful?" Not much of an evil, on the face of it, except that any habit weakened a person's character. This was good advice, though, for the *Youth's Companion* to give its readers: "The habit is unnatural. It meets no normal need, as does the chewing of the cud of the cow and some other animals. Muscles are enlarged by use. Now, the normal use of the masseter muscles tends only to keep them in proper working condition; but their overuse in gum chewing must tend to their undue enlargement and thus to the disfiguration of the face."

Truly, there was a worry for the mother of a girl.

The resentment she had harbored for the past two years against the Health Department, rose up again to make her dark eyes sparkle. What was a mother for, if not to be consulted as to where a vaccination should be placed by the school doctor? A big scar, disfiguring the arm of a girl, isch! No female of the better class in Sweden bore such a scar in such a place. Ellen lifted her skirt and rubbed her finger over the scar high on her thigh. Things were so different—at home—and thinking upon them brought tears.

"Salva-cea," she saw, as she folded the pattern neatly and tied a strip of plaid around it, "for skin diseases, sore throat, *catarrh*, old sores, earache, bruises, sore muscles, ulcers, piles." She would have to get some Salva-cea. Peruna, for all the testimonial by the great Senator from Mississippi, had not helped her catarrh. Neither had Scott's Emulsion, nor Ely's Cream Balm, not even Marshall's Catarrh Snuff.

Ellen sewed. The waist took shape, and she gathered the tops of the sleeves with two rows of running stitches and left the ends of the threads free, so she could fit the gathered part exactly into the spaces between the notches at the top of the armhole and then wind the thread ends around a pin before basting. That always guaranteed that shirrings would fit to a "T." At this rate, she might be able to finish both dresses before school opened next week, the day after Labor Day. There couldn't be much more hot weather, but this summer certainly had been a scorcher! The coolness of the basement was a blessing.

There lay Sigrid, on the junior bed at the foot of their bed, hers and Carl's. How tall she was growing, too big to fib about her age on the streetcar, any more, and save half fare. To think that she would be going into the fourth grade at school! She seemed so old for her age in some ways, a happy enough child, but always with that hurt back of her eyes, almost making a mother feel like a criminal. Ever since the day that she brought home the saloonkeeper's daughter, and her generous hospitality had been blighted in the budding, she had never brought home another playmate. Sometimes she went to Adelaide's house, or to Ruth Swanson's, but they never came home with her.

Ellen dug the needle into a thick seam and pushed hard against the thimble. Her daughter was as good as any of them; the Nilsson family was as fine as any family in Sweden! It was false pride to be ashamed of honest curtain stretchers. She had been unwise in giving in to Sigrid that they should deliver the curtains after dark so none of the youngsters should see the washbasket slung between them.

She found her eyes drifting from her sewing to the clock. Carl should have been home long ago.

Herself—sure—she could wish things were different, that her husband might—but, any man would have some failing.

But what gave a child license to find fault with its parents? Children sometimes overstepped themselves. If her father said it was plum*b*er because it had a "b" in it, that was no skin off Sigrid's nose. Let her respect her father, not ridicule him. There was such a thing as paying too much attention to such little things—"Pope" or "Poop"—what difference did it make? Hanging around like a dog with its tail between its legs—maybe a little swish around her legs with the razor strap would shake her out of it. "Ouch!" The needle stuck her finger and she stopped to suck off the drop of blood.

Why didn't Carl come home? Had he been run over, so he couldn't come home?

Nervously she went to the window to search the darkness. No sign of him.

A wave of guilt swept over her; she leaned over Sigrid and placed a kiss on her forehead. But a wife must uphold her husband. Where would a child land if one parent pulled against the other? In the reform school—that was where.

Oh, blessed relief, there he was at the door. The coffee-pot was ready, and she drew their two chairs to the kitchen table. Not oilcloth spread on it, either, like some careless housewives used, but a hand-hemstitched sugar sack, named "Ingemar." If the fine ladies at home could name their linen tablecloths, she could name this one of hers! Cotton wasn't so far behind linen.

The print still showed a little; she would have to use the milk that the thunderstorm soured yesterday, to try to bleach out the rest of the trademark.

Carl was full of news: four young men, tired of the bleakness of their lives, and the poverty of their homes, had robbed a clerk in the carbarns of the Chicago City Railway at State and Sixty-first streets, and murdered him. They were at large, the bandits! Ellen had better keep the front door hooked. Everybody in Chicago would be on the lookout for them. Carl puffed with importance at the thought of vicarious membership in this large posse searching out murderers. And Sigrid slept.

But on the way home the next day she stopped to watch a measuring worm that was on her sleeve. It clung to the cloth, then raised its whole self up and stood quivering, reached its front part forward as far as it could, humped, and drew its rear end close; repeating, it covered the length of her sleeve. She burst into the house, "I am going to get another new dress!"

"How did you know?" Ellen queried, disappointed that it should not prove a surprise.

"See—a measuring worm—it's a sure sign!"

Ellen grinned and brought out the new dress. "Here, try it on. Do you like it?"

"Oh," the lips were pouty, "I wanted a separate skirt."

Ellen bit her lip. Her chin quivered. "You know you cannot have separate skirts until you are over sixteen. Everything has got to hang from the shoulders, if you don't want to get appendicitis—with things tight around the waist."

"Other girls—"

"Now, don't you sass me! Do you like the dress, or don't you?" Ellen asked impatiently. "Here, I sit up all night to sew it for you, and what thanks do I get? No matter what I do, you always want the earth with a fence around it."

She covered her face with her hands, and sat at the table and wept. Why was she so short with the young one? She didn't mean to be.

It wasn't that she did not care—she cared like everything—but oh, she was so tired. . . .

A good night's sleep did wonders for a person. Ellen saw Sigrid start off to school in her new dress, chewing the knot on the rubber of her leghorn hat with long black velvet streamers down the back. Funny how she could not leave the elastic under her chin where it belonged. But she was happy with her new dress, and she had kissed Ellen good-bye warmly, with, " 'Bye, Ma—thanks!" She liked the dress; she was a good girl.

Ellen turned to the kitchen. Bread certainly smelled appetizing as it came from the oven. It was so easy to make, too, not much dough to handle making only two loaves at a time. The end crusts were the best of all. She guessed she'd cut one off, now, while it was piping hot. M—m—m—with butter melting into it—m—m—

Hard knocks came at the front door, and agitated shakings of the door handle.

"Yes?" She ran to the front. Had anything happened to Carl? Or to Sigrid?

"Give me something to eat, and hurry up about it."

Her legs buckled under her. This young fellow was no ordinary tramp. Then in a flash, she knew. A carbarn bandit. The hunted look, the dime novel sticking out of his pocket, the blood-stained rag around his head—

A murderer!

Shaking, she cut thick slices from the new loaf, and buttered them, and poured out a glass of milk.

"Here," and she unhooked the door.

He sipped the milk. His right hand threw it at her feet. "Half-warm milk, is that the best you've got?" But he grabbed the bread.

She had not fainted for a long time, but anyone might faint at such close brush with a murderer. And the milk was as cool as the running water in the sink would keep it. It was not everybody could afford ice. . . .

On the way home from school Sigrid felt something binding her legs as she walked, and stopped to look down. Shrill voices hollered,

> "I see London,
> I see France,
> I see somebody's
> Underpants."

It wasn't her underpants. It wasn't! It was only her underskirt. The button had snapped off the strap, and let it fall. In spite of Ma's having sewed the thread over a pin laid across the button, to give plenty of thread for play, the button had snapped off.

> "I see somebody's
> Underpants!"

A rush of tears came. If it had been Gracie Shannon, someone would have sidled up to her and whispered softly that her underskirt was showing; but her mother was not a washerwoman.

Sigrid tossed her head. She would just show them she did not care, and so she sang,

> *"I'm just as good as you are,*
> *You are,*
> *You are,*
> *I'm just as good as you are,*
> *For the ransa, tansa, tee!"*

But she knew she wasn't—she knew— Other girls' mothers did not work.

It hurt inside to know the feeling she had; it was not right to be ashamed of your own mother. But how could a person help it? She idled on the way home, and when she reached it, there lay Ellen, still, on the floor, awake but strangely sleepy and shaky.

Remorse stung Sigrid. "You go to bed, Ma. I will get supper." As she had seen her mother do, she set the apron at her waistline at the back, tied the strings into a neat bow in the front where she could see to do it well, and slid the bow to the back. It slid halfway around again as she ran for the doctor.

"You will be all right, from the shock, but, I don't like that cough of yours. I don't think there is any consumption there yet," the doctor said while looking at Ellen's throat, "but you had better find a place to live, away from the lake."

Of course not, she did not have it; there had never been any consumption in her family!

The doctor painted a beautiful picture of a western suburb, where the dampness of the lake did not penetrate, where Sigrid could play in the prairies, where the saloons were fewer and farther between. But it was the lingering memory of the sight of the carbarn bandit that decided her. They would get out of the heart of the big city, away from this flat where she would never again be able to go to that front door without dread halting her footsteps.

"Oh, Ma, won't it be wonderful?" Sigrid hugged her, and forgot that she was going to ask, as soon as she reached home that afternoon, that they change her name. The boys all called her "Cigarette." It would be so much nicer, she had decided, to be named Genevieve or Hildegarde.

Ellen fell asleep, and Sigrid sat at the front window and watched the postman making his last delivery of the day. Wistfully she watched for the lamplighter. The blue asters in the yard across the street faded into the color of the dusk. The air outside grew darker; just as her days at school had darkened, until now they were black, for the pointed fingers helped to paint them so, scraping against each other as their owners sang,

> *"Shame, shame on Sigrid,*
> *Her mother is a washerwoman."*

The older you got, the more it hurt.

Out there, near the city limits, maybe they would have more money to do with. Maybe Ma wouldn't have to work at all. Maybe. How soon could they go? Real soon, she hoped.

Old Mike now came with his short wooden ladder and his stick, whistling through his whiskers, coming like the promise of release.

He leaned his ladder against the lamp post, peered over his spectacles while he opened the gas cock with his stick, waited while the small flame inside its perforated iron head caught, to make the globe beam with a yellow light. Mike waved to Sigrid. He was her friend, almost the first friend of her life that she could remember. Every day since she was born, Old Mike had waved to her. She would have to leave Mike to go to the country. She would miss him, but she would be glad to go.

Autumn was a time to make a person sad; wind whistling through leaves dying on the trees, boys scuffing their feet through fallen leaves blown thick into the curbings, a tall thin thread of smoke rising from a pile of leaves—

A stiff dry leaf hit against the windowpane, in front of her nose, and made her jump.

Going would mean they would have to leave Mr. Ferguson, too. A cheap way to repay him for all he had done for them; who would be the one to tell him? She asked her father when he came home.

She need not worry her little head, he was the father of the house, he would tell Mr. Ferguson when the time came. Now they would let Mama sleep, poor Mama, frightened so!

"But why was my Sigrid crying? No carbarn bandit has frightened you."

She told him of the verses the children sang—to her—about her.

Shame that could never come from scoldings made his face

red to the hair roots. Staring at the floor, he took stock of himself. Was he a man? He must provide for Ellen—better than he had—she must not bend over the washtub. "No help wanted," or no, he would find work; though his shoe sole was thinned to where his foot could feel each pebble on the street, from searching for work—he would find it. He would!

"Come, *lilla vän*," he drew Sigrid to his lap, and blew smoke rings for her to slip her fingers through, as they had done when she was little; and he told her of the trees in Bohuslän.

Oh, there were trees in France or sunny Italy that grew tall and wide; but let a storm come, and the trunks—that were used only to the fairest of weather—got ripped or broken, to let the leafy crowns fall crashing to the ground. But the trees in Bohuslän, so hale they were from being buffeted by wind and storms, that come what may of weather they stood strong, bending but little in a gale.

Those puffings from the mouths of schoolmates, they were the winds to make his Sigrid strong! As Morfar might have done, he made his daughter glad.

They searched in the advertisements in each day's newspaper; they even put their name on the real estate man's list. Oh, yes, he was sure he would turn up something by next Moving Day. They hoped, and yet it seemed unreal that they would ever be leaving this, the first and only home Sigrid had known.

Ah, it was good to leave the home each morning, now, to report for work. Yes, Carl could love this city all the more when she spread her hands wide with Yuletide cheer, giving jobs so jobless men could carry some of her warmth with them to their homes. Not much of a job, perhaps, shoveling snow from a city's streets—but oh, it was a *job*.

Christmas came, and Carl came home jubilant, for he had won a turkey! It was a secondary thing that the whole of his pay had been spent on raffle tickets. It was not squandered; he had won the turkey! This stroke of luck presaged a change in his fortunes, the first time in his whole life he had ever won anything! What matter if Ellen saw it as a bony, blue, and skinny bird. His luck had changed!

Ellen shook her head. She had so hoped that this would be another fine Christmas, that Sigrid growing older in years and thereby in appreciation, should be able to remember this holiday by the association with it of some little gift from her father. But all he had brought home was the turkey and, of course, the man's shoe box under his arm. No woman could begrudge her husband shoes. A man who went out to work had to have shoes on his feet.

"I see you bought shoes," she called to him, hidden behind the yellow screen that he had set in the corner, to make a tiny room, for privacy.

"No, I'll get those my next payday. That was only an empty box." He came into the kitchen, "Have you got the gravy-stuff made yet?"

"Of course not, I'm just mixing the dressing."

He wanted flour and water paste and he took it back, behind the screen. "The bird smells good," he said when he came out again.

Would Christmas, he wondered, always speak of Sweden? There on the table was a centerpiece, a bough of long-needled pine brought in by Mr. Ferguson, a perched in the needles, two little snowbirds made of yarn, by Ellen. The third, a venturesome bird, sat on the white tablecloth; red breast, gray back, black head and wings, and short black tail against the white of "snow."

A vignette, bringing nostalgia—speaking of home—

The turkey wasn't as tender as some, but jiminy, they had teeth with which to chew! Though Ellen always had said, "They never knew the farmer was crazy till he sang and ate," Sigrid so far forgot that as to begin, with a mouthful of drumstick, to sing "Jingle Bells." Someone started it, and soon all were doing it— hitting their glasses with their spoons—each glass with a different level of water in it giving a different tone, keeping time to "Jingle Bells."

Carl wanted so to read the story of "The Fir Tree" from Andersen's book, but he could not bring himself to do it. The story of the tree reminded him too much of himself, dissatisfied with his birthplace, glad to be leaving it, but coming to what end? And so, while Ellen did the dishes, he read Dickens's "A Christmas Carol."

As Americans did, they would hang their stockings for Santa Claus to fill, and open their gifts on Christmas morning. For lack of a fireplace, in back of the Franklin stove five woolen stockings hung with an air of almost human expectancy, as with reluctance their owners found their beds. Ellen's long black stocking could hold aplenty, but the six-three ribbing of Carl's and Mr. Ferguson's shorter ones would stretch! Not a long white stocking from Sigrid's everyday wardrobe kept them company, oh no, hers was a sock that should surprise even a seasoned Santa, for it was of giant size, knit of red yarn, with bright green toe and heel, and "growing" up the leg was a Christmas tree of dark and woodsy green. Big beads and small beads trimmed its boughs; and into the cuff, in white, was knitted *S-I-G-R-I-D* in letters a good three inches tall.

Fifth hung a kitten's sock, a sock striped round and round of every color imaginable and especially of white and orange and black, colors of a kitten grown into a cat.

My, but it was easy to awaken the next morning—to see the stockings bulging, each with an apple, an orange, a winter pear, and best of all, besides the gifts that Ellen's fingers had lingered over, lovingly, making from little—besides the gifts from Mr. Ferguson—a parcel for each of them from Carl, with each a little four-lined verse to speed the giving.

Ah, it was a happy Christmas after all, and Ellen clapped when Mr. Ferguson opened his packet from Carl, to find a bar of scented shaving soap.

A palm-leaf fan for her. A palm-leaf fan in December! She set her lips to smile, but opened them wide at sight of Sigrid's present from her father. It had bulged out from the top of the hanging sock, but now they saw that it was long, and narrower at one end than the other. Sigrid undid the wrapping.

"A violin!"

"Now," and Ellen's voice quivered, "we can play duets, I on my zither—"

"And I on my violin! Oh, Pa, thanks a trillion, trillion times!"

It made a sound like no other violin in all the world. There were no curves forming the waist, for the body was made of a wooden cigar box, varnished. The sound holes were beautifully curlicued, carved with precision into the top; the pegs were hewn by her father's hand, the finger board was screwed to the box. The strings were real. The bow was second-hand, or tenth-hand, maybe, but it was real.

Gladness transfigured Carl's face as he brought forth, "Still another present for my Sigrid." Carefully, he set it on the table.

Inside the cardboard shoe box he had pasted colored papers to make a backdrop, as in a theatre. On the stage, poised on tiptoe, or reclining, one standing on her head, were seven ballet dancers—milkweed seeds—their brown faces topping long full white silken gowns.

There was a cigar box full of extra dancers, some clinging to the outsides of their prickly, pointed cradles; some waiting, in even rows, their gowns close-pressed, for their cues to burst from stiff dry pods.

Carl knelt on the floor beside the table and put his lips to one end of a flattened straw sticking out from the side of the "stage," the straw Sigrid had saved from her first and only ice cream soda. Gently he blew, so very gently, and the theatre became alive with dancing.

"Oh, Pa!" Sigrid hugged him, "It—these are the bestest presents I ever, ever got! Now—let me try?"

Sigrid blew, gently, and Carl sang for the dancing,

> *"Fallera!*
> *Fallera!*
> *Fallera, la, la, la."*

Another year, perhaps, they might revert to the old-country way of gift-giving on Christmas Eve, when the room was warmer from being heated all day, by the candlelight of evening rather than the cold gray light of dawn.

But this was a day to remember. This was a day—

Ellen could not find the heart to tell Mr. Ferguson then, nor later, that they were thinking of moving away; no need, yet, to tell him. There were plenty of houses to rent, and rent-signs standing in every flat building, but it would take a deal of inquiring to find one within their means.

Tomorrow would come New Year's Eve. There was much to thank God for out of this past year. Trying to evade Sigrid's persistent begging to be allowed to go to the real theatre, Ellen sent a special thanks that frequent motherhood, however dutiful, had not been her lot. One child was enough.

"Please, Ma, all the kids from school are going!"

"I told you, we cannot afford it. Now, go on and play or read or do something besides whine! Here is a dustcloth, put it over your finger and dust between the spokes on Pa's rocker." That shoe-box theatre had certainly given the child ideas!

"I never can do anything," Sigrid cried. "I can't skate, because once you broke your shoulder when you skated—I can't swim in the lake because I might drown—I never can do anything! I never can go any place!"

"Even if we could afford it, it would not be good for you to go, as bad as you want to, Sigrid. Anything you want that bad is good for you to learn to do without. That is what builds character." Ellen jerked her head sidewise to give emphasis to the word. "You want character—don't you, Sigrid?"

"I want to see *Mr. Bluebeard*. The teacher is taking all the other kids in the room to the matinée—"

"I said no. Now, march and get your book and sit down and read—march, I said!"

Sigrid cried. Ellen starched and pinned. Noon came and went. Mid-afternoon came; a glow colored Chicago's sky to the south of them. Sigrid and Ellen together rushed into the street to join in the hysterical relay of words: The Iroquois Theatre! Hundreds of children packed, dying, behind doors that did not open outward.

Trampled—Suffocated—Crushed—

Children, like her own little Sigrid. Sigrid and Ellen, together, wept.

It could have happened anywhere. But it had happened to Chicago—growing so fast, like a young girl outgrowing her dresses before a mother could find time to overcast the seams—growing—stretching her fingers out to claim the prairies to the west, the north, the south; a mother, now watching her infants burn before her eyes—

The neighborhood, the whole of Chicago, the nation, wept.

Oh, the glad mothers who had said "no" to childish entreaties! And Ellen was glad. There would be those who would say that some haunting intuition had made them keep their children home. Not so with her. It was because she was poor. If a person searched far enough, he could find a blessing in everything the Lord sent—even in Carl's drinking—robbing his daughter of the price of a ticket to the Iroquois Theatre.

She knelt in humble thanks at her daughter's bed, and watched the even breathing. Sigrid breathed, thank God, she breathed.

"Oh, merciful Father, help those poor mothers who were rich enough to send their children to the Iroquois!"

Carl would be helping at the theatre; she knew him well enough to know that. And so she waited until soon the dawn would come again. Maybe he had tired himself out so in the helping that he collapsed on reaching the corner? Maybe he needed her?

Never had she spied on him, but would it hurt to go to Shannon's this one time and peek under the swinging doors?

Sigrid stirred as Ellen tiptoed from the room. Death and the smell of burning flesh hovered in the air. Ungodly stillness pervaded the night. A bright light shone in Shannon's. She stooped and saw trouser legs and shoes alongside the bar. None moved. No sound came forth. No tinkling of glasses, no raucous laughter, only a stale male smell. She straightened and pushed gently against one half of the swinging, shuttered door, and opened it a crack. There stood the inmates, some covered with soot and grime, some drenched with water; the bartender sat huddled in the far corner, dumb, and a white handkerchief was in the hand that he raised to his eyes.

Fingers were wrapped around liquor glasses, but as Ellen watched, not one glass was raised to thirsty lips.

Carl stood, one foot resting on the brass rail. His clothes bore silent witness to the part he had played in the rescue work at the burning theatre; his head was bowed as with the others he stood, smitten, and their liquor stood before them all, untasted.

TWENTY SIX

"REALLY, MRS. KANT, you will simply have to excuse me now, I want to take a bath before trying to straighten things out," Ellen said, certain this would end the prolonged visit, and she led the way to the door to rid herself of an unwelcome guest.

"Oh, don't mind me," answered the tenant of the flat downstairs, "go ahead and fill it the washtub, I'll just set here," drawing up a chair, "and talk to you while you bathe."

Shocked, Ellen shrank back, "But—"

"We are all women together, and there is so much I have to tell you, you being new here today."

Ellen started to push boxes and pieces of furniture around, and gathered together the head and foot of her white iron bed, and the siderails.

"You won't like Mrs. Allspaugh!" her guest continued. "She is so spoken-out! And comes it the first day of the month, there she stands on your doorstep with her scrawny arms crossed over, and Lord help you if you ain't got your greenbacks ready."

Instinctively Ellen withdrew from the possessive manner of the lady downstairs. This neighbor was no great addition to the flat she had located near the city limits. "If the rent is due on the first, and she is the landlady, what is wrong with that?"

"You don't have to get huffy," the short fat blonde woman said shortly, turning to go. "I was just trying to warn you." Then wheeling around, "You had better be careful of her, she's awful free with the men. She said 'change of life' right out, *right in front of my husband!*"

Ellen's face showed her annoyance. There stood Sigrid, taking it all in. How was a mother to bring up a daughter decently in this day and age? Nervously she reached for the knob and opened the door, "Thank you for coming up, but I must set up the beds so we can sleep tonight."

"Oh, I'll stay and help you."

"I can manage very well," Ellen answered briskly, "with my daughter's help; and my husband will soon be back."

"I'll be up after you get the things unpacked. I just thought if I could borrow a little butter and a cup of sugar I could make a cake for Hjalmar's lunch—well, I'll be up!"

How could Mr. Kant, a Scandinavian, have stooped to marry such a boorish woman. Ellen could not be sure of her nationality, but she was no Swede; she was a peroxide blonde. Mrs. Allspaugh had told Ellen somewhat of the tenant in the lower flat: nosey, she was, and forever borrowing and never remembering to pay back. An egg, a cup of sugar or coffee, it did not seem like much, but come the end of the month, it surely added up. "Stop it before it starts," was the landlady's advice, and Ellen decided that it was good.

"As fresh as the next one, Mrs. Kant," according to Mrs. Allspaugh, "except when her husband has one of his spells." Then she stayed close to her own flat and met any comers with apologetic mien; she said he was sick, but he was one of those periodic drinkers; never a finer man lived, when he was sober, but a fiend from Hell when in a spell.

Ellen liked Mrs. Allspaugh, the little she had seen of her, although she knew Mrs. Kant was not alone in her disapproval of the landlady. Ellen could tell how Carl disliked her by the way he called her "that big woman."

It was to be regretted that their acquaintance should have gotten off to such a poor start. Yet it was because of that, that she had found the flat; just in good time too or they most likely would have had to wait still another year, until next May first. She could smile at recollection of the striking up of their acquaintance, on the train coming from Hillsdale after that wild-goose chase for a house. There she and Carl were sitting listening to Sigrid's vivid description of the racing of the road bed, "A mile a minute, I betcha!" below the hole in the seat behind the little door at the far end of the passenger car, when Carl struck a match on the sole of his shoe and lit a cigar.

Dressed in the latest fashion of tailored suit and high white collared shirtwaist, a militant woman, tall and thin, came and stood beside their seat. A quick jerk to her four-in-hand, a lowering of upper eyelids to squint at him, and in loud voice she spoke, "I say that if a man has to smoke while on a train, let him go forward to the hog car, *pervided* for that express purpose," the huge jeweled ends of two long vicious-pointed hatpins quivered as her straw skimmer kept pace with her nodding, "where all the surroundings will be in *perfeck* harmony with his own tastes."

The passengers had laughed and craned their necks and turned to stare at Carl. A rush of sympathy prompted Ellen to reach for his hand, but he drew it away roughly while muttering of women getting too damned fractious, of loud-mouthed suffragists; and she could tell he was furious by the way he walked to the rear platform, by the way he flicked the unsmoked cigar out onto the moving prairie.

That was the way she had met Mrs. Allspaugh, who sat to fill Carl's seat beside her.

Did Ellen live out Hillsdale way? No? Searching for a place? Then God had brought them together, for she had a flat to rent in Oakhurst. Cheap, too, because it was three and a half upstairs rooms that were actually bedrooms of a big old farmhouse, but they would serve nicely as parlor, bedroom, and kitchen, and the little room could be a bedroom for the girl, for it would take years before the place would pay for itself enough to install a set of plumbing to make it a bathroom as she intended it should be.

"For me?" Sigrid leaned forward. "Did you say something was going to be for me?"

"Sigrid!" Ellen's face flushed with embarrassment. No matter how hard a mother tried, sometimes it seemed it was next to impossible to make the learning stick that "children should be seen and not heard."

The swell-dressed Mrs. Allspaugh continued; there was no running water in the kitchen either, but there was a pump at a good deep-water well in the back yard.

No, she did not live downstairs, she and Hank owned two more houses. It was a wonderful way to save, this buying houses with a small down payment and letting renters finish paying for them, a splendid way to *pervide* for a person's old age. No more banks for her—no sir-ree—she and Hank had lost $357.32 in the Blacktown bank failure. She wasn't the kind who got stung twice on the same backside from sitting on a wasp's nest!

Sigrid and Ellen had looked out of the window as the passengers tittered.

And so today, more than a year since the execution of the

carbarn bandits, one of whom had frightened her enough to make her burn to leave the basement flat, Ellen's furnishings had come by moving van to Oakhurst.

Sigrid held the flatiron upside down under the iron bedrails while her mother hammered them into place in the fittings of head and foot. It was a hollow sound, something like the way her heartbeat sounded in her ears as she bent over. It was not because she was worried about missing a day of school; school did not keep any place on Moving Day. It was not that it would be hard to go to a strange school with all new teachers, nor the mile and a half she would have to walk in rain and snow and winter sleet; it was not even so much the disappointment at finding no bathroom in this new home. Here, when she discreetly asked, in company, to be excused while she "went to visit Mrs. Jones," it would mean going outside to the little privy covered over with pink rambler rose vines. The red-rosed one was for the men. It was not even the distressing memory of the sad look in Mr. Ferguson's eyes, nor the echo of her good-bye in those empty rooms, so starkly bare of everything she had ever known and loved as part of home.

No, none of these. It was a heavy worry, where was her father? Was she getting to be like Ma: "Always expect trouble, then you are never disappointed; you are always ready, then, when trouble comes." For here he came, and oh, he was in a gay mood!

"You must have found a job!" Ellen looked up.

"Well—" he grabbed Ellen by the hands and danced her around, and lifted his one foot after the other, high in the air, doing a schottische, "Not a job, exactly, but now we *are* going to be rich! This time it is a sure thing. Moving out here near the city limits is the best move we ever made! Plenty of ground—nobody cares if we use the prairie—"

"Prairie!" Ellen gasped. "What for?"

They all three sat amid the shambles of moving day and drank coffee while Carl told of his newest venture. He had signed up, with five other fellows, to grow ginseng. They would be in on the ground floor of a project that would sweep the country, for certain shrewd businessmen had collaborated with scientists and found that the Chinese perennial would grow here, in this climate; the Chinese used the herb's aromatic root for medicinal purposes, and they could use all that America could export to them.

Oakhurst, Mrs. Allspaugh, a plant with five-foliolate leaves and scarlet berries, and Chinamen—what a ludicrous combination to make a man rich! Carl slapped his thigh and laughed.

Well, now, here was an undertaking that Ellen could understand, the first of Carl's get-rich ideas that really made good sense. The land always had been a generous partner. Her forebears, his, the entire peasantry of Sweden—and for that matter of Norway, Denmark, France, or Germany—all had been fed and clothed by none other than the land.

"I knew that one day you would find your niche," she stammered, keeping time with his sawing up and down of arms, his two-stepping.

She would help. It would only be for a short time, until the land gave forth. She would be a partner, too, by resuming her little business. It took time for ginseng plants to grow, and there was the rent to pay meanwhile, and food to buy. After Sigrid was asleep they sat like two young lovers and planned all they would do when their ship came in, a Chinese ship, laden with gold in return for the valuable ginseng.

"Maybe, after Sigrid is educated, maybe we could take a trip—home?" Ellen's eyes were pleading.

She saw that look of longing flit over Carl's face; he blew his nose, hard, and then in full control, "I am content to stay here, with my Uncle Sam. But, min lilla Ellen, you shall go—yes—you shall go, first class."

Uncle Sam was a very good uncle, Ellen knew this; but Sweden was their mother-country. Could an uncle ever replace a mother? Not for her.

Day upon day Carl spent in the fields. It was a monotonous work, hoeing ginseng. Again he wondered, thinking on Norden's fields of flax and rye, how far had he come? In all these years he had come no way at all. Look at it any way a person chose, he was a failure.

No rain came: he found no way to irrigate to improve the tilth of the soil, and how could he cultivate when the ground was so hard that when he struck the hoe against it sparks flew?

Drought. The plants shriveled. The worst of it was that he could not now give Ellen all of the things he had promised her. How could he look into her eyes and say, "The land has failed me," knowing it was he, himself, who had failed the land, for that was the blight laid on him by his father, that everything he touched was doomed to failure.

There was no money from the ginseng. Ellen watched the lustre go from Carl's eyes as he faced the truth; there would never be any money from the ginseng. And it was no fun for him, either, to come home day after day, finding no job. She saw his discouragement. Oh, what to do?

Too, she saw Sigrid's amazement that even out as far as Oakhurst there were laundry customers; it was not so bad here though, for the child, for there was a big basement under the whole house and the clothes and curtains dried there and did not have to hang or stand around in the living rooms. Laundry work paid pretty well, but still she could not seem to make ends meet.

"Do you mind if I take in a roomer?" she asked the landlady. "We can set Sigrid's bed up in the hall—and, two dollars a week is two dollars a week."

"Of course, I don't mind. As long as you pay your rent, the place is yours to do what you wish with; but let me give you a good piece of advice. If you have to take a roomer, get a man. Never take in a woman."

"Why not?" and Ellen thought of thin Mrs. Page, bookkeeper at the cracker factory, who had asked to rent a room.

"They're an awful nuisance—always wanting to wash out something."

"We are women, and we would want—"

"It's your funeral!" the white-topped head tossed, "If you want your kitchen cluttered up with some roomer always wanting to make herself a cup of tea, or a piece of toast, take in a woman. But, my advice to you is, get a man."

It was the best thing had ever happened, this taking in a roomer; Sigrid knew, and walked to meet Mrs. Page each evening, and helped her by carrying home the bag of "imperfects," a misnomer for sure. What did a little crack in the chocolate covering of a "marshmallow-walnut" cookie matter? And the soda crackers! Pa broke them up in his soup, anyway, and she didn't mind if the squares were not whole. Nor did Ma. All this was extra, beside the two dollars a week!

Poor Mrs. Page, she could not walk very fast and she could not eat any of the cookies. She did not eat hardly anything since her operation; she had a hole cut in her side and wore a bag there. But in spite of it all, Mrs. Page was such a happy sort, always telling jokes and finding something to laugh at all the time. She was good to have around, for Ma.

What was the matter with Ma, anyway? Why did she give Pa money, and then cry when he spent it? Grown people were so hard to understand.

"Just call me Hattie Allspaugh," she heard the landlady tell her mother, "and I'll call you Ellen. You seem like my own daughter."

Sigrid sat doing her homework, and she saw her mother smile.

"And so I am going to tell you a thing or two. You are no better'n Mrs. Kant, trying to shield that husband of yours—I know."

Ellen hung her head, the smile was gone, "But my husband is only a moderate drinker."

"Moderate drinker! Ha! Well, do you know, then, how a moderate drinker gets to be a drunkard?" Mrs. Allspaugh carefully ran her hands up over her white pompadour. "Just like a pig gets to be a hog—he grows!"

Sigrid's stomach felt queasy at hearing the word; she could not see, clearly, the words in the history book. That word—that awful word—the one that kids put into the shame-jingle—no, no, her father could never grow into that!

She missed some of the talking, and then, "Of course, you realize, Ellen," she heard, "if the girl had been a boy—"

But if she had been a boy, she could not have worn the pretty bridal crown when she got married! That was the thing her mother wanted for her—most of all.

"Every man wants a boy," the landlady said.

Sigrid let the pages of her history book frill from her fingers. It was her fault that her father drank. Mrs. Allspaugh sat there and told it; how a man feels he is wasted when he has not fathered a son, how a daughter never sufficiently proves his manhood. Of course, her and Hank, they lived more or less "plutonic"; she had never had chick nor child, but then Hank had had the mumps when he was young.

Mrs. Allspaugh's words pounded through Sigrid's brain. This was one history date she would never have trouble remembering, June 7, 1905, the day that Norway declared her independence from Sweden, the day she heard that her father would not go to the saloon if she had been a boy! She ran from the house, and walked over the vacant lots and stopped to pluck a bouquet of daisies for Ma; and there were blue fringed gentians, too, to put around the edge. She would hold it behind her back, when she went in, and have Ma guess "Which Hand?" but she would give it to her regardless of which hand she chose.

Poor Ma. She had had a girl when she should have had a boy.

Mrs. Allspaugh had sounded angry when she said, "'A mastiff dog may love a puppy cur for no more reason than that the twain have been tied up together.'"

What was manhood that it had to be proved? How could she have made herself into a boy? She hated Mrs. Allspaugh.

It was good she was getting big; one of these days she would get a job in a department store as a cash girl, and wear a black dress and run to the call, "Cash!" Or maybe she could work in Rice's Dry Goods Store, near home, where she would place the stuff people bought into a small wire basket, and after she put the money into the small leather tube, she would plop it on top of the stuff, pull on the handle at the end of the rope hanging from the ceiling, and watch the basket go up and then scoot along the wires—over the heads of the customers—to the balcony. She would wait, standing importantly, until the purchase came back wrapped, and then she'd count out the change into a lady's hand, "Forty-fifty-a dollar."

Ma would look swell in a new dress that she could buy her if she were working—rustling taffeta—gaslight-green color—maybe even changeable—with purple.

It was good she was getting big. But, so many things changed when a person grew up. Even as with the little verse, "When the evening's gray, and the morning's red, The ewe and the lamb will go wet to bed." It wasn't, as she had believed when she was little, "You and the lamb" who went "wet to bed," but only big people would know about a "ewe." Maybe when she was really big she would see things differently; maybe it wouldn't hurt so much when you knew—things.

Mrs. Allspaugh was all for "Votes for Women." So had he been, before ever he knew of the word "suffragist," learning from old Morfar, at home. But, Carl wondered, what was it about this woman that urged him to reject his life-long championship of woman's cause?

She simply rubbed him the wrong way, rousing his ire to a point where, when she was in the room, he could believe that the influence of women in politics would be the worst thing that ever could happen to America. Suffragists! Was it that only the domineering know-it-alls banded together, making themselves obnoxious in the pushing of their cause? He'd be willing to bet his stovepipe hat on it, if he had one, that even Morfar would forsake their cause if he had to listen to Mrs. Allspaugh.

"A sober woman should be considered as capable of casting a vote as a hog," she said to him.

"A hog! You're crazy. No hog votes," he blurted, disgustedly.

"It is a freak o' nature," she scoffed, "to find only two legs on some hogs."

"Damn it all, are you—" his face was red, and Ellen trembled.

"If the shoe fits, put it on." There was no fear in Mrs. Allspaugh's eyes.

"Women! I suppose you would even ignore the custom that limits a President to two terms—come next election."

"Well, if Teddy would run—"

"Huh! No doubt if Mark Hanna had been a candidate, and you had been voting—"

"Him. He was so crooked he could hide behind a corkscrew! God rest his soul." She raised her eyes toward the ceiling.

Carl smirked. He did not really believe it, but it was this woman's attitude—it would prompt any man to say it—"It would be easy to fool a bunch of women—voting."

"Mr. Christianson," the landlady came close to him, "did you ever read the *Chicago Inter-Ocean?* Did you happen, some time ago, to see the item about the 'Missoura' woman who ran for the School Commission? She was credited with getting only six votes. She thought there was a skunk in the woodpile 'somewheres,' so she inserted an advertisement and offered a reward of fifty dollars if the six men who voted for her would send her their names."

She brought her face close to Carl's, "Just seven hundred and eighty-nine men answered the advertisement!"

She stalked away, her hands on her hips, "Fool the women, eh? Well, naturally the Missoura woman swore that she would contest the election, if she had to prove that exactly half of the men in the county were liars!"

It was a Hell of a note to have that woman hanging around all the time. By golly, he would go again, and not leave the carpenter boss' doorstep until he found him some sort of a job and his first week's pay would be put down on rent somewhere else. Believe him, he was going to move!

He sensed Sigrid's dislike of Mrs. Allspaugh: his daughter

certainly showed good judgment. She was a good girl, Sigrid; for goodness' sake, he had not brought her any little present for a long time! Bravely he jingled the coins in his pocket to help him walk past doors until he came to the book emporium.

"For me?" Sigrid danced up and down. "And it's not my birthday, or anything?" Pa had brought her a copy of Victor Hugo's book.

"Better that he would spend his money on *A Practical View of Marriage* by Marian Harland," Mrs. Allspaugh said sarcastically; but Sigrid loved the book. When he read to her, she could find it in her heart to forget that Pa's tread had ever been unsteady: she could forget those words of Mrs. Allspaugh's while listening to the ones of Victor Hugo. She could forget the poverty that robbed her of a silk dress like Mazie Mann's— brown, with a pale blue dickey—so far was she transported from the cherry rocker that she forgot how Ma cried more now than she did during their first summer in Oakhurst. She was there, at the quays and piers of Toulon, in the crowd, witnessing the accident on the *Orion* when the top man lost his balance; she saw him hanging above the dizzy depth of the sea, swinging at the end of the rope like a stone in a sling. No sailor brave enough to risk his life to save a comrade, and Sigrid wept.

As Pa read on, before her eyes the convict came. She saw him dart up the shrouds and climb the yard and haul the top man up, and deliver him to the sailors.

The convict, was he fatigued, or was he dizzy, that he hesitated, tottered, and fell into the sea!

"You don't have to give me black and blue marks," Carl smiled, loosening the grip of Sigrid's fingers on his arm.

"Go on—Pa—don't stop—" breathless, she begged.

" 'The next day the Toulon paper printed the following lines,—Yesterday a convict, one of the gang on board the *Orion*, fell into the sea and was drowned—and his name was Jean Valjean.' "

Sigrid sighed at the soft, beautiful way Pa said the name.

There were certain of the pages in the book that he skipped over. "Reminded him of things he had to forget," he said, but oh, he was wonderful; he had shown her how she could get away from everything in the world about her that was unkind. Here was a way of escape, by reading books. This could be what Ma had meant when she had read to her about "The Magic Carpet."

She was getting big; she was beginning to understand.

But why did Ma cry? Sigrid helped with the washings, she carried one end of the clothesbasket and even delivered with her mother while still it was daylight, and never batted an eye when Mazie said, "I saw you yesterday, walking with your washwoman."

Especially after visiting with Mrs. Jones, Ma would come up and throw herself on the bed and cry.

"Is there anything I can do?" Sigrid pleaded.

"No. No. Just say a little prayer for me."

Mrs. Allspaugh was good. She gave Ellen cascara for her "ailimentary" canal; she brewed onion syrup on the back of her big kitchen range, for Ellen's cough, "Doctors, bah! I'll eat my hat if it's catarrh! What you need is a soothing syrup for those 'bronical' tubes."

And she laid down the law to Pa.

Sigrid watched a change come over her parents. Pa got a regular job and he got a union card from the "Afe of Ell," which soft-spoken Mr. Allspaugh referred to as The American Federation of Labor. She started to call Ma "Mother" like the rich girls did, being she didn't take in washing any more and seemed somehow more frail and refined. It was all because, as Mrs. Allspaugh said, Mother was "pregnate." Whatever that was, it was good.

"Was Mrs. Kant pumping you?" her mother asked every time she came from out-of-doors and had stopped at the landing downstairs; and the few times Mrs. Kant came up to borrow something for Hjalmar's lunch, Mother nervously shooed her from the room.

It was fun to wander over to where Pa was working on a new house in the subdivision a Mr. Schmitt was building, a whole street length of houses exactly alike; but every one was painted a different color, so they called it Calico Row. She hung wood shavings on her hair, white pine, and they almost matched the whiteness of her own hair. All of her life she had wanted ringlets; but with all the bread crusts that she ate, her hair was still as straight as could be.

Now she tossed her ringlets for Mrs. Kant to admire, and the lady downstairs, unimpressed by the pine curls, asked, "I suppose now that your mother is in the family way, you'll want a little sister?"

As the sky had fallen on Chicken Little's tail in the Holton Primer, this fact of life dawned on Sigrid while Mrs. Kant unfolded it.

Little sister? Oh, no. And no matter what her father said with his lips, his heart must know that there was a God. She had prayed that a boy might come to prove Pa's manhood, so he would not drink. There *was* a God! Mother was right, there was—there was—there was!

She would like to hear about the coming joy from her own mother. Starry-eyed, she flew upstairs, "Mother, where do babies come from?"

Startled, Ellen flushed and bent over the plain white sewing in her lap. "Wait until you are old enough, then you will find out," she answered coldly....

It was God who taught her to love Mrs. Allspaugh; Sigrid wished she could go into a church and kneel and show Him that she was thankful for all the good that had come and was coming. Sometimes, on a Sunday afternoon, she walked past the church, to Harren's Woods, and then she separated the undergrowth and braved the threat of poison ivy so she could be alone with God, and on her knees send Him her thanks.

"Where did you walk to?" Ellen asked one day.

"All the way to Harren's Woods."

"Not—not past that real estate office—on the opposite corner from the woods—not there—surely not there?"

"Why, mother? It is vacant, and there is never a soul around."

"Don't you ever go that way again! Do you hear me? Never!"

Sigrid could see no harm, but she promised. It was Mrs. Kant who told her about the squat building. A girl had been ruined in it.

Someday when she grew really big, Sigrid knew that she would part the bridalwreath fronds in front of the low windows, and peek inside. Would there be anything there to give a clue as to what happened to a girl when she was ruined? She was afraid to ask Mrs. Kant for fear the woman would tell her: it must be a terrible thing, to make her mother fear it so for her. A man always went scot-free, Mrs. Kant said, "The men always have the best of it."

As the months went by, Sigrid knew that this was true. Mothers never got to take vacations, but even though it was winter all of the men in Pa's local were going to have one, all of them planning a trip out to Rockville to ski. Pa whistled as he whittled, making barrel staves into ski—*"she,"* he called them; just as he had told her the skerries off the coast of Sweden were "shares," and she remembered the embarrassment which had flushed her cheeks in the geography class when the kids laughed at her pronunciation.

"Ole Oleson's brother has built a dandy ski slope—from the peak of his barn roof we can go down, onto where he has built up snow to meet the eaves, and away for more than a quarter of a mile."

"Don't go, Carl, please," Ellen begged. "You might get hurt, and then what would become of me?"

"Get hurt? Don't be silly. Why, when I was only a lad I won a pair of little silver ski for 'excellence in competition.'"

Where were they now, those ski? In the big chest in the spare room at Norden, where he had left them?

That look that Ellen loved came into his eyes. She put her arms about him and forgot that Sigrid was there to see; she kissed him and held him close, "Go, have a good time, Carl; but be careful, please be careful, for my sake. You are much older now, perhaps too old."

"Too old! Why we had a woman home who was over eighty and she covered six or seven miles of the mainland every day—delivering eggs—on ski."

"Where," Sigrid interrupted, "where did she carry them?"

"In a knapsack on her back."

"Gee—whizz—zz—"

"And she smoked her pipe besides." He laughed. "Too old, well I like that!"

The sun made diamonds sparkle on the snow as, happily, he waved good-bye. With the feel of the fleeting snow under him, again he was a boy, at home. Snow was made for action! He had forgotten, lately, that he had planned to write, but of this he could write for others to share—the thrill of it, the beauty of the sun on snow, the long blue shadows as the sun grew tired.

He climbed the ladder, his feet found the rungs of a second ladder lying flat on the barn roof and brought him up to brace his back against the louvred cupola while he adjusted his ski. This was the life!

"Twenty-three—skidoo!" he called to the men in front; then down once more, and up again, the others following. But none, he saw, with such grace as he displayed. Up again. Could he slide down the opposite side of the barn roof where no snow had been built up to meet the eaves? He sized it up: like a sheer precipice, this double-story of the barn, but if he could make the jump he would land in the pasture and could slalom all the way to the river!

Relaxed, he stood ready.

Once, he would try it, once—to get the old feel—so he could write it down. With sight of snow, with feel of ski, came thoughts of home. With thought of writing, came thought of his mother. She had wanted him to write.

But, he stiffened, she had not cared enough about him to answer his letter—

Tense, he jumped.

"Christianson! For God's sake!" he heard, and then he spilled.

Why should his leg hurt? For he was at home again, in Sweden, standing proud, holding a little silver trophy—a pair of ski—while a tall and distinguished-looking gentleman said, "Your mother has been a fine teacher, boy."

The "penny for going" to the store for busy neighbors did not go into Sigrid's Salvation Army lassie bank now, for every cent counted since Pa broke his hip and was in a plaster-of-Paris cast. The fifty cents a week she earned at Rice's, working afternoons and all day Saturdays, helped to pay for Mother's medicine, and it lasted pretty long because Mother took it as Mrs. Allspaugh suggested; it was a matter of principle with her, the landlady said, always to take exactly half of a dose of any "perscription."

But even with Mrs. Page's two dollars a week, they were behind on the rent, and every time she went to Benson's grocery he asked her if she did not have a little something to "pay down."

They were poor, but she really did not mind, because Pa was sober all of the time. She did not mind working, either; it was fun to lift the bolts of yardgoods from the shelves at the store and measure it out, or hair ribbon that everyone said was as pretty as any Carson Pirie's carried. But best of all was the meeting with people, fine people like Miss Cooke who gave piano lessons, like Mrs. Parson who never haggled over a cent or two, as Pa said the swells on the North Shore used to do, asking Mr. Schulz to cut off the extra if they had asked for a pound of steak and the piece weighed a pound and two ounces. And there was Pastor Bedell.

He was a minister, but he did not appear to be different from other people, although he wore a black suit and a plain white collar with two stiff tabs hanging from it over the black of his high-necked coat.

"Good afternoon, Miss Sigrid," he always called her "Miss," the only person who ever had. "Why don't you come to our party at the parsonage on Wednesday? We expect to have a stereoscope and plenty of views. We have one of the Grand Canyon that—"

"In the church, it is to be?" She knew Pa would not let her go if it was.

"No, in the parsonage."

"I'll try—I'll try—thank you ever so much!"

"Do come."

She saw his face wrinkle all up in a smile, and when it did, his broad flat nose quivered like a rabbit's.

She was asked to attend a party. In the eighth grade, and this was her first invitation to a party! She had to go. She simply had to go. How could she ask permission? If she mentioned the Pastor, Pa would get mad.

Ever since last summer when she had seen the young people playing in the yard, and Pastor Bedell was playing with them, she had wished to become one of the happy group. From the yard had come giggles, and "Yes sir, you, sir," and "No sir, not I, sir," and "Who, sir, then, sir?" and one boy hollered, "Pastor Bedell," and the Pastor had run to the head of the line like the very dickens, with his swallow-tails following almost straight out behind him, while the children screamed with glee.

Pa was cross; not as bad as he had been at first, but it was not a time to ask him for anything. She did not blame him for being cross, lying there so long without being able to move; but she wouldn't dare ask him.

She did not dare, and Wednesday came.

"My goodness, it's a regular witches' cauldron of a night!" Mrs. Allspaugh spluttered, shaking the rain from her outer coat and removing her rubbers. Even at her age she would not risk getting sore eyes by keeping them on in the house, not for a minute!

"I hate to ask you to come, Ellen, in your condition, but Mr. Knott stopped to say his wife's time has come. He has gone for the doctor," she jumped as a crash of thunder split the air. "Come another year, I am bound I am going to have one of those new-fangled telephones."

"I intend to have one myself," Carl called from the bedroom.

"Humpf! Men!" Disdain filled the air left clear by thunder. "*Sigrid!* Shut that umbrella! *NEVER* open an umbrella in the house. It's bad luck. You're old enough to know that much. Well," turning to Ellen, "it's half after seven, we'd best be going."

"I promised to take Sigrid with me, if I went, Carl," Ellen said, "Will you be all right?"

"As all right as I have been since January," he grumbled.

"Just call Mrs. Page if you need anything. She is so willing."

They would have to walk the long way around, down past the Pastor's house; even in a rainstorm it would not be safe to pass a house where scarlet fever was, as there was at the Swansons'.

"Mother," Sigrid tugged at Ellen's sleeve, "I didn't tell you before, but I was invited to the party at Pastor Bedell's. See all the lights in the parlor? A stereoscope party! Can I go? May I go? Please? Please, can I go—may I?"

"We didn't ask Pa—"

Mrs. Allspaugh snorted, "Of course you can go; here, take your umbrella, and Ellen, you come under mine. The Knotts' is no place for her 'anyways,' Ellen—we are all soaked to the skin already, but nobody will be dressed up on a night like this—go on and have a good time. We will stop for you, or if it gets too late, Sigrid, tell Kristin Bedell to put you to bed for the night. Tell her we have gone to Knotts' and she will understand."

Ellen reached to kiss Sigrid. The child was as tall as she was. My, how time flew! "Don't mention it to Pa until I have a chance to—" she whispered.

"Thanks, Ma! Thanks, Mother! Thanks, Mrs. Allspaugh!"

Drenched and shivering, Sigrid stepped over the threshold of the parsonage. Oh, the warmth of the welcome! She could just have been born, for in this moment life opened up before her—a new life—which, if she behaved herself so that her mother could be proud of her, might even lead to the inside of a church so she could be like other people.

All of the kids were there. And Sigrid "ah-ed" and "oh-ed" when her turn came to see scenes, all the way from Maine to California. All of the guests pared apples, the last at the bottom of a big barrel, and threw the long peelings over their shoulders to learn the initial of the one they some day would marry.

"A 'G'—as big as life!" they screamed as Sigrid's apple peel fell to the carpet. "Must be a George—who is George?"

Sigrid was sure it could not stand for George, because there was no George in her class.

If she ever gave a party, she would wish to have it end in this same way, with all gathered around the organ, singing, while Mrs. Kristin Bedell played.

"They always seem to pick storms or midnight, to come," Hattie Allspaugh remarked as she washed and dried her hands and passed the towel to the doctor.

"It is certainly a fine baby," he said, and turned to where Ellen sat, tired, on a chair, "Now let's see if you can do as well."

A crash, a bang, a flash of lightning, all in the same split second; a little sizzle, and Ellen's eyes followed a ball of fire as it circled the room. It passed under her and the leg of her chair splintered and she fell to the floor. She screamed with fear, then suddenly with searing pain.

The doctor's rig stopped at the parsonage to pick up Sigrid and they went home together, the four of them. Mrs. Allspaugh knew what to do and busied herself doing it.

"Are you going to give her an 'anna-setic,' Doctor?"

Sigrid would be glad to sleep on a blanket on the floor and give her bed to Mother, wouldn't she?

"Just call me Aunt Hattie, and get a big bowl of cold water and put it under the head of the bed." Now she talked more to herself than to Sigrid, "Fresh cold water—a powerful absorbent of gases—we'll change it frequent—purifies the air."

The doctor smiled; but Sigrid sailed on the clouds, so happy was she. She had learned tonight, when the Pastor asked the blessing, how rightly to address God. She would pray, and everything would be all right with Mother.

She slept on the hard floor, but she knew this was almost Heaven. It must be Heaven, for now the sun streamed in and a smiling face, topped by a tall white pompadour, said, "Your mother has a baby boy."

TWENTY SEVEN

TONY. Better than "Legal Tender," as Coxey had named his son, but an odd name for Carl to choose for a boy of Swedish lineage.

Tony Algot. His father thought two names aplenty.

They called him Tony. But he was not baptized. And he was such a frail little thing—the skin over his temples so white and transparent, the veins deep purplish blue.

Why had the babe such little strength, Ellen wondered, when all of her own vitality had gone into his making? Still, the tiny frail baby had a hidden strength that she had never had for, though she had failed to kindle enough of the spark, love at last took her husband by the hand and led him past the swinging doors.

Ellen would choose to believe, with Hattie Allspaugh, that everything was changed because Carl had a son. Hattie had not been born with a veil over her face for nothing!

"Whoop-ee!" Carl picked Tony up and swung him high.

"Upsie-daisy!" On to Carl's shoulders Tony went and they walked forth and back under the portieres, scraping the garlands of corn over Tony's face and head to make him laugh. The portieres were not only a souvenir of the days when Carl was immobilized by a cast—those days when she had tried to encourage him to put pencil to paper, but some secret chip on his shoulder had kept him from writing, or even trying—they represented a sort of triumph for him, who had said his hands were never willing. Thousands and thousands of corn seed strung with a needle and linen thread, to hang like beads at either side of the archway between the dining room and parlor; and more strings hung festooned across the top. Varnished, they shone. "They'll last forever," she had told him, and Carl was pleased with his handiwork.

Steady on the job, too, he was now; so much so that his boss had waived the hundred-dollar down payment on one of the houses in Calico Row.

Yes, the calico cat had moved with them to Calico Row along with a young calico daughter, one of its mother's last litter. Here they were, in their own home. It would take a long, long time to pay twenty-five hundred dollars, paying it off like rent, so little went off on the principal each month especially at first; but it was a start. God bless Hattie Allspaugh for taking up the first mortgage!

Five rooms and bath and a big basement, and an attic that could be made into three more bedrooms when Carl got time, and a nice back yard! Ellen was glad that Sigrid loved flowers. Under her green fingers hollyhocks already bloomed against the blue-gray of the house whose white trim was brilliant in the sunshine. Blue larkspur nestled full against the tall pink and yellow and red saucers of the hollyhock blossoms, with a row in front of yellow columbine, aquilegia, as at home—blue and yellow, like at home—a piece of property a family could call its own, as it had always been at home—even a clump of wild broom growing in the yard, *ginst*, the province flower of Halland. At last her pride would let her write a letter home to her father: now she could truly speak of how well she had it here, in America.

Only one blot, her children were not baptized. The little sickly boy was not baptized.

"What a man don't know won't hurt him," Hattie Allspaugh said firmly. "Go ahead and get some peace of mind, have it done. I say it's about time."

When Hattie Allspaugh used that tone Ellen felt, without being a traitor to her friend, that she could understand why people called Mr. Allspaugh "henpecked."

But, in Sweden it would not have been like this; there an infant was baptized. An infant was born, its christening followed. She had never known of any individual choice in the matter. It was the way. Things were, perhaps, a little too free here in America—

What should a mother do?

There was Sigrid's friend, Pastor Bedell, maybe he would help her; she watched and when she saw him enter Rice's store, she followed and they walked toward Sigrid's counter together. What should she do, she asked the Pastor.

"Never was I one to step between a man and his wife," he patted Ellen on the shoulder.

They sat on two squeaky stools in front of the yardgoods counter. Sigrid showed bolt after bolt of percale, but Ellen only half saw them.

"Nothing would please me more than to welcome your children, and you, into the church. You must know my feelings in this." His head swayed from side to side, "But, if the peace of your home will be disrupted—?" His loose-hanging jowls that hung like scallops at the sides of his deeply dented chin shook, "Would that I had the wisdom of Solomon, to advise you. Such a problem—with a husband who boasts he is an atheist—"

"It is only his tongue that so condemns him," Ellen interrupted quickly.

"Still, you must work this out for yourself. I can only remind you of His words, 'Suffer the little children to come unto me.'"

Tears welled in Ellen's eyes, "About my husband, what can I do?"

"Be kind, Ellen, as I know you are. Help him. I pity him. And yet, I never see him or think of him, but I think of what Lowell said, 'In the parliament of the present every man represents a constituency of the past.' All men have their ancestry; and anyone can see he has so much good in him; he will come out all right."

That's the way the Pastor was, making a person feel equal— educated. If it had not been for Carl, she would not even know who Lowell was!

But the baptism, absently Ellen fingered the printed percale she had asked to see, and ran her finger along its selvage. She wished she could have the Pastor's definite word to lean on, his command. She turned to him, "If one of my children should die—if—oh, not having been—"

The little Pastor rose from his stool and bent over her, "Think you, my dear, that God is any less merciful than a mother?"

Ellen's stool squeaked at her rising. She forgot that she had thought to buy percale, and Sigrid watched her follow the Pastor from the store. Like a little gnome, no taller than her mother, was Pastor Bedell, a friendly troll bringing gladness wherever he walked. Sigrid noticed that she stood taller now than either of them.

She would be willing to work full time to help pay for the

house, but she would know better than to suggest it again, for
Mother had been horrified at the thought. First she must go
through high school. The time had come when nobody could get
any place in this world without a high school diploma. "First
thing you know," Aunt Hattie had echoed, "you'll have to have a
college 'diapluma' to get any kind of a job."

There was not a girl in high school who got higher grades
than she. Not even a boy! It was outside reading, according to
the teachers, which was of invaluable assistance to a pupil. She
and Pa read, all right, and oh, how swell Pa could read aloud! By
the light shed from the cone-shaped Welsbach gas mantle they
studied together, Pa with Tony on his lap, for now Pa was taking
a course from the International Correspondence Schools. A
man never got too old to learn, he always said.

Pastor Bedell was a learned man, but still he spoke in simple
language. She could understand his lessons well. How he was in
the church of course she could not know, but when she met up
with him and they walked together, he showed her how in nature
God sent His messages to him.

Life was good. Ellen could see her daughter enjoying her own
room, as every girl should do, the whole attic! It was hot in the
summer, but at night the breeze through the front and back
windows soon cooled it off; cold in the winter, but Sigrid had
understood at once that it made young people strong and
healthy to sleep without heat in the room. Banking the shiny
nickel-trimmed base burner in the dining room at night cooled it
so much it was like having no fire downstairs, anyhow, and with
Tony sharing Carl's and her room, they needed the second
bedroom for Mrs. Page.

Lettie C. Page. The "C" should stand for courage, Ellen was
certain, watching the little old lady start out to her work six days
a week, in rain or cold, and "dying on her feet," at least to hear
Mrs. Allspaugh tell it.

"You mark my words, Ellen Christianson, you'll have her to
nurse, before you're through," Hattie offered advice to be rid of
the roomer on making the change to the new home.

"I couldn't do that to her!" Ellen had gasped, "Why, she's all
alone in the world."

"You've heard of cancer houses, Ellen. Once cancer enters—"

"Even if she has got it, I couldn't turn her out, alone."

Mrs. Page was a bit too tired to climb the stairs to see Sigrid's room. But Carl went up with Tony on his arm and Ellen was thrilled to see how he liked the way their daughter had fixed it with her precious belongings set here and there—the dark amethyst-colored barbers' bottle, that old lady Muller had given her, catching the sun on the front window sill—the milk glass plate, with openwork fleur-de-lis edge, hanging like a picture from the rafter—the fancy gold-encrusted cups and saucers sitting on a board shelf in front of the rear windows, one set from each of Sigrid's birthdays since they had come to know Aunt Hattie. Carl said the barber's bottle was a kimmel bottle; he knew it, but he could not for the life of him remember how he knew.

Yes, life was good for Ellen. Her daughter's room was not lathed nor plastered, but Sigrid was not ashamed to bring the girls home to see it. She was proud of the bathroom with its beautiful five-foot tub sitting on fancy legs, and the "pull-the-string" toilet. Yes, and Ellen smiled to herself, Sigrid could afford to be proud, because they were practically well-to-do. And now Carl had brought home a gas iron for her birthday! In fun, she quarreled with Sigrid over who was to do the ironing, but she always let Sigrid win out, and stood watching jealously as the young fingers pushed the red rubber end of a bright green silk-wound hose over the gas jet and turned on the cock. Through the little holes in the side of the iron, she and Tony joined Sigrid to watch thin blue flames reach out and pull the fire from a match held close.

"Next I am going to get you one of those automatic washing machines that work by water power!" So good her husband was. "You just attach a hose to the faucet in the sink," he had explained, "and the pressure of the water turns a sort of paddle in the center of the big wooden tub, and the clothes wash themselves!"

He was so enthusiastic about it. But would such a contraption ever replace the good old washboard? Ellen doubted it.

She mounted the attic steps. It was a pretty room, this one of her daughter's. The kerosene lamps from their other house sat with chimneys clean and sparkling; there was no gas connected upstairs yet, but Carl could do that too. He could do anything, even cut threads around and around on pipes.

Sigrid was an odd child, in a way, with her love of all the old things, even old-country things. How she had wanted the old copper tea kettle—the only square tea kettle any of them had ever seen—that the Kants' had buried in the back yard. And the copper pots and pudding molds brought by Mr. Kant's sisters, Greta and Olava, from Sweden; not only the Kants' but the twin sisters themselves were ashamed to have them around, queer-looking and old-countryish as they were. Yet Sigrid had loved them.

Americans used blue and white enamelled ware, and a person could hardly blame the Kants'; although for her part, she would stick to the iron and earthen ware.

Those copper pieces: it was not that she did not want Sigrid to have them, but after they had been buried, how could she have explained her daughter's possessing them? No, they could not possibly have dug them up. Somebody might think they had stolen them.

The doorbell! And Tony was sleeping! She knew the nails in her shoe heel made a swirl into the soft wood floor as she turned, before the bell should ring again.

"It's only me, Ellen, and a coupla friends of mine," Carl picked her up and set her down again and turned to give orders to half a dozen men.

He lent his back to the low end, and seven husky carpenters groaned under the weight of a big black square box, carved with fancy beading all around its shining surface. Set on a narrow side, four yawning screw holes welcomed huge wooden screws topping four heavy carved legs. The men stood the case up, and underneath screwed in a lyre-shaped piece of carving and fitted round strips of wood into cups back of two metal pedals.

Ellen stood with her mouth open. Here, in her own parlor, was a Hallet and Davis square grand piano; Mr. Ferguson's, unless she was sadly mistaken.

"Wh—why—where—how much?"

"For free—" Carl squeezed her hand. "Mr. Ferguson gave it to us, and my friends here all pitched in to help move it!"

They had coffee, and she saw Carl give each one of the men a paper dollar. When Tony wakened she saw him sit with the boy on his lap, and busied herself behind the door of the front bedroom, trying to make herself believe it was not eavesdropping, this reveling in Carl's happiness.

No, not truly eavesdropping; it would have been a shame to

have wasted Carl's words, because the little one could not fully understand. For Carl sat telling of a home he had had acquaintance with, in Geneva, a home in which a piano had been the center of aesthetic training. Such refinement of taste, such enlightenment, such pleasure as he had enjoyed at Mr. Bailey's should come to his son through the home here, patterned as closely as a father could pattern it, after the Bailey home.

> *"Gubba Nuack,*
> *Gubba Nuack,"*

he sang as he depressed *C-C-C-E, D-D-D-F, E-E-D-D-C.*

"Ellen!" he called. "I forgot to tell you, I asked Mr. Ferguson over for supper!"

"And he is coming?" she tripped out from behind the door. "All the way out here?"

"Yes. He seemed glad to come. I think he is lonely."

"We should have asked him more often; he's only been here once."

The imperfects from the biscuit factory sat neglected on the top of the heavy rosewood piano and made a tiny sound, in their paper bag, at the vibrations from Sigrid's squeal of delight upon seeing the addition to the home.

Mrs. Page sat, and her fingers traveled surely over both white keys and black: "Polly-Wolly-Doodle" for Sigrid, "Auld Lang Syne" for Ellen, then briskly she played "Yankee Doodle" for Tony. Carl marched him around on his shoulders, and they all sang "Yankee Doodle."

"Louder! Play it louder!" Carl bent over Mrs. Page, "For here comes our old landlord—and he is deaf."

"Here he is!"

The singing stopped and Ellen and Sigrid ran to clasp, each a hand of their old friend. "Thank you—so much—so very much!"

Of course he did not hear them, but he did not pay any attention to them, either, but looked over their shoulders, and walked toward the roomer.

"You cannot be Lettie—Lettie Cranbrook."

"No," Sigrid interrupted. "This is Mrs. Page. She works at the bis—"

"This is our friend, Mr. Ferguson," Ellen circled her arm around Mrs. Page.

"Mr. Clifton Ferguson," the roomer smiled, and her eyes

danced. "I have met Mr. Ferguson—haven't I, Cliff?"

He could hear Mrs. Page, it seemed, for he replied, "Yes, we have met," and at sight of his smile Ellen beckoned her family to the kitchen.

Oh, what a happy reunion of old friends!

Never was Ellen one to let the dishes go after a meal, but tonight was different. It was time anyway for Sigrid's schoolmates to come; so they would all go out on the front porch and leave the house to the oldsters, so they could relive their youth.

The children liked to come over, especially if Carl was going to help them with their history. In the winter they sat in a circle around the big base-burner and the red fire colored the isinglass squares in the iron doors, but now it was summer. Each evening they gathered on the front steps.

Ellen carried out a pitcher of lemonade, and round sandwiches of homemade bread cut to shape with a cookie-cutter and buttered well, with round fresh nasturtium leaves as filling; and after she served them she sat in the small armless rocker on the porch and sang to little Tony as she rocked him:

"Where did you come from, baby dear?"

And they all sat, swatting at a mosquito or scratching a bite, until Carl began to talk.

He told of how in the old country he asked his great grandfather how it came that they found sea shells up in the mountains? "The sea once covered that land," the old man had told him, for "high on the *fjäll* was the sea sand found," and Ellen saw that Sigrid sat, deep under the spell of her father's voice, listening to the music in the sound of the Swedish word for mountain.

Had the fjäll erupted from the sea? Or had the sea receded from the fjäll? He could not tell. But he told of the mountain range that ran the length of Scandinavia: if they could but visualize a huge boat upside-down, its keel up-ended, then they could see the physical feature of this range in his homeland. He told of waterfalls throwing themselves in wild freedom, from great heights, down the mountainside. And the sea—no goiters there, in Sweden, as so many people had here in the middle west of America. Why? Because the people ate fish from the sea, fish full of iodine. That was why, always, from the Swedish delicatessen the Christiansons' Sunday evening supper came, anchovies, *gaffelbitar*, and caviar!

Eloquent, he was, in the telling of the story of Karl the Twelfth of Sweden. *"Koll den Tolfte,"* he spoke it, as he would if he were speaking to her alone, but the young people looked at him in awe, and did not laugh.

Leif Ericksson sailed westward as they listened, and led the way to North America. The Pilgrims came; together with those eyes that peered from under gray calico bonnets or black silver-buckled hats the eyes of the listeners saw yellow of maples, copper of oaks, against a blue October sky. Carl's voice awakened eyes to clearer sight, made noses keener to smells, and they sat sniffing at talk of wild turkeys roasting on the spit for that first Thanksgiving Day.

Could this be a history lesson? Ellen could sense that not only to her was this more like a combined visit to the Art Institute, the Field Museum, the Library, and the gloriously interesting past.

Lincoln came now, and they could hear Honest Abe's saw cutting through wood for his hearth. She pitched a tune and started singing, and all joined,

> *"He was not of high degree,*
> *Nor of lofty birth,*
> *Yet no grander man than he*
> *Ever trod the earth."*

Silence for a moment, until Carl spoke again, and they rode with Lincoln, attending court throughout the Eighth Judicial Circuit. No, it was not a history lesson as her husband told it; it was a story.

"Nine o'clock, that is all for tonight," Ellen dispersed them and tiptoed toward the door to put Tony in his bed, but as she moved she coughed and awakened him again; he slept so fitfully.

Sigrid went to the back yard to empty the lemon skins into the garbage can. The kids had gotten over calling her the "white-headed Swede." They had forgotten that last December they had twitted her about her ancestry, about *jelling* so they could hear her a block away because King Oskar died. She had not yelled; but they said all Swedes had. Now they marveled because Pa knew other languages than English.

She heard voices and leaned on the fence to listen.

"Jiminy Willikins, I didn't know her father was so educated."
It was the new boy, from the next block.

"Oh, sure, why he never even lets her use a bookmark. Says if
you can't tell instantly where you left off, you couldn't have been
reading very well."

"Gee—"

"She sure has got some 'governor'!" an adolescent male voice
squeaked.

"And *I* always said *Less mis'erables*."

Her breath caught in her throat. She could not bring herself
to go in. She wanted to be alone, to enjoy to the fullest this
beauty of life and living. She set the board into the rope swing
hanging from the limb of the old elm tree, sat, and gave herself a
shove, then "let the old cat die." She had a father to be proud of!
She had a mother who made the kids feel welcome! What more
could a girl ask from life?

Well, maybe that Gordon Crane might notice her. But
everyone said he was "stuck" on Cordelia....

Ellen had not noticed that Sigrid lingered out-of-doors. Mr.
Ferguson was telling a story too: more than a half a century ago,
he and Lettie Cranbrook attended the same high school. They
were in love. After school hours he worked selling papers and
doing odd jobs until he had saved enough to buy a little ring with
a chip diamond in it. In his hand he held her wrinkled one and on
its finger was the ring, worn thin. Those many years ago—or
even now—what parent would give a daughter of fifteen to a
young high school boy?

The Cranbrooks and the ring moved to Iowa. Never, since
the day of their high school graduation, had they laid eyes on
one another, till tonight.

"But, how did you know each other?" Ellen asked, perplexed.

"Her eyes have not changed," the old landlord said. "I would
have known those eyes anywhere."

What made him able to hear? Ellen tried to figure it out and
came to the conclusion that it must have been a lack of interest
that had made him deafer than he really was.

"The only thing that hasn't changed about you, is your
name!" Mrs. Page laughed, addressing Mr. Ferguson, "I'd never
in all the world have recognized you!"

Chicago's North Side was a far distance, but the mail man

covered it for the two old friends. Daily the opening of an envelope brought sparkles to the eyes of the roomer.

"Of course, he'll never marry her," Hattie Allspaugh said, "In her condition. Nobody would expect it but you, Ellen—you romantic simpleton. But it is sort-of nice that she should have this pleasure."

Mrs. Page had to go back to the hospital and Mr. Ferguson chose for her that she should go to the one on the North Side, so he could be near and visit her every day.

"It is like getting a bride ready—" Ellen and Sigrid agreed, as they ironed her nightgowns and helped pack her suitcase.

In a surrey, with a silk fringe on top, Mr. Ferguson called for her. They were going to ride all the way into the city.

"I owe you everything I have," he said to Ellen, "for bringing me to my first love, my only love."

"It was you, yourself—by being so good to us—you earned your own reward."

"But it was you who came to my front door, asking for the key to look at the dirty basement flat. I am ashamed at the memory of that. And it was you, my dear, who took Lettie into your home. I have no illusions as to her condition. I know." He blew his nose. "I know."

"I charged her—"

"Not for all you gave her—not for what you have given us both."

It was fun to make people happy, more fun than anything Ellen could think of.

"Poor, lonely Tom Ryan," she said to Sigrid, later. "Why don't you ask him to join the group and come on over?"

"All the kids snub him."

"I am surprised at you, Sigrid. Can he help that his father worked in the electrician's cage at the Iroquois Theatre on that awful day? It is up to you, Sigrid, to lead the way. You be kind and others will follow your example."

Ellen gritted her teeth. It was plain brutality for parents to jeer, for their young ones to pick up and repeat, that they could see "scenes of burning children" in the very smoke that rose from the chimney above the Ryans' kitchen. And after all, some good had come out of the fire; a law was being worked out to provide that the doors of all public buildings should open outward.

Sigrid should ask Mary Jane, too, the girl whose mother

made her wear blue jean pants while playing after school, with the result that she had been ostracized by boys and girls alike.

"*Some*thing is queer about a girl who wears 'overhawls,'" Aunt Hattie said, but Ellen felt sorry for her, and Mary Jane became one of the study group.

They all gathered at the home and shouted "Bryan's in the teakettle!" when the perennial politician ran for the third time and was defeated again at the polls. Before she could get a chance to gather her wits together to breathe the words, Ellen was astounded to hear Sigrid say, "It will be good for Bryan's *character* that he did not win, as badly as he wanted the Presidency!" Of course, she was right, the child was; but poor Mr. Bryan, Ellen felt a little bit sorry for him too. About the only reminders left of his silver plan were the milk chocolate bars, with "16 to 1" stamped on them, that Sigrid could buy for a cent at the school store where she bought her theme paper and pencils and little black sen-sens shaped like open books.

She listened to Carl tell now of how pencils were being made of late with graphite centers instead of lead. He always kept up with the latest in everything.

"Three hundred and thirty pounds of Taft!" he said. "There certainly is plenty of him to fill the President's chair."

Carl was only a naturalized citizen, but he knew more about politics than all the teachers put together, if these children were any advertisement for their teachers. And when Cordelia Hull boasted that her ancestors came over on the *Mayflower* and her father was born in New York City, Carl squelched her by saying, "I came into this country with clothes on my back and money in my pockets; can your father say as much?" All of the young people screamed with laughter.

"Did she ever get left!" Ellen giggled to herself. It served Cordelia right; she was not really a nice girl, bragging of playing postoffice and spin-the-bottle, and everyone knew they were kissing games.

So they wanted to laugh, eh? Well, she heard Carl say, they had all heard of Professor Metcalf, who considered himself the special agent to preserve the purity of the English language, especially in regard to grammatical construction and absolutely correct spelling and pronunciation *à la* Webster. Surely they were familiar with his book, written in the hope that it would remedy slovenly speech? One of the stories told on him was that he became so exasperated at his rooster who, in crowing his cock-a-doodle-doo, did not sound the long double "o" correctly, that he killed him. He did not wish to have a bad example emanate from his premises!

"Speaking of the sound of 'o' and double 'o'—it is a good thing for me that wives and daughters do not use Professor Metcalf's tactics."

"What? Tell us—" the youngsters demanded.

"No. That is another story." He grinned, like a boy, at Ellen.

They all loved him, and he was her Carl. The grammar school children, and even the younger ones, always gathered around him and clung to his hands and his coat-tails and went so far as to gang up and trail him from the barber shop, singing, "Chippie got a haircut, fifteen cents!"

And he was her Carl.

Sitting with Tony on his lap, saying,

> *"Tumma tutt,*
> *Slika pott,*
> *Långa man,*
> *Hand i strå*
> *Lilla pojke i värm land,"*

his face was so kind-looking. His big clumsy fingers shook the tiny "thumb," went to the next finger, the one that "licked the pot," on to the "long man," tweaked the "one that was in the straw," and finished by tucking the "little boy into the warm land"—the little finger into the folded palm—to keep it warm.

One day, Ellen hoped, perhaps he would tell Sigrid more of his parents' home place, the spot where her forebears had had their living from the soil and the sea; he could do justice to the homeland, such a gift for fine words he had.

More came one night, and unexpectedly. The heavens burst forth into flame and all the people in the subdivision stood with mouths agape to watch the amphitheatre of the sky take on the fierce color of a thousand sunsets.

"It is the end of the world!" someone screamed hysterically, and children wailed. Never before in memory had a winter's night brought such a glow to color each house and tree and living soul a reddish gold. Fear struck at the hearts of the suburbanites.

Doomsday! Dowie's Doomsday!

"Nonsense!" Carl's voice rose, and silence greeted it.

They were the fortunate ones, to be sure, to have this electrical display come to a southern latitude so they might witness it. He stood as the narrator had, in the Town Hall, the night Ellen had gone to see the colored slides from the magic lantern thrown upon a screen. See, Carl pointed—there—where it appeared that an eagle of flame flew, drawing a sky of color after him? Oft had he seen this sight in Sweden, "Thor—proudly with flame and fiery sword he rides his chariot across yon wasteland—see, how the swift-revolving wheels spin the colors round and round—changing the red to gold, the gold to red— and back again!"

Not alone to Ellen, as they listened, did the elms and maples become firs and birches, the cottages in Calico Row become a small red homestead and a large thatched barn, while Carl described his home. Oh, it was good to see him thus. Ellen hugged Tony tighter. But, thinking back on it, it was only when he had been down on his luck that he maligned his homeland. Yes, the better he had it here in America, the more kindly he remembered his birthland.

Thin veils of mauve and green floated across the gold and red; night sky flowed in to take the place of glory before the crowd dispersed.

"The Northern Lights!"

"Just think—'way down here—we have seen the Northern Lights!"

But Carl called it the *aurora borealis*.

"One, two, three, four—" Tony counted his fingers, starting with the thumb. Carl nodded, and rocked the feverish boy.

"When I get to be this," pointing to his little finger, "I go to school. Don't I, Papa?"

"Yes, when you are five."

"You will get me candy, won't you, Papa?"

"Yes, yes, my Tony—as soon as I go to the store."

Carl started his walking fingers up the boy's chest,

> *"Kom en liten lus,*
> *Och villa låna hus—"*

but when they reached his neck, to tickle him under the chin,

Tony did not giggle. Even when Carl started the walking fingers away over on the table before they climbed on Tony, he didn't laugh. Carl tried the zigzag walking to "bring the little louse that wanted to borrow a house," but no—the pupils of the little fellow's eyes rolled upward under drooping lids.

"You'd better keep the shades pulled and keep the room dark," Hattie Allspaugh offered, "because it's measles, you can be pretty sure of that. There is always a lot of it around in March."

"I am never sure of anything until I know for sure," Carl cut her short. An arch-nuisance, that woman, always hanging around; coming for coffee klatch every afternoon. Still, she brought the sugar buns, and she was good to Ellen and the boy—

The doctor pronounced it measles, and a policeman came and, with four tacks, nailed a red sign to the front door; one on the back door, too, for the milkman to see so he would know to break the bottles on the premises.

"If I were you," Hattie confided to Ellen, "I would not 'postprone' it any longer. Have the child baptized."

Ellen nodded. Oh, to *göra hvad Gudi täckt är*—to do what is right in the eyes of the Lord!

"I don't want to be a crape-hanger, but you know he is so overly bright, and he has never been strong, always like a little angel, so pure, never even a bit of cradle-*crap* on his head from the day he was born."

"I know."

Hattie Allspaugh could have saved her words, for it was her own heart's urging that prompted Ellen and brought the Pastor to the quarantined home while Carl was downtown at the store. Three times on the brow of the little one, three times on the head of the young woman already of an age to be making her confirmation, Pastor Bedell sprinkled the blessed water "in the Name of the Father, and of the Son, and of the Holy Ghost. Amen."

Tony was better. As soon as he was baptized, Ellen saw a difference. She greeted Carl at the door to tell him the boy seemed brighter. She wished she could tell him the other; if he were not so kind and good she would not regret, so much, her deceit.

"Watch him closely," the doctor warned, "the urinalysis showed a heavy content of sugar. Feed him, if he will take food, but only the items I have listed here. No sweets. No sweets, whatever."

"You're the doctor!" Carl agreed, but what was that look Ellen saw on his face, a sly look that was like the children's when they would say, "I know something you don't know." Promptly she forgot it, for he turned to play "Knock on the door, peep in, turn the knob, walk in," with his son.

Yes, Tony was better; and so they must celebrate. As Carl pinched one cheek, "Take a seat here," and the other, "Take a seat there," Hattie Allspaugh spread the dining-room table. As Carl moved Tony's chin up and down and chanted, "Take a seat in the rocking chair!" Ellen cooked a fresh pot of coffee, and by the time Carl had gone over "Teedle-eedle umplings, my son," not John, but "Tony!" for the second time, it was ready and they all sat and ate the Swedish tea ring fresh from the oven.

Ellen's bliss was complete.

Carl stepped softly to lay Tony on the couch, "Sh-h-h," he cautioned, "I think he's going to sleep," and drew his arm a fraction of an inch at a time from under the boy's neck.

"Sh-h-h." They talked in whispers as they drank and ate.

"Yes, coffee is the best—"

Carl grinned as though he expected Ellen's interruption and might have been disappointed if it had not come, "Kaffetåren den bästa—"

Oh, dear God in Heaven, Ellen grasped the table edge, why had Sigrid to spoil the serenity of this hour? She knew better than to bring up this subject; but Ellen heard, "I want to join the Lutheran Church."

And Sigrid could have swallowed her tongue. What in the world could have made her say those words? She had not meant to speak them. She had been thinking them so hard, they just came out.

"What?" Carl did not whisper.

Sigrid gulped.

"What did you say?" he spoke to his daughter, but he looked toward Mrs. Allspaugh; it was the way that woman pursed her lips that was so irritating. "What did you say?"

"Sh-h-h," Ellen warned and nodded toward the drowsy baby on the couch.

"The other kids have—they have—so—so much—fun—" Sigrid groped for words now; she could not explain her real reason to ears unfriendly to the church, how she did not seem to belong unless she was a part of that living that included the church.

"Fun! In church? Are you dippy entirely?"

Ellen breathed deeply as Carl took a large bite of coffee cake; at least Sigrid had the common sense not to carry this on. The worst of it seemed to have passed over. If only Hattie Allspaugh would stay out of it now; Carl always put his worst foot forward whenever she was around. But no, that was too much to ask. Ellen heard her friend say, "Why do you want to deny your children the knowledge of God?"

Deny! The woman was crazy. There was not a thing in this world that he would deny to Tony; Carl opened his mouth to speak, but she kept him from interrupting her, "They are entitled to know the power of prayer—"

"Prayer?" His head slumped forward. Prayer, a thing synonymous with his father—that woman's lips, thin, like his father's—and so positive, so damned positive! "Holy Smoke!" He laughed, and a bitter laugh it was. "What a job a God would have, of answering millions of prayers. On the same day, you pray for rain so your garden will grow, he prays for a clear day because he wants to paint his house, she prays for a hot sunshiny day because she wants her clothes on the line to dry, or a child is going on a picnic. They all believe. They all pray! But how could all of those prayers be answered, all at the same time?"

"Of course, you would not know," Mrs. Allspaugh answered him, quietly for her, "but there is more to prayer than the mere asking for something. But rain or shine, I am content to let God work out my destiny."

"Destiny, destiny—all right—*your* destiny, but not mine. *I* am the master of my own life! I am no less than Hugo's 'serene and lofty soul who only feels the profound and subterranean heavings of destiny as the summits of mountains feel earthquakes.'"

"But God—" Ellen broke in, softly. Let her remind him that God had sent dear little Tony. But Carl did not give her the chance.

"God." In full measure all of the old bitterness returned, the hate he held for his father and the God his father worshipped. If there had been a God—

"There is no God!" Like a ten-pound paper sack blown up

and then smacked against an unyielding surface, he exploded.

The room swam for Ellen, but she saw Hattie Allspaugh stand, "There is a God. For Ellen and Sigrid and Tony and me, there is a God."

"Very well," Carl conceded, but his face was crimson. "If there is a God, let him show me." He stood. If it was the last thing he did, he would disprove this—this female standing here. "I am not afraid; if there is a God, let Him prove Himself; let Him come and strike me dead—here and now." He beat his chest, then sauntered toward the door. "I dare Him!"

Hattie Allspaugh looked at Carl askance and blurted, "He is an ass!"

Pathetically loyal to her husband, Ellen panted, "But he is earnest—he is sincere."

Hattie flounced from the room, "Aren't *all* asses?"

"Oomp-pah-pah, oomp-pah-pah," the large bassoon, the tuba too, played outside the door, played little Tony's favorite piece, *"Ach Der Liebe Augustin', Augustin', Augustin'."*

"Please go away," Sigrid begged The Hungry Five. Tears streamed down her face, but through them she saw incredulity in the faces of the five Germans at sight of her empty hand; before they turned the backs of their gold-braid-embroidered red coats on her.

"Zum Teufel mit das plebs!" and the German band leader turned the corner.

Little Tony lay in a state of coma. The doctor had warned about the sweets, and almost a half of the chocolates were gone from the box.

Could Carl, in his indulgence to the boy, have brought them and fed them to Tony? No one else. "Perhaps it would have happened so anyway," the doctor had said. But—perhaps not—? Or was it Carl's blasphemy? Ellen shuddered.

"Acidosis" was the grave diagnosis.

She obeyed the doctor's instructions to the letter: a teaspoonful of baking soda water every ten minutes, through the day and through the night, slipped into the mouth of the unconscious boy. No. No one could do it but her; not Hattie Allspaugh, who stayed to help, nor Sigrid, nor Carl. They may as well sleep. This was her job.

Midnight. One o'clock. Two.

The onyx mantle-clock with brass-winged serpents at each side struck the hours, the quarter hours, the halves; and the cast bronze author sat on top with his pen and manuscript in hand, his wide-brimmed ostrich-plumed hat set at a jaunty angle, and he was smiling.

Morning. Every ten minutes—every ten minutes—

One, two, three, Ellen counted the strikes until the hour had struck eight. Quietly, tiredly, came Tony's last breath.

Quietly, tiredly, Ellen laid the spoon beside the glass of soda water. "Good-bye, little Tony. You will never know how much you gave me—so much—so much—"

She dared not cry, for crying made her cough.

The little hand; she bent and kissed the finger-tip where she had slapped it—but only gently—only gently—the day Tony had toddled over and stuffed it up the wooden spigot of the molasses barrel in the grocery store, and then licked it off.

Life was full of regrets—

Carl had built the teeder-todder for the back yard, but not in time. Tony would never sit on it now. And he had wanted it so—

Tony was gone. In that other world he would be alone, without her, without his mother. Loss penetrated now to the depths of her. How could he get along all by himself—he who had never as much as crossed a street alone?

How—how could he get along—alone?

"Carl! Oh, Carl!" she called, and he came running, disheveled, half-shaved. She swayed into his arms, "Oh, Carl—Carl—"

He sat her gently on the bed, and then he looked at his son. He ran his fingers over the boy's face and arms and hands, begging them to tell him the truth was not true, trying to prove his sight had told him wrong.

"Tony!" he wailed, and fell to his knees and hid his crying eyes on the bed.

"Tony. Oh, my Tony," he turned, bewildered, to Ellen. "It was the best candy—and I had promised it to him—the very best candy—"

Ellen sat and with unseeing eyes watched a circle of water spread over the pine kitchen floor, white from its daily scrubbing. She had forgotten to empty the icebox water. She must do something about that.

Carl did not think it necessary to buy a cemetery lot.

"Cremation?" he was saying. "That is not new; as long as two thousand years ago, the custom prevailed in the North. Certainly much to be preferred over burial, where worms can eat the bodies."

"Carl!" How could he be so cruel, so heartless, here at the death of his own flesh and blood? He had been so kind at Algot's death. He loved Tony. She knew he loved Tony. Was it that he wanted to believe, so desperately, that this was not the end—and could not make himself believe—that he put on this brusque and carefree front?

Her mouth drooped at sight of him in the new hound's-tooth checkered suit. A black suit, she had told him to buy, suitably to be dressed for the funeral, a black suit, not one to make him look like a circus crier, for the funeral of their son.

She stooped to slide the pan from under the refrigerator, and left it pulled halfway out and stood again. Clinging to the lapels of the flamboyant suit, she sobbed, "How could you, Carl; how could you drink at a time like this?"

And yet she knew. He could not face his loss. She who had prided herself, always, on having character—even she could cry out now for forgetfulness.

If the glassy film over his eyes helped him not to see how the carnations in the little white crape on the front door had shriveled after their first night in the March cold, so let it be. If it helped him when he looked upon the small white coffin, sitting on a folding metal standard loaned by the undertaker, in the parlor where a sheet was draped over the console mirror above the mantle clock, let him be helped. It was too hard to see a big man cry.

Still his tears fell when Mrs. Allspaugh came and knelt before the casket and made the sign of the cross over her breast, and said a prayer.

Ellen was thankful that he could sleep. What could her training do for her, but keep her half awake, listening as she had been accustomed, for the turn of a little body in the crib so she could rise and see that Tony was covered? So hard to break, a habit of love; deep in the night she rose and then, remembering, passed by the little empty bed and walked barefooted into the parlor.

The light from the tall taper made shadows play on Tony's face. There had to be a candle—fire restrictions or no—there had to be a candle, as there would be at home....

One foot moved forward to step into the room, but she stopped. Accustomed to the light now, she saw the slight, white-nightgowned figure of Sigrid kneeling before the casket.

"Oh, God!" She felt her way back to the bedroom. It was not only a mother's heart, or a father's which could be torn by loss. Sigrid, too, had loved Tony.

There were burying grounds closer to Calico Row, but a white hearse led the way to Rose Hill. Ellen sat dry-eyed during the long ride. Tony should sleep near to Algot; she could not let him go from her on his lonely journey to lie entirely by himself.

Only two cabs were in the small procession; all of the neighbors would have liked to come, but who could afford five dollars for a carriage that accommodated only four, paying for their houses as they were?

Ellen smiled toward Sigrid sitting opposite Carl and her, in the mourner's carriage, and shifted her legs to give her daughter knee room. The Allspaughs and Pastor and Mrs. Bedell were in the carriage behind. Carl had not noticed the Pastor's coming, or if he had, had said nothing. Mr. Ferguson would meet them at the cemetery.

"Go ahead and cry, Sigrid, or you'll bite holes into your lips," she leaned forward and pressed a handkerchief into her daughter's hand.

They walked, but Tony was carried, out there at Rose Hill. And she had promised to take Tony to the Barnum and Bailey's circus when summer came; they would march in step to the band music as the elephants and camels walked along in the street parade; and they would see the girls, standing on one toe on horseback, and hear the crunch of wheels as red and gold wagons rolled by, with lions and tigers in—all this she had promised Tony—

"Safe in the arms of Jesus,"

Ah! How glad she was that he had been baptized.

"Safe on His tender breast—"

Pastor Bedell sang, and his spoken words committed little Tony to his grave.

The Pastor's arms turned Ellen around, and Sigrid saw her

mother throw one last heartbreaking look over her shoulder.

Yes, Ellen looked. Would that she could follow her look, and go back there and lie beside her son. Tony was gone. She had lost a child of her own body. What greater loss, on earth, than this?

But she had to be strong: there was Sigrid, and there was Carl. If ever anyone needed the help that strength could give, it was Carl. He, too, had lost his son. All are not born alike, she told herself. Of what use to have strength to give help, if there were no one needing it? Balance was everywhere in Nature. Balance. For every loss, then, there must be gain. There had to be! Was it God's whisper, answering these clasped hands of hers that told her, yes, she had gained?

But what? What? A son of immortal youth. As he had been, a child of love, unspoiled, so he would remain always. Of him would she never have to wonder, "Where is my wandering boy tonight?" Never would she see disappointment stunt his ambitions, nor temptation lower his standards. Tony would be—always—Tony, the fair child—young, and pure forever. This, she had gained.

She coughed. The sky was heavy, it was as if it pressed, heavy with snow, against her chest; the sky was low, so low that the gnarled fingers of the trees trembled in trying to hold it above them.

Inly she begged the sky to let fall its burden,

> *"Fall lightly, snowflake, fall*
> *And bed the grave so small."*

Sigrid took her father's hand. This was too deep for her to grasp, Death. It meant they would never see the little brother again. It meant she, too, would cry into her pillow at night as her mother had used to do; but it meant more than that, more than the terrible tragedies of childhood, the devastating loss when Mother had thrown her precious paper dolls into the fire that time when she failed to answer the first time she was called, more than the sorrow at seeing the long brown lashes follow the eyes of her lovely doll—to fall back into the papier-mâché head—it meant—

"Death." Carl shuddered. "Death is the end. Of everything, the end. There is nothing beyond. So hopelessly, so irremediably, the end."

She stood with him after the others left the grave. He was sobered now, as slinking in from Lake Michigan fog heavied the air and dripped from the bare branches of a catalpa tree on to their heads and shoulders. Beyond the cemetery's edge, peeking out of the mist, a square of light hung suspended; no window frame, no bricks, no siding, only fog around the lighted pane.

"Dead. My little Tony is dead. The only things I ever loved are dead." Carl's head swayed. "I should have remembered, and not gone lax and allowed myself to love him, but I forgot—I forgot—"

Sigrid pressed his hand. Never, in all her life, would she forget the sadness in his eyes.

"Dead, like this tree here."

It was still winter. All of the trees were bare, not only this one; she tugged at his arm to try to tell him so, but he shrugged her off. Pastor Bedell said that believing a thing made it so. Pa believed the tree was dead, and so to him the tree was lifeless.

"Dead," his voice trailed off into a whisper.

Yes, all he could see was the arthritic-looking fingers of an old dead tree.

Sigrid edged him gently toward the waiting carriage, away from the sight of leaden fingers clawing at a sky of lead.

TWENTY EIGHT

MR. KAYE was a living example of the theorem he taught, "walking is the process of falling forward." Sigrid's eyes followed the cadaverous-appearing physics teacher as he strode across the front of the laboratory, back and forth, his long arms hanging like an ape's and swinging as he walked.

Back and forth. Pa wouldn't like it if he knew she used that expression, even to herself. "You cannot go back before you go forth," he insisted.

Pa. He was different now than he had been when Tony lived.

Mr. Kaye walked forth and back. His black eyes popped a little; the lids looked as though they were struggling to keep the eyeballs within bounds; his coarse black hair hung straight from a cowlick at the front center of his head.

"There should be a way to treat milady's hair," the teacher's broad mouth moved, but Sigrid noticed that his upper lip remained at rest while his full lower one flopped up and down exactly like the mouth of the dummy on the ventriloquist's lap at the Suburban Business Men's Fair.

"Now, I have perfected, I believe, a formula which when applied will obviate the necessity of putting a lady's hair up in crimpers every night, or using a damaging hot curling iron every morning." Mr. Kaye held up a bottle of milky-looking liquid, "But I need a volunteer on whom I can try it."

He was a good physics teacher, but Sigrid knew that everyone agreed that as a disciplinarian he was nil.

"A volunteer! A volunteer! His kingdom for a volunteer!" Dan Armstrong yelled, and stood raising his arm and pointing to the ceiling. "It is my humble opinion that at Mr. Kaye's age he should be married." And bowing to the teacher, "Then you could try it on your wife."

"These girls have seen some of your experiments before, Mr. Kaye," laughed LeRoy, at the worktable next to Sigrid's. "Why don't you ask one of the Seven Sutherland Sisters?"

Sigrid sat daydreaming. Here was her chance. She ran her hand over the back of her neck and brought forward the long, scraggly blonde hair. She was tired of trying to look like the Swedish nobility: so pitifully plain-looking, her hair was, hanging loose and straight, even braided it would look nicer, so the plaiting of one length of hair over the other would make lights and shadows; but so much nicer yet if it were curly. Mother notwithstanding, she looked like a stepchild with it this way.

At last, here was her chance to have ringlets. Maybe she was getting a little old for them, some of the girls were starting to wear their hair up, with pins; but ringlets were something she had always wanted, all of her life.

She raised her hand.

"Good!" Delighted, Mr. Kaye sat her at his desk, and in front of all the class parted her long hair into twelves, stroked the evil-smelling liquid on each strand, one strand at a time.

"Vanity, thy name is woman!" Dan orated, while the teacher's fingers wound her hair down around a core of linen cloth, then wound the linen around the outside, up to meet the beginning of the core, and tied the two ends of the rags into single bows. Now misgivings made Sigrid's insides flutter: what would Mother say if she could see what was happening to her daughter's "crowning glory"?

Twelve bows, twelve white linen ringlets, went home with Sigrid after school.

It was worse than she had feared.

"We'll take those rags off, right now," Ellen said.

"Oh no, Mother, I could never go back to school if I spoiled the teacher's experiment! No—no—*don't touch them!*"

Ellen backed away. Not go back to school! Could the child really mean that? "Very well, but you are not too old to thrash," Ellen said, with tightening lips. "Just wait till your father gets home, he'll take care of you."

Stealthily, Sigrid went for the razor strop and hid it under the edge of the parlor carpet. "I am too old to be spanked. I am."

"Pa will have to take care of you in the morning." Ellen surrendered reluctantly, "It's late. You had better go to bed."

The ringlets stiffened, and during the night Sigrid tried to lie comfortably, first on one side, then on the other, and on her back, but it was like trying to rest on a dozen iron pipes. Finally, she turned over on her face and fell asleep.

"Where is my razor strop?" Carl thundered, next morning. "I've got an appointment, early."

Ellen searched. She sensed that Sigrid's was only a play at searching. "Tell the truth and shame the devil, Sigrid, have you seen Pa's strop?"

"I don't see it," Sigrid was evasive, but her face was red. Fear struck into the heart of Ellen. Worry. Had Sigrid inherited a taint of weakness of character that she would stoop to lie?

Shivering, Ellen came close to her daughter and looked up into her face, "You find that strop this instant, or I'll break every bone in your body!"

"Here," shamefacedly Sigrid took the strop from its hiding place.

"Here, Carl," Ellen controlled herself with effort. "She is a junior in high school—too old to get a licking—but not too old to lie. Isch!"

Carl took the strop, and when Ellen had reached the kitchen he said in a gruff voice, "Here, here's one for lying," and brought down the strop. "Here's one for taking my razor strop; and here is the thrashing of your life for submitting to such an experiment at the school without first asking your mother!" But the strop came down lightly, and the noise of its striking was made when he hit against the heavy wool of his trouser leg. "Always ask your mother, Sigrid, she knows best," he finished kindly.

"Not dry behind the ears yet," bemoaned Ellen, "and making such decisions for herself." She couldn't bring herself to ask Sigrid about them, but she hoped the strop had not left blistered marks on the child's legs, blisters in the shape of the handhold. It was good that young girls' skirts reached the floor, for marks like that could show through stockings, heavy cotton though they were. Too bad to have to have Sigrid chastised, but never let it be said of Ellen Christianson that she had spared the rod to spoil her child.

Carl's appointment was at the back door to receive cans, hundreds of them, with small screw tops. Tucked under the topmost can, Ellen saw an unpaid bill; but if this could put him back on his feet again, it would be worth it. For the carpenter boss had had to let him go. "When a man starts needing a drink in the mornings, he is no good to us," and what a shame, the boss said, for Carl was the smartest figurer he had ever seen; could look at a set of plans and estimate the board feet of lumber required so close that later figuring would prove his mental calculation to be tip-top! "Such a brain! But of what use is it when he doesn't have sense enough to keep his senses?" He was sorry, the carpenter boss was, but—

Ellen could believe, though, that all of this might be for the best. Building trades work was so flighty; a man could leave for the job on a bright sunshiny morning, and no more than get there, than it might rain like the Old Harry. Who could know if it would turn out to be only a short shower? Should the men go all the way home and lose a whole workday, or wait around to see if it would clear up in an hour or so?

She understood perfectly: where else could they go, to wait and see, except under cover of the saloon? It was not all that Carl tried to drown his late sorrow; the class of work was at least partially responsible for the way he was. But, with so many out of work—and jobs so scarce—

Well, anyway, it was good to see him take interest again, even in cans!

"I'm having a telephone installed," he announced eagerly.

Sigrid had never been late for school, but Ellen would let her chance it this morning, so she could hear about the new business. Metal polish. He could not lose because he had a good name for it, "White Star."

Soon he would have to buy a roll-top executive desk, with lots of pigeonholes inside, to take care of all the paperwork, and Sigrid should study typewriting and shorthand, and be his secretary!

"This won't come to nothing," he assured them, "like the jobs have in Schenectady and Portland and Frisco and—"

"Nothing? Carl," Ellen comforted. "How can you say, 'Come to nothing'? What do you suppose has gotten Sigrid the highest marks in geography that they ever gave at the school? Going to Schenectady and Portland and—"

"But never on the train," discouraged, he answered her.

"On the map though! 'Come to nothing.' Why Carl, I am surprised at you, seeing no further than the end of your nose. 'Come to nothing'—eh!"

"Ellen—" he stretched his arms out to her.

Her face flushed. "Sigrid, better get going! You'll have to run the whole way, so's not to be tardy!"

Sigrid ran, and slid into her homeroom seat just under the bell. They were going to have a telephone! She found it hard to keep her mind on her lessons, with that, and the white rags, and the joshing that went with the rags. She wished for the sixth period to hurry up and come. At last, to the physics class to have the white rags removed.

But they would not come off. Mr. Kaye tried solution after solution; the rags would not loosen.

Thread by thread, shred by shred, the fingers of thirty physics students pulled the linen rags from iron-stiff ringlets. "Curly-locks." Forever and a day she would be known as Curlylocks. But then, that was no worse than being called "Cigarette."

She ran home. Breathless, bursting into the house, she called, "Mother, Mother, Mr. Kaye says you will have to cut it off!"

"Cut it off!" Ellen's voice was cold with horror, "Indeed not. Decent girls don't go around with their hair cut short."

"But I can't go around with it *this* way!"

"This is exactly the way you wanted it. You chose to have ringlets. All right, now you live with your ringlets. Let this be a lesson to you. Such a foolhardy thing to do!"

The whole world was going to the dogs, Ellen grieved. It was growing harder and harder all the time to bring up a girl. She hung her head with shame at the thought of the *New York Herald* printing an advertisement for clothes for expectant mothers—she had seen the advertisement, herself, with her own eyes; no modesty, no modesty at all, printing such things for everyone to read, even growing girls. No wonder they grew more difficult to teach, disregarding parents to the extent of letting such a thing as this happen. Ringlets. Ringlets, indeed.

"You will be a fine sight to go in to Chicago, with those ringlets."

"Are we going to Chicago?" Sigrid's pleasure at the thought was so great she could forget the hair, "What for?"

"I ought to make you stay at home."

But, of course, they all three had to go to Chicago, and Ellen perched Sigrid's hat on top of twelve stiff ringlets. No daughter of hers would ever be allowed to wear a scarf over her head, like a mere peasant in the old country, and certainly not to a wedding.

No ordinary wedding was this one of their old landlord's,

Ellen helped to prop up Lettie Page against the pillows on her hospital bed, and slipped her wedding gift over the wasted arms and shoulders, a soft rose-colored bedjacket.

"Till Death do us part," they took each other, and oh, the look she saw in Lettie's eyes! Ellen could know her joy, even at this late date, in being wed to the one she loved.

"And beyond—" Ellen heard Mr. Ferguson say, as she slipped from the white-walled room and beckoned Carl and Sigrid to follow. She need not be ashamed to cry, for she saw that the minister drew the back of his hand over his eyes.

"I never knew *old* people got married?" Sigrid could not quite understand.

"Sh—h— you are not old enough to ask questions about marriage," Ellen cut in.

"I suppose there are people who will say she must have money, Mrs. Page," Carl addressed Ellen.

"Why? Of course she hasn't."

"Why? That he should marry her, in her condition. It is not everyone, Ellen," and his eyes took on that look she loved, "who understands, as we do."

Though she could not afford to serve lemonade and sandwiches, the young people came as usual, and the telephone was an added attraction. On the evenings that Sigrid did not work at Rice's, they came and heard Dan call "Parkside 3201, please!—Is this the grocery? Yes? Well, do you have any dry fish? You do? Well, why don't you give them a drink?"

There was the call to the zoo, asking for Mr. Wolf, that caused so much hilarity that Mother and Pa came from the basement and put a stop to it, for good and all, but before Pa left the room he promised them, each and every one, a penny apiece for wrapping and pasting labels on his metal polish cans.

They were not to use the phone for nonsense. What if an important call came through for him while it was so employed? So the visitors left the house singing,

> *"I should worry, I should fret,*
> *I should marry a suffragette—"*

The phone bell rang. There was a wild scramble from the basement. "I'll bet it's a big order!" Carl panted.

"Hello!" he screamed.

"It's for you." Perplexed, he handed the receiver to Ellen and she put her lips up close and yelled, "Hello!"

She stood still and listened. Mr. Ferguson spoke in low tones: Lettie had slipped into her deep sleep. He was not sad, only happy that his sole mission in life had been accomplished, to find his love and to make her his wife. The days that they had been together had brought reward beyond telling—for she had surrendered herself into his keeping—strong, true, steadfast character that she was. All so worth while, every moment they had had together, and with deep gratitude both had lived those moments.

"I do not grieve, my friend Ellen, for she still lives for me. Our promises and commitments are for all time. Death does not part."

Ellen placed the receiver gently on its hook. Somehow she felt bigger than she had been before, no more confined by one small earth; through Mr. Ferguson's words she felt to be a part of the universe, part of the whole creation.

Carl sat undoing his shoe laces from over the metal hooks above the sets of eyelets, and Ellen watched him. In a year, the metal polish had not started paying. She could not keep going much longer, providing all they needed over and above what Carl could earn at odd jobs. There were so many men out of work, not only Carl.

Who could that be at the door, this time of night? "Sigrid, please see who's there?"

"Aunt Hattie—"

Carl walked toward the doorway; it was that woman again. Showing his lack of respect, he leaned close to the jamb and scratched his back against it.

"All I need now is the automobile," Mrs. Allspaugh tripped into the room. "See my new duster and auto veil?" Quickly she drew up the chair Carl had vacated, "I did not come to show you these. I came to tell you that Mr. Kant has been *fined*," she looked in Carl's direction, "for being drunk!"

"Oh!" Sigrid and Ellen, together, gasped.

"He deserved it, no doubt about that; but I say let the magistrate fine the saloonkeeper who receives the money, not the poor fool who has already spent his pile—and my rent money—on internal irrigation."

"Well," said Carl, "you can't exactly find fault with the

saloonkeeper; what is he to do when one man has treated. He can't very well refuse to sell when then another wants to treat."

"Treat." Hattie Allspaugh interrupted, disdainfully, "This custom of treating, this bibulous generosity, what is it if not purely a creature of the saloon? Certainly it was never born in sober sense!

"Did you ever hear of it except in the soggy good nature of a man half full, or more, of liquor? Did you ever find this 'code of honor' any place except inside of a saloon? Did you, by any chance, ever see a man walk into a dry-goods store and say, 'Set 'em up, all around, to *underdrawers!*'?"

Carl started time and again to speak, but Hattie Allspaugh continued at a pace that aborted his utterances so they ended in intakes of breath.

"It is in the saloon, and only in the saloon, that this treating business has got into popular usage, making men funnels through which to pour alcohol." She drew her new duster up close about her neck, "There is a lesson there for others," glancing toward Carl, "Kant's getting fined."

Sigrid drifted to the piano and started playing one of the three pieces she knew without notes, "Home Sweet Home," but after the first note she changed to "Tenting on the Old Camp Ground." No, that would not do, either, so she played her mother's favorite piece, "In the Sweet Bye and Bye, with Variations." Her left hand crossed over her right.

"Heart-'rendering,'" Hattie Allspaugh said as she left. "For having had no lessons, she does right well."

Ellen resumed her reverie. Soon Sigrid would be through high school; that was a good foundation, and every parent owed a child a high school education. Then Sigrid could take care of herself. But Carl; she had loved him too well, perhaps. Would it have been better never to have shown him that she cared? That had been her mother's teaching; and "No man runs after a streetcar after he's caught it," Hattie advised. "Keep 'em guessing." But how could she have hid the love she had for Carl? Too little unity of purpose in this marriage, and yet—when Tony lived—

Tony. Oh, that Sweet Bye and Bye when she would meet him.

"'On that beautiful shore,'" Sigrid's clear voice rose.

Ellen sighed. She watched the uneven heaving of Carl's chest, and knew he sobbed within. If she could only help him! If only one of his many works had panned out all right! It was hard on him, this not getting orders for his metal polish, and he worked so faithfully at it; harder on him to see her find customers when he could not. How could she help him?

Praying for inspiration, inspiration must come.

It came. A square, dark-colored envelope came, with darker hairs pressed into the surface, with the picture of the Swedish King on the stamp in the upper right hand corner. And it was postmarked, "Falkenberg."

Her trembling fingers slit an opening, with the kitchen knife. Ah, if she could share this with Carl, this letter come from her old father in Falkenberg; only a bit of paper with some inky scrawls upon it, but having the power to bring back sights of beech and willow, the smell of woodland in the spring, the sound of vines murmuring as, clinging to a little house, they sang of summer, the taste of wild berries, the memory of children running, hand in hand—she and Algot—

But to Carl no letter from home had come. She could not show him this, and make it seem that she was "rubbing it in" because he had none.

Home. If only she could go home.

She straightened, as if a poker had been slid between her corset and her skin. "A wishbone where your backbone ought to be, is that what you've got, Ellen Christianson?" she asked herself, gruffly. "Even if you had the money, you couldn't go until Sigrid is through high school. And that's that!"

But thoughts of home could show the way to help Carl. There was no job for Carl. His metal polish did not sell. All right, then, let him make his adversities work for him, not against. Let the kicks he received be kicks upward, not always down. Let him use this time constructively, for writing. Had he not always said he yearned for sufficient time in which to write? Who could tell what might come from the pencil of a man as capable of deep feeling as her Carl? If only she could get him to write of the Homeland!

Sometimes he seemed never to have really grown up, some little perversity there, that when she said one thing he took the opposite side, perhaps only for argument; but she could try a ruse:

"Du gamla, du fria—"

She started the national anthem, and, sure of his attention, went on, "Du gamla—ha! America certainly owes nothing to Sweden, with all of us immigrants coming here, eating off of her land, really giving nothing in return. I'd sure like to write a book about that, if I was smart enough to write!"

"How can you speak so, Ellen?" his voice was almost harsh. "Why, if I should write a book, I should write it to tell of all that the immigrants have done to build America." He picked up a pencil and made petal marks at each upper corner of a sheet of paper, and little triangles and dots across the paper to join them. "It is their heritage, come over here in the hands and minds and gifts of the immigrants that has helped to make America the wonderful country that it is."

Oh, this was reward to Ellen, for it was love of homeland made him speak as now he spoke. Yes, he would write, of the hills and firs of home! A fine beginning for a book, the anthem,

"Du gamla, du fria—"

He wrote; each day he wrote, but after so long a time each day, he threw the pencil down, discouraged.

"The words—they are not the same in English, Ellen."

She glanced over his shoulder. "I think it sounds beautiful, 'Thou ancient, thou free—'"

"But you'd have to finish it, 'Thou fjäll-crested north!' How does it sound, 'Thou mountain-crested north'? All of the rhythm is lost—using the word 'mountain.'"

He threw his pencil down, "I can't write, Ellen.

"No. I can't find the words. Even 'Du gamla,' saying it 'Thou ancient'—it loses its feeling. None of the words have the same—the same something. Take *'din sol.'* Every land, Ellen, has its sun. But 'din sol,' that is different. It is something grander than just 'your sun.'"

He picked up his pencil, but let it fall. "The meaning may be the same, but the words in English speak only from the tongue; but take 'du fjäll höga nord,'" passionately he said the words. "They speak from the heart."

"Write it in Swedish, then, completely in Swedish, and we can translate it afterward."

"No, Ellen, it takes a Selma Lagerlöf to write of Sweden. I can't do it. I can't write. It's no use, I can't."

He looked at his wife. She was disappointed in him. No more, though, than he was in himself. It was no easy thing to look into a mirror and see a failure, always a failure—a misfit, torn by the roots from his native land, and never able in the transplanting to make his roots take hold—and of late, something worse. Oh, God, she said she understood, but how could she understand the torture that came to a father who had brought candy to his son. "It might have happened so, anyway," the doctor had said. But again, *it might not have!*

In her kind way, Ellen had thought to interest him in writing, he was not so dumb but he could figure that out. How could he expect her to understand, she who had never crossed the threshold of a Family Entrance, the release from misery and remorse?

Yet Ellen knew she understood; but why did he care so little for his health? Only gulping down a couple of raw eggs in a little whiskey, that's all he took. "Not hurting anyone but myself," he answered her remonstrance. How could he be that unseeing?

He was so kind in other ways. It was only yesterday that she had watched him go, at the sound of the pipe of the waffleman's whistle, to bring a cube of sugar to the horse. The little mare's straw hat had slid down too far frontward, and Carl had taken it off and brushed the front short hairs of the mane back out of her eyes, so tenderly, and fitted the little hat with its peaked crown over the long ears again.

That was her real Carl, tender, as he had been with Tony, as he was with her except in the cruelty of his intemperance.

On a Friday he went to Chicago, hopefully, to follow up on an order for polish. A wild-goose chase, it turned out to be. "Why had I to bump into the shoemaker from Geneva," he grumbled to himself on the way home. So John Peterson was retired. Satisfied with himself because he had played a part in others' successful lives; or so he made himself believe. Jack Johnson: thirty dollars he had paid for custom-made shoes—the lasts were still sitting right there on the shelves, in Geneva. Lillian Russell, too, had reached the top. "And I made the shoes that carried them there," John had boasted. Did such second-hand participation entitle a man to bathe in glory? Let him brag; who cared?

So John thought that Carl should have stayed in Geneva; he

might have been a head guy in the big starch company, grown out of the glucose? And that lot Joseph had wanted him to buy had tripled in value. Joseph—Martina—Mr. Bailey—a whole flood of memories— If he had stayed in Geneva—if—

Carl stopped. On the sidewalk a little child stood crying, rubbing his fists into his eyes. Only wailing answered Carl's questions, but the boy was lost, that was obvious.

"Well, sonny, don't you cry any more, we shall go to the Police Station, and they will find your papa." He stooped and little fingers wrapped themselves around his big ones.

"We'll look for Mama." At that magic word the boy stopped crying, and looked with trustful eyes into Carl's.

"I should like to telephone my wife," Carl said to the desk-sergeant at the station, "why I have been delayed." He could afford to feel a little puffed up; it was not every man who had a telephone in his home.

"Hello?"

"Ellen?"

"Yes, and where are you?"

"At the Police Station!" If she could only see the twinkle in his eyes at this.

"*Now* what have you done?" she cried.

He dropped the receiver on to the hook. Ellen didn't trust him. How could a man ever amount to anything when his own wife did not trust him?

He didn't care if he never went home.

Cordelia's family had a talking machine, with a huge horn shaped like a morning-glory flower. It was the newest thing out; naturally the kids would flock to her house. But Sigrid did not join them. Not after that last time.

"Speech! Speech!" they had demanded of Cordelia after she won a love game at tennis; and she stood like a soap-box orator: "I believe in a man taking a drink—sure, I believe in a man taking a drink, but there is such a thing as going too far!" She flailed her arms about and finished shrilly, facetiously, "There ought to be a saloon in every block!"

The laughter died, but every eye had turned toward Sigrid.

What had Pa said? "As long as I am not hurting anybody but myself."

Little did he know.

Why did mother martyr herself—fear-ridden, trembling at

the sound of an ambulance siren, "Maybe Pa has been hurt!"—afraid of everything—leaving the front door open on their return to the house after absence, so they could run out "if anything was wrong."

There must be something between them that made her willing to live with him the way he was. She must have something.

Yes, of course, Mother did have something: the memory of how he was, before. Though it was March, who could forget the blue sky of last summer? Who could forget the sight of Pa's eyes that day a year ago at Rose Hill?

But how did his mind work that he should come home lugging a small keg of salt herring, sheepishly suggesting that on Good Friday they not eat meat, but sill, when he always denied the church? Never would she be able to understand grown people. But books, they were something else again, and Sigrid buried herself in them. And as time went on, the blonde ringlets kept getting softer.

She liked Miss Lowe, her mathematics teacher. Some of the pupils were afraid of Miss Lowe; without meaning to, she frightened the members of her classes the first day she met them.

Beneath the forbidding blankness of the teacher's facial expression, Sigrid found a most kindly personality. Miss Lowe was no ogre, as the boys said, but she had never learned how to wear her real self on the outside.

She became Sigrid's friend; fitting that she should be the one to tell her, "You are to be the valedictorian."

"Oh." What else could a person say to that?

"You may have first choice of the scholarships to these universities—"

Miss Lowe was genuinely sad to learn that the prize pupil would not be going on to school. "There is always a way," she said.

Sigrid knew better. There was no way.

"You could earn your board and room, and with the scholarship—"

She was big and strong; it was time she took the burden of work from her mother. There were bills, bills. No, there was no way.

Outwardly she pretended to be glad to think of getting a job; and Miss Lowe was bewildered to see that she had been mistaken in believing Sigrid to be a student.

Inwardly, the heart of Sigrid was broken.

"The Senior Prom?" Ellen asked, "What sort of thing is that?" It could not be necessary, surely, in order to obtain a diploma. "Dancing! Funny school system they have in this country!"

"Never mind, Mother, I was only wishing. I couldn't go in my school clothes, anyway."

"It is *at* the school, isn't it?" Ellen asked, as Hattie Allspaugh walked in for her daily visit.

"If it is the thing to do, I think she should go," Carl interrupted. "But try to be home before nine o'clock," he smiled toward Sigrid.

Tomorrow he would get a job, somehow, somewhere. If there was only one job in the whole country, by God, he'd get it. His daughter should have clothes as good as the rest of them.

"I couldn't go without a new dress," Sigrid pouted. It was bad enough to have to go to Commencement in the dress cut down from Aunt Hattie's white dress, the one she had gotten for "enstallation" in her lodge.

Sigrid's pouting lip hung low. She had voted for caps and gowns; but it was voted down, because all of the other girls wanted to show off their new dresses.

Hattie Allspaugh patted Sigrid's shoulder, "You are young yet. There is plenty of time for you to party. And the dancing. Are you sure you want any part of that? I say, never can the country be free of shameless women until the decent women and girls refuse to let a fella put their arms around them to music when they know full well they'd let no whippersnapper handle them like that if there was no band playing. Come on, we'll all go to the new nickel show. My treat," and she sent a grin in Carl's direction.

In the semi-darkness, they found their seats; Sigrid pushed down the sitting part of her chair with her buttocks. Her eyes were glued to the front of the theatre. There was a moving picture, life-sized; a dog was running, the scene changed, he started at the lower left of the picture and ran, ran until he was only a dot leaving the upper right. The scene changed again and again, the dog ran and kept on running, at times diagonally across the screen, again straight up, from bottom to top and out of sight over a hill.

At first she sat forward, her mouth wide open, grabbing the front of the seat with both hands, then she settled down to enjoy this wonderful new experience, the seeing of a moving picture! It was not so bad, not to go to the Prom; she did not know how to dance, anyway.

She leaned back against the seat, comfortable, for the "iron" at last was gone from her ringlets.

Sigrid had been graduated now from a Ferris Waist to a corset; graduated too from high school, and working in a printing office. It took a smart girl to hold copy for a union proofreader, and Sigrid was smart. These Mondays, Wednesdays, and Fridays seemed over long to Ellen, with Sigrid away all day and staying downtown after work to go to business college to study typewriting. Tuesdays, Thursdays, and Saturdays were long, too, because she had to work at Rice's then in order to get the money to pay for her typewriting lessons. My, what a thing a high school diploma was! Mr. Rice was paying Sigrid four dollars a week now.

Yes, Sigrid could take care of herself, she had a good foundation of schooling.

But Carl, what about Carl?

Ellen took from her bosom the letter that had come from her father. She had tried to write in reply so many times, but tonight she would try again. How many times she had read this letter. The large angular writing showed the trembling in his aged hands, "I take my pen in hand to write to you," she read again, and reading, compensation came to Ellen for all the puzzling years, for all the hurts, for the sorrow. "Come home," his letter said, "so I may see you once again. If only for a day, come home.

"Maybe it takes a man ninety years of living to get some sense into his head; it is so hard to say to a daughter who has other ties, but please come home so I may see once more my *lilla skälmaktiga Elin.*"

She had written, in that first letter home, of how good she had it here. He could not know that passage money had been as far removed from her possession as the crown jewels of Sweden—until today—

The coffee pot cover danced on top of boiling grounds. Bubbles came out of the lip of the pot, making brown streaks until a sizzling sound came from the gas burner. Ellen sat unheeding.

Sigrid could take care of herself. But who would take care of Carl?

If she went home, no one would ever finish the petit-point

shelf scallops for the china closet in the dining room. Would Sigrid want to be bothered finding homes for all of the kittens as they came? Would Sigrid find time to set the fern out in the rain in summer, and sprinkle it in the bathtub in the winter? And the palm; would Sigrid wash it off with watered milk, loving it as she stroked its leaves?

Oh, they were dear, Sigrid was dear, but not so dear as the old home.

And all of the property owners in Calico Row had signed to have sewers put in, and curbings, and paved streets. She had signed, thinking of the day the ambulance had been stuck in the mud outside her door—with the MacKenzie girl inside—and all the sand and gravel and boards had been used vainly; the wheels went deeper and deeper into the mire and ruts. They needed paved streets, and she had signed. But she was too weary now to think of meeting assessment payments, too sick.

But who would look after Carl?

Rain, quietly falling outside the door, hummed as the door opened and Carl came in.

"Someone has been here! A man!" He took Ellen in his arms and tipped her chin so she should look at him, "Confess!"

Ellen pulled herself from him and went to the stove, and took the dishcloth to the gas burner, and washed the brown streaks from the side of the coffee pot. "Oh, you Sherlock Holmes, you," she smiled and sniffed of the air in the room. "Yes, it is Mr. Ferguson's pipe you smell."

Sigrid came to hear her tell of his visit. Her mouth opened, wide, "But I thought only millionaires left wills!"

Mr. Ferguson had brought the word of Lettie's bequest: that her good friend, Ellen, should have the wish her heart craved most, a trip to Sweden.

"Of course, I can't go—"

"Of course you can, Ellen! You should, of course. Shouldn't she, Sigrid?"

Yes. Ellen must go.

Without giving thought to the words, Sigrid played "The Old Oaken Bucket." Her mother had been remembered in a will. It set them apart, as a family.

Carl knew the words of the song, and he sat and looked at Ellen. Drink deep of the sight of her, he told himself, for she is going home. Never would he have one thought of staying her, for it was right that she should go; she longed so for home.

"If you would go with me, Carl—"

"We are as one, Ellen. You go. Through you I shall visit the homeland too. Go to the land that gave us birth, Ellen, but I shall stay. I got a job today."

Why did he urge her to go, when all the while his whole being cried out to her to stay?

Oh, to go with her! "The scenes of my childhood." Nostalgia, beckoning to him from the past, called him home too. But he was an American.

Anyway, he had received no letter from home.

Ellen, though, she belonged at home. She never should have left. If he had been a man, he should have furnished passage to her, years ago, to bring this light of glad anticipation to her eyes.

"You can *helsa flitight* to Sweden for me, Ellen." Yes, she would give his best compliments to the old home.

"I will work hard while you are gone, Ellen, and when you come back you can tell me all about—about everything—"

"When I come back," she smiled. Could Carl not guess why she had to go?

Only so recently had she awakened to the truth. How could she have been as unknowing as not to have realized long ago why she was weary, ill, and frail. One who had cared for Sara Osgood should have known at the very first; was it that a person never did see his own self failing? Looking back, the weakness before Tony's coming, the gain in weight when Carl was working and there was plenty to eat, the awful weakness when she started taking in washing again, working too hard for her strength; there was no excuse for her not knowing it then. She should have known, then, that there was very little time left.

But now, she would see her father once again. She would go home, before it was too late.

"The best is none too good for my Ellen," and Ellen's eyes filled when Carl came home next day with a suitcase, a nightgown, and a brush and comb set.

"It will take you the rest of the year to pay for it all!" she remonstrated.

"And who better should I work for?"

A bright red umbrella with little ruffles all over it kept the rain off Ellen as she stood and waved good-bye.

"Take good care of Sigrid, Carl!" she called, and smiled in answer to her daughter's knowing smile.

"Hurry back, Mother!"

Sigrid had a high school education. She would be all right. But oh, what about Carl? The click-click over the rails sang, "What about Carl?"

So good he was, to wire to Dr. Osgood to meet her in New York. It showed how big he was, how thoughtful.

"Are you sure you are equal to the trip, Ellen?" Doctor John asked, "Let me take care of you, as you took care of Sara?"

He guessed her secret. He knew consumption and how it galloped toward the end.

The Atlantic was unkind. She remembered how Carl had thought everyone loved the ocean. But not Ellen Christianson! Hemorrhage followed retching and in a wheelchair, pale, wan, Ellen was disembarked at Liverpool. On a stretcher she made the journey to Göteborg—to Falkenberg—

Returning, it was as if she had never been away. Somehow the home she had known in America was an extraneous thing—not really a part of her life—even Sigrid—even little Tony, for now she was home. Under the Gamla Bron the water flowed; with vibrant tones it sang a welcome.

"Min lilla Elin," her father greeted her, and she answered by telling him that in America the sky had never been so blue as here; there could no green match these glorious leaves of home.

"The vines," on the little house, "grown here for more than a hundred years," she whispered, and remembering, she pointed to the red parasol, "My husband gave it to me."

"Has he been a good husband to you, Elin?"

"The best," she smiled, "the best in all the world—the very best."

Her father bent over her, "Min lilla skälmaktiga Elin—God keep you."

She saw him smile. It would be sacrilege, now, ever to rest her eyes on any other sight. She pressed his hand. Into the blue depths of her eyes she pressed the sight of her aged father's face, smiling.

Here was forgiveness.

Here was home.

Here was God's blessing.

Ellen closed her eyes.

* * *

Four feet, eleven inches, the height of Ellen lay in her warm earth bed. Winter would come, and summer, but no more would Ellen stand to the cool breezes of hill or valley, America or Sweden.

Six feet, four inches, the height of her widowed husband lay on the bed, a cablegram clutched and crushed in his left hand. Only one balm for heart-pain such as this, for conscience driven to despair; only one surcease that he knew, for wretchedness.

Five feet, seven inches, the height of Sigrid bent over him to urge him up to partake of nourishment.

Opposite Sigrid, sitting at the kitchen table, after black coffee, Carl drew his head back, better to see, as an old man who has mislaid his bifocal lenses must do, finding his arms not long enough.

"Translate it again, Pa."

Elin lay beside her own mother, in her hand the little dried bunch of wildflowers—buttercups, berry leaves, all the same color which she had kept these many years, now come home again with her.

Sigrid had seen and held that poor bouquet.

It had rained when her mother left. Raining, when she was a tot, Mother had said it was "Angels washing the floors up in Heaven, and there are cracks so the water comes dripping through to us. And the thunder is the noise the Angels make in moving the furniture around." There must be many cracks in the floor up above, and scrubbing must be done often, for now it rained again.

Sigrid walked into the dripping day. Forlorn, forsaken, and alone, she let her feet take her where they would, and they led her toward the church.

Outside, on the asphalt street, a duck lay; a depression the width of a solid rubber automobile tire made a mark across its body. Sigrid stood and looked at it. A strong wind blew the rain into her face, and blew the feathers up from the still breast on the pavement.

Death for the poor duck. The end. Ducks had no souls—had they?

Souls. "Souls are built as temples are," she repeated aloud. "Here the picture of a saint, there a carving queer and quaint."

A drake came now and walked around and around. The

short feathers on his head stood upright as he stared, unbelieving. He stopped and with his bill smoothed down one feather, defying the wind, smoothed down another and the first stood up again. Repeating, over and over, he tried; and failing, laid the side of his head down on the duck's, so his head and breast covered hers, keeping her feathers smooth. Then he got up again and walked around and around her, cocking his head to one side so with one eye he stared at the unfamiliar sight of blood. He tried again, with his bill, to stroke her feathers smooth against the wind.

It was futile; he smoothed as best he could, then covered her with his body; he laid himself across her, laid his neck along her neck, his head above her head, his bill along her bill, there in the rain. And the rain made bubbles as it joined the depth of water on the asphalt.

Before Sigrid noticed that the drops no longer hit against her face, she felt a presence beside her.

"It is going to clear," the Pastor said.

"But not for the poor duck. For her it is the end," and Sigrid threw herself into Pastor Bedell's arms to sob. "My mother—she will never come back to me—she went only for a little while, but now I shall never see her again."

"You heard so?"

"Yes, a cablegram. She died as she reached her father's home."

The Pastor stood silent, his head bowed. Then he turned to Sigrid, "Why do we have to think death is the end? Why can we not think of death as an incident? Can we say for certain if it is the end of one phase, or the beginning of another?"

A bird came from behind them and settled on a low branch, preening itself after the rain.

"From whence it came, we know not," the Pastor said. "It rests here for a while—even as we—"

The bird took wing and Sigrid followed its flight, a smaller and smaller speck, until it disappeared.

"Standing here, on the ground, in the present, we can see it no more."

"It is gone." Sigrid said.

"So, too, is your mother gone," the Pastor said, and she nodded sadly.

"The bird is gone—gone from our sight," he added, "but it will appear elsewhere."

Sigrid walked home, and entered the empty house. So was the duck gone, but it would not appear elsewhere.

Confused, she sat at the piano to play her mother's favorite piece before she watered the palm and the fern.

TWENTY NINE

LIKE A TIRED GULL, beating against an angry sea-wind, Carl battled his all-consuming thirst. For days now he had had no help, no help at all.

Sigrid was a good girl, no doubt about that, but not like Ellen. Too big, not dainty and petite, like Ellen. And stingy.

His hand shook in reaching to wipe the sweat from his upper lip. His forehead, too, ran with perspiration. Sweat broke out all over him and left him panting. Both physical and mental suffering had exhausted him. Oh, the anguish of the thought that at best he had given stinted, meagre affection in return for love. Oh, the agony of it, that now it was too late to atone to Ellen.

Sigrid was a good girl, yes, yes; he panted now so that it took all of his strength to lift his hand to the table in front of him to touch her mechanical bank. But not generous, like Ellen.

His head swam and his stomach was sickened. "No, not even a quarter's worth," his daughter had said; denying her poor old father, who needed medicine to ease his pain. Only a quarter's worth of whiskey and he would be all right again. He knew that.

Nobody trusted him. Even the bartender at the North Pole laughed when he asked for a quarter's worth on the cuff. He, who had always been such a good customer!

His shaking fingers played over the blue bonnet on the cast-metal Salvation Army lassie, traced the shape of the shepherd dog, lifted its hinged tail and flicked it up and down. Why should it take almost superhuman effort to lift a bank, to see if it rattled?

Saliva drooled from the corners of his mouth: all he had to do was to slide the bottom off, and there would be the price of what he needed. He would not buy it by the glass—not enough, that way, for your money—no, he would buy a pint bottle and bring

337

it home and portion it out, like the medicine that it was.

And after that was gone? What then?

He drained a glàss of water and reached again, gingerly, for the bank. Growing dark already, but it was only noon! He blinked his eyes; clouds heavied with rain hung from the ceiling, inside of the room! Was it Ellen sat there across from him, lifting the coffee pot?

"Ellen!"

The truth came to him; he had loved her. How he had fought against loving—afraid of losing her, too.

Parents. What would his life have been if his father had not sold his horse? And his mother—wanting him to write—that was a farce, with as little education as they had given him, his parents; and he had wanted so, a higher education.

His eyes, his mind, were playing tricks on him. It was Ellen sitting there pouring his coffee, but it seemed to be Tony, too, and his mother—

The clouds at the ceiling broke and rain fell. He swam in perspiration; he felt refreshed. It was hard to know how he had managed to exist through all these days without the help of the courage-giving fluid, but the torture was easing now.

Limp fingers that had lain across the metal lassie strengthened and shoved the bank from him. He stood and grasped the edge of the table.

"Börja med en knappnål—"

He nodded to where his mind had seen his mother sitting, and picked up the bank and returned it to its place on the shelf.

"Nay, mor." He smiled; he would never, never steal.

He stood more solidly now, and walked to the icebox, and broke four eggs into a glass and gulped them down. His hand dug into the pocket of the old pants he had just slipped on. Ah! A coin! His eyes lighted with anticipation; a smile of deepest satisfaction spread over his features at the thought of reaching for a bottle—tearing off the foil—and lifting it to his lips.

The coin; but it was his Columbian half-dollar.

Maybe before he had swallowed the eggs he might have spent it, but he was stronger now; that should not be spent for drink. He had suffered through these past days, God knew how he had suffered for want of it, but now that he held the means for it in his hand, he did not really need it. No, he was over the worst. He had given it up once, when he had Tony. He could do it again.

Sigrid was a good girl, all right, keeping up the house since Ellen was gone—

If only he had known before what he knew now, he who had promised Ellen so many times that he would stop; but he must admit he always had, to himself, surrounded his promises with reservations.

He knew now why he had not given up drinking; he had not really wanted to. No man stops drinking unless he *wants* to.

He knew he would never spend the Columbian half-dollar for liquor. He would never touch another drop, as long as he lived.

But now, at this instant, he knew what he would do. Sigrid was a good girl, too good to be burdened longer with such a father as he. There was nothing he could do now about the past, that was as water spilt, but he had brought her misery enough. This was the least he could do for her—his daughter—the very least. It would be a shock to her at first, this thing that came now as the answer to his problem, but she would get over it. The half-dollar would help him by buying a strong, strong rope.

Neatly, into a cardboard shoe box, went his belongings, the deed to the house, the mortgage papers, paid tax bills, receipts, oil stock certificates, gold stock—indictments of his judgment— his mother's address, right on top, so Sigrid should be able to inform her of his demise.

Down into the basement of a theatre building under construction Carl went, over a steel beam he slipped the strong, strong rope. He was not afraid. A moment, and then it would be over: not afraid, there was nothing beyond, to hope for, or to fear.

His fingers fumbled with a slip knot.

"There is a God above who sees." He looked up, sharply; had Ellen spoken?

The rope. He would have to fix the rope. Once he had heard his mother tell of a guide rope, laid and battened to the ground from house to barn before deep snows fell, so she could find her way to tunnel to the barn to feed the animals. There she had been, following the rope, tunneling in the snow, on the morning he was born.

Had she gazed at his infant face and yearned to give him all of the things he had wished for, for Tony?

His eyes moistened, and still his fingers fumbled. Now it was ready; one foot forward, to leave the turned-over American Family soap box on which he stood.

Mist has a way of clearing; he saw familiar words—a page in Victor Hugo's book—and the vignette came to life for him: "The bishop, who had laid stress on the words, continued solemnly, 'Jean Valjean, my brother, you no longer belong to evil, but to good. I have bought your soul of you. I withdraw it from black thoughts and the spirit of perdition, and give it to God!'"

Carl closed his eyes. He reeled at sight of his mind's change of scene.

It was not the bishop! Nor Jean Valjean!

It was his mother speaking, and she spoke the words to *him*.

All of his wasted life rose up to tell him now that it was he who had chosen the path of misery, not Life which had betrayed him, not Luck who had denied him.

He had cheated himself.

The fault was his and his alone. The same path had opened up before him as had welcomed the immigrant shoes of Joseph, who now rounded out his years in comfort in Geneva; of John Peterson, who had soled the feet of those who walked the road to Fame; of Mr. Seastrom, the biggest building contractor in the Middle West.

Was it too late? Was there still time to prove he was his mother's son?

What was the thing he sought to do? No! Not this! God could never forgive such a sin as this! He flung the rope from him.

The carpenter boss was plumb crazy to think he was not steady enough to do the work. A risk on the job? He'd show the boss! He would show Sigrid, too, what a father he could be; again, together, they would read in Hugo's book. Of profound significance, the realization came, were some of the excerpts he had memorized without conscious intent. His voice vibrated with feeling as he repeated, "I feel in myself the future life. I am like a forest that has been more than once cut down. The new shoots are stronger and livelier than ever. I am rising, I know, toward the sky. The sunshine is over my head. The earth gives me its sap, but heaven lights me with the reflection of unknown worlds."

The sun was in the west. Sigrid would be coming from work soon, and he must find her.

Daughter—mother—he could not quite distinguish which,

now; only to find her. She would take care of him until he could take care of her.

He must find Sigrid.

Here, she passed this downtown corner on her way home. He would wait here.

Times certainly were changing, more automobiles passed than horse-drawn vehicles. An old-time one passed, "A Buick Model Eight, I'll wager," he said to himself, and rubbed his bare hands together to keep them warm. March was bitter cold this year; if snow would fall, maybe the temperature might rise. Andersen's poor Little Match Girl had no colder hands than his, but alas, he had no matches. An ulster was not protection enough on a day like this; he shivered, and drew it closer around him.

The old Buick spit and back-fired, more than a block away, but everyone on the street corner jumped.

"Help!"

"Stop them!"

"A runaway! Look out!" a policeman shouted.

Carl saw a team of horses coming, running wildly away from the horseless carriage, a piece of harness leather flying wild as they bolted.

His hands were stiff. His brain was numb from weariness and cold. Why should he care? Let them run, the horses, let them bring destruction to others' lives, as a horse had brought to his.

"Bobby! For God's sake, someone—" a woman screamed.

A small boy stood, bewildered, directly in the path of the frenzied team.

The child! Carl came to life.

Horses? Of course he knew how to stop them; he stepped from the curb and in the fleeting instant that the team was abreast of him he grabbed the bit of one, twisted it, and set the big horse down on its haunches, stopping them both before his deep-rooted reserve of muscle strength gave out.

"Bravo!" the crowd cheered.

"Magnificent!" they said, of Carl; then, "Oh-h-h, oh-h," when they saw him being trampled under the hooves of the nervous animal while the team resisted the restraining hands of policemen.

"He saved my son! Oh, save him! He saved my son—*save him!*"

"Pa," Sigrid kneeled beside him and stroked his hair back

from his forehead. Blood streamed from his mouth. His eyes opened, and closed again.

"I saw, Pa. I am Sigrid; Sigrid—don't you know me?"

"Sigrid—" a feeble smile broke.

"Yes—yes, your Sigrid."

"Min mor?"

"No—your Sigrid—"

"Min mor—min lilla mor—*ah, förlåta mej*—förlåta mej—*i Hans Heliga Nam*—"

"My mother—my little mother," he had breathed, "ah, forgive me—forgive me—*in His Holy Name.*"

Sigrid prayed, a prayer of thanks; at last his soul had grown to match the height of his tall body, freeing those lips to speak the words they longed to speak.

Only the good would she remember; how he had run down the street after the balloon man, on Sunday mornings, his suspenders flying straight behind him like a bird's tail, at first sound of the sad piping tune blown from the balloon man's horn, his coming back with one, red, for her and one, blue, for Tony. "Never too big to play with a red balloon," he'd grin; and the Easter egg he brought, with a little window at its one end—and when she put an eye up close, there inside the egg were lambs and sheep, grazing on green meadows.

Bare was the catalpa tree as Carl was lowered beside his son.

Sigrid glanced about, through her tears. The family of little Bobby Schmotzer stood near by. The heavy oaken coffin with silver handles, red roses blanketing its top, all paid for by Bobby's father, sunk out of sight. Six pallbearers, members of Mr. Schmotzer's lodge, their white gloves accentuating the gray of the day, stood motionless. There was dear Hattie Allspaugh, and her eyes were red. Mrs. Kant stood near; people spoke of her, now, behind the backs of hands because she had been divorced. Half of the whole city of Chicago, it seemed, was gathered here.

All through his years, no mark was made by Pa, until the end. Most of his life he had lived in trivial and unwise ways, until in that one grand moment he had grown majestic, and people came now to look at him and pay respect and tribute to a hero.

And he was her father.

Sigrid clasped her hands. She had been proud of him before,

in those wonderful days when he had read to her, and studied with her. She was proud, now, of the deed which had cost him his life; but prouder still of his last words, those which bravado had locked so long within his heart.

His mother would be sad to receive the letter she was going to write—telling what she would have to tell—but surely balm must spread over the wound when her grandmother would read the clippings from the newspapers, telling of her son and his heroic deed, and those last words.

Her own grandmother—a Sigrid, too, and she was named for her—

Sigrid looked up at the catalpa tree etching a pattern, gray against a sky of gray.

Slow falling snow, in large white fluffy flakes, fell now and melted on the bared heads of men as Pastor Bedell dropped small handfuls of earth into the grave, saying slowly, "From dust unto dust."

Wet snow clung in the crevices of the rough bark of the catalpa tree. If Pa could stand here now, beside her, he would not say, "Dead, as that tree is dead." Not after the reverence on his lips.

The Pastor watched her face, and it reminded him of his mother, how her face had looked one day while sitting at her window that was frozen over by the winter. Gloom surrounded her, the purple sadness of a winter's dusk; her shawl fell from her shoulders and she shivered; but her face, it was like sun shining on bright marigolds, and when he had peeked to see what lay in her lap, it was a seed catalog. So it was now that Sigrid's face appeared as the Pastor watched her.

For Sigrid saw her father's words blend in some mysterious way with the catalpa tree. The intricate pattern of twigs and branches spoke of broad heart-shaped leaves, spelling shade in summer's heat; blossoms came, cream, striped inside with yellow and dotted with little flecks, tinges of lavender; the summer done, long dry pods hung from every bough, "cigars" for boys to smoke; winter again, and here would stand a stark, gaunt tree.

Faith, it was, that told her spring would come again, again, and yet again.

"In His Holy Name—"

As Sigrid stood, spring came to her; the silent tree gave

music, the rustle of its leaves in tune with birds' songs; the gathered clumps of snow changed into large clusters of bell-shaped, cream-white blossoms.

Here was the wondrous answer to it all—

Immortality—

Divinity—

Eternity—

God.